THE PAINTED BRIDGE

A NOVEL

WENDY WALLACE

SCRIBNER

New York   London   Toronto   Sydney   New Delhi

S

SCRIBNER
A Division of Simon & Schuster, Inc.
1230 Avenue of the Americas
New York, NY 10020

First Scribner hardcover edition July 2012

SCRIBNER and design are registered trademarks of The Gale Group, Inc., used under license by Simon & Schuster, Inc., the publisher of this work.

For information about special discounts for bulk purchases, please contact Simon & Schuster Special Sales at 1-866-506-1949 or business@simonandschuster.com.

The Simon & Schuster Speakers Bureau can bring authors to your live event. For more information or to book an event contact the Simon & Schuster Speakers Bureau at 1-866-248-3049 or visit our website at www.simonspeakers.com.

DESIGNED BY ERICH HOBBING

Manufactured in the United States of America

1   3   5   7   9   10   8   6   4   2

ISBN 978-1-4516-6082-1
ISBN 978-1-4516-7530-6 (ebook)

For Sylvia Wallace

Oh it was summer when I slept,
It's winter now I waken.
—From *A Daughter of Eve*
by Christina Rossetti

THE PAINTED BRIDGE

ONE

Lizzie Button was upside-down. The crown of her head rested on the floor; her feet, in black laced boots, floated above her. Lucas St. Clair leaned his eye closer to the ground glass and brought her face into sharper focus, moving the brass knob back and forth to sharpen the grain of her skin, the strands of cropped hair that lay across her forehead. Her expression was wary. Lucas had trained himself to read eyes that signaled from below mouths, frowns that mimicked smiles. He ducked out from underneath the cloth, replaced the lens cap and looked at her in the flesh, right way up.

"Are you comfortable, Mrs. Button?" he said, inserting the plate into the back of the camera. "Warm enough? Will you be able to keep still?"

"Yes, Doctor," she said, her lips barely moving. "Go on. Make my picture."

"Let us begin."

Tugging out the dark slide, he removed the lens cap with a flourish and began to count out the exposure.

". . . Two. Three. Four."

He could feel the familiar excitement rising in him. The hope that the picture would succeed even beyond his expectations and reveal Mrs. Button's mind. "Eight, nine, ten." That it would offer up the secrets of the world inside her head. "Sixteen. Seventeen." Illuminate the mental landscape, the population of unseen persecutors and innocents with whom Mrs. Button conversed. "Twenty-three. Twenty . . ."

The fernery door flew open behind him and the patient swung round toward it with a look of alarm in her eyes. Her hands began to pluck at a piece of wood, wrapped in a ragged white shawl, on her lap. Lucas heard a pair of feet wipe themselves repeatedly on the sack thrown over the threshold behind him as a voice rang through the air.

"Stuck. Swollen from the rain, I suppose. Afternoon, St. Clair."

Lucas held up his hand for silence.

"Thirty-one. Thirty-two. One minute, please." Querios Abse crossed the brick floor and stood beside him. Abse wore old-fashioned trousers strapped under the instep and shoes that had molded themselves to the forward press of his big toes. His body was padded with an even layer of flesh, with his own mortal armor. He stood watching as Lucas continued. "Forty-nine. Fifty."

"That must be long enough," he said. "Surely to goodness."

Lucas St. Clair counted on. "Seventy-one. Seventy-two."

His eyes, steady and clear, held the whole picture before him: Lizzie Button—her shoulders hunched now, her gaze fastened upon him; the carved wooden chair on which she sat; the plain canvas strung from the wall behind her and the spider that clambered over it.

"Ninety-nine. One hundred. You can relax now, Mrs. Button. Thank you." He flung the square of black velvet over the front of the camera and turned to Abse. "What can I do for you?"

"Just dropped in as I was passing. How are you getting on?"

"I'm making progress, thank you."

The cheer in Lucas's voice belied his disappointment. The picture was spoiled, he knew already, the spell broken when Abse crossed the threshold. The patient had moved. On the plate, she would appear to have half a dozen heads and a score of ghostly hands fluttering over her lap. He wouldn't develop the photograph. It would disturb Mrs. Button further to see an image of herself that looked as if it came from a freak show. He'd finished the exposure only to make the point to Abse that he ought not to be disturbed.

"And what's your opinion of Button here?" Abse jabbed a hand toward her. She was rocking back and forth on the chair, cradling the stick in her arms and humming. Abse lowered his voice a fraction. "Incurable, Higgins reckons."

"I can't say yet, sir. I haven't had a chance to make a print or to study her image."

"You've met the woman, haven't you? You've read her notes. What difference does it make to see the wretched creature on glass?"

Lucas had explained to him in detail the difference he believed the new science might make. The opportunity it offered to see the face in a settled expression, reduced to two dimensions, with all the accompanying clarity and possibility for close reading. Was Abse baiting him? Or did he just not listen?

"It's a scientific way of looking," he said. "Free of the old prejudices and preconceptions. It can lead us into the minds of patients. Mind if I carry on, Abse? We can talk while I'm working."

Lucas stepped inside the dark cupboard and closed the door behind him, glad of the flimsy removal from Abse. He wore a long apron over his trousers, the pale canvas stained with what looked like sepia. His sleeves were rolled to the elbows and the neck of his shirt unbuttoned behind a lopsided blue cravat. His brown hair reached to his shoulders and his whiskers, his only vanity, were razored in a sharp line that reached from his ears to his chin.

He inhaled the sweetish smell of ether as he lifted the plate out of the dark slide and lowered it into a bath of water. He would clean it off, reuse it another time. By the orange gloom of the safe light he prepared a new plate, gripping it between the thumb and forefinger of his left hand, using the other to pour the collodion, tilting the surface back and forth, watching as the gummy tide rolled over the glass, then draining the surplus from one corner, drop by drop, back into the neck of the flask. Abse's face loomed toward him from the other side of the small window of amber glass, his flesh and silver hair turned a sulfurous yellow, his red waistcoat the same tone as his black jacket. He dangled his watch in the air and tapped the face of it.

"I haven't got all day, St. Clair," he called. "I'm expecting a new patient."

Lucas retrieved the fresh plate from the silver bath and secured it in the dark slide. He rinsed his long fingers with water from an old kettle that he kept on the shelf for the purpose and stepped out, blinking in the glare.

The fernery had been an enthusiasm of Abse's late mother but had long ago fallen into disuse. Empty of plants and with the stove in the middle lit only for his visits, the air in the old glasshouse felt damp

3

and chilly year-round. The light was good though. It was shadow-less north light, as scientific as light could be. It poured through the cracked panes of the sloping glass roof in a pristine abundance that Lucas found, despite his atheism, miraculous. *Lux aeterna.*

"Finished with the dark arts, have you?"

"Not yet." He wished that Abse would take his leave. Mrs. Button wouldn't be able to settle until he did. Nor would he, come to think of it. "You expect a new patient, Mr. Abse?"

"Yes, she's due any time." Abse cleared his throat and rocked on his heels. "There was something actually, St. Clair. We've got the inspectors coming in again before long. Of course, they never say when. I want more of the pictures on display, in the dayroom. Gives the place an up-to-date look."

Lucas hesitated. "Very well. I'll hang them myself, on my next visit."

Abse walked toward the door. "Good. Best be off," he said. "Oh, and St. Clair!"

"Yes, sir?"

"Don't forget to tell me what ails Mrs. Button. If your photograph speaks to you in the privacy of your darkened room. Tells you any more than doctors with a lifetime of experience have been able to see unaided."

Lucas cleared his throat.

"Shall do."

"Bloody old sod," Mrs. Button said over the sound of Abse's departing chuckle as the fernery door banged shut.

Lucas watched as Abse made his way along a path edged with box and out of the walled garden. He disliked the idea of his pictures being pressed into the service of a publicity campaign, pasted up like advertisements for cocoa powder or soap flakes before their true utility in diagnosis had been properly established. There was something dishonest about it. He squashed the objection. He had to keep Abse in favor of the project, needed his agreement in order to continue visiting Lake House. It was a small price to pay for the opportunity to pursue his research.

He stooped under the cloth again and began to readjust the focus of the expensive French lens. Poised on her head, her old print dress sailing above her, Lizzie Button had grown still. Her expression had changed, her mouth curving downward in a slight smile, her eyebrows lifted quizzically toward the ground. She looked almost hopeful. Lucas threw off the velvet and straightened up, inserting the dark slide into the camera back with one practiced movement.

"I'm so sorry for the interruption, Mrs. Button. Shall we start again?"

The cab lurched through the gates and along a driveway edged with tall trees that still clung to the last of their foliage. Red and gold leaves fluttered on near-naked branches as if the stately oaks and beeches were down to their undergarments, to petticoats and one stocking. Anna glimpsed the house through the glass and got an impression of its great flat front, of ivy encroaching on the top windows. It had a half-blind look that reminded her of the flint house.

"As you see," Vincent said, "it's a fine place. Comfortable. Well situated."

"Very fine. Who are your friends?"

"You'll find out soon enough."

He climbed out, his feet crunching on the scatter of gravel as he headed for the studded double door. Glad to escape the confines of the cab, Anna jumped down onto the mossy stones and followed Vincent to the porch. She hoped she looked sufficiently presentable. Her boots were still stained with salt from the trip to the coast; she had on her old blue velvet dress, with the lace collar. She disliked the two new dresses Vincent had bought her on their marriage. The wool irritated her skin and the dark hues drained her face of color. She pushed a few escaped strands of hair back into her tortoiseshell combs, while Vincent heaved on the bell.

A maid led them through a hallway and on into a room lined from skirting board to ceiling with shelves crammed with books and ledgers, heaps of yellowing papers pushed in like thatch on their tops. The floor was as crowded as the walls: curios, chairs stacked with more files, a stuffed fox in a glass cabinet.

"What a funny old place," she said, glancing around. "It doesn't look as if anyone ever reads the books."

"Good afternoon, Reverend."

She jumped. The voice came from a man halfway up a ladder propped against one of the bookshelves. He climbed down and hurried across the room toward her, brushing a hand on his red waistcoat, extending it. His hair was silver, brushed upward on both sides of his head; he had a signet ring jammed onto his little finger.

"Querios Abse. Welcome to Lake House." He shook Vincent's hand then hers, holding it a moment too long as he regarded her. Anna disentangled her hand, turned away from his avid stare. "I take it this is she?" the man said to Vincent. He pulled Vincent toward the door and they began to talk in low voices, facing away from her.

The wind gusted again outside; threadbare curtains belled inward from the windows then subsided. Anna felt a rising sense of indignation. She'd missed her appointment with her sister, traveled all this way and wasn't even going to be invited to sit down. She pretended to examine a globe on a stand, spun it on its axis through China, Persia, Abyssinia, until she found England, its dear, peculiar outline. Wheeling it more slowly, she trailed her fingers over the lumpy surface of the Atlantic. She would visit Louisa tomorrow. She'd go early.

She looked up to find both men regarding her.

"Oh, yes," Vincent said. "Excellent physical health."

He came toward her with a look of regret, holding his hat against his chest.

"Anna, I believe it best if . . . *Thou knowest not what a day may bring forth.*"

"What do you mean, Vincent?"

Anna was perplexed but her voice was eager. She wanted to offer forgiveness, even before she knew for what. For what didn't matter. What mattered was that they pulled together, each played their part. That was what marriage was, as far as she could make out.

"Good-bye, Anna."

He made a stiff little bow, walked backward to the door and disappeared through it. He was there and then not there, like one of Louisa's phantoms. She began to follow but the man called Querios Abse stepped in front of her, holding out both arms as if he herded an unwilling sheep.

"One minute, Mrs. Palmer. I'd like to introduce you to someone."

"Where's my husband gone?"

Another door opened at the far end of the room and a woman crossed the floor, the clip of her heels on the boards deadened as she reached the rug.

"This is Fanny Makepeace," said Abse. "Our matron."

"Good afternoon, Mrs. Makepeace. I'm leaving now, if you'll excuse me."

"Your bonnet, Mrs. Palmer," the woman said, holding out a hand crowded with rings. "Your cloak."

Everything about Makepeace appeared ordinary. She was in middle age and of medium height, her brownish hair drawn tightly back to display a pair of deep-set eyes that looked at Anna without expression. Yet Anna's skin prickled with unease at the woman's proximity; she was unable to meet her cool stare.

"I'm going," she repeated. "I'm not staying."

TWO

Anna barely knew how, afterward, but without laying a hand on her, Abse and Makepeace had seemed to carry her along, to sweep her up a grand staircase, through a huge and faded salon where a fire smoldered in the grate. More stairs, steeper now, the handrail narrow and plain; she felt herself moving down a corridor, propelled by the force of their combined will. There were windows on the right-hand side— glimpses of a courtyard far below, crossed with narrow paths. On the left were numbered doors, all closed, each with its own letterbox, curiously situated at eye level.

Querios Abse stopped at number 9 and pushed open the door with his outstretched arm. The last of the afternoon light filtered dim and gray into a small room; some ill-matched pieces of furniture huddled around the walls. Despite the open window, the smell of mold hit Anna like a blow and she stepped back, covered her nose with her hand.

"The chamber has been uninhabited," Abse said, "which accounts for any mustiness in the atmosphere." He gestured again for her to enter. "Many ladies have found solace within these walls, Mrs. Palmer. Peace of mind."

"I don't need solace."

He was still talking. Lake House was a retreat and there was no shame in a period of necessary seclusion. Moral management was suitable for most guests although regrettably not all. The antiphlogistic diet was efficacious in soothing feminine emotions.

The words rushed by her, impossible to grasp. Anna felt as if she'd already been in the house too long and needed urgently to escape it.

Her legs had grown weak. She breathed in to the bottom of her lungs, clenched her nails into her palms. She'd never been a fainter. She and Louisa, all of the Newlove girls, had been brought up to be strong as boys. Stronger, if necessary.

She braced her back against the wall of the passage and spread her hands on the soft undulation of the plaster. She was almost as tall as he, could look straight into his sharp gray eyes before they darted away.

"I'm not going in there, Mr. Abse."

"Step inside, Mrs. Palmer."

Anna turned to Makepeace for help. The woman put an arm round her waist, took hold of her wrist and thrust her forward so fast and hard that she stumbled and fell on her hands and knees into the room. The door shut behind her. Anna got to her feet, felt blindly up and down the wood for the handle. There was no handle. Only a keyhole that as she stooped and looked through it was covered over from the outside.

"Let me out," she shouted, standing up. "How dare you?"

She flung herself against the door, felt it slam into the side of her face and began to beat on it with her fists. In the moments that followed, anger gave way to fear, to a feeling that she was drowning, that something fluid and dark was rising inside and choking the breath out of her. She heard her own voice calling Vincent's name. Calling for help. Asking if anyone was there. After some time, the screaming gave way to silence.

Her throat was raw, her cheek throbbing. She got off the floor and straightened her skirts, felt her face with the palm of her hand. She kicked the door again, more to vent her feelings than from any hope of its giving way, and stood on one foot rubbing her toe with her hand and looking around her.

The room was taller than it was wide, the walls covered in green patterned paper up to a picture rail. The iron bed was as low as a child's, not more than a foot off the floor. On the wall opposite the bed was a chest, its oak veneer peeling up from the deal wood underneath, and at the end of the bed stood a washstand with a marble top; a chair was pulled up to it. There was a writing case on the mantelpiece and just one picture, a watercolor of a fisher girl, on the wall over the bed. Anna peered at it, hugging her arms over her chest. It was a back view. The girl stood on the sands looking out over a flat, gray sea, her hair in a plait on her shoulders, her shrimp net empty beside her.

It was growing dark. She pulled the chair to the sash window, lifted an inch at the bottom and prevented from further opening by two rusty nails driven into the frame higher up. Kneeling on the chair, she looked out at a pearl and mauve sky, the long, low clouds lit from below like the shining bellies of fish, a crescent moon floating above one bright star. The ground underneath the window sloped away to a pale shape, a lake or a river. The wind had dropped.

Anna stayed at the window for some time and as she gazed out, the picture in front of her changed. She saw not the night sky but the image that had come to her so often throughout that year—of a boy, a bright-haired boy, standing on top of a rock. He was still for a moment and then he jumped, leapt off the rock to what appeared to be a solid surface below. For an instant, it held him. But as she watched, it cracked and broke up beneath his feet. What had been solid land turned into the sea and the boy disappeared into the water. He slid from view, slowly, an expression of surprise visible on his face until the moment he vanished, leaving only a circle of hair floating on the water.

Noises began outside in the corridor. Keys turning, footsteps, an instruction to be quick. Anna got off the chair. She felt in her pocket for her handkerchief and found she was carrying her penknife. It was a childhood present, from her father. She wrapped it in the handkerchief, wondering if they would try to take it away from her. Anna and her sisters had had iron beds in the flint house, had always used the legs as hiding places. She lifted one leg of the bed and finding it hollow, slid the knife inside. As she set the bed back down, there was a tap on the door. A key turned in the lock and a woman with a blanket over her shoulders marched in. The woman banged down the window, dragged out a straw mattress from under the bed and thrust a chamber pot in its place as the door slammed behind her.

"Night air, miss," she said, flinging down the blanket. "I don't agree with it. I'm Martha Lovely. I'll be yer companion tonight and most likely fer a good few nights to come."

"I don't need a companion. I'm not staying here."

"You're here now, miss, far as I can see. And I'm here with yer. Best get into bed fer some shut-eye."

The woman spread the blanket on the mattress. She lit two candles then kneeled down, pressing her hands together in front of her nose. Anna studied her as Lovely rushed through the Lord's Prayer, eyes closed. She wore a plain, calico nightdress; a whistle and a key hung on separate strings around her neck. Her face was pitted with pale, shallow scars from her hairline to the neck of her nightdress. Martha Lovely opened her eyes.

"Time you laid yer head on the piller."

"I am not getting into that bed."

"As you like. Good night, miss. God bless."

"It's not 'miss.' I'm a married woman."

Too late. Lovely had disappeared under the blanket.

People always took Anna for unmarried, despite her twenty-four years. She had a ring that she'd chosen herself in a jewelers in Holborn, hadn't taken it off since the day of the wedding, but it made no difference. Everywhere she went, she was "miss."

Lifting the chair to the hearth, she pulled her cloak around her and stretched her feet almost into the grate. She had refused Makepeace's request to hand over her cloak, although the woman had seized her bonnet from her head. The fire was small and the flames blue and cold-looking. She peered into the scuttle, empty except for a thin heap of dust. Flexing her toes inside her boots, she pushed her icy fingers up the sleeves of her dress and tried to think what to do.

Write to Vincent, that much was obvious. But she didn't know what to say to him. He'd barely spoken to her since she got back from the coast. Hadn't laughed when she unintentionally said something funny or reached for her in the dusty four poster. Her husband was implacable.

Anna didn't understand his anger. They had first met at a Missions to Seamen Society meeting; he knew of her concern for sailors. She'd thought that Vincent would approve of what she'd done, that he would see it as an act of charity, a proper response to the devastation all around the coast that the great storm had brought about. She imagined that he'd be glad to part with a few items of clothing that he hardly wore, a stopped watch that lay in the drawer, unconsulted from one month to the next. A little money. It was little compared to the need of the survivors, anyway.

It was rash of her, she realized now, not to have sought his permission before she left. But caught up in the awful drama, she had behaved as her every instinct urged. She'd been gone five days. When she arrived back in London, her dress stained to the waist with white rings of salt, hair smelling of pipe smoke, fingers red and raw, it was Sunday. She went directly to the church, slipping as quietly as she could through the Gothic door, dipping her fingers in the font as she passed. She hurried along the aisle to her place in the front pew, breathing in the familiar scent of stone and frankincense and nodding at a few familiar faces.

Vincent stopped his sermon in midsentence and gazed down from the pulpit as she rose from her knees and settled herself on the seat. He was silent so long, regarded her with such fierce intention, the thought entered Anna's mind that he was going to greet her, commend her action publicly. But as she smiled up at him she began to feel his fury, so large and present it seemed to fill the church. The congregation had been craning their necks to get a better look at her. One by one, their heads turned. They began to stare up at Vincent as if they'd never seen him before and to whisper to each other. There was laughter. The organist struck up and the most stalwart members of the congregation embarked on a hymn, one elderly female voice striking out ahead of the rest. Vincent descended from the pulpit, straight and stiff as a waxwork.

Anna had been mortified. As the service limped to a halt, she hurried out through the robing room, ignoring the curate's solicitous inquiries as to her well-being, the eager curiosity on the faces of some of the women. Cook was off-duty and she let herself into the Vicarage. By the time Vincent returned from evensong, hours later, Anna was undressed and in bed. She woke from a doze as he kicked open the bedroom door, ducked under its low frame and flung his hat on the chair with a carelessness quite unlike him.

Anna sat up, rubbing her eyes, unsure of what to say.

"Hello, Vincent. Were there many at the service?"

"More than usual. Anticipating a further spectacle, no doubt."

"I'm sorry," she said. "I never meant to embarrass you."

He gave a bark of laughter.

"I can't think what you did mean, then. Where the hell do you think you've been?"

She had never heard him curse.

"You surely saw the note? I went to offer assistance to shipwrecked sailors. Was it wrong?"

Vincent pulled his crucifix over his head, trickled the chain into a puddle on the dressing table.

"Was it wrong?" he repeated.

He turned toward her with a sudden movement and she flinched and pressed her body back into the pillow. Vincent looked at her for a moment then seized his dose of chloral from the nightstand.

"I am not a wife-beater, Anna. I shall retire to the study."

She lay awake after he was gone, listening to the drunks outside in the street. The mattress was full of pebbles and the pillow as unforgiving as the pew. The birds started early, their calls in the first glimmers of dawn singular and intimate, the way she had imagined marriage would be.

In the gloom of the little bedroom, Anna stepped over Lovely's feet and assembled the writing case and candlesticks on the washstand, drew up the chair. The pen was worn, the few sheets of paper dog-eared. But there were envelopes. A stub of red wax. She tested the nib on the back of her hand, felt its cold, light scratch on her skin and dipped it in the ink.

My dear Vincent,

I am writing to implore you most urgently to remove me from this place.

Please forgive my hastiness in departing for the coast before seeking your blessing. In future, I will be sure to obtain your consent for any such missions.

You intended this retreat for the best, of that I am sure. But you know that there is nothing at all wrong with my nerves.

I wish only to be back at the Vicarage with you and will do my utmost to avoid embarrassing you in any way again.

Until that time, I remain your loving and obedient . . .

Anna paused for so long that the ink dried on the nib. After nearly seven months, she still didn't feel like Vincent's wife. She signed herself his loving and obedient Anna, read the letter over and folded it into an envelope, resisting the impulse to throw it on the embers.

Picking up the pen again, she warmed the underside of the nib over the candle, loaded it with the remains of the ink and began an account to Louisa of everything that had happened since she read in a newspaper of the ship wrecked off the Welsh coast, the boy who had been pulled from the water still breathing. How she'd felt impelled to travel there, see if she could help.

She explained how Vincent had misunderstood her actions, and expressed her pressing need of rescue from this gloomy and godforsaken *madhouse*. As best she could reckon it, Lake House was some three miles north of the brickworks at the top of the Hollow Way, could be reached in a couple of hours by carriage from Louisa's house at Wren Street.

She sat for a moment resting her head in her hands. A madhouse was what it was, however Mr. Abse tried to dress it up. Her husband had put her in a place meant for lunatics and hysterics. The thought prompted a stab of pain in Anna's chest. She'd never set foot in any place like this, had only hurried past the walls of the large asylum near the Vicarage on occasion, hearing the awful cries that came from inside the place and feeling a mixture of relief that she wasn't in there and horror that others were. Wondered what afflicted them. Back in Dover, where she grew up, such people tended to remain at large. There was a simpleton who wandered the cliffs, a woman who lived in a hut in the woods, feeding the birds better than she fed herself, and whom some of the local lads tormented as a witch.

Anna rubbed her eyes and grasped the pen. She'd run out of space. She needed to keep one sheet of paper for the other letter. She sent her love to her sister, her nephews. Remembered her brother-in-law and added him too. "Please, Lou, come quickly, I beg you," she wrote up the margin. The *you* was squeezed, almost illegible. She would have to trust in Louisa to grasp the seriousness of the situation. Sometimes, Louisa saw gravity only in things that related to herself. Still, she was the closest of Anna's sisters. The others were so much older, all so far away. Anna couldn't think how she would even begin to explain her predicament to them.

She got up and stretched, put her finger to the pane and slid it back and forth in squeaky lines. Drops of moisture were running down the inside of the window, joining and separating. It was pitch dark outside; she could see nothing, only feel the night pressing in on her, adding its weight to the walls, to the pervasive odor of damp. She had to get out.

Both candles were guttering, sending up curls of black smoke. Martha Lovely was a woollen mountain, her breathing steady. Anna stood and watched her, followed the rise and fall of the blanket, then crept to the end of the bed and eased the leg off the floor. The little knife fell out of the handkerchief into her hand, its pearl handle cool and smooth in her palm.

"Are you awake?"

The rhythm didn't falter. Anna kneeled down by Lovely's head and lifted the edge of the blanket. The woman's cheek rested on the palm of one hand, her mouth open. Anna pulled the blanket down farther. The string that held the key was clearly visible above the neck of her nightdress. Anna sat back on her heels and pulled out the blade, silently. Her heart raced as she leaned forward and felt in the candlelight for the string.

She started and jumped back as Lovely sat bolt upright, one hand clamped around the key and the other holding the whistle to her lips.

"One blast o' this and they'll all come running. You lie down, miss. Go to sleep now."

Lovely's voice was calm, her tone determined. She didn't sound like someone waking from sleep. Anna wondered if she'd been tricked for a second time that day as she scrambled to her feet and slid the knife up her sleeve.

"I'm still writing letters."

She was shaking as she sat down again at the washstand. The blade had come within an inch of the woman's neck; it could have hurt her. Anna hugged her arms around herself trying to get warm, to slow her thumping heart.

There was another letter she must write but she would not do it tonight.

Querios Abse climbed the back stairs and trudged along the corridor to his own parlor, flung himself into his chair. In her smaller, matching, armless chair on the other side of the hearth, Emmeline tinkled the bell in a long, uninterrupted note that he took to mean she was annoyed.

"I told Cook to delay supper," she called out over the ringing. "Where have you been?"

"Working," he mouthed back. "On the books."

She stilled the bell in the palm of her hand and put it down on the hearth tiles.

"I do wish you'd come up earlier, Q. In the evenings."

"I was occupied. New patient kicked up a rumpus."

"I want to talk to you about our daughter."

Querios felt his heart sink. He had real worries, important concerns and responsibilities, yet Emmeline persisted in burdening him with trivial domestic matters. The more he tried to explain the financial situation to her, the less she wanted to understand. He wasn't certain that Lake House could stay in business. Government asylums were being built all around, taking in private patients as well as pauper lunatics. The old ways, the restraints, the rotatory chair, were out of fashion but it cost money to keep patients safe without shackling or frightening them. The wages bill kept rising and the amount patients' relatives were willing to pay did not.

Private madhouses were closing down all over the country—thirty in ten years. Lake House might be one of them if things didn't pick up. Emmeline didn't see it. Nor did their eldest son, Benedict. The younger ones were children still, away at school. Querios had only himself to talk to about it. He slept badly. He had a ringing in his ears that could drive him barmy, if he let it. Rushing like a waterfall, sometimes. Like swarms of insects, at others.

"Wasps," he said aloud. "Or crickets. That awful sawing."

"Pardon?"

"Nothing, Emmy. Nothing."

It was a good decision, to allow St. Clair to test out his theory on the guests. Lake House had to move with the times. He'd kitted out the old fernery with blinds, ordered Fludd to build the dark cupboard St. Clair required. Patients liked to see themselves in photographs, drawn from the life, and relatives considered it progressive, although more than one inquired after the cost. He didn't tell the families that there was no cost. That Dr. St. Clair was conducting a private experiment which in his own opinion was a sheer waste of time.

Querios's efforts hadn't increased business enough. Patients arrived infrequently, despite the newspaper advertisements, the brochures. Some were withdrawn by their relatives almost immediately, others abandoned by husbands or brothers who would neither pay their costs nor remove them. A good cure rate impressed the families but depressed the revenue. The ones with puerperal mania, out of their right minds after childbirth, often improved within weeks and had to be discharged back to their infants. A few lived on at Lake House, neither fully well nor fully deranged; they passed as normal inside the asylum but as lunatics outside it. One or two, like poor, wronged Fanny Makepeace, ended up as staff.

The good thing was, he reminded himself as they proceeded into the dining room, sat down at their respective ends of the table, that the new patient was likely to remain for at least a couple of years. Hysterics often did and the woman's husband hadn't balked when he'd indicated as much. Querios had made a rough calculation earlier of what Mrs. Palmer would mean for the business if she proved an average case. Totted up what sum might be added to that if she had the full range of treatments. It had improved his mood.

Stewed rabbit with puréed parsnip cheered it further. He lifted a loaded forkful of meat and commenced chewing. The dull gleam of the brass candelabra, the soft lines of the old willow pattern china that he'd eaten off since he was a boy, seemed to speak to him, offer their reassurance that life would continue, unchanged. Extracting pieces of shot from the mouthful of flesh, lining them up like plum stones on the rim of the plate, he experienced a rare feeling of confidence. Lake House would be up to the mark by the next time the magistrates called. All spick-and-span. Good enough, at least.

At the far end of the table, Emmeline was speaking. Her face was set in the frown that was becoming habitual and the wide white streaks at her temple shone in the halo of candlelight. She was as dear to him, as reassuring, as the old carver chair on which he sat, the gate-legged table on which he rested his elbows.

"What was that, Em?"

"I said that Catherine is poorly." She spoke up, enunciating as if he was deaf. He was not. He heard too much, not too little. "She isn't coming down tonight."

"Again?" he said, matching her volume, outstripping it. "She seems to be making a habit of it."

He embarked on a dish of tapioca, added a dense layer of sugar from the silver sifter, flooded the edges with yellow cream and watched as an island appeared. He held the empty cream jug aloft, waggled it and the maid came forward with a startled air. Emmeline was looking at him again. They always wanted something from you, women. A chap could have no clue as to what it might be.

"Benedict is out with his guttersnipes this evening, no doubt. Where on earth is our daughter?" He scraped the last traces of pudding from the inside of the bowl, relishing the smooth, bland sweetness. He licked clean the front and the back of the spoon, laid it down and looked at his wife. "Hmmm?"

From the expression on her face, he gathered that the answer had already been given.

THREE

A dozen or more women were gathered around a long table, roughly laid for breakfast. Lovely gave Anna a little push, pointed at a chair at the far end, a spoon and tin mug positioned on the oilcloth. As she sat down, the woman in the next seat looked up from a piece of wood wrapped in a scrap of white shawl, on her lap. She wore a print dress and her hair was cropped like a boy's, with tufts sticking out over her ears. Her brown eyes were intense, searching, as she looked at Anna.

"Forgive me," she said. "I tried my best."

"I'm sorry but you're mistaken. We have never met."

The woman's expression changed; Anna thought for a moment she was going to strike her.

"You were always a heartless creature, Ma Button. I saw it in your eyes, the first time I ever met you. I knew then what you were."

Anna took a sip of water from the mug, rolled its iron taste around her mouth. An old woman opposite was collecting bread crumbs in the corner of a handkerchief; farther down the table, another one called for her mother. The air was thick with the taint of unwashed clothes and untreated hair.

On the far wall was a large fireplace in a marble surround. Next to it, a collection of portraits hung in two lines, some singly, others in pairs, all on long, fine strings attached to picture hooks on the rail above. Their arrangement on the wall was purposeful, had a pattern and order at odds with the rest of the room.

"The tea will be here soon," her neighbor said in a different, lighter voice. "I expect you'll be glad of it on such a cold morning. How d'you do anyway, I'm Mrs. Lizzie Button."

She shifted the bundle on her lap and held out a hand. Anna felt an impulse to grasp it, beg the woman to tell her what this place was, who these others were. Why they'd taken her cloak and boots, by the time she awoke. How she could escape. Checking the urge, she fixed her eyes on the wall in front of her and made her face expressionless. She wouldn't—couldn't—utter a word to any of them. She must keep herself separate, prove that she wasn't one of them, that she didn't belong here and never would.

Lizzie Button was undeterred. She carried on talking, between mouthfuls of herring. The tea was strong but never hot enough. She longed for a cup of coffee, they all did, and there was plenty wanted something stronger. All you got was a glass of beer once in a blue moon. Not that she took a drop herself. The fare was unappetizing right enough but the young lady ought to eat something if only to keep up her strength. She would need all of her strength in this place, especially if they decided to try to cure her. Mrs. Button yelped with laughter then started to cry again, dragging a handkerchief from her cuff, sniffing.

The woman turned to Anna and grabbed her hands, squeezing her fingers with unnatural strength.

"Let me see them," she said, her voice charged. "My angels. Just once, Ma. I'm begging you."

Anna shook herself free as a maid arrived with cakes, tipped upside-down from the tin and heaped on a platter. A hum rose over the table, hands reaching in from all sides. The plate emptied and a scuffle broke out at the other end of the room. As Makepeace's clipping, approaching heels made themselves heard above the din, coming from along the corridor, the women fell silent. They rose one by one and formed a line by the wall, holding the cakes like robins' eggs in cupped hands, then began to file out of the door.

Anna felt someone looking at her. A woman stood at the end of a sideboard, stacking side plates like a deck of brittle cards. She was dark-haired, with a pleated white ruff around the neck of her dress, pushing up under her chin. Her face was dusted white, with black arched brows high over her eyes and reddened lips. She looked like an elderly doll.

The woman picked up a small brush and pan and began sweeping the table, flicking shards of eggshell, fish bones, and cake crumbs into the pan, the bristles making light, stroking sounds on the oilcloth.

"You'll grow accustomed to the routine, Mrs. Palmer," she said, in a gentle, cultivated voice. "Mr. Abse leads prayers in the dayroom after breakfast. Some of us take the air at ten-thirty in what they call the airing grounds. It's a courtyard, behind the house. After that, we occupy ourselves with handwork till luncheon. Mrs. Makepeace will provide you with silks. It's the same every day, except Sunday. Then there's no sewing. The time passes somehow. If I can help you with anything, let me know. My name is Talitha Batt."

Anna wanted to ask the woman how she knew to address her as Mrs. Palmer, how long she had been here, who Abse really was. She opened her mouth to speak then again quelled the impulse to respond to a lunatic. Turning her head away, she surveyed the room, the oversize sideboard running along the wall opposite the windows, the mismatched chairs around the table.

Anna found herself looking again at the pictures on the wall and got up to examine them more closely. They were photographs, she discovered to her surprise, oddly modern in this old place. Each one was six or seven inches tall and four or five wide, cut into an oval shape and pasted on card. Photographs of women. Every one of them was alone, pictured against a plain background that made them seem as if they might have been anywhere or nowhere. Some looked afraid, others angry. Amused. Some seemed to have retreated inside themselves and their expressions gave away nothing at all.

An old country woman caught her attention. She had a spotted scarf tied around her neck and was clasping a pigeon against her breast; bird and woman looked out with the same brightness of eye. Studying the face, the white hair springing out from under the edges of a man's cap, she recognized the woman who'd been sitting opposite her at the table. She could see her more clearly in the photograph than she had with her own eyes.

"Mrs. Valentine. Violet Valentine. A good likeness, don't you think?"

Anna felt a hand on her arm and turned to see Makepeace beside her. Her gaze was neutral, unyielding, and she wore the same dark dress as on the previous day but with the addition of a small cameo hanging from a ribbon around her neck. Anna shrugged off her hand and stepped back. Makepeace had shoved her into the room with the strength of a kicking horse; she intended from now on to stay out of her reach.

"Did you want something, Mrs. Makepeace?"

"If you'd care to follow me, Mrs. Palmer."

Anna glanced around the room, empty now. She had no option but to walk behind Makepeace, past the staircase to the bedrooms, past a room where a maid on her knees sorted through a heap of dresses all made from the same sprigged cotton as Mrs. Button's. The sound of rain pounding on a tin roof was coming from farther along the corridor. It was peculiar, that rain should fall indoors. It wasn't raining outside. She strained her ears and clearly heard the echoing splash of water hitting tin.

"What's that?"

"What is what, Mrs. Palmer?"

"That sound."

Makepeace stopped in front of a door and selected a key from a silver contraption at her waist.

"I don't hear anything. Come in and sit down."

Makepeace held open the door, then closed it behind them so that only the crackling of a fire could be heard.

The room smelled of something familiar. Anna breathed in deeply, inhaled a bitter aroma that cheered her before she knew what it was. Coffee. Just to smell it made her feel hopeful. The situation was about to be resolved. Makepeace had brought her here to apologize for the mistake, to inform her that a cab waited for her outside in the driveway and that she was free to leave. Anna ignored the chair Makepeace pulled out for her on one side of a table.

"I'd like my cloak, Mrs. Makepeace. My boots. I need to return to London this morning."

"Be seated."

At the tone of her voice, Anna felt the hope drain away. She sat down, keeping her eyes on her lap. The ring on her finger seemed to belong to another woman, in another life. It was in the shape of a snake, curled around her finger, gold, studded with tiny turquoise stones. Vincent had said he feared it might be blasphemous and urged her to select a plain band. "Remember the serpent, Anna, *more subtil than any beast of the field.*" It was only when the jeweler pointed out that the Queen had one similar that he'd agreed to her choice.

"There was general hysteria this morning."

"Was there?"

"Yours, Mrs. Palmer. It spread along the corridor, to the other guests."

"I wasn't in the least hysterical. I was calling for help."

"You've been entrusted to our care."

"I don't need care, thank you, Mrs. Makepeace. All I want is to be allowed to go. I've written to my husband and my sister to arrange it."

Anna reached into her bodice and pulled out the envelopes. They looked porous by the light of day, inadequate vessels for her hopes. The wax seal was soft from the warmth of her body, too substantial for the flimsy paper.

"I need to post my letters, urgently."

Makepeace glanced at the window.

"I will deal with your correspondence," she said.

"I'd prefer to do it myself."

"There is no post box inside Lake House, Mrs. Palmer."

"I can walk. There must be one nearby."

Makepeace seemed to suppress a smile.

"Guests do not leave the grounds," she said. "The cost of stamps will be added to your bill."

Vincent was paying for her to be here. The light coming through the window lost what tinge of sun it held as Anna looked again at Makepeace—at her doughy face, the brown tide mark across the top of her forehead where she dyed her hair. Makepeace used a mirror, Anna thought, had an opinion about what she saw there. She was a woman like other women, with desires and fears and vanities. She would appeal to her humanity.

"Mrs. Makepeace, I went to try to help the survivors of a shipwreck, after the hurricane. It was a reasonable thing to do. A good thing, some might believe. My husband doesn't come from a maritime family, as I do. He never set eyes on the sea until he was an adult man." She gave a small laugh and forced herself to meet the woman's eyes. "It is understandable that he could misinterpret my state of mind. But surely you can see for yourself that there's nothing wrong with me?"

Makepeace's mouth remained set.

"It is not just your husband who is concerned for you, Mrs. Palmer. Two doctors confirmed his view."

Anna pressed the letters to her chest, feeling her spirits lift like a hot air balloon.

"I haven't seen any doctors. It's all a mistake, Mrs. Makepeace, just as I thought. You've no right to detain me."

"They signed the certificate, after their interview with you."

The two women's eyes met again and this time it was Anna's that slid away as she remembered the visitors who came to the house some days after her return from the coast. It was late afternoon; Vincent had asked her to join them in the study. He poured her a glass of sherry from the decanter, invited her to tell the two men, old friends of his from the university, about her *mission of mercy*. He'd understood, she thought. At last.

She'd set about explaining the tragedy to the men. Most of the survivors had already gone by the time she reached the Welsh harbortown, sailed for their far-flung homelands on a Cuban clipper. Only the worst-injured remained, living off brandy from salvaged barrels, sleeping under sheepskins in the cottages of the fishermen. They had lost everything. Comrades. Possessions. Eyes or limbs or teeth, in the darkness, in the water. The captain bit off his own tongue before he drowned. Farther down the coast, corpses were still washing in on the tide.

Relief had made Anna voluble. She took another sip of the sherry and continued. The sailors were wiry, hardy men, Vincent's trousers were too large around the middle for them, his shirts too broad in the neck. She told Vincent's companions about the first mate's hands, the size of shovels. The way he held his lacerated fingers in front of him as if they weren't part of him and demonstrated how he'd grasped at the rocks and been swept back by the waves time and time again until finally he managed to get a hold.

The sight of his injuries had turned her stomach; there was a smell in the room like rotting meat. When she held out the silver watch, the first mate turned away.

"I didn't have a chance to clean it," she'd explained. "It only needs winding."

He let loose a torrent of words in his own, throaty language and looked at her with eyes that seemed to see something other than her or the humble room. She'd left the watch on the locker among the grains of spilled sugar and strands of tobacco. It only occurred to her afterward that he didn't want it. Not because it was tarnished but because it was charity.

She fell silent. Looked at the men, hungry for some explanation of how God could allow such suffering. One adjusted his bow tie; the other stifled a yawn.

"Tell them why you went, Anna," Vincent said, drumming his own, intact fingers on the desk. "Explain what you believed you were doing."

So she told them, how she'd read in the newspaper about the wrecked ship, the boy brought out of the waves still breathing. And that as she read she felt certain she was called to play a part, could offer some help. Vincent might perhaps have explained that she came from a seafaring family, that her own father lost his life in just such a tragedy. If, as a woman, she was able to make any contribution to society, she'd always prayed that it should be in assistance to sailors. The men made notes, nodding and glancing at each other.

"Is that everything you wish to impart, Anna?" Vincent said. "Nothing more? About the strange things you've seen?"

"I think we've heard enough," the one in the bow tie said, getting out of his chair and tugging on his fingers, making the joints crack into the silence that had descended in the study. The bells of All Hallows sounded outside as they rose and made their good-byes.

Vincent had betrayed her. Anna felt as shaken as if she'd slipped and fallen in the street. She struggled to compose herself, to meet Makepeace's look of satisfaction.

"In that case," she said, "I must see another doctor. An independent one whose opinion is impartial."

"You'll be seeing Dr. Higgins, Mrs. Palmer. All our guests do."

"When? How soon can I meet him?"

"Next time he comes to Lake House. By then, we can hope for an improvement in your state of mind."

"I don't need improvement. There is nothing wrong with my mind."

Makepeace smiled properly for the first time and reached out her hand.

"You are hardly in a position to be the judge of that." She took the letters from Anna, dropped them into a drawer on the far side of the table and closed it. "Now, if you would care to rejoin the other guests, you can start to acquaint yourself with everyone."

FOUR

In the parlor, Catherine lay on a chaise longue, her head resting against its buttoned back, her fingers supporting the book balanced on her chest. The book was bound in crimson linen, the pages roughly cut like the end of a loaf.

"Are you going to change, Catty? You can't spend the whole day in a morning dress."

"Why not?"

"Your father likes to see you looking pretty."

"No, he doesn't." Emmeline Abse opened her mouth to protest but Catherine spoke first. "He never notices what I look like, Mother."

Catherine turned a page and as her eyes traveled down it, her face took on a wistful look.

"'Ten nights and days we voyaged on the deep; / Ten nights and days, without the common face / Of any day or night . . .'" she read. "Isn't that beautiful?"

"I'm sure it is, dear." Emmeline held her own book at arm's length. "'Moisten the celery with cream. Place a thin layer between slices of bread and butter and serve.' I've always been fonder of cucumber in sandwiches, myself." Poetry would not triumph over sustenance. She wouldn't allow it. She stole a look at her daughter. "There's a recipe here for custard tarts, darling, with grated nutmeg. You used to relish them."

"I still do. I'd like one now."

"I'll get Cook to make you a batch tomorrow."

"I won't want them tomorrow."

"Why ever not?"

Catherine groaned, laid the book face down on her chest and closed her eyes. Her white fingers set themselves first to stroking the horse-hair upholstery then to plucking out strands.

"It's too far off," she said. "Look how many hours this day's got left in it, Mother. How many minutes."

Emmeline concentrated on preventing the frown in her mind from reaching her face. The room was warm, the wide wooden floorboards covered with worn Persian runners whose creams and rusts and plums glowed in the light from the lamps. Time had accelerated for her and she felt it most acutely in winter. It was half past three by the clock on the mantelpiece, which was reliably fifteen minutes slow. She glanced at the window, at the line of violet sky overlaid by a lace of black, sil-houetted branches, and braced herself.

"There's a whole section here on damsons," she announced. "Dam-son cheese. Damson jelly. Damson wine."

Catherine made a noise of disgust as she brought her own book parallel to her face.

"I hate damsons. Listen to this!

"'She had lived we'll say, / A harmless life, she called a virtuous life, / A quiet life, which was not life at all.'" Catherine closed her book with a soft, hollow slap. "Did you ever have an adventure, Mother? Before you were married?"

"Marriage is an adventure."

"Not with Father it isn't."

"Catherine. It isn't good for you."

"I know . . ." Catherine swung her feet to the floor and jumped up. "Burying myself like this in books."

She had an angular look; her bones were the fastest-growing part of her and her flesh struggled to keep pace with the hard fact of them. Her stockings were wrinkled around the ankles with one heel twisted to the front. She stood before Emmeline, looking down on her. Her complexion was so white most of the time that it could appear almost blue. But in a passion, as she was now, she turned crimson. Like a sheet of watercolor paper, thought Emmeline, flooded with rose madder.

"I'd die without books, Mother. Can't you see that?"

Catherine turned and rushed from the room, stooping to pick up the poetry book, catching the claw-footed table with her own long foot as she passed, sending a glass case crashing to the floor.

Ringing the bell with short, emphatic swings of her wrist, Emmeline let the frown invade the whole of her face. She had paid too little attention to Catherine's constitution when she was a small child. She'd loved sweet things. Milk and honey, crystallized pears, sugarplums. Emmeline had allowed her to carry on eating pap long after the age the boys had given it up. She hadn't thought it mattered. Catherine had been like some edible delicacy herself, her breath like violets, her limbs marzipan. She used to sit beside her when she slept, wondering at her, inhaling her, raising a plump, cool fist to her lips for worship. It had spoiled her. She'd grown willful on love and sugar.

No sign of Hannah Smith. Emmeline maneuvered herself down to the floor, one knee at a time and felt the rough press of the rug against the palms of her hands. The glass dome had cracked. Close up, the flowers looked scarcely worthy of display, the petals melted out of shape, their pinks and apricots and mauves bleached almost white. It wasn't right that wax flowers should fade. That was the point of *immortelles*. That they should remain beautiful.

She lifted the case onto Querios's chair, hoisted herself back to her feet, and as she straightened up caught sight of a woman she half-recognized, in the mirror over the mantelpiece. Her hair had begun to show silver strands not long after Catherine was born. This year, the two white streaks at the front had become broad stripes. A portent of things to come. On bad days, she thought she looked as if she'd been struck by lightning. On better ones, she tried to consider it distinguished.

Emmeline felt sometimes that something inside had faded with her hair, some quality of imagination that had once been vivid. At Catherine's age, she too had been a dreamy girl, with a head full of longings for *la belle France* inspired by her brothers' language tutor, Monsieur Pierre.

Replacing the flowers on the table, she turned the crack toward the wall, slowly rubbing off the fingerprints with her cuff. It made her uncomfortable, her own daughter thinking that she knew more of life than Emmeline did. And Catherine appeared determined to help herself to more of it even as she became increasingly contrary about what she ate. Emmeline was worried about her. She must talk to Querios.

She rang the bell again and added her own voice.

"Hannah Smith! Where are you?"

FIVE

$$\asymp$$

"Doctor's attending today, miss," Lovely said, escorting Anna back to the bedroom after breakfast. "Mrs. Makepeace says you're to wait here. I'll be up for yer soon as he's ready."

"Thank you, Lovely. I'm hoping he'll help me."

Lovely sniffed and wiped her nose on her cuff.

"Daresay you are," she said, pulling the bedroom door closed behind her and locking it.

Anna felt too impatient to sit down. She had been in Lake House for one week and felt she could not tolerate another day. Another hour. She pulled one of the rough brown blankets off the bed, wrapped it around herself and went to the window, leaning her elbows on the sill, feeling the cold air streaming in around the edges of the frame.

The view was the only comfort the room offered. In front of her was a spacious downward sweep of grass with an ancient oak that stood to the right of her window. The tree's shedding leaves created the impression of a rich, golden shadow in a circle underneath it. Beyond the lawn, marked off by iron rails, was a sheep field and at its boundary a row of breeze-tossed willows leaned out over the fringes of a body of water. It could have been a river but from its stillness she took it to be a lake, a cool reflective eye staring up at the sky, filled with it. On the other side of the lake were woods and open land and on the far horizon, beyond everything, the dome of St. Paul's Cathedral, small and softly round, as if fashioned from cloud.

Anna's eye was drawn again to the bridge beyond a thicket of trees farther along the shore of the lake. It was a white bridge, stretching from one side of the lake to the other, delicate and ethereal, its three shallow arches a row of half-moons that seemed to float on the surface of the water. The bridge was the most beautiful she'd ever seen, like something from a painting or an illustration for a fairy tale.

As she stared out, a girl in a red cloak appeared from the direction of the house. She wove a path across the grass, her head bowed, moving in an erratic line. She was about to collide with the railings when she stopped and raised her head. As she turned toward the gate, Anna saw the reason for her strange progress. The girl was reading a book.

She passed into the field and continued her meandering way to the edge of the water. A line of ducks swam to meet her and she began to throw scraps to them, swinging her arm again and again. She reopened the book and walked back toward the house, still reading, oblivious to the sheep that followed her through the open gate.

On impulse, Anna tapped on the glass and lifted her hand in a wave. The girl stopped and looked up, pressing the open pages against her chest. Anna saw a still, pointed face, thin fair hair. Suddenly, as if she heard someone call her, the girl thrust the book under her cloak and darted out of sight.

A minute later, Lovely arrived and led Anna down the stairs to Abse's study.

Anna paused in the doorway, casting her eyes over the cliffs of books, the fox in its glass cabinet. It seemed wrong to her that she should be entering the room from inside Lake House, from the patients' quarters, instead of from the outside like the accidental visitor she felt herself to be. A man sat writing behind Abse's desk.

"Best o' luck," Lovely muttered from behind her. "I'll be back to collect yer in ten minutes." Lovely departed, closing the door behind her.

Anna reminded herself that this was her chance to get out. She might even be free today if the physician gave her a fair hearing. Digging her nails into the palms of her hands, she readied herself to tell the whole story, calmly, from the beginning.

"Good morning, Doctor."

He raised his head, looked her up and down as she walked toward him.

"Come in, come in. I won't bite."

"You are Dr. Higgins?"

"Indeed I am. Sit yourself down."

He rose and took hold of her hand, two fingers pressed to her wrist while looking at his watch. She smiled at him.

"I am not ill, you know. I need to explain to you what has happened."

"Open your mouth."

"Doctor, I'm perfectly well. If I could just recount to you . . ."

He bent his face close to hers and opened his own mouth to reveal a white-coated tongue. She averted her eyes as he flattened her tongue with a spoon, peered into her throat. He was old, fifty or more, to judge by the slump of his shoulders, the corrugated skin of his forehead, but he had the hair of a boy, glinting chestnut, smooth and shining on his head.

"Throat looks normal."

"My throat isn't important," she said when he removed the spoon. "But I must talk to you."

"Now, Mrs.—Mrs.?"

"Palmer."

"I believe the doctor is generally considered the one who knows what's important. Eh? Do you know what year it is?"

The wind was gusting outside; she could see what might have been leaves or birds whirling through the sky on the other side of the glass. The globe stood on the floor by the window, tilting on its stand, swaths of pink glowing in the gloom.

"It is 1859, sir. The first of December. But Mrs. Makepeace said I would only have a few minutes with you and I want—"

He interrupted with more questions. Anna supplied the name of the monarch and the Prime Minister, told him how many fingers she had. How many toes.

"There was distress, on admission, according to the notes," he said.

"Distress?"

"You were out of control. Hysterical. Have you any recollection of it?"

"It wasn't hysteria, Doctor. I was alarmed to be locked in a room by two strangers. Frightened. I was angry too. Wouldn't you be?"

"It is you that is under discussion. Not I."

He put a trumpet against her chest, leaned his ear against the end of it. His head was so close she could feel its warmth under her chin, see the hairs growing out of his ears, the line of grime on the inside of his collar.

"Rapid heart rate," he said, straightening up. "Not unexpected."

She took a deep breath.

"Dr. Higgins, I am here only because my husband didn't understand why I acted as I did."

He resumed his seat, scanned a piece of paper in front of him.

"Says here he's a man of the cloth. A vicar must know something of human nature even if he knows more of God. Eh?"

He looked at her, pleased. She felt a sense of disbelief that the interview should be going so awry. She must make him hear her.

"Listen! There were hundreds drowned that night, all around the coast. I still believe it was right for me to try to help."

He shook his head, held up a finger to his lips.

"A young woman has no reason to think about death. A young woman should contemplate life. Increased life in the case of a married woman like yourself."

His gaze shifted to her breasts.

"When did you last have your monthly bleeding? Do you recall?"

It had added to her difficulties on the journey back to London. She'd felt the usual relief, despite the jolting pains in her belly, echoing the jolting of the carriage, mile after mile. She somehow couldn't imagine having Vincent's child. The eyes looking up at her from the crib, hard and opaque as black marbles. Vincent never mentioned children, which she found odd. Anna shook her head. She didn't want to talk to this man about it.

"I see. Suppressed catamenia. Uterine disturbance."

"I am well, Doctor. In all respects."

"On the contrary. You are suffering from hysteria. Most of your sex do, at some time in their lives."

He crushed a blue pill on a scrap of paper with the back of a spoon, mixed it in a tumbler of water. The solution flew round and round, grains descending to the bottom in a slow fall.

"Oh no, Doctor. I don't want any medicine," she said, her hand rising to her mouth. "I never . . ."

"Emetics are helpful in cooling the blood, restoring the proper balance."

He had stood up, was pressing the tumbler to her lips, holding back her head with the other hand as he tipped the contents of the glass into her mouth. "Count yourself lucky," he said, addressing the ceiling, ignoring her choking. "Abse believes in restraint from within. There are no shackles here, no bridles. The tea isn't laced with antimony and you won't find yourself in the strait waistcoat, unless strictly necessary."

She spat out what she could, then swallowed and wiped her mouth on the back of her hand. The liquid was bitter on her tongue, undissolved fragments catching in her throat. Higgins sat down again, picked up his pencil and focused on the sheet of foolscap in front of him.

Anna thought of their doctor at Dover, his kindly prescriptions of syrups and tonics. Morphine, *in extremis*. Words, sometimes. She pictured his quiet nodding, as his patients told him what ailed them. She had never known a doctor could be a brute. She felt as if the world had spun upside-down, as if she had failed to understand something important.

Curbing the urge to reach across the desk and grab his lapels, demand to know how this man dared call himself a physician and disgrace an honorable profession. She took a deep breath. Swallowed again.

"You haven't given me a chance to explain."

The pencil scratched its way across the rough weave of the paper; Higgins's stomach rumbled.

"I've heard all I need. Good day, Mrs. Farmer."

"I told you, my name is Anna Pa—"

Lovely was back. She pulled Anna from the room, hurrying her up the stairs to the bedroom. When they got there, she said she'd be back in two shakes of a lamb's tail and left again, banging the door shut, running down the corridor in her heavy clogs.

The fire was out and the room felt dead too, the air still and cold and stale. Anna sat down on the bed and looked at her feet in the pair of shapeless slippers they'd supplied in place of her boots. She felt sick with disappointment.

The feeling grew stronger. She got up and clutched at the washstand, leaned against the wall then stumbled to the bed to lie down. Waves of nausea rose from her stomach up through her chest, her head. She jumped up from the bed as Lovely rushed in and set down a tin bowl. A stream of liquid spurted out through Anna's mouth, spattered across the bottom of the bowl. The sickness ceased and returned immediately, more strongly. Lovely stood beside her, holding her hair out of the way, wiping her mouth, as Anna vomited again and again.

"How does anyone get out of this place?" Anna said, between heaves of her stomach. Lovely held a cup of water to her lips.

"They get out sooner or later, miss, most of 'em. It depends mainly on what happens outside. Who wants them out. Who wants them in."

Anna continued retching, violently, though nothing came. Black spots danced in front of her eyes; her stomach muscles ached.

"Damn you, Higgins," she said, leaning on the bed frame, gripping it with both hands. "And damn you, Querios Abse. Damn you to hell."

Lovely put the bowl outside the door, came back and squeezed out a flannel with water from the ewer, smoothed it over her lips, her ears, her neck. Anna didn't resist, as Lovely helped her into a nightdress.

"It'll pass, miss. Lie down a minute."

It was dusk when Anna woke. The light glowed violet through the flimsy curtains; outside, sheep were complaining in long plaintive cries. Someone had laid the fire and the bedroom door had been left ajar, kept open by a wedge of wood. She could get off the bed and walk through it. She pictured herself doing that, gripped the mattress and tried to sit up. At the sound of footsteps in the passageway, she fell back on the pillow and closed her eyes.

Lovely returned and busied about the room. She struck a lucifer and the air grew sharp with the smell of sulfur. Anna heard her blowing into the sticks, then the sound of liquid splashing into a cup. The rattle of a teaspoon, followed by the double tap of it. Her mother, Amelia

Newlove, used to make the same sound. Stir, stir, stir. Tap, tap. Her own little tune.

"You feeling any better, miss?" Lovely laid a hand on her shoulder. Her touch was gentle, despite her brawn. "I brought sweet tea and Cook's spared a dash of brandy. Sit up and take it while it's hot."

Tears sprang from Anna's eyes and rolled toward her ears. She couldn't accept pity from Lovely or from anyone else. The only strength she still had was to rely on herself and keep everyone here at a distance. Rolling over toward the wall, she stared at the reflection of the fire, the flames in the glass licking at the fisher girl's back.

"I don't want tea. Just leave me alone, will you."

"As yer like."

Lovely dragged the mattress out from under the bed and threw herself down on it. Anna lay still, waiting to hear the Lord's Prayer in the fervent whisper that made her feel as if she'd never properly heard the words before. Nothing. Only, after a while, a creaking and rustling of the straw. An *Amen*.

When she judged Lovely was asleep, Anna sat up. The door was locked again. Lovely had left the tea on the chair, drawn up by the bed. Anna reached for the cup and took a sip. The tea was lukewarm but the brandy felt fiery in her throat, heated her from inside. She drained it and eased herself back down under the blankets, hugging them around her ears, her feet tucked up under the rough nightdress.

She thought back over recent events, trying to see them clearly. The mission to the coast had not been what she had imagined. It was the first time since her marriage that she'd traveled alone, and when she set out on the Tuesday after the great storm she'd felt sure of herself, had a sense of invulnerability that was new to her. The feeling ebbed away as the train tore past cottages with their roofs blown off, trees lying on their sides, their roots in the air, festooned with mud.

Taking coaches from Birmingham, she traveled north and west toward the Welsh coast, through mountain passes where the road was scattered with fallen boulders. Three times, all the passengers had to disembark, the women huddled in the wind by the side of the track while the men lent a hand shifting rocks. The world seemed to have been torn up, thrown around like a plaything by the storm.

By the time the coach reached the harbortown it was dark. The exhausted horses had ceased to respond to the driver's whip. They trundled at walking pace past windows lit with rushlights, past leaning hovels with people clustered round their open doors, dogs barking and snapping at the wheels of the coach. Peering out from her seat by the window, Anna felt afraid. She gripped the handles of the carpet bag for reassurance. It was heavy, stuffed with her new clothes and Vincent's old ones. Hidden right in the middle was his second-best watch, the silver one.

She'd rummaged in the drawers in the wardrobe before she left, pulling out shirts with signs of wear on the necks, socks in need of darning. The drawers were labeled but the contents did not match the labels. There had been socks in the Shirts drawer, shirts in the one for Cravats. They had nothing for children in the Vicarage. She had run down to the kitchen before she left, requested a pound of currants, some loaf sugar. It was all she could think of.

"Could you hurry, please? It's urgent. Actually, it's a matter of life or death."

Cook had looked at her oddly but for once she hadn't cared. The image of the boy brought from the water was so clear in Anna's mind that it seemed to outshine ordinary life. Vincent was conducting a funeral and although she hadn't intended to conceal the trip from him, she found she wanted to get away before he returned. She scratched a hasty note and left it for him in the study, propped against his dictionary. Slipping out through the side door, which led directly to the street, she climbed aboard an omnibus in the direction of the railway station.

By the time she got off the coach in the main square of the Welsh town, Anna was hungry, her hands freezing. She couldn't put down the bag; the filth was inches deep under her feet, clinging to her boots. She felt relieved when she found a room in an inn. It bore no trace of the sea view it was named for and a salty dampness pervaded the air, the walls, the bedding—but it was a place to lay her head and make a plan.

The first morning, she woke early. It was a fine day, clear and still with not a breath of wind. She hid her bag under the bed and paid a boy a farthing to guide her to the bay where the ship had gone down, picking her way behind him through alleys where pigs ran free and the stench from the flooded ditches made her retch. There were chimney pots lying smashed in the cottage gardens, walls and fences blown down so what had been private, a broken-doored privy, a three-legged chair balanced under a kitchen window, was exposed for all to see.

The *Katerina* lay a little distance away from the land, half submerged, sinking as the waves broke over her then rising up between the swells, water pouring out of her portholes like tea from a pot. Anna hesitated, standing at the water's edge. The sea under the morning sun did not appear a killer. It advanced playfully, surge by small surge, retreated again. She knew what she must do. She took a deep breath and waded into the shallows, first gasping then crying out loud from the cold, sifting branches of podded seaweed and splintered lengths of driftwood through her hands, plunging her arms in deeper. She knew even as her empty hands trawled through the water, her fingers in violent pain from the cold, that she would find nothing. The sea had swallowed hundreds of adult men, without trace. And the newspaper report had said that the boy had been rescued alive. Yet she'd been compelled to search for him in the water. She couldn't quite understand it.

A crowd of children had gathered to watch from the rocks and were throwing pebbles in the water around her. The ship's cat bobbed on the tide—inflated, water-slicked. If she ever had to drown, please God let it not be by a black beach, she prayed, as she walked out, her skirts heavy, and her heart, asking herself what she'd imagined she might find.

The children followed Anna back to the Sea View Inn, jeering, pulling at her soaked clothes. Back in the privacy of her room, she sent down for hot water for a bath. The water was plentiful when it came and smelled of wood smoke; it left a residue of grit in the bottom of the tub like pepper in a soup bowl. She left her sodden skirts drying by the window, put on her other dress and made her way down the creaking, wooden stairs to a snug off the saloon bar and ordered a chicken sandwich, warming herself by the fire, trying to think what she should do next.

Anna felt a growing awareness of the oddness of her situation. An awareness brought about not just by the stiff politeness of the landlord, the guarded looks of the other residents at the inn, but by the utter novelty of the experience. She had never traveled such a great distance alone before or stayed in a hotel on her own. Yet this was the response she was impelled to make to the storm, to the wrecked ships and lives it had left in its wake.

In the afternoon, she set off around the cottages with the bag, intending to give away the things she'd brought and make inquiries about the boy at the same time. Some of the survivors turned down what she offered, refusing the sober shirts and jackets as not what they would wear even if they were about to be buried six feet under. One pointed out the worn knees on the trousers. Another grabbed her from his sickbed, took her by surprise. There were better things than socks to offer a man back from the dead, he said when she escaped to the other side of the room, the skin around her mouth rising in a rash of protest, her breast throbbing.

No one knew anything of a small boy, brought from the water still breathing.

SIX

Grace Jephcote's brow was contracted, the gaze in her large eyes fixed. The muscles on each side of her mouth appeared rigid and her hands grasped each other under her chin, the tendons taut. She had a daisy chain on her head, slipping down her dark hair.

"What d'you think?" Lucas St. Clair said.

James Maddox picked up the photograph, brought it within inches of his face, then held it at arm's length.

"Looks nervy. Then there's the crown, of course. Why do they all fancy themselves as queens? I don't know, St. Clair. Hysteria?" He dropped the picture back on the table. "I find it easier when I can see 'em in front of me."

Lucas picked up the picture again and held it to the light still filtering through the dining room window. He blew particles of dust from the face and neck. The corners of the print displayed the fragile, curling boundaries of the collodion; the whole image appeared as if it could peel up off the paper like a layer of skin. He looked at the eyes, the dilated pupils. He'd done his best to reassure her but Mrs. Jephcote had crouched on the edge of the posing chair and scarcely drawn breath during the long exposure. She'd crossed herself again and again when it was over and hurried from the room.

"She's suffering from religious mania, Dox. Can't you see it? The raised, curved brows. The tension in the jaw and that terrified look in her eyes. The poor woman is possessed by some fearful vision, incited by her crackpot preacher, you won't be surprised to learn. The daisy chain is her crown of thorns."

"How on earth am I meant to know that?"

Lucas laid down the print again.

"By careful observation. The point is, Dox, that if you can diagnose patients, you might stand a better chance of treating them effectively. I got them to take away her Bible and set her to work in the gardens, planting beans. That was back in the summer. She's much improved. They discharged her last week. If she stays away from the parson she might do well."

Maddox ran a finger over his front teeth. He'd had a new one wired in, Lucas saw, filling the crater at the front of his mouth.

"Purging seems to do most of 'em a power of good," he said. "Leeches, on occasion."

"Women hate leeches," Lucas said.

"Even so. She might have benefited from a cooling of the blood."

They walked along the passageway and into the parlor, where Lucas lit both lamps, adjusted the wicks and poured whisky into two crystal tumblers. Keeping the glass with the chipped rim, he passed over the other.

"Cheers."

"To your experiments," Maddox said, raising his glass.

There was a tap at the door and a head wearing a red scarf appeared around the edge of it.

"I'm off now, sir, if there's nothing more you want."

"Good night, Stickles."

The basement door banged as both men sat down by the fire. A dustbin lid clattered to the ground outside in the darkness, followed by a curse. Footsteps receded down the pavement. Lucas had taken on Stickles as a plain cook, which she proved not to be. Downstairs in her kitchen empire she didn't so much cook as conduct experiments. She concocted salve from beeswax and insisted he apply it to his hands, to counter the effects of the chemicals; produced unidentifiable jams involving petals and bits of aromatic bark, or pickled nuts and root vegetables in jars, occasionally serving one up on a plate. The lumpy defeat in their shapes reminded Lucas of the preserved hearts and kidneys in the labs at university.

He lived on bread and cheese but kept Stickles on because she didn't insist on getting the skivvy to clean the darkroom or tidy up. He stored his periodicals and case notes on the dining room table in what looked to others like random heaps but were in fact a carefully calibrated system, foolproof until some other hand interfered in it. All he asked, he told her, was that she should keep down the dust in the house and especially on the second floor. Stickles laughed. He would have to remove to the countryside, if he wanted to get away from dust. "It's what Lunnon's made of, sir," she said.

The lamplighter climbed down from the post in the street outside; a round-topped rectangle of flickering light appeared across the floorboards. The heat in the sole of Lucas's foot, the smell of singeing leather, had become impossible to ignore. He shifted his leg along the fender, emptied the last drops of whisky down his throat and got up to jerk the heavy curtain along its pole. It always got dark earlier on Sundays.

"Time you went, Dox. I'm on duty in the morning and I've got work to do tonight."

"In a minute. Have a look at this."

Maddox dug in his breast pocket and passed over a small card. It was a photograph of two girls lifting their skirts, showing bandy legs and childish pudenda. The print was amateurish, with no contrast and no detail, the flesh crudely colored with carmine. Lucas grimaced and passed it back.

"No thanks."

"Come on, old man. Every chap enjoys looking at pictures of naked women. Especially drawn from the life."

"I don't disagree with that. But not when I'm thinking about work. Anyway, these aren't women." He exhaled and looked at his friend through the softening drift of smoke. "It's time you found a wife."

Maddox grunted. He was fingering his tooth again, tracing its outline, his top lip drawn up like a snarling dog. He looked like the old statue of a raving maniac, outside Bedlam. Maddox bared his teeth further, lifting his top lip on both sides.

"Got it done by a chap in Holborn. Swore it was ivory. D'you think women care, about teeth?"

"Some of them might, I suppose."

Lucas himself had no interest in marriage. He was too busy for social life. And if he wasn't, he would want a woman he could talk to. Not some creature who spent her energies on stitching and sketching and tinkling the piano keys. Half the female patients in his care had been driven to the edge of reason by their limited lives, in his private opinion. Human beings needed a purpose.

While Maddox entertained a string of women at his rooms at Regent's Park, female callers at Popham Street were restricted to Lucas's mother, on her annual visit to London from the Cotswolds, and his sister, who claimed to find the parlor more comfortable than any other in town and who if she called without her husband smoked a Turkish cigarette while Lucas puffed on his pipe.

He leased the house from a silver merchant. It was adequate and the rent reasonable. On the top floor, where other men had bedrooms for children and servants, he had his darkroom. He'd had water piped up for the purpose and although he had not bothered to install a water closet, he was particular about the long basin, the drain that carried away the spent materials. The back bedroom was for dry work, varnishing and retouching, as well as storing the plates. Whatever time he didn't spend at his post at St. Mark's, Lucas spent on his research. He'd agreed to give a lecture in the spring to the Alienists' Association on photography in the diagnosis of lunatics. The members of the Association were like-minded, progressives in tune with himself and hungry for new approaches to mental disease. He had been working on his research in every spare minute, trying to take further the science that Dr. Diamond had begun.

Lucas put his glass down on the floor and rubbed his eyes with the tips of his long fingers. Most of the older generation were resistant. The superintendent of his own hospital, Sir Harry Grieve, was downright hostile. "The human eye does a better job of assessing a lunatic than a glass one ever will," he liked to pronounce from behind his half-moons. He'd refused Lucas permission to take photographs at St. Mark's, which forced him to seek out private asylums.

As soon as he was able to establish his research more firmly, he planned to leave St. Mark's. With luck, he would get a superintendent's post himself and with it the chance to build a progressive retreat. In the four years he had spent working with the insane, Lucas had come to believe that mental pain was the worst kind of pain. It was worse than bullet wounds or gangrene. More agonizing than cancers or dropsy. And there was no consensus on how to alleviate it. Blistering was an agony. Purging weakened patients and left them depleted. Cold showers could kill. The intricate variations in medicines were more articles of faith than proven treatments.

Lucas was convinced that photography could constitute a decisive break with the old ways. That it could lead to improved diagnosis, which in turn would inform better-judged treatments. But if he couldn't even persuade Maddox of the utility of the method, what chance did he have with the medical establishment?

Evidence. It was the only way. He had to come up with the evidence. He must get back up to Lake House at the first opportunity to discuss Mrs. Button's picture with her; he owed his subjects that much, he believed. And he wanted to meet the new patient Abse mentioned and see if she would agree to being photographed.

Maddox was dozing. His head lolled on the antimacassar and his jaw was slack. The tooth gleamed in the lamplight, whiter and larger than its intended twin. Lucas and Maddox both had posts at St. Mark's; they had been at the same university and before that, boys at school together. The event that had bonded them more deeply than friendship, than shared history, was the one thing of which they spoke with difficulty and usually only when both were drunk. Maddox too had lost an older brother in the Crimea. George Maddox was mowed down alongside Archibald St. Clair in the slaughter at Balaclava. Lucas and James were older now than those men had been when they met their deaths. They had no right to squander even a minute of their lives.

Maddox gave a thunderous snore and Lucas nudged his shin with the toe of his boot and stood up.

"Bugger off home, Dox," he said. "I've got things to do."

SEVEN

A fox emerged from the trees on the edge of the lake, made its way up the side of the field and broke cover, heading across the grass for the house. It reached the gravel path that led to the airing grounds and stopped, its tail a flag of intent.

Querios Abse watched from the study window, stroking the quill of his pen against his chin, enjoying its sharp, soft edge. He'd been too busy to get out again with the gun, occupied as he was with readying Lake House for the next visit from the inspectors. He'd had the whirling chair dismantled at last. Jethro Fludd carried it up through the servants' quarters into the roof space between the attic rooms and laid it piece by piece across the rafters. Querios had ordered dried lavender from Baldwin's and supplies of chloroform in fluted bottles that couldn't be mistaken. He'd permitted the introduction of ham, once a week, to be served with English mustard. The photographic portraits were now up in the dayroom as well as the dining room. The magistrates were sure to be impressed by Dr. St. Clair's techniques, even if the art critics found such pictures offensive.

He'd rehearsed with Fanny Makepeace the code of whistle blasts by which, the instant that the magistrates' carriage reached the gates, every member of the staff at Lake House could be alerted. On hearing the signal, the groundsman was to release the peacock, the attendants were to throw the lavender on the fires and Makepeace was to take the agreed measures to subdue any patient who threatened to embarrass the visitors.

The birds were the only part of the preparations that gave him personal satisfaction. He liked peacocks and when the magistrates had complained last time of too few diversions for patients, amongst other things, he'd had an idea. He'd ordered a silver one, with two hens, from a man in Suffolk. They arrived in a wooden crate and the cock began immediately to molt. A week later, one of the females was found dead in the run, her head detached from her body. Querios had been out then with the .12-bore and an oil lamp, taken potshots in the direction of movement in the shrubs. The noise disturbed the patients, Makepeace reported; in particular, Talitha Batt.

The fox was raising its leg against the old oak. He banged on the glass and it took off in a leisurely canter up toward the walled garden, the groundsman's cottage, the coop. His father, Septimus Abse, had shot a whole family of foxes. The dog prowled forever in a case in the study, stuffed fuller than he had ever been in life; the vixen was made into a stole, for his mother. The ineffable softness of the tips of fur flicking against his cheek, the feel of the lifeless paws and claws in the palms of his hands, had been a motif of his childhood, a symbol of all that was inexplicable about the adult state.

Returning to his desk, Querios put down the pen and picked up the new brochure. It featured Lake House on the cover, looking solid and dignified as a country hotel. In the engraving, the windows were bigger and the walls lower. Three women walked together toward the lake, their skirts and bonnets a deep rose pink. The edges of the picture were soft, as if the house was shrouded in fog or floated, unanchored, above the city it surveyed.

The paragraphs inside described a comfortable, well-situated retreat in the district favored by poets and philosophers, near enough to London to be accessible for visitors but far enough away to be removed from cares, smogs and the din of construction. The notion that they were interested in poets flattered the families. Relatives liked to think they could visit patients, if time allowed. They were less keen on the idea that patients could take it into their heads to visit them. He hadn't included the rates in the brochure. The accountant's plan was to raise them but so far Querios hadn't dared. Losing existing guests could be disastrous.

A log fell in the fire and he put aside the brochure, opened up a series of ledgers and once again began to go over columns of numbers that denoted reasons for admission, conditions, modes of treatment, cures, lengths of stay. The figures were an attempt to explain something that Querios Abse increasingly believed was not subject to explanation: the female mind.

The dayroom was the gloomiest Anna had ever seen. The high ceiling, the length of the room and the doors at each end gave it the air of a grand and static corridor. Brocade curtains soaked up the light from three long windows. A line of gas lamps suspended from the ceiling gave off more noise than illumination, the mantles hissing overhead, spent fumes souring the air.

Fifteen or twenty women sat at intervals around the room. Mrs. Violet Valentine and the other old ones clustered by the fire. The rest were stationed either alone or in groups of two or three on chairs and sofas. Lizzie Button paced about most of the time. Two of the women, Miss Todd and Miss Little, were inseparable except after one of their frequent quarrels. Then they made sure to sit at opposite ends of the salon.

"Are you feeling stronger, Mrs. Palmer?"

Talitha Batt's face was composed under a mask of powder that to Anna looked suspiciously like flour; her hands unspooled a length of vermilion silk in rapid, efficient movements.

"I'm perfectly well, thank you."

Anna answered without thinking, despite her resolution not to talk to anyone. Batt bit off a length of thread and smoothed out the fabric on her lap. The embroidered piece was large and densely worked, a complex, deep-colored tableau of exotic-looking flowers and insects. It was almost finished. She brought the tip of a needle up through a half-completed petal.

"Generally, one is out of sorts after an emetic. The muscles ache. One feels fatigued. Low in spirits and without appetite."

She glanced at Anna again, her darkened brows raised. The ruff standing up under her chin gave her an old-fashioned look; a Queen Elizabeth with a pointed chin and small ears. She could have been carved on a cameo, she was definite and distinct.

Batt had described so precisely how Anna felt that she might have been inside her body.

"You needn't bother about how I am, thank you. In fact, I would rather you didn't."

"Why is that, Mrs. Palmer? We are thrown together in this place, after all."

"I won't be staying long. I shouldn't be here but my husband has misunderstood my state of mind."

"Husbands so often do."

Her voice was mild. Anna flushed.

"He's a clergyman. He'll be coming soon to take me . . ." She thought she would say *home* but her lips refused. "Out."

"I do hope so. This is no place for a young woman. For any woman."

Lizzie Button was walking up and down, singing a lullaby, patting the piece of wood cradled against her chest. She moved like a mother in a nursery, her hand rhythmic, her voice soft. Anna made a long, low intake of breath. Poor thing had lost a child. It was obvious. She threw her a look of sympathy. Button glared at her.

More photographs had appeared in this room, arranged in two long lines on the wall opposite the windows. Anna got up to look at them. Like the others, they were of women alone, against blank backgrounds. Some looked into the eyes of the viewer, others gazed at something or someone unseen, or gave the impression they saw nothing at all. All had names or initials written on them; some were also labeled by their illnesses. "Hysteria." "Epileptic mania." "Habits of intemperance."

Anna stopped at a picture in the middle of the top row. The woman's face was grave, her eyes amused. She was sitting in a chair, her arms contained within its arms, a book open on her lap. Her hair, beginning to show the signs of age, was undressed. The photograph had the initials *LM* in ink, written in a fine italic hand and followed by "Melancholia."

Hanging next to it was a photograph of a different woman. Her hair was piled on each side of her head in stiff ringlets. She wore a shiny, checked dress with mandarin sleeves slit to the elbow, white lace undersleeves. She stood at an angle, her face half turned, eyes raised to some far horizon. The picture was titled "Convalescence." It was labeled with the same initials, *LM*. Anna looked back at the other picture; saw the duplicate almond shape of the eyes.

She turned away from the photographs, went back to the window seat and sat down. Picking up a magazine, she looked without interest at the advertisements for eiderdown petticoats, juniper hair tonic and skin creams that filled the back pages. She disagreed with the diagnosis. In the first picture, LM looked human. As if she might step off the wall and sit down for a proper talk such as women could find themselves having sometimes, one where something true or funny was said, some sorrow eased or laughter shared. In her convalescence, LM looked as stiff as the carved prow of a sailing ship. There was a dishonesty in her expression that hadn't been there before.

The door opened and a stout woman with white stripes like a badger's in the front of her hair bustled through the room, nodding at Batt as she passed. The room came briefly to life, a current of interest running through the occupants; it subsided into torpor in her wake. Anna looked at the old grandfather clock again. It was eleven-forty. She dropped the magazine and covered her face with her hands. Someone must be ill. One of the children had whooping cough. Or Louisa had gone away for a few days, summoned by her mother-in-law. She would return to London at the weekend, come for her on Monday or Tuesday.

Anna's sense of expectancy was becoming weary. She could barely call it hope anymore. She loved her sister but Louisa wasn't altogether reliable. Anna had always felt more like the older one, despite the four years between them. She must write to her again.

Had Vincent been to see Louisa? Was it possible that he had persuaded her that Anna was ill? Had lost her reason? Anna had once told Lou, after their father died, that she believed God wanted her to go to the aid of seafarers.

"Are you mad?" Louisa had said, screwing up her face. "Are you out of your mind, Anastasia?"

The drizzle outside thickened to rain, coming down with a dreary insistence. Anna stretched her arms in the air and reached down to retrieve the magazine from the floor. She avoided being indoors for long stretches, disliked closed windows and the lingering odor of past meals. Her father used to say she suffered from cabin fever. She wouldn't spend another day waiting for the creak of the door on its hinges. If the door opened, she intended to take no notice at all. Louisa would have to squash up next to her on the seat, throw her arms around her, pinch her, scream her name, before she even knew she was there. Anna stared down at the magazine, wiped her eyes with the back of her hand as a tear fell and formed a wrinkled circle on the print.

"I find it is easier to escape Lake House by accepting one's situation than by struggling against it," she heard Batt say, quietly. "Enjoying what companionship one may find."

Anna looked up.

"I will never accept it. I need to see a doctor. Not Higgins, a proper physician, Mrs. Batt."

"It is Miss Batt. I am unmarried. You could make an appeal to the other doctor. Present your case to him."

"Which other doctor?"

"He visits occasionally." Batt inclined her head toward the wall. "Those are his photographs. I notice that you found them of interest."

"I won't be photographed as a specimen, Miss Batt. Labeled like a butterfly and put on display."

The door squeaked open and despite herself, Anna's head flew up. It was a man. He stood in the doorway looking around with an air of purpose and interest. He was dressed in an old tweed coat, its collar turned up around a carelessly tied bow at his neck. His long hair was beaded with rain and his whiskers reached to his chin in the style that Vincent said denoted bad character, which he called Piccadilly weepers.

"Good afternoon to you all," he said.

Makepeace was behind him.

"She's over there, Doctor," she said, pointing at Anna.

He brushed rain off his shoulders and pulled off his gloves, looking at her curiously. For a minute, Anna couldn't think who he was or where she knew him from. Then she understood. Louisa had sent him. Louisa had sent her a proper doctor. How could she have doubted her?

She clapped her hands as he crossed the room toward her, laughed with relief as she jumped up from the window seat.

"Thank God you've come. Isn't it strange, that a week or two can take forever?"

"Yes," he said. "Isn't it? You must be the new patient."

His eyes rested on her for a long moment and traveled on. She became aware of Lizzie Button, leaning against the wall next to the window seat, her bundle in her arms.

"Greetings, Mrs. Button. I am Lucas St. Clair, come to see you again."

"I know very well who you are," Button said, laying one hand on his forearm. "What do you take me for, a cupboard head?"

"Not at all, I . . ."

"I am teasing you, Dr. St. Clair. Did you have a comfortable journey?"

They left, the man closing the door behind them with a last glance in Anna's direction.

Anna sat down. She felt sick with disappointment. Foolish too. The silence in the room was deeper than it had been, punctured by the uneven tick of the clock. Something had caused Miss Batt to smile. Her teeth emerged, small and white and straight-edged, between parted lips, as she held up the cloth to the light and examined it, a silver thimble stuck on the tip of one finger. She seemed in no mood for further conversation.

Anna decided to make an exception to her rule.

"Who was that?" she said.

Batt glanced around, her eyebrows lifted so high it appeared they might depart her face altogether.

"Are you speaking to me?"

"Yes. Who was that man?"

"He announced himself to Lizzie. You can hardly have failed to hear his name."

"I heard his name. But who is he?"

"He is a doctor, Mrs. Palmer. The one you decline to see. The photographer. He may also be a miracle worker."

"What do you mean?"

"It seems Dr. St. Clair has induced you to speak."

"I am perfectly able to speak, Miss Batt. It's just that I . . . Well, I . . ."

"You don't wish to associate yourself with the insane. Quite understandable, Mrs. Palmer. I felt the same myself once."

Her voice was dry and Anna felt the beginnings of a blush creeping onto her face.

She changed her mind about not talking to anyone; she was longing for some company. Asking Miss Batt about herself she learned to her surprise that Batt was the oldest in a family of eight, born in India in a bungalow among mountains whose tops disappeared in the mist. She'd grown up listening to the roars of tigers and being cooled by servants fanning her with banana leaves bigger than she was. In England, she worked as a milliner. Had her own little place in Fulham and spent her days plaiting straw and gluing feathers.

"I'm a practical woman, Mrs. Palmer," she said. "I do what needs to be done."

They lapsed for a while into silence. Mrs. Button had not returned. Anna glanced at the images on the wall.

"I may agree to be photographed after all. Do you think it might help me prove my rationality?"

Miss Batt stitched on for some time without speaking.

"Dr. St. Clair is a well-intentioned young man," she said, eventually. "Whether he holds any sway with Mr. Abse is another matter. And then of course there is the question of his techniques."

"What do you mean?"

"I mean that they may be misguided," said Miss Batt. "That there is always the possibility of their doing more harm than good."

EIGHT

⤬

Anna breathed in the fog, felt it on her cheeks, her lips, her tongue. It was white and tasteless, different from London fog. It was different from sea fog too—thick and unmoving. Abse had agreed to her request for a walk in the grounds. She could go where she liked, he said, with a poor sort of laugh. Within reason. Lovely would follow behind.

She walked along the gravel path at the back of the house, felt her way past the brickwork of a walled garden and arrived in front of a cottage, a curl of blue smoke from its crooked chimney pot merging with the white blanket that pressed down on the roof. A bird was calling somewhere nearby, making a high, harsh shriek that hurt her ears. She stopped to look at the cottage, leaning on its fence of wooden palings, peering toward the latticed windows for signs of normal life being lived by someone.

"Hello?" she said, experimentally, keeping down her voice so Lovely shouldn't hear.

At the side of the cottage, something red appeared to turn in her direction.

"Who's that?" came a high, clear voice. Anna made her way up the path and saw the girl. She was younger than she'd realized, pale and graceful inside her cloak, her eyes large and serious under a high forehead. She was standing in front of an enclosure, a book balanced on a fence post beside her. On the other side of the woven fence was a large, grubby bird with a crest of small quills like pins on top of its head and a long ragged tail stretched out behind. The mud in its run was marked

54

with angular footprints and scattered with bits of what appeared to be dumpling.

"Even he hates suet," said the girl. "Peacocks usually eat anything."

"Is that what it is? A peacock?"

"A silver peacock. That's what my father calls it but it's not really silver. More of a dirty white, don't you think? Poor creature. I don't know why he has to be penned in like this. It's so unfair."

The girl held her hand over the fence, dropped another lump; the bird shifted backward on scaly feet.

"My father's afraid he'll be eaten."

Anna cast a glance over her shoulder and Lovely clapped her hands, the sound muffled.

"Come along, miss. Best get going," she called.

The girl picked up her book.

"We can walk together." She took Anna's arm and they passed back down the path and set off across the grass that led to the field. Anna had a sense of unreality that she should be next to the girl, feeling the light grip of her fingers.

"I've seen you from my window. What's your name?"

"Catherine Abse. I'm not allowed to talk to lunatics but you look alright."

"I'm Anna. Mrs. Anna Palmer. I'm not a lunatic. You must be Mr. Abse's daughter?"

"Yes. I suppose I must be." Catherine let go of Anna's arm and peered at her out of the vapor, her white face coming nearer. "How old are you? Let me guess. Twenty-seven."

"Twenty-four, if you must know. How old are you?"

"Nearly sixteen. At what age should a girl marry, do you think?"

"I've never thought it mattered much. Why? Do you intend to marry?"

Catherine let out a noisy breath.

"One day I might. Not many men would want to marry a girl from a loony house."

They continued toward the lake under looming trees, their top branches amputated by the fog. The grass was thick and soft along the edges of the mud path, wet with dew. The hem of Anna's dress began to slap at her ankles, dampen her stockings. She'd wanted to use the walk to find out if the high wall went all the way around the grounds of Lake House, whether the bridge and the gates were the only ways out, but the visibility was too poor.

"Do you love birds? Is that why you come out to feed them? I've seen the ducks all coming to meet you."

"Not really," Catherine said. "I can't eat the food we have at home so I give it to the ducks. Most things stick in my throat. I can feel them choking me, even after chewing fifty times."

"Really? I would have thought that was impossible."

"Mother says it's impossible too. How many times do you chew things, Mrs. Palmer?"

Anna laughed. "I'm afraid I've never counted."

They went through the gate and on in the direction of the lake. Catherine began talking about an Indian man she'd read about in the *Illustrated News,* who fell in love with an elephant. She could understand it because she had fallen in love with Italy—"The white walls, the blue hills, my Italy"—even though she'd never been there. But she supposed falling in love with a country wasn't the same as falling in love with an elephant. Or a man. She stopped, turned her head toward Anna.

"Is it?"

"I don't know. I don't have the time to think about that kind of thing."

"What do you think about, Mrs. Palmer?"

Anna glanced around. She couldn't see Lovely or hear her but it didn't mean she was not near. The fog clothed everything.

"Since I was brought here, I have found it difficult to think of anything, Miss Abse, except how to get away."

"Call me Catherine. Please."

The edge of the lake presented itself suddenly, its surface still and black, dotted with white feathers, the clean, muddy tang of it penetrating through the fog. Anna stepped down a shallow bank and pulled off her glove; the water was soft and cold, lapped around her fingers,

magnified them. The white bridge gleamed through the vapor from
farther down the lake, the far side of it vanished in the mist. She gestured toward it and made her voice casual.

"What a pretty bridge. Where does it lead?"

"Nowhere."

Catherine tossed something out of her umbrella. It splashed into
the water and two dim shapes nosed their way to the surface. Anna
heard Lovely's voice calling from a distance. She had a sense that she
had been given another chance, in place of the one Higgins denied her.

"Catherine!" She put her hand on the girl's arm and met her eyes. "I
know we've only just met but I need to ask for your assistance. Would
you help me escape?"

"Why should I? Oh—I suppose you miss your husband too, too
desperately, Mrs. Palmer."

"Not really, I . . ." Anna lapsed into silence, looking at Catherine's
eager expression, the sympathy on her face. "Yes, I do. Miss him. Of
course, I do—most terribly."

"But how could I help you?"

"You might speak with your father. Persuade him that I am perfectly well. Do you have any influence with him?"

"No," Catherine said, abruptly. "He never listens to me."

Anna cast around in her mind.

"Could I pass as one of your friends, next time you go somewhere?
Slip out of the gates with you? Or hide in a corner of the carriage?"

"I don't go out. Except to church, sometimes. And we don't keep a
carriage anymore."

"I'll think of another way, then. But you don't refuse?"

Catherine leaned on a silver birch, resting the back of her head
against the peeling trunk, picking at the side of one of her nails. Her
skin was as pale as the bark, her hair lank where it emerged from her
bonnet. She looked like a woman, where a moment before she had
appeared a child.

"It would be an adventure," she said. "I long for adventure. A quiet
life isn't life at all, don't you think? Who was it that had you locked up?
Was it a jealous sister? His mother?"

Lovely's outline approached, slow and steady, growing more definite with every step. Anna and Catherine stopped speaking as she appeared in front of them, rubbing her bare hands together, her shawl pulled up over her head.

"There you are." She looked from face to face. "Thought I'd lost the pair of you."

They began to move back through the trees toward the field. Catherine told Anna how her brother was teaching boys from the slums of the Rookeries, instructing them in reading and arithmetic, how she planned once she reached twenty-one to change her name to Aurora, like her heroine, Aurora Leigh, and go to live in Italy. She intended to travel about freely by train, might even dress as a boy to achieve it, although the truth was that despite everything, she'd never wanted to be a boy. She sighed and turned her serious eyes to Anna again.

"Do you believe that life for a woman begins when she marries?"

"For some, perhaps. I don't know much about marriage."

Catherine giggled as she tightened her bonnet strings. Her hands were small as a child's, the fingers tapered, the nails flecked with white.

"But you are married. You must know about it."

"I haven't been married long. And my husband—well, he's not the easiest man to know."

He was impossible to know, Anna thought to herself. More remote and silent with every month that had passed. Catherine clapped her hands.

"Is he mysterious like Mr. Rochester? Older than you and broody? Passionate?"

"I wouldn't call him passionate, exactly."

"Why did you marry him then?"

A pair of swans flew low over their heads, their outstretched wings beating hard on the air, necks craned toward the water. They heard the splash of their long, skidding landing on the lake's surface. Both Anna and Catherine turned to see it but could not.

"There are many reasons to marry, Catherine, apart from passion."

"I know that. I'm not a child."

They made their way up through the field in silence, keeping to the sheep path. Anna felt an unexpected impatience to get back inside. Catherine was a sweet and likable girl but she couldn't help her. It was foolish to imagine she might be able to do anything, and Anna ought to be at her post in the window seat in the dayroom—able to see Louisa or Vincent the very moment they arrived to collect her.

On the higher ground, the mist had thinned; Lake House had come back into view. It looked perfectly flat up on its ridge, like a piece of scenery that she could reach out and topple with a shove of her hand. Lovely had gone on ahead and was opening the side door, wiping her clogs on the boot scraper. Next to Anna, Catherine's cloak rustled against her skirts. Her boots squeaked on the wet grass.

"What did you say was the matter with you, Mrs. Palmer?"

"Nothing. My husband got it into his head that I needed a rest. And your father"—she kept her tone light—"so far hasn't seen fit to let me go."

"There must be something wrong," Catherine objected. "Or you wouldn't be here."

Anna paused. She didn't intend to embark on the story of recent events with Catherine Abse but she wanted to give her an answer.

"Catherine, I am called to help the drowned." She was about to tell her about the boy but Catherine interrupted.

"You really are a lunatic. No one can help the drowned."

She stalked ahead through the open door and into the house, the flash of red vanishing into the dim interior.

Back in the dayroom, on the window seat, Anna wrapped her arms around her knees, closed her eyes and made herself think about her marriage. Vincent was almost twenty years older than she, and since being in Lake House she'd wondered if that was the difficulty, if it was impossible to bridge the years between them. But it wasn't only that.

She met Vincent in London, at a Missions to Seamen Society meeting organized by Louisa's sister-in-law. The sister-in-law was a bossy little woman, Louisa said, unmarried and much concerned with good works. It threw Louisa into a panic when she asked for her help because Lou wasn't by instinct a do-gooder. She spent her spare time at the house of her spirit medium, to the scorn of her sister-in-law.

Louisa wrote begging Anna to get her out of a tight spot, to come up to London for a week and prove that the Newloves were decent people with charitable urges. Anna, who was the last of the sisters and stranded at home with their widowed mother in Dover, jumped at the chance. She disliked London but she needed a change of scene and she welcomed the opportunity to try to help mariners and their families. Even before their father lost his life at sea, she'd had a particular feeling for sailors, for their courage in entrusting themselves to the uncertain oceans.

The day arrived. In a meeting room off Piccadilly, Anna spoke easily—about the need for help for sailors of all nations, not just spiritual aid but practical assistance. She didn't talk long but she described cases she knew from Dover, even including their own in a disguised form. Storms and hurricanes were no respecter of persons, could swallow the captain as readily as a cabin boy. Some sailors came ashore maimed in body or mind or both, unable to work. Some never came home at all. And the heartbreak and hardship that were the legacy to women of men's deaths at sea never eased.

Afterward, a tall man dressed in a black coat almost to his ankles approached her. He had a cup of tea on a saucer in one hand and a curious old-fashioned hat adorned with cords in the other. He handed her the tea, professed himself in full agreement with her sentiments and introduced himself as Reverend Vincent Palmer. He was austere-looking, serious, talking about his parish, his vocation. Anna was thirsty, her throat parched and the tea was nectar. Vincent Palmer fetched her another cup, talked on.

Elated from her speech, her head spinning from the novelty of it, she felt that this man recognized her. He saw past her dress and boots that seemed unremarkable in Dover but that in London looked downright shabby. Past her direct way of speaking, that Louisa insisted was unfashionable. And he shared her concern for seamen.

Her feeling was confirmed by what followed. Reverend Palmer called at her sister's house the following day, to pay his kind regards, showed an interest in their background. Louisa tittered, after he departed.

"Careful, Anna," she'd said. "He'll have you up the aisle before you know it. He's measuring you up for a wife."

"What if he is?" Anna had said, coldly. Louisa's beauty had always made it easy for her to scorn suitors, men in general.

Vincent Palmer called again the next day, with a gift of a small hymnbook bound in calfskin, and on the morning she was due to travel back to Dover, he came to the railway station. Anna was alone on the platform; Louisa hadn't wanted to get smuts on the children's outfits and had said good-bye outside the station. Anna looked up from her suitcase and saw a tall man in a tall hat, raising his arm to her in a proprietorial wave, striding down the platform. From afar, Vincent Palmer looked distinguished. Energetic. She felt a visceral response to his maleness. He drew nearer, accidentally knocking a small child out of his way, his eyes fixed on her.

"Miss Newlove," he said. "I've come straight from a meeting with the Canon. I am so glad . . . I mean, I hope I am not too late. I have come to inquire whether you wish to become"—he paused, removed the hat from his head—"Mrs. Vincent Palmer."

Anna could smell the frankincense lingering in his clothes, feel the tension in him as all around them the impatient engines roared and sighed. He was obscured for a long moment by a billowing blast of steam, then appeared again, his face eager. Waiting.

"Yes," she said. "Yes, I will."

The whistle blew and she had no choice but to board the train. Vincent passed up her bag behind her, slammed the door, waved through the sooty glass. She found her seat and as the train drew away watched him hurry in the other direction along the platform.

Anna sat without stirring all the way to Dover. Everything around her, the crowded carriage, the families with their boxes and rugs and walking sticks, was the same but she had changed utterly. A man who had reached middle age without finding a woman suitable to be his wife had chosen her, without hesitation. And he wanted to marry as soon as possible.

Anna had never been much interested in marriage. She'd seen too much of her mother's suffering, left alone for months at a time with five children and never quite enough money, then widowed in the middle years. Anyway, isolated as their family had become, Anna had never met anyone she wished to marry. She'd acted out of character in accepting, she told herself sternly. But the alarm she felt was matched by an unexpected elation. A man wanted desperately to marry her. She would escape from the house on the cliff, from her mother's bitter, circling ruminations.

Anna saw Vincent only twice in the months before the ceremony. He came to Dover to meet her mother; Anna went to London once and spent three days with Louisa. Meanwhile, he remained in London in his new parish. He wrote a few times, notes, more than letters, and said he was busy preparing things for their life together. The idea that there was a life waiting for her made her dizzy. She tried not to think about living in the East End. Shoreditch could not be very far from the river, she told herself. And judging by his interest in the Seamen's Mission, Vincent might even be as glad as she would to move to a seaside parish when the opportunity arose.

When Anna arrived at the Vicarage in May, after the wedding, she couldn't see any evidence of preparations. The house was tucked in between the churchyard of All Hallows and a busy road. Spring appeared to have passed by the little house, which was unadorned by blossom or even ivy. It had a worn, white gravestone set over the front of a ground-floor window, bearing the names of a series of girl children who'd died of diphtheria, one after another, quickly followed by their mother. From the way the stone was set, she had the impression they might be interred within the walls of the house but Vincent had said not to be fanciful and of course they were not. She took a deep breath, stepped over the threshold straight into a parlor, and looked around for something she could not identify exactly except by the fact that it was missing.

The truth was that she hadn't felt ready for marriage when it came to it. She met Vincent in October. The following January, Anna's mother, Amelia Newlove, had fallen ill. She lay in her bedroom in the flint house, the curtains drawn night and day, complaining that she could hear the sea through her earplugs. Even when the wind outside dropped and the sea grew limpid, she heard waves dashing on the old chest of drawers, the carved headboard, felt them lapping at her ankles if she lowered them to the floor. She clung to Anna, begging her not to let her go, not to let her drown too; her nails left small, curved wounds on Anna's wrists.

By March, Amelia said she'd had enough. She cursed every new morning, refused to open her eyes to it. Begged the sea to take her, raged at it for leaving her in the dry place, marooned, cut off from the tides. In the middle of one such lament, she stopped. "No matter," she said. "What a beautiful day." And she was gone. Anna emerged from the sickroom disoriented. Death had become a constant companion, a trickster hiding behind the curtains with the toes of his shoes in full view.

Vincent favored proceeding as planned with the wedding, soon after the funeral. Not as an occasion for jollity, he said, but as a holy sacrament. The Bishop was anxious that he regularize his domestic situation. Louisa, grieving, begged her to postpone. Anna could come and live with her, she insisted. She needed help with the children. Anna, who had been wavering, saw clearly the choices that lay ahead of her and decided to proceed with the ceremony. She told Louisa she could not help her with the children. And asked Vincent for two months in which to ready herself.

By then, she thought of the marriage as necessary. Like the boys who jumped from the clifftop at high tide on summer days to get money from trippers, she was jumping into life. She had to. She had no inheritance, no skill in nursing or governessing. Her father, Amos Newlove, had quarreled with his family when he went to sea; her mother's line was far-flung—the only things Anna had inherited from her were pride and a resistance to being beholden. She would marry Vincent, and even if she did not yet love him she could be a good wife to him. Love would come to her in her life. She felt certain of it.

The bell for luncheon ended Anna's reverie. She unwrapped her arms from her knees and stood up, stretching her arms over her head, pushing back her escaping hair. Following the others into the dining room, she looked without enthusiasm at a tureen of stew, a crowd of drowning dumplings. She knew what she must do next.

That night, once Lovely was prone under her blanket, Anna got out of bed and drew up the chair to the washstand. She would be defying Vincent's wishes but she had to write the letter. She couldn't think of any other course of action. She dipped the pen in the last drops of ink and inscribed on an envelope the name and address that were imprinted in her memory: Miss Maud Sulten, 59 Sebastopol Street, London SW.

She put the envelope aside to dry and in a careful hand, making sure to avoid blots and smudges, began the letter.

Dear Miss Sulten,

You do not know me. You may not even know my name. But I am writing to plead for your help . . . .

She continued to the end in small, deliberate characters intended to ensure that not one word could be misread.

NINE

The great hall of the Bishop's palace was lined with benches. The stone construction of the walls and the vaulted timber ceiling overhead gave the place an ecclesiastical atmosphere but the urgency of the muttered conversations underneath, the quick eyes of the clerk and the purposeful strides with which some men entered and departed, contradicted that holy air and gave the echoing hall the atmosphere of a marketplace.

Vincent Palmer sat on one of the benches, disliking equally the warmth from the bodies of the men pressed up on each side of him and the chill in his kidneys from the stone wall at his back. Worse than the physical discomfort was the fact of having to look at the other petitioners, at the assorted crowd of clerics, politicians, parishioners and paupers. He wondered again why the Bishop wished to see him.

The clerk emerged at intervals from behind the door to the private chambers, scanned the crowd and called people in according to a system of his own that had nothing to do with either rank or length of time served sitting on the bench. It was right, Vincent supposed, that as in Matthew, chapter 20, verse 16, *the last shall be first, and the first last*. Nonetheless, the fellow ought to acknowledge that some men had more pressing calls on their time than others. On top of which, he was hungry. He'd been there more than an hour already. He imagined himself walking through the Bishop's door and allowed his mind to drift to thoughts of the hoped-for promotion.

"Morning, Palmer."

Solomon Saville was standing in front of him.

"Morning, Saville."

The clerk tapped Saville on the shoulder and hurried him away toward the door to the chamber. Saville disappeared through it. Vincent ran his little finger over the undulating stiffness that was the top of his moustache. The Canon had appointed Solomon Saville as Deputy Minor Canon—even though he had less experience than Vincent and no authority in the pulpit. The burning sensation in his guts intensified. Youth and an easy manner with the congregation were surely not the proper qualifications for advancement.

Vincent wondered whether it would appear ungodly to sample the pork pie he had in his pocket. He'd left the Vicarage early and, in too much of a hurry to stop in a coffee shop, had bought the pie from a boy at the gates of the palace. He rejected the idea of taking a bite. He would fast until he had an audience with the Bishop, whatever hour of the day that might be. Vincent shifted on the wooden seat and cast his mind over the events of the last few days that had brought him here.

On Monday, the Canon had called at the Vicarage. Some helpful soul had evidently alerted him to Anna's absence.

"Where's the missus, Palmer?" Rosebury said, standing on the step.

"Come in, Canon Rosebury," Vincent replied, holding open the door. "Come in." Rosebury raised both hands in front of him.

"Can't stop," he said. "I'm in a hurry. What have you done with her?"

"She has gone away. For a short stay. With friends," Vincent said, in a tone meant to discourage further nosiness.

"Had enough of you already, has she?" Rosebury chuckled.

Vincent diverted him to the subject of the church roof and, despite some reluctance on the Canon's part, took him into All Hallows to see for himself the deplorable state of the rafters. They said an affable enough good-bye, half an hour later; Rosebury hadn't mentioned Anna again.

Several people had inquired after her. It irritated Vincent. She was at the Vicarage as his wife. If she wasn't there—no matter. Women did go to the country. Make long visits. Mother used to. It could not be allowed to emerge that his wife was suffering from nerves. It would have serious repercussions for his career. Anyway, Anna had been prying. Concerning herself with matters that didn't concern her.

He shifted on the bench. His palms were clammy, despite the deep frost outside and the chill at his back. The day after Rosebury's call, he'd received a summons to the palace. There was no cause for worry. The Bishop was after all a blood relation although he had not pressed the point with the clerk when he presented himself, had simply mentioned it in passing. They had a great-grandfather in common, a connection tracked down by Mother while Vincent was still at university.

The Bishop was obviously alert to the significance of the bond. It was he who a year ago had urged, through the medium of the Canon, that Vincent marry. He'd even penned a note. A charitable woman could add a good deal to parish duties and minister to wives, et cetera. Anna had seemed a good candidate, with her concern for the seamen so passionately expressed, when he first encountered her. Not that there were undue numbers of seamen in the congregation of All Hallows; he couldn't think of any, offhand. But no one could call Anna worldly, even if she wasn't properly pious either. Her notion of religiousness had turned out to be very unorthodox.

A promotion might be the Bishop's way of rewarding his prompt action in finding a suitable wife. The parish offered a poor living, only five hundred pounds a year, and his private means were limited and under pressure. Securing his familial tie with the Bishop, advancing their personal relationship, could only be advantageous.

Vincent banged the silver tip of his cane on the stone flags. The room fell quiet, the clerk raised his pale face from his ledger. Vincent had had an idea. He would issue a personal invitation. On behalf not only of himself but of all members of the parish, inviting the Bishop to matins at All Hallows. Spring might be best. He didn't want him to witness a leak, however powerfully it upheld his case. If the Bishop cared to take the pulpit, the honor would be all theirs. If he preferred simply to share in their humble proceedings, listen to his own inadequate preaching, they would be equally thankful.

Vincent looked around him. The room had all but emptied. Only a handful of petitioners remained and most were elderly women. The clerk called his name and he got to his feet, stiff from the cold and feeling unprepared, despite the age he'd spent on the bench.

"Please, God," he murmured as he made his way across the smoothed and hollowed stone flags, stooped through the small door cut into one of the pair of larger, ceremonial doors. "Help me."

"Reverend," said the Bishop, holding out his hand. Vincent took the hand in both his own, bowed his head, kissed the ring.

"Are you in health, Your Lordship?" he said, pushing the pie deeper into his pocket with a sudden, awful presentiment that the Bishop could smell it.

The ring-bearing hand appeared to wave away a fly. Vincent felt his hopes intensify. He decided to issue the invitation before the Bishop had a chance to state his business. He would take the initiative.

"I wanted to raise something with you, Bishop," he said.

"If it's funds I can't help you, Palmer. You will have to make your own arrangements. And if it is spiritual direction you're after, apply to the Canon. If you wish to pursue our family connection, tenuous as it is, I have to advise you that this is not the place to do so."

"None of these, Lordship. I come as the bearer of an invitation. From my flock."

The Bishop laughed. "Really?"

"They wish for you to attend a service of worship with us at All Hallows and partake of refreshments afterward."

The Bishop seemed to sigh. It occurred to Vincent that he looked tired. The skin under his eyes drooped and the hem of his purple robe trailed on the stone floor in a way that made Vincent think of a too-large nightshirt he'd had as a boy.

"As you know," the Bishop said, "I wanted to see you. Rosebury is of the opinion that your wife has disappeared. Has she?"

He had half expected it but the question caught Vincent off-guard.

"Disappeared? She is visiting friends in the countryside, as I told the Canon."

"Well, bring her back from the countryside, Palmer. You need her."

"My wife is indisposed, Your Lordship. Female troubles."

"Look here, Palmer. You've been married less than a year. A clergyman is meant to set an example. Wife by his side, loyal helpmeet and all that. If you've made a mistake, my advice to you is to pack her off back to her family and make the fact public. If not, recall her from wherever she's run away to. Expecting, is she?"

"We thought perhaps Easter. . . . I do hope I shall not have to disappoint the congregation?"

"If you disappoint the congregation, Palmer, it won't be my doing. I might call on you and I might not. Either way, make haste and put your affairs in order. People are talking."

The ringed hand gestured toward the door and Vincent walked backward out of the chamber, his eyes fixed on the dusty hem of the Bishop's robe.

TEN

Makepeace sat behind the same round table with her back to the window, a pince-nez perched like a small bird on the end of her nose.

"I can't understand why my sister hasn't replied to me," Anna said. "Nor my husband. Did you post the second batch of letters?"

"They were dispatched immediately."

"And the third?"

Makepeace nodded.

"And nothing arrived for me with the letter carrier this morning? No one has called for me?"

Makepeace shook her head and settled herself back on her chair, locked her fingers in an arch in front of her chin, her rings lined up in front of her knuckles. Only the wedding finger was bare.

"Sometimes relatives don't appreciate the true nature of a retreat such as this one."

"What do you mean?"

"In a better world than this, families would understand the value of rest for the mind. But unfortunately some are . . ." She smiled at Anna, without warmth. "How can I put it?"

"You mean they're ashamed? To have a lunatic in their midst?"

"We're very blunt, aren't we, Mrs. Palmer."

"Louisa would never think me a lunatic. So she could not feel embarrassed," Anna said.

She had a feeling every time she encountered Makepeace of struggle. As if in her company it was vital not to show weakness or even to feel it. She met the woman's soft-edged eyes. Even looking straight into them she couldn't say exactly what color they were. Not black nor blue nor brown nor quite gray. They were the color of money—the same shade as an old bun penny. Makepeace's stare flickered away toward a dusty arrangement of everlasting flowers on the mantelpiece.

"I daresay your sister's letter will arrive shortly. She may even come and visit you." Makepeace smiled again, more coldly, if it were possible, than the last time.

"I wish she would. I so long to see her."

Anna was delaying what she had to do. She felt nervous. It was irrational, she told herself, to fear that Makepeace might inform Vincent whom she wrote to. She must hand over the letter without showing any anxiety. If Makepeace inquired, she would tell her that Maud Sulten was a former governess with whom she'd stayed friendly.

"Oh! I almost forgot, Mrs. Makepeace. I have another letter here."

She pulled it out from her bodice and tossed it on the table. Maud Sulten's name and address were written in a hand so careful and constrained Anna barely recognized it as her own. "I would like it posted immediately."

"Very well."

Makepeace's buttons shivered and glittered as she took the envelope and unlocked the drawer on the other side of the table, placing the letter inside. She got up and went to the hearth.

"The wind is in the wrong direction," she said, stabbing at the coals with unnecessary force, her rounded back turned to Anna. Fragments of ash fell through the grate into the cinders, floated out over the fender. She clattered the poker down on the hearth tiles and straightened up. "This Miss Sulten is a friend of yours?"

"Yes. A former governess. We correspond occasionally. Be sure to post it promptly, won't you? I haven't written to her for an age."

"Indeed, Mrs. Palmer. I will deal with it immediately."

Makepeace was looking at her again with an expression of malice that did not change as Anna thanked her and left.

Alone in the room, Frances Makepeace tipped back her head and poured the last drops of her cup of coffee down her throat. She enjoyed those final drops, thick and sweet, almost syrup, as much as she enjoyed the initial stinging sip. Makepeace made coffee every morning in her housekeeper's room, pushing the rug up against the door to keep the smell of it from seeping into the corridor. It made patients restive if they caught a whiff of it on the way to the treatment room. It could create hysteria in the susceptible—their longing for coffee.

She rinsed out the cup, dried it and replaced it on the mantelpiece. The cup and saucer were mismatched, oddly if inescapably paired. Like a husband and wife, she thought, bitterly. Her dislike of couples was extending beyond human beings to all paired things. She could tolerate items only in ones or threes. Not twos or fours. Like the animals, trooping into the ark.

Returning to her table, she got out the letter, adjusted her pince-nez and slit open the top of the envelope with a paper knife. It was an affectation of Mr. Abse's to keep the ramblings of patients with the same care he would apply to legal documents or his own extensive and unnecessary records and logs. The ledgers he thought so much of were infested with weevils and decomposing from within. She dealt with patients' correspondence in her own way, keeping back any she found of interest or that made complaints about herself. As Lizzie Button was in the habit of doing.

If she passed all the letters on to Abse as he'd instructed, the shelves in the study would have fallen from the walls by now with the weight of useless paperwork. She stood for a moment by the window contemplating the image of Lake House collapsing from the inside, falling in on itself with the weight of its own history like a vast failed cake.

The wind had changed again and the fire was showing signs of life. The coal sent up a mustard-colored stream of smoke, the back draft forcing wisps of it down the chimney. She put her handkerchief over her mouth and nose as she pulled out Mrs. Palmer's letter from the envelope. "Dear Miss Sulten," she murmured aloud. "You do not know me. You may not even know my name."

She read the rest in silence, reached the end and remained motionless. She was back ten years and still married to Jack Makepeace. Back in all the fresh horror of his disappearance. She felt a sudden urge to weep as she clenched her fingers around the letter and then threw it down on the floor. It settled lightly on the wide boards, immune to the violence of her gesture.

Makepeace permitted herself a rare moment of self-pity. She worked so hard at putting the past behind her, maintained a constant vigilance against its intrusion. It was unfair that it should ambush her like this. Picking up the poker again, she jabbed at the coals, trying to usher them toward the fireback and keep the smoke going up the chimney. Mrs. Palmer was disturbing everyone. She'd seduced Talitha with her pretended lack of guile. When she tried to warn Talitha that Palmer was a troublemaker if ever she'd seen one, Talitha just smiled.

"I like her, Fanny," she said. "That's all there is to it. Anyway, people do make trouble. Everyone does sooner or later."

She was trying to wheedle her way into the Abse family. Makepeace had told Mrs. Abse that she'd seen Catherine talking with her. Emmeline Abse had frowned. Said she didn't like the idea of her darling girl "tête-à-tête"—there was another one who gave herself airs and graces— with a patient.

The clatter of clogs approaching along the corridor grew louder. Makepeace flung down the poker, picked up the letter from the floor and shoved it to the back of the drawer. She tried with a shaking hand to fit the key into the tiny lock but couldn't see clearly. Her eyes were stinging as if they had soap in them. It was the smoke, she told herself. The smoke.

Lovely made a spirited if unnecessary tap on the door.

"What is it?" Makepeace shouted. "And can't you stop your blasted singing, woman?"

ELEVEN

The air was filled with the scent of hyacinths; the winter sun threw a slanting rectangle over the dining table. Emmeline felt a sense of pleasure that they should be all together for breakfast, gathered round the table, even if Ben's fingers were stained with ink and Catherine's hair uncombed. Catherine had laid her knife across her book to keep the pages open and was picking at a piece of bread, giggling occasionally, taking sips from her water glass.

"Don't read at the table, Catty. It's bad manners."

Catherine looked up and scowled at her.

"Does Father know that? Why don't you remind him?"

Querios shook the pages of his newspaper into formation and folded it into one quarter of its size, smoothing and creasing it as if he might be able to subdue its contents at the same time.

"The place at Colney Hatch is in the news again. They've got more patients than they know what to do with and the whole system is crumbling under the weight of numbers. They didn't think about that, did they? When they built their monster asylums and put the little men out of business."

Emmeline looked at him along the length of the table, willing him to respond to her meaningful glance. He slapped down the paper and turned his attention to the plaice on his plate, scraping off the flesh on the top, lifting out its spine in one supple piece.

"Benny is here, Querios."

"I know that, Emmeline."

"He wants to speak to you."

Querios sighed.

"Well, Benedict? Do your tribe of scallywags need my support?"

"The boys are doing well. They're not scallyw-w-w-ags and if you intend to ridicule my p-p-petition, I will not m-m-make it."

Benedict's face contorted as if every last muscle was involved in the effort to get out the words. Emmeline felt her own face stiffen in sympathy. Ben's stammer was worst at the table. But the table was the only place they ever saw each other all together, these days, with Querios working all hours and Ben out of the house so much.

"Until I have heard the plea," Querios said pleasantly, "I don't know whether I shall ridicule it or not."

"We want to start a second school for g-g—young ladies, F-f-father. We have a room, in G-g—Golden Lane. We need benefactors."

Emmeline braced herself for the answer, resting her elbows in the soft furrows of the tablecloth. She sometimes had a feeling that the trust she placed in Querios, had always placed in him, to know better than she did, to have a surer sense of what to do, was not justified. The idea gave her the same swimming sensation as a dream she'd had recently—where they all lived in France, in a house of papier-mâché, built on ground of blancmange. She was often in France in her dreams.

"It's a marvelous thing, persuading others to be the instruments of your charity," Querios said to Ben. "How you can call yourself a teacher looking like that, hair all over your face, I don't know."

"If you still had hair, Father, how would you wear it?"

Catherine's voice was innocent.

"Catty, darling," Emmeline interrupted. "Pass me the marmalade, would you?"

Querios didn't seem to have noticed Catherine's remark. He was in full flow, his fish forgotten.

"At your age, Benedict, I was working with my father. You might have the luxury of indulging your conscience with the poor but I am obliged to labor alone to keep your brothers in school as I dimly remember I once kept you in school."

Emmeline listened with half an ear. She took a sip of China tea and felt the bite and smokiness assuage her sinking spirits. The truth was that Querios had feared Septimus Abse. Even in middle age he used to become nauseous before an audience with the old man. But when Septimus died, Querios was lost. Grief-stricken. The ringing in his ears had begun that hard, cold spring. Could it be five years ago already?

If Benedict wanted to give his time to the ragged school movement, she had no objection. He would grow out of it soon enough. Querios had wanted to be a teacher himself when she first met him. He believed it was his vocation. Sometimes she thought that Querios felt reproached by Benedict, by his good heart and his desire to help people, and that his son reminded him of his own younger, better self.

She returned her empty cup to its saucer with a sharpness that caused the teaspoon to jump.

"You might consider my nerves," she said. "It is distressing to see you quarreling over trivial matters."

"We're not quarreling, Em."

"They're not trivial, Ma."

Emmeline looked down the table at Querios again.

"He's not asking for very much, Q. Only a contribution."

"A contribution, eh? That's all any of us want."

Emmeline felt a pulse in her temple begin to throb. He was getting more and more impossible lately, still refusing to talk to her about Catherine—sidestepping every conversation she tried to begin on the subject.

Catherine picked fragments of shell from the sides of a boiled egg.

"I'll give you some books for the girls, Ben," she said. "I think it's an admirable idea to teach them to read and write."

"Not r-r—read, Cath. They are going to learn to cook and s-sew."

"Why not teach them to read? What are they meant to do in their leisure time?"

"They don't have any l-l-l . . . Anyway, Cath, I've got a new book for you."

"Oh, Ben, I love you. You are the best possible brother. What is it?"

Catherine jumped off her seat and ran to him as Ben finished off his third plate of mushrooms and, dropping his fork on the cloth, extracted a book from his pocket. She threw her arms round his neck, kissed him, and dashed out of the room with the volume, her feet pounding on the stairs.

Hannah stepped sideways through the door with an empty tray in her hands and began collecting plates. Querios rolled up his newspaper, stuck it into his pocket and pushed back his chair. Benedict folded another rasher of bacon into his mouth with his fingers and got up.

"Thank you, Hannah," he said, as she took away his plate. "How are you this morning?"

Emmeline could never get used to Ben's height. He'd outstripped her own five feet three inches when he was fourteen and now at over six feet he towered over Querios as well. He was tall and straight and handsome despite the old clothes he affected, his unkempt hair and the holes in the toes of his shoes. She felt a rush of pride and love for him. Gratitude too. It was such a simple matter to love sons. Catching hold of his hand as he passed, she pressed it against her cheek.

"Your father means well. I'll talk to him later."

"I know, Ma. Don't trouble yourself."

"Ben? Do you think it's a good idea, bringing Catherine all these books?"

"Yes, I do. She enjoys them. I'm off to school."

And he went. They were all gone, before the longed-for togetherness had ever quite arrived. Emmeline felt sticky even though she hadn't touched the marmalade in the end. She sat on, alone at the table, as the golden rectangle of sun narrowed and disappeared, dabbing at her mouth again with the square of damask. The hyacinths lolled against each other in the bowl as if overpowered by their own scent. She got up and went around the table, lifted the top of Catherine's egg. It was untouched, the yolk hardened and opaque in its soft white collar.

Emmeline climbed the stairs toward Catherine's room. She intended to ask what she meant to do with the day and suggest that they pay some morning calls. If they wanted any society, they had to go and find it. People didn't like to visit Lake House. They feared being seen coming through the gates—feared the whispers about confined relatives, contaminated bloodlines and unmarriageable daughters. She'd felt the same herself the first time she came to meet Abse Senior and his wife. It was hard to shake off the feeling as the carriage passed through the high gates that the air on the inside of the walls of Lake House was different air, the ground a far country. That she might not escape.

Catherine didn't understand the handicap with which she was setting out in life. She was unaware of the prejudice she was likely to meet when she did finally decide to go out and about in society more. Perhaps it was for the best.

"*Rejoice,*" Emmeline muttered, approaching the closed door. "*This is the day the Lord hath made.*"

She prayed often, not from the staunchness of her belief but from its feebleness; she felt that faith must be like good grooming—desirable definitely and achievable possibly, through hard work.

"Catherine! Dear!"

The good humor in her voice sounded forced. Sometimes she wondered whether she feared her own daughter. She pushed open the door without waiting for an answer and walked in. The air was stuffy; dresses were strewn over the backs of chairs and silk shawls lay in puddles on the floor alongside unpaired shoes that looked as if they had been running around independently. Catherine had taken off her wrapper and was lying on the bed on her stomach, dressed in a chemise and a pair of red flannel drawers, a book propped on the pillow.

"What a mess it is in here. Hasn't Hannah been up?"

"I told her not to."

Emmeline stepped farther into the room and the loose board creaked under her foot—louder here than when she heard it from underneath, in her own bedroom. She stooped to pick up a stocking, considered whether she might risk sitting on the edge of the bed and decided against it. She would wait for an invitation.

"You didn't eat your egg. Are you unwell?"

"I'm perfectly well, Mother. I'm reading Mrs. Barrett Browning. Listen to this! 'Some people always sigh in thanking God.' Just like Aunt Flo does."

She laughed and for an instant something in her face looked just as it did when she was five years old. Emmeline smiled.

"I've told Cook to make the biscuits you like."

Catherine repositioned her book but made no response.

"I thought we might pay some calls this morning."

"You go, Mother. I'm busy."

Emmeline sighed.

"You can't let your life slip away, Catty, while you lie in the gloom reading books."

"This isn't my life. And don't call me that."

"You know your cousins wish to see you. Especially Henry."

Catherine rolled onto her back and pulled the pillow over her face.

"Stop it, Mother," she said, her voice stifled by down. She removed the pillow. "If I get married, it will be to a poet. An Italian poet."

"But we don't know any Italians."

Her daughter burst into laughter and Emmeline stood by the glass-fronted bookcase wondering what was funny. She felt rather like crying. She steadied her voice and spoke levelly.

"Darling, I want to pay some calls. I would like you to come with me. I worry about you not seeing anyone your own age. And of course I hope you'll marry one day but not everything I say is about finding you a husband."

"All right, Mother," Catherine said, quietly. "I'll come down soon."

Emmeline descended the stairs, one at a time. She felt more tired going down them than she had going up. She straightened her spine, trying to remember her deportment, reached the landing and stopped, leaning both elbows on the banisters. Once, Catherine had loved nothing more than to be by her side. Even at seven, eight years old she used to beg Emmeline to stay with her at night to tell her stories and sing to her. Clung to her limbs with the whole of her fierce strength if she tried to leave her bedroom before she fell asleep.

It was all happening so quickly, Catherine growing up.

TWELVE

Lunch was two thin slices of ham, served with boiled potatoes and a dollop of yellow mustard that made Anna feel as if the top of her head was on fire. There were small burrowings around the heel of the loaf where mice or worse had been feeding on it. The scrape of spoons on china, the coughing and the banging of chair legs on floorboards were louder and more discordant than usual. The pudding, stewed apples still in their bitter, green skins under a white blanket of corn flour, set her teeth on edge.

"No appetite today, Mrs. Palmer? Are the apples too sharp for you?" Talitha Batt was standing by her with a bowl of sugar and a teaspoon in her hand. Anna pushed away her dish.

"I'm not hungry, Miss Batt, thank you all the same."

Anna was in low spirits. She had delayed writing the letter to Maud Sulten from a belief that when she did, something must happen. She'd thought that even if she provoked Vincent's wrath she would through Miss Sulten find a way to free herself. Eleven days later, there had been no response. She felt a sharp humiliation every morning as she asked whether any letters had arrived for her and Makepeace shook her head, affecting sympathy while her eyes gleamed with satisfaction.

Most of the others had left the table for the dayroom. Only Anna and Lizzie Button remained in their places. Mrs. Button seemed oblivious to the fact that lunch was over. She rocked to and fro on her chair next to Anna, muttering about her angels, her arms folded tight over the piece of wood held against her chest. Occasionally, a moan escaped her. Anna turned to her. She'd been waiting for an opportunity to say something.

"Mrs. Button, I'm sorry for your loss. You have my deepest sympathy."

Button put both hands in front of her face. "Leave me alone."

"Mrs. Button, I only wanted to say that I'm so sorry you—"

Button dropped the stick, clamped her hands to her ears, and let out a wail that gave Anna goose pimples along the length of her arms.

"Let me alone, Mrs. Palmer. You know nothing about anything."

Anna took a mouthful of water and pushed back her chair, her jaw clenched. She made her way into the dayroom and threw herself into the window seat, preparing to endure another interminable afternoon. Was it true what Button said, that she didn't know about anything? It couldn't be. But perhaps it was. The photographer doctor had not returned. Maud Sulten had not replied to her letter. Even her own sister made no response to her. She was completely alone.

She became aware of Makepeace standing in front of her.

"Visitor for you, Mrs. Palmer. In the office." She jerked her eyes to indicate the door that led out of the dayroom and began leading the way toward it. "Come along, please."

Anna followed on Makepeace's heels down the stairs, almost tripping on the hem of the woman's skirt. At the bottom of the stairs, in the short corridor that led to Abse's office, she couldn't contain her impatience. She pulled up her skirts and flew past Makepeace, almost falling through the door into the office.

"Where is she? Let me see her. Lou? Oh . . ." She stopped dead. "It's you, Vincent."

He was standing in the very spot from which he'd disappeared, dressed in the same long coat, his hat held over his chest.

"Good morning, Anna." He took off his gloves and put his hat down on Abse's desk, balancing it on its brim. "How are you getting along?"

She'd thought that when Vincent came she'd fly to him, kiss his hands, beg him to see reason. But she couldn't take a single step toward him. She took in his hair, slick with bear's grease, the fresh tone of his skin and his air of wary benevolence. He wasn't suffering from her absence. He didn't share her anguish.

Her head felt light and hollow. She put out her hands to steady herself and Makepeace stepped forward, propelled her onto a chair.

"Mr. Abse will be here shortly," she said. "Try not to upset yourself, Mrs. Palmer. The visit should not be a prolonged one, Reverend, if you'll pardon me for observing. Visits meant to comfort can result in disturbed emotions."

Anna interrupted her.

"I am dying here, Vincent. You have to take me out of this place."

Vincent ran his finger along the top of his moustache.

"Come, Anna, please. Don't exaggerate. A retreat is intended to provide respite for the nerves, not to inflame them."

"I did not need to retreat anywhere, from anything. You . . . you tricked me into coming here."

"Calm yourself, Anna."

"Don't tell me to be calm when you've taken my life from me. Have you been speaking to my sister? Trying to turn her against me? I've written to her again and again and heard nothing."

Vincent's air of smugness faltered. He turned to Makepeace.

"Are you the housekeeper? I understood from Dr. Abse that guests were able to remain in seclusion here? Without, er, unwelcome contact with the world outside?"

Makepeace's face was at war with itself—her mouth opening and closing, waves of unexpressed thoughts passing over her features. She cleared her throat, loudly and at length.

"That's right, sir," she said. "I'm the matron. I'll fetch Mr. Abse."

Her mind racing, Anna barely heard their exchange. Makepeace left and Anna and Vincent were alone in the room. Vincent walked around it, tipping back his head as he surveyed the highest shelves of ledgers. He pulled a handkerchief from his pocket and dabbed at his forehead.

"Marvelous collection the doctor has."

"Vincent, please. Why are you doing this to me? I don't understand."

"Have you got out for walks much? Wonderful countryside."

"I'm begging you." Her voice sounded shrill. She took a deep breath.

"I'll lose my mind, any woman would. Your own mother would go mad here."

"'The Lord will not suffer the soul of the righteous to famish.' Please don't speak about Mother, Anna."

Abse hurried in.

"Welcome, Reverend. This is an unexpected pleasure. I thought for a moment you were another party of visitors."

"Good day, Doctor. God bless you."

Vincent pumped Abse's hand. Abse walked behind his desk, began shifting the papers around, leafing through piles. Vincent glanced at the door. He wasn't staying, Anna understood. He had no intention of taking her away. She had the odd feelings in her body that had become familiar at Lake House—an ache in her lungs and a sense of her blood stopping in her veins, with the wrongness of things. She made a low, animal howl.

"You shouldn't have come, Vincent, if you only intend to go away again and leave me here. Why have you come?"

"My wife appears emotionally excited still, Dr. Abse. I'd hoped to find her more rational."

"She has made fair progress," said Abse. "She hasn't been troubled by any more *visions*." He pronounced the word with a flourish, turned to her. "Have you, Mrs. Palmer? No boys jumping from rocks or anything of that nature. Eh?"

Anna turned away, feeling the words like slingshot. So Vincent had informed Abse about her visions. She had tried to explain to Vincent before they were married about what she saw. She'd thought he ought to know. Sometimes they came regularly, sometimes there were gaps of a year or more. Waking dreams that she'd had from the time she was a young girl. She'd never thought they were anything to be ashamed of. She thought of them as God speaking to her.

At first, they were always set down on the chalk shore, below the house. Sometimes she waded in the water. Picked and slithered her way over the rock pools or climbed the sheer white cliff in a way she never could in life—surefooted, supported.

Jesus had appeared in the very first one, pulling his boat up out of the waves, His bell-bottom trousers rolled to the knees. The boat was narrow, painted green, with two wooden benches across the width of it. She'd run to help Him bail the water out of the bottom but found there was none. The boat was dry. Jesus had laughed at her surprise, although not unkindly. He had told her to expect the unexpected. He said He had work for her.

Vincent said it was impossible that Jesus should have laughed.

The study door opened and Makepeace returned with a maid carrying a tea tray that the girl set down on the table, looking nervously about the room. The maid left and Makepeace poured the tea and passed round the cups, while Querios Abse read from a ledger. "Full-blown hysteria on admission. Some lesser episodes since. Emetics have contributed to a slow but steady improvement. Matron has noted a lack of cooperation. Full cure likely to take some time." He looked up from the ledger with sharp eyes. "It might be wise to think in terms of months rather than weeks, Reverend. We can review your wife's case in the spring."

"I see, Doctor." Vincent was nodding, vigorously, as though he wanted to hear that she should be detained. "Yes, I do see."

Anna gripped the teacup in the palm of her hand as Abse closed the ledger, opened another.

"I don't believe that I ever informed the Reverend Palmer that I was a medical doctor although I have long experience with mental affliction. I am a doctor of the school of life. Some extra monies are owing for treatments, Reverend," she heard him say. "As well as the regular monthly fee."

Vincent emptied his cup and dabbed at the underside of his moustache with the handkerchief. He was still sweating, the perspiration on his face catching the light. For the first time, his eyes met hers and she saw again the regret in them that she had glimpsed on the day he brought her here. Regret and guilt.

"It's for the best, Anna. Believe me, it's for the best."

"Why didn't you tell me those men were doctors?"

"The heart of her husband doth safely trust in her. She will do him good and not evil all the days of her life." He smiled at her, tight-lipped. "Proverbs. Chapter thirty-one, verses eleven. And twelve."

She felt a desire to hurl the teacup at him.

"What are you talking about? You deceived me, Vincent."

His eyes slid away like fishes.

"You must try to curb your passions. For your own sake."

Abse got to his feet. "Leave your wife in our hands, Reverend. A full cure may take longer than all of us here had hoped but I am optimistic. I am always optimistic. Further treatments can be employed."

Vincent rose too. He picked up his hat and adjusted the cords between crown and brim.

"The Bishop asked very kindly after you, Anna. I hope to find you more composed next time. God bless and keep all of you."

"Vincent, tell me why you're doing this to me. You have no right—"

He was gone.

Abse made a noise of satisfaction as the door closed behind him.

"Fine man, your husband, Mrs. Palmer. Knows his scripture too. Aaaah . . ."

He gasped as the cup hit him in the middle of the chest and bounced back onto the desk. Tea flooded over the open ledger, the dissolving ink creating a gray tide over the page. It dripped from the edges of the desk onto the rug, where it steadily darkened the pattern of chrysan-themums.

Abse stood looking down at the desk. He leaned over it and began to blot the ledger with his sleeve in small, fussy movements.

"Take her back up, Fanny," he said. "We'll commence further treat-ments straightaway."

A Proverb of her own came to Anna as Makepeace ushered her out of the room. She repeated it silently to herself all the way up the stairs. *"Therefore shall his calamity come suddenly; suddenly shall he be broken without remedy."*

She hardly knew on whose head she wished greater calamity—Vincent's or Querios Abse's.

Anna couldn't sleep. She didn't want to be in Dover. But often since she arrived at Lake House she found herself there—in the garden, on the clifftop. In her bed. In her self, as she had been as a young child.

There were things that she knew as a child without knowing how she knew them, that were never presented by a governess. All the important things were like that. What she knew was that her place was on the edge of things. On the edge of England, where the earth broke its solid promise and surrendered to the sea. On the edge of her family, not snugly bracketed between sisters.

She knew that girls were lesser beings. Her mother's voice whispered that she had been a chance of what they longed for—a son and heir. She heard the word as *air*, felt the light, expansive promise of the male line. The earthy disappointment of girl children. Her parents even had a name ready for him; Antony without an *h*. They'd substituted Anastasia, in their disappointment. Shortened it to Anna by the time she was old enough to hear it. A fifth daughter did not merit five syllables.

She decided early that she liked to be on the edge of things. Slid into a bench seat in the kitchen, pressing her spine against the wall, with the only route out under the table. She would sit on her ankles behind the wing chair in Captain Newlove's study, eyes smarting from tobacco smoke, looking at a book about shells. *Conchology*. It was a long time before she connected the drawings of shells in the book with the shells on the shore. When she did, it was with a secret passionate thrill that ran all the way through her.

More often, the air was innocent of smoke. Their father was missing. He was a word, an empty chair, an anticipation. He was one of the pelagic birds he told them about, that lived at sea, drifted on the currents for months at a time, swimming in the skies, held there by the eye of the water.

She knew him best through his study. He had charts pinned up of the waters off the coasts of England, Spain, the Cape of Good Hope. Maps in which the dry lands were sketchy, rudimentary spaces, almost blank, but the waters teemed with detail—with the reefs and wrecks that could cause vessels to founder, the buoys and lighthouses that could save them. He had a globe of the stars that he said must be looked at as if from inside it, looking at the sphere all around, from the center.

A spiked pink shell was marooned on a shelf, a red shell from the Red Sea whose inside curled in on itself, to a secret place. After he died, Anna took it out of the study. Ran down the path with it and hurled it with both hands into the sea. Her sea, that was gray and bronze and black like its shells. At ebb tide, she looked for the exiled casing. Walked over the muddy sand, her toes resisting its hungry suck. The worms left piled casts on the surface, traces of where they were not.

She knew the bay as she knew her own body, knew its soft and tough places, its sweet and rank smells. She arrived in it fast, magically, sliding down the path from the clifftop, sending flying showers of small stones, grabbing at roots of thrift and mallow. It was a path too undignified for adult use, too direct and dangerous, necessitating at some points sliding and at others a headlong rush that could be undertaken only in a spirit of faith, that the rusher would remain upright, regain her balance farther down and meanwhile half run, half plunge to the bottom of the cliff.

The adult route to the shore was through a passageway hacked down through the cliff. The descent was sinister to her, the cliff in relief unsettling. It was alarming to know that the earth was so thin, endured only inches below the turf, that it gave way to a pebbly compromise of shale before the strata of chalk began, jagged, piled on top of one another as if they fought for position, trapping the great helpless flints that jutted from them.

The passage indicated that she might keep walking, down into the earth. She could walk under the bottom of the sea, under the underneath of things, and what would she find there? Would it be the sky, again, would she fall through into nowhere, unsupported, floating or swimming? Or vanish, like a jellyfish carried home in a pail?

Walking down through the passageway alarmed her more than swimming as far as she could toward the horizon, while any of the succession of disoriented governesses who passed through the Newlove household watched from the shore, eyes shaded by their hands, calling in voices of which no trace, no echo, could be heard. The sound of the sea canceled out the sounds of the earth, rendered them futile and plaintive. Anna floated on her back with her ears under the water, the noise of the pulsing depths like shattering glass, high-pitched evidence of things exploding.

*   *   *

Sometimes she felt like the survivor of a wreck herself. They lived in a flint house on the clifftop; the smell of earth and salt and wind defined the meaning of home. She shared a room with Louisa. At night, Anna lay in her bed next to the wall, looking at the rose-patterned paper, considering whether the paper at night was different from the paper in the day, whether it was possible that the roses were all the same. She'd never found any two things exactly the same. Moonlight fell through the uncurtained window, threw a pillar of light over the blooms. She raised her hand, made a dog's head or a starfish, marveled at the shadow she cast.

The window of the parlor on the first floor looked straight out to sea. In winter, they kept a vigil for blue lights, slept with the sound of the lonely raging waters in their ears, a sense that the ground of their lives was being dragged out from underneath them.

Captain Amos Newlove died within sight of home, his ship wrecked in the English Channel on the Goodwin Sands. The maps hadn't saved him, nor the globe or the brass telescope. Her mother covered up every window in the house that looked directly out to sea. She blocked the one in the parlor with a bookcase so the room was always dark. In the garden, surrounded by glossy-leaved bushes, she burned the pea jackets and calfskin shoes, the logbooks, the foreign banknotes. The flames were orange, transparent in the sunlight; the smoke blew sideways into their faces. Anna and Louisa, girls of ten and fourteen, left behind by their older, married sisters, retrieved a few blackened treasures from the ashes, contemplated their warmth in silence. Later, they forgot where they'd hidden them.

Amelia Newlove grew old overnight. She announced that she loathed the water, hated the sight of it, the smell of it and worst of all the sound of it. She wore cork stoppers in her ears at night and never referred to the sea, to ships or to sailors. She marooned herself in the flint house, looking inland toward Canterbury and the spires of the cathedral, which even on the clearest day could not be seen, although the coast of France looked sometimes as if you could reach out an arm and stroke it. One by one, neighbors stopped visiting. The ship's bell by the front door, Captain Newlove's jest, fell silent.

The sea was to be feared. Anna knew that before she knew anything. The sea took its due. Swallowed whole what it would have. Must have.

* * *

The morning after Vincent's visit was drizzly, the day as dull outside as it was inside. The fire was out when Anna woke and the stockings Lovely brought each had a different name written in the top. Neither of the names was hers. Anna flung them aside and they landed in the chamber pot. Lovely gasped.

"I do my level best, miss. To make sure yer get what yer need."

"I need my own stockings."

"These are the only ones that came up from the laundry."

"I'm not putting on other people's."

"Go without, then." Lovely's face was pink.

"I will," Anna shouted, as Lovely left the room, banging the door behind her. "I will go without."

She sat on the edge of the bed and stretched her legs out in front of her. It had shocked her when she arrived to see the women's naked ankles in the slippers, their cracked, spreading heels. Now she was the same as them. She was being undone, pulled apart like a piece of knitting. Personhood came down to small things. One's own clothes. A letter in a familiar hand. The opportunity to step out of the door, rain or shine. The parts of life Anna had believed were details were turning out to be its most important elements.

Sitting at the washstand, she brushed her hair one hundred times, piled it up at the back of her head in a loose knot secured by the two tortoiseshell combs. She must keep hold of herself. She must not allow them to break her.

After breakfast, as Anna got up to move toward the dayroom, Makepeace stepped in front of her. She wore a pinafore over her costume in a drab fabric, thick and coarse. Anna shook off the hand on her arm and stepped back. She had a lingering fear of Makepeace's touch, almost a horror of it.

"Come with me, Mrs. Palmer."

"Why? Where to?"

"Dr. Higgins believes a shower may be beneficial."

Talitha Batt knocked a metal dish cover off the sideboard; it landed on the floor and rolled from side to side making a mournful, dying echo.

"Not a prolonged shower, I trust, Mrs. Makepeace," Batt said, her voice sharp. "Not in this weather."

Makepeace, summoning Lovely with a peremptory shout, didn't hear her.

The shower room was beyond Makepeace's room, in a part of the house Anna hadn't seen before. Thin wooden lathes like ribs showed through patches of fallen plaster and the floor was carpeted in old flour sacks. There was a narrow wooden box in one corner with a tin tank over the top of it, its door secured by an iron bar. It looked like an upended coffin. Anna supposed it was the shower. She wouldn't be defeated by a shower. She'd walked into the sea in November—she wasn't afraid of cold water.

Lovely shivered and cast her eyes to the floor. Anna looked at Makepeace as coolly as she could.

"Yes? What now?"

"Take off your things, Mrs. Palmer."

Anna turned her back to them as she undid the bodice of her old velvet dress. She draped its skirt on the chair Lovely put by her, wordlessly. She slipped her feet out of the slippers, felt the rough texture of sacking under her feet and stood there in her petticoats.

"All of them, please," Makepeace said.

Anna took off her petticoats, pulled her chemise over her head, then stepped out of her drawers and folded them on the chair. She had never fully undressed in front of another person before. She felt as if she was someone else, watching this Anna from a distance. As if it was she, not Makepeace, who observed the white curve of her belly, the protruding hip bones, the dark triangle below. Her hair was warm over her breasts, and her feet, even more than the rest of her, looked naked, on the dusty floor.

"Step inside, Mrs. Palmer. We should find two minutes sufficient."

Anna glanced at Lovely for reassurance as she stepped inside, saw the stricken look on her face. The cupboard was smaller inside than it appeared and lined with tin. With the door shut, she couldn't raise her arms. She looked up, saw a perforated roof and gasped as the first streams of water hit her face. Her mouth jerked open, icy water flooded into it, down her throat. She struggled for breath, her chest made a strange hoarse noise. The cold was violent; the sound of the crashing water confused her. The sea had been warm, by comparison. Benevolent. She craned her head, trying to remove it from the rush of the water but she couldn't get away from it.

She closed her eyes and tried to remember which side the door had been on. She must knock on it and make them let her out. This couldn't be how it was intended. This was torture. The water kept coming in a relentless flow, hard as metal. Anna couldn't think clearly. Water was rising above her knees and her feet felt as if they were being beaten, as if the bones were breaking from the inside out. She lifted up one foot, trying to remove it from the pain and overbalanced against the tin wall. Clawed her way upright again.

The water rose to her thighs, reached the tops of her legs, then in between them. It seemed not to be liquid but some punishing solid thing. It continued, past her waist, her breasts. Fear overtook the physical pain. She was going to drown. It was she who would die this way. Her hair that would float on the water; her eyes that would remain open as she went under the surface.

The flow subsided. Stopped. The water had covered her shoulders, almost reached her chin. There was silence, then voices from outside that mingled with her own awful cries. A trap was opened in the bottom of the door and the level began to drop. Before the cupboard was quite empty, the door opened and Lovely hurried forward with a blanket and caught Anna as she fell through it. The outside went as dark as the inside.

Anna slept and dreamed of a letter. A letter that she pulled from the water, that she read again and again but could not understand, even though it was in her own language. When she woke she thought about another letter. The one she needed to talk to Louisa about, had been intending to discuss with her on the day Vincent brought her to Lake House.

She had found it in the drawer marked Sundries, in a pink envelope addressed to Vincent. She picked it up, felt the thin, cheap paper. It smelled of soap, a faded, floral sweetness that seemed to carry some wistful message. Anna pulled out the letter, read it, then replaced it where it was. She intended to say nothing. But the question escaped her, two days after she returned from the coast.

"Who is Maud Sulten?"

Vincent had been on his way to a service. He closed the door very precisely and gestured for her to step into the study.

"Who is who? I don't know what you're talking about, Anna."

His voice was as low and cold as she'd ever heard it. He didn't want Cook to hear, nor the curate. Anna continued to speak, her face burning. She told him that she'd understood from her mother that men had mistresses and wanted to know if Vincent had one. A woman who had come back to London from some other place. Who wanted urgently to see him. Who had a mind to come to All Hallows for a service, if she had to.

"I am surprised at you, Anna. That your mind should run along such lines as those. You are imagining things again. I want to hear nothing more of this, do you understand? I forbid you to speak of it to me or anyone else."

She watched him from the window of the study, hurrying toward the church, his legs moving like scissors across the rough ground. After he was inside All Hallows, she went upstairs to the bedroom and looked for the letter. Sundries was empty apart from a candle snuffer and a handful of coins, light and bent, smooth around their edges. Counterfeit. She closed the drawer and sat down on the bed. She had a feeling that something had ended in her marriage even before it had begun.

Anna brought herself back to where she was, opening her eyes and seeing the bowed ceiling of the room in Lake House. Her feet were cold and felt a great distance away, as if they were no longer part of her body. The nightdress, the sheet underneath her, were clammy. She dragged herself out of the bed, took the blanket, climbed onto the chair and rested her elbows on the sill. The sheep were huddled together in a spot halfway down the slope, one down on its knees as if it prayed. There was no sign of Catherine Abse.

She pressed her forehead against the cold glass, drank in the clean, damp air blowing around the ill-fitting frame. The eye of the lake looked unblinkingly up at the sky, the surface black and inky. The white bridge stood out in the dusk, more luminous and bold than when she first saw it, as if it was made of whalebone or ivory—something that could not be destroyed.

THIRTEEN

Lovely's clear eyes scanned Anna's face. She pushed a strand of Anna's hair back into its comb and straightened her lace collar with two big, gentle hands.

"He's waiting for yer, miss. You go on in and I'll take a turn around the garden." Anna opened the door to the glasshouse and saw Lucas St. Clair down on one knee, adjusting a wooden stand, a pipe clamped between his teeth. He got up and walked toward her with one hand outstretched. He was taller than she'd realized and the sharp line along his whiskers left the shaved parts of his cheeks looking smooth and naked.

"Mrs. Palmer? We met once before, I think. I'm Lucas St. Clair."

"Yes. I mistook you for someone else." His fingers were splashed with ragged black stains, their grip strong. She felt embarrassed at the memory of their previous encounter. "You must have thought my behavior odd, Dr. St. Clair, but I was expecting another physician. I thought perhaps my sister had asked you to come and see me. To help me get out."

He nodded. He was looking at her still.

"It generally takes people a few weeks to settle in," he said. "Feel comfortable."

She laughed.

"I won't feel comfortable here if I stay for a thousand years."

"I know what you mean. How long have you been here?"

"Three weeks. My husband brought me without my consent."

He frowned.

"Oh, really? That doesn't make it any easier. Thank you for agreeing to be photographed, Mrs. Palmer."

"I didn't agree to it. I asked to be photographed. I've seen your pictures on the walls."

"What do you make of them?"

Dr. St. Clair didn't seem part of Lake House. Anna wanted to be able to trust him, to believe in him and his methods. She would tell him what she thought.

"Some of the pictures are good. They show people as they are. I don't agree with the labels you put on them, though. Dr. St. Clair, I don't want my picture on the wall with the others. I'm not like them."

He was still looking at her with the same intense interest. His eyes seemed to see right into her, make her forget what she had to say to him. She felt herself coloring and walked away, found an old garden bench and sat down on it, next to a stack of terra-cotta pots. The worn brick floor of the fernery was covered in a thin layer of dry sandy soil and the place smelled like the old conservatory at the flint house, the pleasing smell that as a child she had thought of as the breath of plants.

Dr. St. Clair was in front of her again, a velvet cloth thrown over his shoulders, one knee of his dark trousers smudged with sand.

"You said you asked to be photographed. Would you mind explaining why?"

"Isn't it obvious, Dr. St. Clair? I want you to prove that there's nothing wrong with me. So that I can get away." She looked down at her hands. "You don't have to try to make me look beautiful or anything. Just please don't make me look mad. That's all I ask."

"I can't make you look anything, Mrs. Palmer. Photography is the art of truth. The camera draws from nature, without interference from man. That is the beauty of it. Oh, Lord!" He swiped his forehead with his hand. "The collodion! Damn! I left off the lid. Please excuse me."

He turned on his heel, rushed across the fernery and disappeared into what looked like a cupboard in the corner.

There were rusted hoes and rakes hanging on the walls, their wooden handles like long legs. A woodstove in the center of the room, the chimney running up and out of the glass roof, the flames visible behind an alabaster door. In the middle of it all, a grand, carved chair with a leather seat stood in front of a blank sheet of canvas suspended on the wall. She listened to the sound of Dr. St. Clair stirring and pouring and rattling in his cupboard just as if he was in a kitchen. She could see him through its yellow glass window, his head bent over a line of bottles, intent on something.

The last time she'd been photographed was before the wedding. She and Vincent stopped on the way to the church, at a studio in Hoxton. They stood in front of a canvas of Roman pillars and the photographer gave her a bunch of silk roses to hold. When the pictures were delivered afterward, she had been startled to see herself standing next to Vincent, so close that their arms appeared to be touching although they had not been. She never thought of herself as joined to him. She always saw Vincent as separate.

The photograph was taken outside, the canvas strung on a wooden frame and then hung so that the plain part of it covered the spring grass. There was no horizon; the canvas changed from painted to plain under their feet. She'd smoothed her hair in the mirror beforehand, as the photographer suggested. He was a lucky man, he'd told Vincent. Her husband-to-be had been embarrassed. Taking the mirror, he'd pretended to check his teeth for greens, looking at his moustache, the way the crucifix hung over his cravat. She couldn't help thinking it wasn't godly, or even manly, to mind the way Vincent did about his appearance.

The photographs were her idea. She had wanted a record of the day and she insisted, despite Vincent's protests that it was a waste of money, that the ceremony was for God's eyes, not the eyes of man. When Vincent asked about the cost, the photographer offered to make small pictures. *Cartes de visite* were cheaper, he said. Anna didn't want that. She wanted one big picture, to put in a frame. Evidence of her marriage. Something to make it real. Afterward, she thought it never was so real again as it was for that minute in front of the Roman pillars with the roses that were soft from other people's hands around the stems, the wire poking through green sugar paper.

The service was an anticlimax. Only the curate and Louisa as witnesses, the Vicar hurrying through the words as if they might wear out in his mouth. Anna herself, standing there with a sense of not knowing what it was she didn't know. Thinking about God's eyes.

St. Clair was out of the cupboard, his fingers blacker than ever, holding a lit pipe in one hand and a dark slide in the other. Tobacco smoke joined the smell of soil and brick and leaf mold.

"Are you ready? We're always working against time. The collodion dries out and the light . . . it fades fast on winter afternoons. Did you know it was almost the shortest day?"

"I suppose it must be close to the solstice. Every day is long here, though, Dr. St. Clair. Incurably long—I think I could go mad just from boredom."

"Are you not a needlewoman or a watercolorist?"

"Not really. I never have been, actually."

She wouldn't try to explain to Lucas St. Clair that she had a calling. Catherine Abse's response had shown her how easy it was to be misunderstood here. To unwittingly provide evidence for what people already assumed. He shifted the carved chair forward slightly and gestured for her to sit down. In front of the chair was a camera on a tripod, its round brass lens covered in a leather cap. He began moving from one side of her to the other, coming close and retreating, holding up a white board. He put down the dark slide on a trestle and stood behind her. She felt the touch of his fingers as he adjusted the set of her head against the posing stand behind the chair; the warmth gave way to the press of two cold metal thumbs behind her ears.

"It's meant to help you keep steady, Mrs. Palmer. Just adopt the expression that comes naturally to you. When you've found it, try to hold still."

He threw the cloth over the back of the camera and stepped under it. Anna didn't know what she looked like, what he saw. Should she stare straight at the camera? Gaze into the distance, as if she saw nothing? She couldn't think what a rational female face looked like. She would not adopt Mrs. Button's trusting cooperation, LM's furtive, convalescent glance. She would look as her mother had when she was dead. Like a person free of trouble. A Sphinx. Arranging her face in a rigid composition, eyebrows slightly raised, mouth unsmiling, she tried to empty her mind.

"Do I look rational?"

Lucas St. Clair poked his head out from the back of the cloth.

"The face contains muscles of expression. If the mind is troubled, so are the features."

"Does it mean one is a lunatic, if the mind is unquiet?"

"No, no . . . I don't believe it does." He had disappeared again; the glass eye on the front of the camera was shifting back and forth in tiny movements. "But the face is the mind unveiled. It is the best aid to diagnosis we have, in my opinion."

Anna's mouth began to tremble with the effort of keeping it stiff. Her hands felt clumsy on her lap. Empty.

"Can't you give me a flower? Something to hold?"

Dr. St. Clair ducked out from under the velvet, reached the low brick wall of the glasshouse in two strides and pulled a last, late fern from the mortar. He came toward her, brushing dust off its root and bowed as he presented it.

"Will this do? Granted, it has no scent."

"Thank you. The scent won't show on the image—or can you even see that, Doctor?"

He gave a muffled laugh from back inside his velvet tent, adjusted the lens again and emerged, replacing the cap over the eye of the camera and inserting the dark slide.

"Ready? We must proceed before the plate spoils."

"Wait a moment."

She wouldn't try to look like her mother. She would look like herself. Her true self. Anna jerked her neck free of the stand and pulled out her combs. Her hair fell around her, to her waist. She held the fern across her chest, raised her chin and looked at the glass, her gaze strong and steady. She could see herself reflected in the lens—upside-down and shrunk inside a circle.

"I'm ready. If you really can photograph the mind, Dr. St. Clair, you'll discover there is nothing wrong with mine."

He pulled out the slide cover, removed the lens cap and began to count.

It was easy now to keep still. Anna felt more comfortable in the fernery than she'd ever felt in the dayroom, despite the draft whistling through the broken windows, the chill penetrating her feet from the brick floor. Sitting on the chair with her hand on the cool spine of the leaf, her heart beating steadily behind it, breathing in the odor of earth and smoke, she had a feeling she hadn't had for a long time. As Lucas St. Clair reached sixty and replaced the cap on his camera, announcing that the exposure was complete, she realized what it was.

She felt at ease.

FOURTEEN

Catherine had arranged the slices of peach around the edge of her plate and was eating them in order. She picked one up with her fingers, slid its glistening tip into her mouth.

"I could live on peaches," she said, swallowing, selecting another piece.

"No one can live on peaches, Catty."

"Fruit bats can. Please don't call me that, Mother."

Querios looked up from his Stilton.

"Surely it isn't necessary to have them every night of the week?"

"We don't, Father. We haven't had them since Sunday."

"Catherine enjoys them. Use a spoon, darling, please."

"Why? What difference does it make?"

"It is not a question of enjoyment, Em. It is a question of household economy. Balancing the budget."

Querios smiled at her, a benign, affectionate smile, and Emmeline wished he was sitting nearer. She wanted to pinch him or kick his shin under the table. Didn't he understand that if Catherine craved peaches, she should have them? Even if they had to be brought fresh on the back of a donkey from wherever it was they grew. Spain. Arabia. China. It wouldn't matter.

Hannah Smith was taking her time brushing the crumbs from around Benedict's place, leaning over his shoulder.

"From the right, Hannah. And not so close."

Catherine wiped a dribble of juice from her chin with the back of her hand and Emmeline picked her own napkin off her lap, offered it to her. Catherine didn't take it. Her elbow appeared to be glued to the table. It was unnatural, the way it didn't move.

"Can you think of a fruit that you like better than peaches, Mother?"

"I like strawberries. With cream and sugar."

"Strawberries are boring. Everything English is."

Catherine inserted another slice of peach between her lips. She'd had beautiful lips from the day she was born. Pink and shapely, a rosebud mouth, like a girl from an advertisement. She'd loved playing at being a woman, trailing around in Emmeline's shoes with the heels clopping on the floorboards, draping strings of beads around her neck or cooling herself with an ostrich-feather fan. As soon as she became old enough to start the rehearsals for womanhood in earnest, she'd stopped. It was as if she lost all interest in female life. One might almost think she'd begun to despise it.

"Some of them have never even seen a p-p-piece of f-f-fruit." Benedict's head was bent over a heap of peach slices, a thick wedge of Stilton. At least he had a healthy appetite. Hannah finally left the room, filling the doorway with her back view as she did so. Emmeline could swear she had on a crinoline. She would have to speak to her.

"I had to explain to them the d-d-difference between an orange and a l-l—"

"Lemon," Querios said. "I suppose you want me to supply your urchins with tropical fruits as well."

"What a good idea," Catherine said.

Catherine had dressed, at least, was wearing the primrose-yellow lawn. Emmeline had chosen the simple gown for the rounded neckline that flattered girls of her age, made a subtle allusion to the bust without vulgar display, the wide sleeves that accentuated dainty hands. But what bosom Catherine had developed seemed to be disappearing. She'd trailed one sleeve in the soup and had the other wrapped tightly around her wrist.

"Fox has been sniffing around again," Querios said. "The question is whether the peacock will survive long enough for the magistrates to see it."

"He doesn't like to be penned in," Catherine said. "I feel sorry for him."

"The bird told you so itself, I suppose," said Querios. "Did it?"

"Do you think any living creature can thrive in captivity, Father?"

"Catherine!"

Emmeline gave her a look. Querios couldn't get over the fact that the magistrates had described the airing grounds as "gloom-filled" the last time they came. The chief magistrate had added a note suggesting they offer patients rides out, in a carriage. She'd laughed when Querios showed her the report. They didn't even keep a carriage for themselves anymore. Only the pony and trap for going to the village or the station.

Emmeline resented the patients. Even if you didn't see them, you always knew they were there. They were like ghosts—more present for being invisible. Sometimes, in bed at night, she heard them wailing or singing. It was one of the reasons she'd insisted that the boys be sent away to school. In her heart, she cherished a wish that the inspectors would close down Lake House. They could sell it, move somewhere else, and live like normal people.

Two years before, a patient had jumped out of a window. She took it into her head that her husband waited for her down on the lawn with a lit candle in his hand, and threw herself right through the glass from one of the bedrooms on the second floor. She and Querios had been preparing to retire for the night when they heard a noise like a sack of turnips falling from a cart. Emmeline had grabbed the first thing that came to hand, which happened to be her opera cloak, and had run down the stairs behind Querios, out into the moonlit garden.

The woman was already dead. She was naked. One breast pointed upward and her head rested on the gravel at an impossible angle. Her feet were bare and dirty. Emmeline threw her cloak over the body while Querios fetched Fludd. Ever since, she couldn't walk past the oak without seeing a pair of startled eyes looking up at the moon. It had been full, of course, they were always worse then.

Catherine was often out and about in the grounds and she must see things, hear things. It probably accounted for some of her notions. Emmeline could have sworn she saw Catherine push her chop into the sleeve of her dress a moment before Hannah cleared away the main course. The chop was there one minute and next time she looked, Catherine's plate was empty. Not even a bone. She could be mistaken.

Her eyes weren't what they had been. She made a mental note to tell Cook to order more tinned peaches. It was astonishing, the things they put in cans. Oysters. Peas. The idea of preservation in a dark safety soothed her.

"I shall retire early," she announced. "Good night, Ben, sleep well. Good night, Catty, darling."

The moon was unnaturally small and a cold blue-white. It looked like a harvest moon in reverse. Emmeline tiptoed around the side of the house across the gravel and along the edge of the grass. She'd made herself stay awake, propped up on the bolster making lists of matters to which she must attend. She was wearing her opera cloak over her nightgown and had pulled a pair of shoes onto her bare feet. An owl swooped somewhere out of sight, its call written across the night, and she shivered. The garden in the darkness was a different place—wild territory in which she was a trespasser.

Catherine's window was lit, the curtains parted and the frame lifted a few inches at the bottom. She crept toward it, barely breathing, trying not to dislodge any stones. Under the window, Emmeline turned so that her shadow fell behind her, bent down and began to pat the ground. The stones were sharp and damp against the tips of her fingers. Nothing. She got onto all fours, padding the ground under her knees as best she could with the folds of the cloak, and spread her arms in a wider circle—out toward the path, patting, checking the earth around the roots of the magnolia, feeling between the stones.

Still nothing. She was about to give up and go inside when her fingers encountered something large and greasy, both soft and hard. It was the chop bone, still heavy with meat. Picking it up with her thumb and forefinger, she dropped it in her pocket. Emmeline felt on in the darkness, blind and determined as a mole, and her fingers pressed into something spongy and congealed. She shuddered with disgust and felt a little of her own dinner rise sourly in her throat. Dead man's eyeballs. Her brothers used to force her to play that game, blindfolding her and pushing her hands into aspic or creamed potato. She had forgotten that sensation for thirty years.

She picked up the chilly lump, added it to the pocket, grasped a branch of the magnolia and heaved herself back onto her feet, shaking out her cloak. There was no cloud in the night sky and the stars were profuse, scattered diamonds. Emmeline tipped back her head, searching for the elusive, flashing triangle. She treasured the Seven Sisters. Her father had shown them to her when she was small and ever since she'd thought of them as his gift to her. It was one way of looking at things. The entire estate had gone to her younger brothers, but she had inherited the galaxy.

Back in her bedroom, she washed her hands, rubbing and rinsing them for some time. Afterward she sat at her dressing table, smoothing cold cream upward over her cheeks. It soothed her to sit at the dressing table, readying herself alternately for the day and for the night, knowing that one would follow the other. There were some certainties in life. Her fingers smelled of lavender and underneath was the faint, unmistakable sweetness of pork.

The soft shuffle of Querios's slippered feet on the carpet made itself heard and Emmeline put down the pot with a brittle tap on the rosewood. She felt the need to alert him to her presence; she couldn't rely on him to notice her. It hadn't always been like that.

"Q. It isn't often I ask something of you." She glimpsed his creased face in the mirror, saw it stiffen.

"I've got accounts outstanding, Em. Peaches are an extravagance."

She turned on the stool and caught hold of his hand.

"I'm not talking about groceries. Catherine ignores my advice. Contradicts everything I say to her. I'm worried about her. I want you to talk to her."

"There's nothing wrong with Catherine. Young women always want their own way."

"I am not talking about what she reads or what she wears. Even the friends she associates with, although lately she's become so solitary. I'm talking about . . ." Emmeline stopped. She had not spoken of her fears to anyone. She'd kept quiet, on a superstition that if she voiced what she saw it would confirm it. "I'm talking about her figure."

Querios sat down on the edge of the bed in his nightshirt. The springs lurched and resettled themselves in twanging complaint.

"What about it?"

She held up the pocket. It was stained around the bottom and bulged in unreadable shapes.

"I found this under her window. It's a chop. A pork chop and a slice of suet pudding. It's her dinner, Querios."

"Really, Emmy, this is something for the maids. I have told you time and time again that I have larger concerns."

He banged his ear down to the pillow and pulled up the red satin eiderdown around his head.

Emmeline put down the bag on the hearth tiles and sat looking at nothing in particular. She suspected that Catherine's monthlies had ceased. When she asked her, Hannah Smith had confirmed that nothing of that nature had come to the laundry for some time. In fact, she could remember the last time, Smith had murmured, as if she spoke to herself. Then she said, well, it didn't matter how she recalled it, but it was a few months ago. Something snagged Emmeline's attention as she remembered Hannah saying that. She pictured Hannah's eyes. Her averted face as she served Querios his kippers and her fingers swollen around the curtain ring she'd taken to wearing on the left hand.

"Oh, dear God."

Hannah Smith was expecting. Why was it that one only ever understood things backward? Querios stirred and subsided in the bed as Emmeline's mind roamed over the possibilities. She supposed it must be the groundsman. Her heart sank at the thought of the squalid cottage with its earthen floors. Or it could be Jethro Fludd, the only male attendant. Fludd had something in his eyes. Something . . . well, *animal* was the word that came to mind. She remembered the sun-browned man who came to sharpen the knives every year. Oh, please, Hannah, not him. In that shelter on the heath where they all camped. When was it that the knives had been sharp?

By one in the morning, Emmeline's only comfort was the memory of the Pleiades. She lay on her back, absorbing the silence all around her and picturing the far, flashing stars.

FIFTEEN

Anna had agreed to Makepeace's demand that she find something to occupy her hands. A handkerchief-size square of cambric lay on her lap alongside a limp cotton bag of silks. Makepeace had instructed her to embroider a letter *V* on the squeaking, starched piece of fabric. Anna had made the first tentative stitches but the line refused to take shape. She dragged the needle off its thread and began to unpick a line of puckered chain stitch.

"Miss Batt?"

"I am listening, Mrs. Palmer."

"Will you call me Anna?"

"I would rather not."

"Why?"

"Habit. My family always took comfort in formality. It does not preclude close acquaintance."

"It's just that I don't feel like a Mrs. Palmer. I never have."

She was sitting between Talitha Batt and the fire, driven off the window seat by the draft. It was over a fortnight since the cold shower and six days since Lucas St. Clair took her picture. She barely knew how, but she'd somehow begun talking often and easily to Batt. What she'd told Dr. St. Clair, that she hadn't laughed since she got here, was no longer true.

Miss Batt was thirty-six years old. She had been in Lake House three years and eleven months. The only thing Anna hadn't discovered was why. She hadn't liked to ask and Miss Batt had not volunteered the information—or asked Anna what had brought her here.

"May I ask you a personal question?" Anna said.

Batt pursed her mulberry lips. "If you must."

Anna hesitated and substituted another inquiry. "Do you see madness in my face?"

She turned to Batt as if braced for a photograph, eyes wide and unblinking. Miss Batt looked back at her with cool gray eyes and smiled.

"We can all look at times as if we're losing our wits," she said. "It helps not to be idle, although I have observed that you have no aptitude for handwork. Do you enjoy sketching?"

Anna shook her head.

"What do you like to do?"

"Almost anything apart from sketching and sewing, Miss Batt. I'm not much of a pianist either. What I really love is dancing."

"Not much of that goes on here, unfortunately."

Batt selected a golden silk from the tangle of colors and drew out a length of it. A long-trumpeted orange lily was taking shape beneath her fingers in a succession of neat, slanting stitches.

Anna looked up at the ceiling and examined the deep, molded frieze that ran around its edge. The plasterwork was discolored, blackened with smoke and chipped, with some of its cherubs missing toes or noses. She brought her eyes back down into the room. She had to know.

"If you don't mind my inquiring, Miss Batt, what is the nature of your affliction?"

Batt was tying the end of the silk in a double knot, using the tip of her needle to tighten one on top of the other. She pulled the thread taut with both hands.

"That is a question one does not ask in Lake House, Mrs. Palmer."

"I'm sorry. It's just that I can't see anything the matter with you." Anna looked at Miss Batt's white, powdered face and the exaggerated, drawn-in features. "Not really."

"I suppose I should be glad of that."

Batt's voice was vexed. Anna rethreaded her own needle and began again on the cambric, in a different corner. She felt reproached. She ought to have stuck to her original impulse and not said anything. She jabbed the point through the resistant weave and gasped as it pierced her thumb. The blood when it came was profuse, disproportionate to the wound. Anna sucked it, tasting it on the tip of her tongue, and looked up to find Batt watching her again.

"I committed a mortal sin, Mrs. Palmer. My family convinced themselves that I must be ill. They didn't believe that in my right mind I could do what I did."

"I see."

Had Batt killed? Was she a murderess? A flurry of sleet splattered against the window like a handful of thrown gravel and Anna's skin crawled under her clothes. She couldn't suppress the shudder that ran through her. Miss Batt laughed.

"I fell in love."

"That's hardly a crime." Anna could hear the relief in her own voice. "Wasn't it possible to marry?"

"No."

"But why? If you loved each other so? Couldn't your family have accepted your choice?"

"No. And nor could his. You see, Mrs. Palmer, my lover was not a Christian. There was no possibility on either side of our marrying. I lived with him for a year without the shelter of the law or the consent of a single human being other than myself. We lived in mutual happiness until the day my family came and took me away from him, using the methods they thought necessary."

Batt's hand was shaking. Anna felt herself turning scarlet and for a minute neither spoke.

"I'm so sorry if I intruded, Miss Batt. I haven't . . . I didn't . . . the truth is that I haven't known love. Only marriage."

"You're not alone in that, Mrs. Palmer. My observation is that few women experience both."

"Do you regret it? Living with him?"

Batt studied the world that had come into bloom under her fingers. The pattern of vivid, exuberant flowers and diaphanous insects in jewel-like colors—gold and fuchsia and sapphire and purple and behind it all a bright, cooling green the color of fresh limes.

"For that one year, I was alive, Mrs. Palmer. I was alive in my heart and soul, in my body, too, as I never had been before and never expect to be again. I cannot regret it."

Anna smoothed the material on her own knees and stared at its virginal blankness. Miss Batt had loved. She had known passion and given herself to it, regardless of the price she would pay. Anna knew as little about love as she'd known before she was married.

She and Vincent hadn't touched before the wedding. There had been the opportunity; Vincent had stayed at the flint house overnight when he came to meet her mother, had slept in Lavinia's old room. Anna had always been curious about the sexual act. They didn't know men, in their house, but there were sometimes sailors who wandered along the bay, stopped to smoke and watch as they played on the shore. One had taken out his penis, long and blue-looking in his hand. Anna had been grinding chalk to make milk, rubbing together two smooth-edged stones, sitting on the ground with her pail between her knees. She looked up and saw the member bob upward clumsily as if it floated in the air.

She overturned the milk on the pebbles, watched for an instant as it spilled and dissipated, then she scrambled back up the path, the path that adults never took. Next day, she came back with Lou. Her pail was still there, lying on its side. Nothing had changed.

She had waited for Vincent's advance, expecting him to attempt to step over the bounds of propriety, as Louisa said all men did. She would have let him. She was impatient to explore the mystery. And she needed a way to know this man, who in conversation revealed little of himself, preferring to quote from the Bible rather than from his own mind and heart. Anna waited for him, listening to the creaks and sighs of the timbers, the night barking of the dogs beyond her window. He didn't come.

It was because he was a clergyman, she told herself in the morning. A good man, better than other men. She sat opposite him at the old drop-leaf table in the dining room of the flint house and watched him chew his way through a pile of toast. It was burned, had arrived at the table scraped and the air smelled of carbon. Anna thanked God, while he said the longest grace she'd ever heard, that he was unaware of her impure thoughts.

It would be different once they were married. The physical act would make them intimate, Louisa said, with a little smile. But it had not. The first night, in the Vicarage, Vincent undressed as if he was alone, taking time to hang his trousers on a wooden hanger, lining up the hems, putting in his shoe trees while she lay in the bed watching him.

He got between the sheets and turned to her purposefully as if she was a job that needed doing. Pulled up her nightdress, explored between her legs with one impatient hand and pushed himself into her without a word, his face over her shoulder, while she bit on a hank of her hair with the effort of not crying out. He had finished with a prolonged, internal groan and rolled off her.

Anna lay in the dark, waiting for him to say something. She felt proud. It had been achieved, after all. The great mystery had been accomplished and she had been present. For some reason, she felt like laughing. But he hadn't said anything at all.

Over the weeks that followed, she wondered whether she might have understood it all better with a man closer to her own age. She found Vincent physically—well, not quite repulsive, but somehow she didn't much like the smell of him. The feel of his skin, always slightly chilly, almost damp, against hers. The whiff of frankincense that reminded her of church.

She didn't love Vincent, she understood, sitting on the wobbly bentwood chair in the dayroom watching Miss Batt's flying, fluent needle. She didn't want him. She never had.

Anna felt someone watching and looked up to see Makepeace surveying her and Batt from the other end of the room. Makepeace's face was set and her arms hung rigidly by her sides. The woman didn't like the developing friendship between Anna and Miss Batt. Preferred to claim Talitha Batt as her own friend, when she could. And Miss Batt obliged, had a kind word for everybody.

Anna shivered, rubbed her own arms and breathed in the smell of fish rising from the kitchen. She was feeling more than usually restless. They couldn't walk in the grounds, because of the rain, and the air in the room was close. She lowered her voice.

"Did you ever consider escape from here, Miss Batt?"

Batt gave a laugh that was over as soon as it began.

"Of course. I thought of nothing else for a long time."

"What happened? Did you ever try?"

"There is no escape. Not in the way you're thinking. Not through scaling walls and so on."

Her voice was subdued; Anna had to strain to hear her over the squawking of Violet's bird and the maid banging around the skirting boards with a dustpan.

"What other way is there?"

Batt didn't answer.

"I believe this place is enough to drive one mad," Anna said, leaning toward the fire, lifting her skirts to warm her ankles. "Sometimes, I think it would be better not to live at all than to live where there is no life. Death must surely be better than this hell."

Batt looked her fiercely in the eye. "Our life on this earth is given to us by a greater power, Mrs. Palmer. Ending it is not to be contemplated. Not ever."

"You are right. Until we can get out we must find a way to escape inside Lake House. Within ourselves."

Anna dropped the handkerchief on the floor and stood up. She kicked the slippers off her feet and conjured in her head the opening notes of a polka, a rough country polka played on fiddles as the Gypsy players did at the Christmas fairs in Dover. She bowed to an imaginary partner and began, slowly at first, skipping forward and retreating again, turning in circles, raising her hand for twirling. The music in her head picked up speed and so did she, moving along the length of the frayed rugs, spinning in circles as she engraved a larger pattern over the whole room, her stockinged feet moving fast, her skirts swinging out around her. The music filled her head—the lilting, turning rhythm of the polka that promised life's continuance through good times and bad, that expressed its endless, unstoppable movement.

She danced until she could stay upright no more and came back to the chair, laughing, collapsed down onto it with her chest heaving and her limbs loose, eyes shining. Miss Batt and Violet Valentine clapped their hands; Miss Todd and Miss Little stared at her. Makepeace turned on her heel and left the room, banging the door behind her.

Anna picked up her workbag. She wouldn't surrender. She and her sisters had been brought up to be as bold and strong as boys. Taught by their father when his ship was in to swear and spit and whistle. To endure. Survive anything that came. She licked the end of her thread, inserted the fine tail into the eye of the needle and dragged the length of silk through the cloth. She would get outside the walls of Lake House. Free herself. If her own sister wouldn't help her, Dr. St. Clair would. She was sure of it.

SIXTEEN

Lucas St. Clair stood by the mantelpiece in the dining room, looking at the photographs on the wall. He had on the same worn coat as on the first time she'd seen him and carried a portfolio under his arm. Anna sensed life in the air that surrounded him, felt it hanging on him like a strong, enticing scent. He looked as out of place in the utilitarian room as a banquet would have looked on the old oilcloth.

"Hello, Doctor."

He turned and smiled at her.

"Hello."

He put down the portfolio and they both looked at it. Anna felt dizzy, to think that the means of escape might be right there in front of her, lying flat and contained as a rail ticket, tied up by the buff-colored tapes. She held on to the back of a chair.

"How are you, Mrs. Palmer?"

"I'm perfectly well, Doctor. Except for being here, of course. How are you?"

"Me? Oh, I'm all right, thank you. Overworked and underpaid."

His whiskers were newly shaved, the line of them precise and jaunty, contradicting tired eyes that looked past her to the window. She turned to find out what caught his attention, saw only the sheep in the field, the lake beyond, its surface ruffled and unsettled under the tossing willow fronds. In the distance, the bridge looked dull and small, its silvery promise dimmed.

"What did you find in my picture, Dr. St. Clair? Am I fit to rejoin the world?"

He appeared to grope for his words.

"Mrs. Palmer . . . everyone who comes here does so for a reason."

"Of course, Doctor. My husband's concern for me was genuine, I know. He didn't intend to drive me mad by bringing me here."

He didn't return her smile. She pulled out the chair and sat down as he untied the tapes of the folder and drew out a photograph carefully, holding it by its edges. He looked at it for a moment, frowning, then came around to where she sat and laid it on the table in front of her.

Anna saw a woman sitting in a carved wooden chair twice as wide as she was. Her hair fell down over her shoulders to her waist in waves, crinkled from its night-time plaiting. Her complexion was chalky and her eyes pale, almost translucent. A fern lay across her chest like a skeletal, many-fingered hand and her dress looked white. The woman appeared as if her whole being was centered around the unspoken plea that signaled itself from the points of light in her troubled eyes.

"Is it me?" Anna said, at length. "I suppose it is."

Lucas St. Clair cleared his throat.

"Yes, it is. What do you think of it?"

"I hardly recognize myself."

He was close behind her, looking at the picture over her shoulder. He picked up one corner and tilted it to the light.

"The focus is sharp, the light even. The tones are better than I'd hoped and the print clear and rich. But those are technical matters."

Anna turned her head and looked up at him.

"Dr. St. Clair, can't you see that I am well? I mean, with your own eyes?"

"Mrs. Palmer, disorders of the mind can pass. They can heal. There is no shame in mental illness despite the prejudices of the general public."

He thought her a lunatic. He thought she was one of them. Anna felt more undone by St. Clair's thinking she was deranged than by her husband's thinking the same thing. She'd thought she could trust him. That was the difference. The idea came to Anna as if a stone had hit her between the eyes. She didn't trust Vincent. She never had.

She made herself look again at the picture.

"So what is your diagnosis?"

"Do you not see the slightly fixed stare? The tension of the muscles by the jaw? The face—alight with nervous energy." He was touching the photograph as he spoke, his finger resting on her eyes, her cheeks, her lips. He smelled of pipe smoke and something musty and sweet that reminded her of apples stored over the winter. "These are the classic signs of hysteria, Mrs. Palmer."

She rose from the chair.

"I was keeping still, for the camera. If I seem to stare, that's why. And who would not be tense, in my situation? I am a prisoner here, Dr. St. Clair. A prisoner who has committed no crime."

Her voice was as flat as if it had been ironed. He walked back to the fireplace and pulled a pipe out of his coat pocket.

"You are troubled by visions, according to your notes?"

She watched as he struck a match on the bottom of a small silver case and held the flame over the tamped tobacco, making small, regular inhalations, throwing the match into the hearth. Blue smoke rose and hazed the air, stung her eyes, transported her for a sharp instant to the study in the flint house. Anna began to pace up and down the dining room.

"I am not *troubled* by visions. I see them. I have done since I was a child."

"Would you like to tell me about them?"

"I don't know." She stopped by the window, folded her arms and stood with her back to him, looking out. The trees waved and thrashed. Strands of hay tumbled in the wind over the sheep field. Only the bridge was still. She turned around to face him again. "Lately, just one vision comes to me, Doctor. And yes, I admit that it does trouble me. I see a boy, disappearing."

She began to explain how all through the summer the image of the boy came to her again and again. Then, after the storm that battered the nation's coasts, wrecked scores of ships, she read of a child rescued from the water still breathing and brought ashore in the Welsh harbortown. She explained to Dr. St. Clair her sense that she was meant to help the child. Her hurry to reach the site of the wreck and how when she got there she could not find him.

The little town was overwhelmed by the numbers of dead, its mortuary overflowing. Anna made herself go there, searching, and found it a horror beyond words. The bodies were strapped to planks because the drowned could twitch back into life, leap up, animated by exploding gases. Some had lost the skin of their hands, slipped off like a pair of gloves after days in the water. Others had lips and eyes eaten by the fishes; skin grazed by the sand as they bumped to and fro on the tides. A few had disintegrated altogether. The boy wasn't there.

Anna heard her own voice, became aware of the torrent of words pouring out of her mouth and stopped.

"Forgive me, Doctor. I know people find it distasteful to hear a woman speak of these things."

"Not at all. Most of us never face unnatural death on such a scale, Mrs. Palmer." His voice was somber and gentle. She remembered Vincent's cold tone when she had tried to tell him about her experience and the way he'd turned his head from her as if repulsed. Tears sprang to her eyes.

"I saw terrible sights but wanting to help does not make me mad—does it?"

"No. It does not."

Silence descended in the room and for a minute only the light moved, causing the shadowed outlines of the window frames on the wall to tremble in golden squares, illuminating the stretching wreaths of pipe smoke.

"Dr. St. Clair, I'd hoped your theory was right. That you would discover from looking at the photograph that I am well. But it seems that you weren't able to see the truth in it." Anna picked up the print, tried to inject some hope into her voice. "Perhaps your theory is wrong. Will you make another picture? It might tell you something different."

"Gladly, Mrs. Palmer."

Their eyes met and there seemed to be an exchange between them that was different from the words that had been spoken, as if in the same room two other people had, for an instant, encountered each other. Dr. St. Clair's eyes were as troubled as hers as they said goodbye, stiffly, with a prolonged grasp of hands but with none of the ease they had shared in the fernery.

* * *

Christmas Eve fell on a Saturday. Lizzie Button, in the dayroom, cradled her baby on her lap, wrapped in a new napkin. She rocked back and forth, dropping kisses on it and crooning. She wore her laced boots and had her bonnet upside-down on a footstool next to her.

"I'm going home," she called out to the new patient, Mrs. Featherstone. "My husband's coming to get me, I feel it in my bones."

"Lucky for you," the woman replied. "I'd be off myself but it isn't safe. They're waiting for me out there behind the trees. I'm Her Majesty's Person, you know."

Talitha Batt was dressed for travel in a severe, woollen dress, enlivened by her usual white ruff. She had a fringed, embroidered shawl of gold flowers on a red ground over her shoulders and polished, old-fashioned navy shoes on her feet with buckles on their sides. Her sewing was nowhere to be seen and she sat with her hands folded in her lap, in silence. She seemed distracted, did not inquire whether Anna was going home for Christmas, as Violet Valentine did, half a dozen times, her interest as fresh with each asking as it had been the first time.

All through the morning, men strode into the dayroom, looked around with a mix of embarrassment and impatience on their faces, then claimed one or other of the women. They extended broad arms, inquired, loudly and too cheerfully, after Mother's or Aunt's well-being. The visitors left more slowly than they arrived, pulling their relatives through the door and out, down the stairs.

At eleven o'clock, a man with the same dark hair as Batt's arrived.

"Ready?" he said, without preamble.

Miss Batt raised her flying eyebrows in response, rose from her chair, and came over to Anna.

"Good-bye, Mrs. Palmer. My brother is here. I cannot wish you a merry Christmas." She smiled, one of her rare smiles, showing her neat white teeth. "But I hope it passes tolerably. I will be thinking of you."

"Thank you, Miss Batt," Anna said. "I hope you *do* have a happy Christmas. And I suppose I must hope that you don't return, even though I should miss you very much."

Batt stooped and squeezed her hand with cool, bony fingers, kissed her on the cheek.

"Farewell, Anna." She left with her back straight, her step as precise and light as always.

The room looked more disorderly after she had gone. Batt's chair appeared emptier than the other vacant seats. Anna sat without moving, her hands still around her embroidery as, at intervals, loud, cracking explosions from within the grate threw out showers of sparks that glowed on the hearth rug, and died, leaving behind a smell of burning wool.

By midday, only Anna, Lizzie Button, Violet Valentine and five others remained. Lizzie Button had begun to cry—gulping sobs that racked her body. She kept on crying as they walked through into the dining room to face a lunch of boiled bacon and beetroot. Anna put an arm round Lizzie's shoulder and leaned her cheek against the side of her cropped head.

"It's alright, Mrs. Button," she said. "You'll be alright. We all will."

By the time the food was cleared uneaten from the table, Anna felt tired. She walked through the door in small steps, her legs as weak as the day she came. She'd thought there was no doubt that they would come. If Louisa didn't arrive, Vincent would. If Vincent didn't, then it would be Louisa who rushed in, brimming with apologies for having taken so long. It was impossible that she would be left here over Christmas.

Throughout the afternoon, she tried to keep up her spirits. Vincent was occupied with services, would come late and get the cab to wait. Louisa was expecting twins this time, they thought from the size of her. She'd send her husband, Blundell, in her place. By three in the afternoon, the house was still and silent; outside, nothing moved.

The door opened and all of them in the room raised their heads at the same moment. Makepeace's voice sawed into the air; her rings clashed as she clapped her hands together. She had an unsteady look about her, her cheeks rouged, a sprig of holly pinned to her buttoned bodice.

"We are an intimate party, aren't we, ladies? What a pleasant time we shall spend together. For now, we must return to our rooms."

*　*　*

On Christmas morning, when she woke up, Anna saw the boy again.

He was so very present as he disappeared. He was small, young enough still to have rounded limbs. He stood on a rock, a prince surveying his kingdom. A moment later, he jumped, landing on both feet on the opaque surface. He paused, as if for an imagined instant he walked as he expected he would. Then began the toppling descent. He went under quickly, the look on his face changing from delight to something that she could not describe as fear but only as incomprehension. His eyes remained wide open. Then, she saw the top of a round head, the way the hair floated out around it.

She stood in the sea, searching it with her hands, pulling her open fingers through its widths. In the bed at Lake House, she relived the sensation of trawling her hands through the water, the water slipping through without resistance—pulling them this way and that, plunging her arms deeper. She could feel the cold and smell its sharpness, hear it sigh and suck. The water stretched around her, the broken surface becoming solid again before her eyes.

Since her marriage the picture had come to her so clearly and often. It haunted her.

Anna got out of bed and kneeled on the chair at the window. Outside, the sky was pink and gold and the grass leading down to the field beaded with dew. The sheep had gathered around a pile of hay and were eating steadily. Beyond the field, the lake was still and long ribbons of white mist hung over the water. The bridge shimmered in the radiant light, tinged with rose. It felt to Anna as if every time she saw it was the first time, as if she could never grow tired of it. She gazed at it through the window until her feet became so icy that she had to get back into bed. Curling up under the covers, her arms wrapped around her legs, she held her toes in her fingers and tried to warm them.

As she lay there, she pictured the bridge, studying the photograph of it that her mind had made. She saw its three arches, leading to the far bank. The pretty, upright pillars of the baluster and the smooth handrail that ran along their tops. The reflection the bridge cast on the water, each arch the shape of a new moon.

Anna heard Makepeace approaching, banging along the corridor unlocking doors. She climbed out of bed again, rinsed her face in the cold water left in the jug. Combing her fingers through her hair, she swept it forward over one shoulder and twisted it into a plait, watching herself in the mirror. The bridge was her way out. As soon as Christmas was over, she would find a means to get across it.

SEVENTEEN

Querios Abse came up the stairs with a tin of bonbons in one hand. He could hear laughter coming from the dayroom. He listened intently to the unfamiliar sound. No doubt about it, it was female gaiety. He stopped in front of the door. The guests were much reduced in numbers; a dozen of 'em had been taken home for the festivities, he explained to an imaginary magistrate at his side. He provided as well as he could for those who were left, within the constraints of the anti-phlogistic diet. Believed they had almost as much enjoyment as they might have had around their own hearths.

The word *hearth* had a cheery, comforting sound about it, *heart* and *earth* put together. He would weave it into the next brochure. *Offers all the comforts of the home hearth.* More comforts than most of them had ever had at home, in his estimation.

Querios opened the door with a declamatory gesture and as he stepped through it his satisfaction drained away. Violet Valentine's bird had escaped from its cage and was in panicked flight around the ceiling, banging against the tops of the windows and the chimney breast. Some of the women were chasing after it, pursuing it with raised hands, cooing to it, shouting with laughter as they caught at the feathers that fluttered down from the ceiling. The bird landed on the gasolier and splashed its waste onto the rug below.

The rest of the guests were grouped around the fireplace in unseemly postures, their hair stuck with ribbons and pieces of tinsel borrowed from the fir tree. Violet Valentine, seemingly unconcerned about the plight of her pet, had her legs resting on the fender, her head wreathed in mistletoe. Lizzie Button crouched next to her on a footstool with a blue tablecloth thrown around her shoulders. Makepeace occupied Talitha Batt's wing chair. Her head was tipped back and her mouth open, he saw, with a sickening sense of apprehension. A Madeira bottle lolled at her feet.

Anna Palmer stood a little distance away from the others. She was wearing the dress that she'd arrived in, unsuitable for a vicar's wife, although he couldn't say why exactly. It was a blue-green material with some sort of sheen to it. Unfashionable, he suspected, but it flattered her, with its quaint lace collar hanging down in two points, the buttons leading like stepping-stones from her neck down to her narrow waist. Her eyes were swollen from weeping. Mrs. Palmer's condition had worsened since she'd arrived, he informed the magistrate. Sometimes that was the trajectory. It couldn't be helped. Illness was unpredictable, just as health was. Neither could be relied upon. Of course, they made every effort and he himself was always optimistic.

"I trust everyone has passed a pleasant evening?"

The laughter had ceased as he stood there, the bird catchers grown still. He gave a smile he hoped was encouraging but reproving and tucked his thumb into his watch chain, resting the weight of his hand on the blunt links. He had been called "Vicar" by his contemporaries at school. At the time, he took the nickname as a compliment to his upstanding nature. Only later did it occur to him that others saw him as self-righteous.

He felt suddenly awkward, did not know where to put the bonbons. The lid of the tin was embossed with a picture of a tree crammed with glass trinkets, sugared fruits and candles, surrounded by rosy children in their nightgowns. It mocked what he saw in front of him. The branches of the tree he'd procured at some expense looked like the bony arms of old women. A carpet of needles sprinkled around it gave off a resinous odor that reminded him of a forest. The candles on it were lit and burning low. He saw the possibility of immolation, the locked door at the other end of the room, imagined the magistrate scratching a sharp and indelible little note.

A torrent of the kind of feelings that he didn't normally permit himself coursed through Querios. Was it his fault if these women were mad? He did his best to help them, keep them safe in Lake House, protected from censure and their own abominable desires and passions. He had never wanted to work in an asylum but had been forced to assume the mantle bequeathed by his father. It dawned on him with a startling clarity that he disliked lunatics above all other kinds of people. They were devious. Cunning. Untrustworthy. Parasites on the body of healthy society, without higher thoughts or aims other than to secure their own individual liberty.

He looked again at the tableau in front of him. Something about the Button woman's pose on the low stool, some humbleness in it, was designed to reproach him. It was intolerable.

"Mrs. Button. Get up off that stool."

He banged down the tin on a vacant plant stand, seized the piece of wood out of Button's hands and flung it on the fire. There was a moment of silence broken by a hiss as the dry wood caught and flared. Mrs. Palmer ran forward, stooped in front of the leaping flames and reached one hand into the grate. She pulled out the wood and doused it with water from the holly vase on the mantelpiece. Querios flinched as she turned, afraid for a moment that she intended to empty the rest of it over his head. She brushed off the charred edges of the wood and handed it back to Button as carefully as if it was a live child. He almost laughed.

"What do you think you're doing?"

"Mrs. Button is playing the Virgin Mary, sir."

Now, he did laugh, long and loud. Tears of mirth sprang from his eyes and his breath came in wheezing gasps, preventing him from getting out his words.

"Button here hardly resembles our Lord's mother, Mrs. Palmer. Wretched creature that she is."

From a foot away, she spat in his face—coolly and accurately, exactly like a man might, as if she were some jack-tar rolling out of a tavern in Wapping. He groped for his handkerchief and dabbed at his eye, maintaining an expression of unconcern, for the sake of his own dignity as much as the impression on the imaginary magistrate. The Reverend was likely to visit over the festive season. It would be awkward to have to inform him that his wife was more hysterical than ever but there it was. He was always optimistic.

Violet had found the sweets. She was sucking the white, powdery sugar off the bonbons with rapid movements of her jaw and spitting glistening toffees back in the tin. Her bird, returned to her shoulder, pecked at the berries that dangled from her ears. Querios wished Talitha Batt had remained over Christmas. Miss Batt set a standard. He retrieved the tin, jammed the lid back on and rapped on it with his signet ring.

"Fanny! Bring this regrettable soirée to a close."

He repeated the instruction, more loudly, but she didn't so much as raise her head. He felt a spurt of anger. Quelled it. It was the season and one had to make allowances. There weren't many females who could do Fanny Makepeace's job. There weren't many who wanted to try. He would leave them to it. That was it. Let them sort themselves out.

Outside in the passageway he leaned against the wall, trying to overcome the roaring in his head, the crash and thunder of it. There was no sign of when the magistrates would come and he was haunted by them. Permanently under inspection. Permanently found wanting.

Emmeline was nagging him about getting a physician to Catherine. He would not, he decided, looking at his feet, the way they were planted on the carpet, toes turned out. His mother used to scold him for walking with his toes at a quarter to three. He'd never understood why. He didn't now. He strained after some saying about a cobbler's children. Couldn't remember it. He would not risk the business by letting word get out that his own daughter was unbalanced.

On the other side of the door, voices had resumed. There seemed to be some merriment again. The women were singing and he could hear the boards creaking and bowing—it sounded as if they might be dancing. He could go back to his own parlor and sit with the family, Emmeline's sister Florence and her children, but he didn't feel inclined.

Querios felt his way down the unlit stairs to the office. The curtains were open and the moonlight sufficient to display the objects in the room quite plainly. A lot of old junk, he thought. And none of it chosen by him. He sat down and rested his eyes on the piles of ledgers on the front of the desk, contemplated the white quills laid out on a stand next to the ink bottle.

They'd planned to leave Lake House once the old man died. When it happened, it had not after all been possible. Querios knew no other trade and even with Emmeline behind him lacked the courage to sell up, take a chance on a new life. Unable to discharge himself, he had no choice but to stay on and look after the guests, imprisoned for longer than any of them. He wondered if they saw the irony. Some did, he thought, although on the whole it passed the families by.

The cobbler's children go barefoot. That was it. Once he remembered the homily, he couldn't dislodge it. He caught some movement from outside out of the corner of his eye, got up and stood at the dark glass. The fox bounded toward the house with its shadow reaching ahead of it on the moonlit grass. He raised a fist, banged on the window and it swerved and carried on—toward the cottage, the peacock's enclosure.

Bloody creature was getting bolder.

EIGHTEEN

Lucas St. Clair bought a bag of hazelnuts from a boy with his feet wrapped in bundles of pudding cloth and told him to keep the change. Regent Street curved away in front of him, alive with people. He would have liked to seize the beauty of the moment but the exposure would be too long. By the time they'd left their mark on the plate, the women in their colorful shawls and cloaks would appear to be wraiths; the strolling men, specters.

He continued on his way, eating as he went. He wasn't due at Vigo Street, at the gallery, until eleven, but it was hard to rid himself of the permanent sense of hurry with which he lived. Lucas couldn't remember the last time he had taken a morning off but he was fulfilling his resolution for the new year—to get out for at least a couple of hours on Saturdays and do something that was not work.

Some of the shops still had Christmas fir trees over their doorways; others displayed curling branches of pine and laurel in their windows. New photography studios were opening everywhere. At the point where the wide street swerved toward Piccadilly, he stopped in front of one. The *p* had come off the painted sign outside; it advertised *hotography*. He found himself looking at an image in the window of a girl wearing a dress tied with a satin sash. She was aged about ten and had been pictured stepping through a huge, ornately carved frame as big as she was, passing through it as if it was a doorway. She was half in the frame, half out of it, in the act of escaping it even as it captured her. The picture was a jest at photography's expense. He stared at it, throwing nuts into his mouth from the palm of his hand until he'd emptied the bag.

* * *

At the gallery, there were too many pictures. Landscapes sat shoulder to shoulder with still lifes; portraits jostled Eastern antiquities for space. They hung five or six deep around the walls of the long room, with more propped against the skirting boards. The profusion irritated Lucas; it suggested that the merit of photographs lay in their existing at all, that no selection procedures were appropriate.

Maddox hadn't arrived. The only other visitor was an elderly man, baby-faced with a bald head and ebullient salt-and-pepper whiskers framing his face. He walked around the room stooped forward with his hands linked behind his back and his nose pointed at the pictures.

The early photographs were grouped together. Mr. Fox Talbot had supplied both the calotype negative and the print for his study of an oak tree in winter. They hung side by side, the eerie beauty of the paper negative perfectly matched by the delicate fascination of the positive.

The old gentleman had appeared beside him.

"Wonderful work, isn't it, sir?" Lucas said.

The man nodded. "I'm glad you think so."

Lucas wandered on. Was it Fox Talbot himself? Just to think about Fox Talbot, his persistent experiments with silver and salts, his lace and leaves offered up to the sun in the Wiltshire countryside, made him cheerful. Fox Talbot was part of the magical quality of photography, its human alchemy. He had assisted at the birth of the medium; it was up to the next generation to develop the uses to which it could be put.

As schoolboys, Lucas and his friends had coated pieces of paper with silver nitrate, held them up to the classroom window with their hands in front of them, watched the outlines of their fingers take shape like white gloves as the surrounding paper turned black and dense. The image was fugitive; like childhood afternoons, their hands quickly disappeared, darkened to nothingness. He'd found it entrancing—the apparition of a negative shadow, a faithful record. Its subtle vanishing. His father, when he informed him of his desire to become a photographer, had let him know it was out of the question. Lucas had put aside his passion and concentrated on his medical studies.

After Archie died it didn't seem to matter anymore what his father or anyone else thought. The smudgy picture of Archie that Lucas had made with a pinhole camera on the day he left for the Crimea was the only image of him they had. It became his mother's most precious possession, carried with her everywhere in a locket. That was when he'd taken up photography again—seriously.

He felt tired. He sat down on the Chesterfield in the middle of the gallery, wincing as his fingertip encountered the leather. He'd given himself a splinter while cutting plates and had tried to extract it with a scalpel tip but his flesh had closed stubbornly around it. And he'd slept badly. The talk to the Alienists' Association was approaching fast. It loomed up at him in the night asking what he planned to say and whether it was true.

He was rattled by Mrs. Palmer's rejection of her image and her insistence that she didn't recognize herself in it. He hadn't been able to forget her face or the look in her eyes—not in the photograph but by the filtered light of the dining room, gold on her hair, her skin, the shadows moving, changing with every passing minute and her face changing too, her expression as fluid and evanescent as the unscientific, beautiful light.

Lucas rose to examine the modern work. Wet collodion provided far greater detail than the old paper negatives; the exposures were much decreased. He admired a picture by Frith, each huge slab of the Cheops pyramid sharp as lump sugar. But he felt dissatisfied with the portraits. The camera was faithful in its way and yet it recorded a world that no one had ever seen. The qualities he found inspirational about the medium, the way it ordered life, flattened and clarified the world into planes of light and shade, stopped time, also frustrated him.

He stopped in front of a picture of a man propped in a chair, his eyes closed, chest bare. The man's torso looked as vulnerable as the flesh in one of the Old Masters, his pale body contrasting with his darkened face and hands. He was slumped at right angles to the camera. It was refreshing to see a man who wasn't standing like a statue, moustache waxed, wife clamped to arm. A man who wasn't trying to prove he was a fine fellow. *Self-portrait as a Drowned Man*, he read, and he felt his faith strengthen again. Photographs could show the inner man, the inner woman, display the deeper truth of human existence. It was possible.

"What kind of fellow would make an image of himself dead?" came a voice from behind. "Is that how he wants to be remembered?" Lucas turned as Maddox clapped him on the back. Maddox gestured toward the room, his eyes sweeping the walls. "There's a damned lot of them. Quite remarkable what they can do these days."

The old gentleman was still stooped in front of the two oak trees. He straightened his back and left, tipping his hat at them. Maddox made a quick turn about the room and flung himself down on the couch in front of a tableau of a group of women draped in wet gauze, their hair parted over their breasts. The title on the mat was *The Water Nymphs*.

"You've got to admit it's a thing of beauty, the female form," Maddox sighed.

Lucas did admit it but not to Maddox. And the way he wanted to appreciate it wasn't behind glass, posed by another man—or posed at all. Not that there were other options open to him. He stared at a picture of a foam-topped sea, two dark and distinct clouds sailing across the sky above. Something about the image didn't convince. The line between sea and sky was confused, overlapping. In the next one, the waves were stilled and flat but the sky contained the same two sailing clouds. It had been constructed in the dark chamber.

"Do you think it's right, to take two different photographs on two different days and splice them together? Present them as one?"

Maddox dragged his eyes away from the nymphs.

"Don't see the harm in it if it makes a better picture."

"Yes, but is it true? Don't you think when you look at a photograph that you're looking at a record of the truth?"

"Depends what you mean by truth, old man."

Maddox looked tired too, Lucas noticed.

Lucas had seen a photograph that meant something to him. It wasn't the Drowned Man. He puzzled over it as they walked out into a light rain and along Regent Street, racked his brain while Maddox hailed a cab.

"Grieve had a word with me the other day," Maddox said, once they were in the cab. "Reckons you're not pulling your weight."

"What do you mean?"

Maddox looked out of the square of smeared glass at a couple of women hanging on to umbrellas turned out by the wind, the ribbons of their bonnets streaming.

"You know Grieve. He plays the numbers game. Makes him look good to the commissioners. He's after fifty percent of patients discharged within a year, certified as cured. Says you're marking too many *discharged uncured*, and keeping too many more of them in."

St. Clair snorted in disbelief.

"Where's the merit in discharging people when they're still ill? Or saying they're well when they're not? It's pointless. It's dangerous."

Maddox shrugged.

"It isn't about patients' welfare. It isn't even about getting the diagnosis right. It's about what the politicians want."

"I know but I don't accept it, Doxy. I can't work like that."

Maddox sighed.

"It's not easy for any of us, Lucas. How's your research coming along?"

"I'm working on it. I thought you weren't interested."

"I told you I'd keep an open mind. I'm not saying it doesn't have a use—only that you'll have to convince me."

"I intend to. You and a lot of other people. Remember, I'm making a presentation shortly, to the Alienists. Shall I reserve you a seat?"

Over a late breakfast of coffee and kedgeree at the Pall Mall Club, talking with Maddox and some friends they encountered about the new anesthesia, smoking his pipe and wondering whether leisure was really worthwhile after all, it came to Lucas. It wasn't any of the pictures at the exhibition. It was the girl in the window, stepping through the frame. She'd given him an idea.

NINETEEN

Emmeline heard Catherine's light, running footsteps and followed the sound through the open door of her sewing room. The old cedar chest was pulled out from the wall, its lid thrown back on its hinges. Catherine kneeled on the rug in front of it, still in her nightdress at midmorning, the soles of her bare feet exposed.

She sat back on her heels and held up a pair of slippers, dangled them by their straps.

"Look at these, Mother." She ran her thumbs over the unscarred leather soles. They were for an infant too young to put its foot to the ground, never worn by the look of them. "Were they mine?"

"Probably, darling." Emmeline sat down in her sewing chair. "Catty, I need to talk to you."

Catherine rummaged in the chest, pulled out an embroidered baby dress, held it up by the shoulders. White and translucent in the morning light, with a long fall of skirt, it looked like a child ghost.

"Did I wear this?"

"You must have done. It's the christening dress. You all wore it. Can you imagine Benedict, dressed in that?"

Catherine laughed. "Not really. Why do you keep it, Mother?"

"It's a memento. Anyway"—Emmeline kept her tone light—"one day there will be babies in the family again. You might want it for your own children."

Catherine ignored her and continued digging around in the dark interior. Emmeline had had the chest since her own childhood. It was carved over its rounded top with leaves and flowers, the inside full of snipped curls and milk teeth and sailor suits. The polished coral rings on which the children had cut their teeth. She never opened it. Even to lift the lid, breathe in a scent so faint it seemed always on the point of vanishing, flooded her with a persistent, immovable melancholy. Keeping objects was useless, she'd belatedly come to understand. It only accentuated all that was lost.

Emmeline opened her workbag and took out a table napkin. She had set aside her lacework. Darning was all she could do at present, making connections where there were rents and tears. She resumed a line of small anchoring stitches along the side of the rip and tried to remember some detail of Catherine's infancy.

"Your first curls are in there somewhere. You were born with a whole head of hair, you know, and so pretty."

"Was I?"

"Yes. You still are."

"You don't really think that. You think I ought to be like Cousin Alice." Catherine picked out a silver spoon with an ornately traced handle. "CVA. This must be mine."

"It was a present from Granny. She used to feed you milk jelly with it."

"How sickening."

"You adored cold puddings. Junket. Egg custard. Tapioca. You used to beg for more. Such a plump little thing, you were."

"Why do you always talk about what I used to be? I'm not six years old anymore, Mother."

"I know you aren't."

"Why do you sigh?"

"I didn't."

"You did. You always do."

Emmeline suppressed another that rose in her like a gale. Catherine had refused to come to the table for lunch. Complained of stomach cramps and requested soup on a tray in her bedroom. Emmeline had insisted that she take the consommé in the parlor. She wanted to see it slipping down Catherine's throat, make sure it wasn't lying in a puddle outside her window. She'd found a hedgehog out there the other night, eating steak.

She stole a glance at her daughter, took in the long sweep of her lashes, the sullen set of her mouth. It was difficult sometimes to remember that she was almost sixteen. A woman. Emmeline's eyes flickered away. Catherine didn't like to be observed—it was one of her refrains. Don't *stare* at me, Mother. Stop *looking* at me.

Catherine was sitting back on her heels, tapping the spoon on the palm of her hand.

"I want to talk to you too, Mother."

Emmeline felt her spirits lift.

"Oh, darling. I'm so glad. I haven't known how to—"

"I want to go somewhere. Somewhere special."

"Wonderful!" Emmeline restrained herself from jumping up to kiss her. "We can go anywhere you like, Catty. Call on Aunt Flo. Or go shopping. You need gloves. A dress for spring."

"I don't want to go shopping. I want to go to the fair."

"The fair? What on earth for?"

"Other people go. Why shouldn't I?"

Emmeline's own mother would have been scandalized if she'd spoken like that to her. She didn't feel scandalized. She felt helpless.

"Your father wouldn't allow it."

"What about you, Mother? Would you allow it?"

Catherine's eyes were burning in her pale face. Emmeline didn't understand Catherine's resentment of her—where it came from. She'd never raised a hand to her, had only ever wanted what was best for her. She shook her head.

"I would not, Catherine. No."

Catherine slammed down the lid of the chest and rushed from the room. Emmeline heard her footsteps again, fast and furious on the stairs, then her bedroom door banging. The key to the chest lay on the rug. Emmeline picked it up and put it back in the lock. She folded the dress and replaced it, paired the slippers and returned them to the disorderly cavern of the past. She locked the chest, inhaling the woody odor of cedar.

Sometimes she wished Catherine was a child again and that they could go back to the laughing years, when she had loved her without fear or any kind of reserve. Too much, Querios had said.

* * *

It rained every day after Christmas, from early in the morning and on into the afternoon. Anna was not allowed out-of-doors, even to the airing grounds—the miserable closed courtyard designated for patients' exercise. She watched from the window as water cascaded over the rims of the gutters, dripped from the bare branches of the trees, collected in pools on the grass in front of Lake House. It made its way inside—dripping through ceilings into buckets and bowls, sending sooty splashes over the hearth tiles. It was still raining in the small hours when Anna woke with a start, a sense of urgency running through her whole body. The rain came down more quietly at night, as if it talked to itself. She lay eavesdropping on it. Thinking about her plan.

The guests came back one by one, returned by husbands, sons or fathers, clasping small bottles of cologne, lavender bags, boxes of dried fruits, but most of the scullions and housemaids stayed away. By the end of the old year, Lake House felt like an abandoned ship. The windows and doors were swollen with damp, crumbs collected around the chair legs in the dining room, and dust furred the slats of the blinds. The grates were unblackened, the water for washing in the mornings cold. Lovely went about her tasks at a run, muttering that she was expected to do the work of six.

On the first day of the new year, on Sunday morning, Talitha Batt reappeared. She sat at the head of the table in the dining room but did not take any breakfast. Miss Little and Miss Todd were on either side of her, tussling over a saucer of gooseberry jam, tugging it between them. One of them let go and the saucer flew in the air, emptied itself onto the floor. Miss Batt pushed back her chair and walked into the dayroom, her back straight and narrow as ever.

The others followed, one by one. Anna finished her tea alone at the table, feeling glad that Miss Batt was back. Talitha changed Lake House by her presence. She dignified it. And Anna could talk with her. She enjoyed her company. A yawning scullion arrived and began to drag a cloth through the jam with her foot. Anna rose from her chair and walked around the end of the table, felt the soles of her slippers stick to the floor, the stickiness pursue her into the next room.

Miss Batt was in her green velvet chair, one hand fingering the edges of a new collar. Anna shifted a chair nearer to hers and Talitha Batt looked at her dully. Anna could feel an invisible "Do not trespass" notice. She wouldn't ask about Batt's time with her family. She threw herself down in the chair and rubbed her hands together. Smiled.

"Welcome back, Miss Batt. And a happy new year to you." Anna got out the square of cambric and selected a skein of gray silk. "Will it ever stop, do you think?"

"Will what ever stop?"

"The downpour, Miss Batt. The rain."

Batt lifted her shoulders minutely and lowered them again. Her movements were stiffer than ever, as if she operated under some increasing internal constriction.

"I daresay."

"I do hope so. I'm anxious to get out for a walk."

Miss Batt didn't answer.

"I can't say we had much of a festive season here," Anna said. "Although Mrs. Makepeace did a bit of singing on Christmas Day. Quite a bit, actually; Mr. Abse had to intervene. They served up what they claimed was a goose and Mrs. Valentine set fire to the plum pudding."

"Singing? Who was singing?"

Miss Batt looked at Anna, a haunted expression in her eyes, and clenched her sewing on her lap as if she would wring it out.

"Mrs. Makepeace," Anna said, wondering how she had disturbed Miss Batt, wishing she could make her feel better. She parodied Mrs. Makepeace's singing, trilled a couple of lines, "Oh, never leave me, Oh, don't deceive me." Stopped. "I cannot say that I am glad you're back, Miss Batt. But you know I am most awfully pleased to see you."

A tear made its way out of one eye and rolled down through the white powder on Miss Batt's face as she shook her head slowly from side to side.

"Don't, Mrs. Palmer. Please don't say such things."

"I'm sorry. I didn't mean to distress you."

Miss Batt didn't answer.

"We could have a game of drafts, perhaps, if you would like a little

135

diversion. I suppose it is difficult to return. Forgive me if I was insensitive."

"Pardon me?" said Miss Batt, her voice a whisper.

Miss Batt's polished, navy shoes were gone; she wore the same blunt slippers on her feet as they all did, that could be worn on either foot, by anyone. Anna fixed her eyes on her sewing.

"Miss Batt, what has happened to you?"

"It is four years, Mrs. Palmer."

Miss Batt's voice was tremulous and Anna lowered her own.

"What do you mean?" she said, gently, looking up from the cloth and reaching for Miss Batt's hand. "What is four years?"

"Four years since they brought me here. I decided then that I would tolerate it for four years. No less. And no more."

"I see."

Anna looked at Miss Batt, at the rows of photographs behind her on the wall. It was as if Miss Batt had returned as a black-and-white rendering of herself, flat and colorless, the life in her gone. Anna was close enough to her to hear her shallow breaths and catch the note of naphthalene that escaped from her clothes but she had the sense that Talitha Batt was far away, absent from all that surrounded her.

TWENTY

In a room on the first floor of a small house to the south of the river Thames, some miles from the Vicarage, Vincent Palmer sat on the end of a bed. He was dressed in dark trousers and a white shirt and the expression on his face as he dragged a gray sock over his naked left foot and secured it with a garter was one of absorbed concentration.

The room was dim and warmed by a small fire in the grate, the air he breathed imbued with a faded, female sweetness. Two sash windows were hidden behind lace hangings, further obscured by curtains that had long ago surrendered their designs to the sun. On the walls, theater posters had been stuck over wallpaper printed with exotic birds. The paper extended to the top of the walls and on over the ceiling as if the birds had long ago flown up there to roost and never left.

Vincent leaned toward the dressing table mirror and coaxed the ends of his moustache into their upward curl. Lately he had encountered white hairs in his moustache; the sight of them filled him with a disgust of a different order from that which he felt for the ones on his head.

"Why don't you stay awhile?" came a voice from behind him. "You could see the boy, Vince. He'll be awake soon."

"Not possible," he said, bringing his face in closer to the mirror, dragging down the corners of his mouth. He opened a small drawer and rummaged through its contents; hairpins, buttons, a desiccated rosebud from a bunch he had once presented her with, after a performance. "Don't you have any tweezers?"

He peered harder, felt the strain in his eyes and gave up. He couldn't see well enough to attempt the operation and there was no aggravation like accidentally pulling out perfectly serviceable black hairs and then seeing the silver one lurking, resistant to capture. The edge of the mirror was draped with strings of beads—carnelian, cinnabar, lapis lazuli—all of them semiprecious. Poor Maud. He had the satisfaction at least of knowing he had done the right thing by her.

He stood up, knocked his shin against the leg of the dressing table and assumed the impenetrably cheerful smile that he found himself using more and more.

"*Tempus fugit*. I must return to my flock. Much though I would like to stay and breakfast with you. My dearest."

Maud didn't answer and he felt a surge of annoyance. Really, she became more and more tiresome. Christmas might be over but still he had very little opportunity for visiting her, as he had often explained.

"Time flies," he repeated, picking up his hat and brushing dust off the rim.

"I know what it means," came the voice. "Better than you do."

"Please, Maud. Not that again. Do you have everything you need?"

She sat up in the bed and reached around to plump a flattened feather pillow behind her back.

"No, I don't."

Vincent looked at her in the mirror. Her hair stood out from her head and her face and breast were still flushed. He disliked seeing her in a state of dishevelment. Preferred to see her costumed, made-up, in character. It barely mattered as what. The role was the thing that released his desire, fueled his excitement.

Over her head, on the wall behind the bed, was the painting of her as Cleopatra—as she had been when he first saw her, on the stage. She wore a black wig and her skin was arsenic-whitened. Milk and jet. The poster displayed her silhouette as he had seen it at the Empire, the unruly swellings above and below the waist, the shape that had branded itself on his imagination.

"I've given you all that I can, for now."

"It's not only about our keep, Vincent. You never take me anywhere or see the boy. We never have any amusement. Just . . . this."

"It was your own decision to return to London. I was against it as you well know. I can hardly be blamed for your disappointment."

He smoothed his hair down over his ears and retrieved his gloves from the dressing table, knocking over a couple of scent bottles. He could hardly be blamed for that either, she had so many of them—all dusty-shouldered and half-empty. A sweet, musk-ridden smell seeped into the air. He felt an urgent desire to get away. The room had been thrilling to him once. He'd found it almost unbearably exotic. Now it felt suffocating and, harder to bear, pathetic.

He made for the door, past the little wardrobe stuffed with Maud's feathers and furbelows and kicked the draft excluder out of the way.

"Duty calls. God bless you both."

"Don't you have any natural feelings?"

"I will look in on him, Maud. I was intending to do just that."

He was almost at the nursery door when he remembered his cane. He was forced to go back for it, stooping to retrieve it from behind the door, blowing fluff off the handle. Maud didn't say a word, just looked at him. Her face in its natural state looked positively ugly. He wondered why it had taken him so long to notice. Women did not age as well as men, generally. In temperament as well as in the flesh. Their weaker brains deteriorated rather than strengthened with the passing of the years.

"Good-bye, Maud."

He took the stairs briskly, swung open the front door and emerged, banging the door behind him. Hurrying down the street, he felt more harried than when he arrived. That was the effect Maud had on him these days. He felt a moment of deep compassion for himself. Of course he had natural feelings.

"*Man that is born of a woman is of few days and full of trouble,*" he muttered to himself, turning out of Sebastopol Street, reaching the main road. He stopped to reposition his hat in the reflection from the baker's window. "*For a whore is a deep ditch; and a strange woman is a narrow pit.*" He was far enough away to risk raising his face from the ground and looking about at will. "*She increaseth the transgressors among men.*"

Not that Maud was a whore. She didn't even work in the theater anymore. She said that he made her feel like a whore, coming and going, leaving the money on the dressing table the way he did. She had

actually used the word. It had offended him because if she was a har-
lot, then what did that make him? Wives, whores, women. They were
inexplicable, troublesome, and all of them *lieth in wait as for a prey.*
He had a picture of himself as healthy red meat, butchered, his internal
organs laid bare and a crowd of winged harpies screaming and circling
in the air overhead.

It wasn't until he approached Shoreditch that he remembered he
had forgotten to see the boy. Next time. Gabriel was still too young
to benefit from the company of a man—barely speaking and prone to
dribbles and leaks of all descriptions. Certainly, he was too immature
to benefit from any religious instruction. But more often than not,
when Vincent picked him up or tried to entertain him with a game of
peekaboo, the child wept and shrieked for his mother.

Maud should not ask so much of him. He had too many people to
look after and his flock came first. They had to come first, whatever
the personal cost to himself. He supposed he could take Maud out for
some entertainment, to one of the pleasure grounds she liked so much
or perhaps a play. He had to keep her happy—he was always afraid she
might arrive unannounced at All Hallows. A chap could turn away callers from his own front door but it was a different matter to bar entry to
God's house. He felt a shudder crawl down his back under his long coat.

At Curtain Road, he slowed his step. Stiffened his features in anticipation of encountering parishioners, demanding help in forms that he
had no intention of providing. It was they, in truth, who should give to
him. Their respect for him was God's due. He nodded at a man rushing toward him, wringing his hands, sidestepped him and proceeded
through the lych-gate, still afflicted with a sense of unease prompted
by the idea of Maud appearing under the leaking roof of All Hallows.
He would take her out soon.

Rain had given way for several days to a bitter cold. The grass in front
of the house was white with frost, the weeds along the edge of the path
stiff with crystals. Anna's heart was thudding. It was the first time she
had been able to get out since Christmas. But now the moment had
arrived, she felt unprepared, despite all the rehearsals in her mind.

Lovely lingered on the step, looking up at the pewter sky. Anna avoided her eye as she pulled on her gloves. She tried to keep her voice normal.

"Let's go, Lovely."

"You sure it ain't too cold, miss?"

Anna looked at her suspiciously. "What do you mean?"

"For walking."

"Oh. Yes. I'm sure."

"My chilblains is terrible," Lovely said, blowing on her fingers.

"Stay here then, if you like."

"I'm duty bound to come with yer, miss."

"All right. We won't stay out long."

Anna hugged her cloak around her and set off over the grass. The earth struck up hard against her feet and everything was hushed—the atmosphere, the light, the sounds. The birds were quiet and there was a smell like metal in the air, no shadow on the ground. She walked down over the grass, absorbing the strangeness of the morning, its peculiar deathly stillness, wondering why it made her feel afraid.

Arriving at the gate, she let herself into the field, and made her way along the narrow path, still visible even in the frost, passing a huddle of sheep with icicles dangling from their coats. Lovely followed behind, at a distance.

The lake was transformed into a white expanse of ice, solid and secretive-looking. Stilled. Anna picked her way down over the stiff tussocks of grass and onto the shore. Close up, the ice was not white but a translucent gray. The ends of the willow fronds were trapped, held in a drowning embrace.

She hesitated, standing by the side of the lake with her hands clamped under her armpits for warmth. The ice frightened her. It needn't change anything, she told herself. There was no reason why it should. She picked up a twig and threw it out over the frozen surface, watched as it skittered to a halt in the middle. Beyond it, on the far side, the trees were still and patient, their branches jeweled. Waiting for her.

A group of ducks wandered confusedly on the lake and another flew in to join them and landed, skidding along, leaving parallel tracks. A duck skated toward her, slipping at every step, its naked feet seemingly impervious to the cold. As she watched, a piece of bread flew through the air; the duck craned its sinuous neck and caught it.

"Hello, Mrs. Palmer."

Catherine's nose was pink, a fur muff swung on a cord round her neck. For a moment, Anna couldn't say a word.

"What in heaven's name are you doing here?"

"Don't sound so indignant." Catherine tossed half a muffin at the ducks congregated in front of them. "I could ask you the same question."

"I'm out for a walk. Some air. Shouldn't you be inside, in the warm?"

Before Catherine could answer, Anna began walking along the shore, toward the bridge. Catherine followed behind and their feet crunched in step on the frozen ground.

"I'm not meant to be out," she called. "Mother says the cold is bad for the complexion. But I saw you from my bedroom window and came to wish you a happy new year."

"How kind."

"Please, Mrs. Palmer, don't be nasty. I haven't seen you for ages. Where've you been?"

Anna stopped and turned to face her.

"Where do you think? I've been in the dayroom. The dining room. The little cell called a bedroom."

Catherine's eyes met hers then flickered on past her.

"I'm just as much a prisoner as you are."

Anna laughed.

"No, you're not, Catherine."

"'I kept the life, thrust on me, on the outside / Of the inner life, with all its ample room,'" Catherine said. "That's what Aurora Leigh does. It's what I do, when I remember. You could try it too, Mrs. Palmer."

They were at the edge of the thicket, closer to the bridge than Anna had ever been. The scarlet holly berries were magical-looking; beyond them was a clump of bare yellow stems the color of mustard powder, some beech saplings clinging to their crisp brown leaves. She couldn't wait for another chance. She must act and it must be today while she still had the strength and the will to free herself. Anna wrapped her cloak more tightly round her body and imagined herself plunging through the tangle of branches, head lowered against the thorns.

Lovely had stayed back in the field, hopping from foot to foot, rubbing her hands together and pressing them against her cheeks, her suffering evident. Catherine was talking about an American. She waved the hands that she'd freed from her muff, eyes shining.

"She's traveled all the way across the Atlantic Ocean, from Boston, Mrs. Palmer. I absolutely have to go and see her. I'll never get another chance in my whole life."

"Catherine! Listen to me for a minute. It's not true, what I said to you about my husband. I don't miss him at all. He won't be coming for me."

"What's that got to do with me?" Catherine's voice was flat, her breath a wisp of vapor in front of her lips.

"I have to escape. Will you help me?"

"I said I would, didn't I?" Catherine's tone was sulky. "Even though I don't know why I should."

They glanced simultaneously over the lake toward the other bank. The bridge was to their left, not more than a couple of hundred yards farther along. It was as ethereal and still as if it was carved from the ice or had bloomed from its dull surface. Anna gestured toward it.

"I'm going to run away. Over the bridge."

Catherine blinked and her face colored.

"You can't, I told you before."

"I've got to."

Catherine stamped her foot.

"Why doesn't anyone ever listen to me?" she shouted. "It's not a bridge. My grandfather had the bridge pulled down after one of the guests fell off it. They say she fell but she didn't. She jumped with her babies, one in each arm. I saw her."

Catherine hurled the last crust out over the ice; two ducks skated after it, their shrieks tearing the air.

"I don't believe you. I can see it with my own eyes." Anna felt winded.

She turned and saw Lovely, almost upon them. Lovely arrived, her face scarlet, contorted with pain.

"Good morning, Miss Catherine. Let's go indoors now, miss," she said to Anna.

Anna looked at her.

"In a moment, Lovely. I'm freezing too. Didn't you hear Mrs. Makepeace shouting for you? She was blowing her whistle."

"Were she?" Lovely looked suspicious.

"Oh, yes," Catherine said, her voice high and clear. "Father was calling for you too. I never heard such a bellowing."

"Gawd. They must be 'ere at long last." Lovely began to toil up the bank. "Hurry along, miss," she called over her shoulder.

"Coming," Anna said. "I'll be right behind you."

"You can still get away," Catherine hissed, her eyes alert. "Look."

She plunged forward through a fringe of bulrushes taller than her and lowered a foot over the frozen surface. For a moment she stood like a skater with one boot on the ice and the other lifted behind her.

"Catherine, don't. It's not safe."

Catherine didn't seem to hear. She took another step, placing the second foot down flat in front of her.

"Come on, Mrs. Palmer." Her voice was full of pleasure as she glanced back toward Anna, then went on, slipping and rebalancing in an odd, stiff-footed dance, laughing as she wobbled and regained her balance. Her white neck was caught by the light and her arms emerged from her cloak like two stiff wings.

Catherine was so slight, not fully grown. The ice would hold her. Even the water might have held her. Anna pictured herself stepping out onto the frozen surface—walking to the halfway point and on, until she arrived at the far bank. She looked over her shoulder. Lovely had got almost to the gate into the field. It would be faster to walk straight across from here, if she could, than it would be to fight her way through to the bridge.

She pushed through the rushes and put her foot out onto the ice, felt the chill of it seeping through the sole of her boot. Leaning forward, she put more weight on it, waiting for a fearsome cracking sound. Nothing. Anna held her breath as she brought the other foot in front of her and started to make her way out over the glassy surface. Drowned leaves and branches pressed up underneath the ice as if they fought for air. The dim, blunt-nosed shape of a fish glided underneath her. She raised her eyes and took another step, holding out her arms.

Catherine was almost at the far bank. Anna followed, hardly daring to breathe, putting down her whole foot at each step, spreading her weight over the length of it. Hearing a shout, she stopped and turned around. Her shadow lay in front of her, long and faint on the ice, stretching back toward the shore.

Lovely was careering down the bank, beckoning frantically for their return. Anna spread her hands in front of her, palms upturned.

"I can't, dear Lovely," she said aloud. "I've got to go."

Lovely reached the edge of the lake and dragged up her skirts, showing her bare legs, the ends of her drawers. She screwed up her face, eyes closed, then jumped with both clogs onto the ice and plunged forward, falling. Anna heard the cracking sound she'd dreaded. Lovely screamed as she floundered, a high scream of shock and pain. She scrambled to get one bare foot onto the ice, then capsized again into the reeds. She crawled back onto the shore, righted herself and got to her feet. With her sodden skirts clinging to her round form, Lovely began to make a different gesture—throwing both hands out from her body as if urging Anna to make haste toward the other bank.

Anna lifted her hand in a wave, turned and carried on, moving quickly now, skating on the worn leather soles of her boots, trusting the solid support of the ice underneath her, a wave of excitement coursing through her from her toes to her fingertips. She reached the far side and jumped onto a frozen, muddy shore churned by cattle hooves. There was wood smoke on the air, a dog barking in the distance.

She glanced back toward Lake House. The rise of the land obscured the lower part of it; she could see only the dayroom windows on the first floor and above that the bedrooms, lit by the sun breaking through now, tinged with pink. The shore of the lake was empty, Lovely gone. They had fifteen minutes at least before she would get back and raise the alarm. Anna lifted her skirts and scrambled up the far bank to a vista of open heathland.

Catherine was sitting on a log, blowing on her fingers. She smiled up at her.

"You took your time, Mrs. Palmer."

Anna grabbed her hands and kissed them.

"I don't know how to thank you. I'll never forget this as long as I live. Go back now, Catherine, quickly. You'll have to get on the bank in a different spot; Lovely's broken the ice. Hurry and I'll watch till you're safe."

Catherine looked straight past her to the horizon, her face lit up.

"Who's going back? Not me."

She jumped to her feet and set off, her hem trailing on the glittering earth.

TWENTY-ONE

Anna fell into step with Catherine and got hold of her arm.

"What do you think you're doing?"

"Coming with you, of course."

"Why?"

"I knew you weren't listening. I have to go to the fair tonight. I must see the Fasting Girl before she goes back to America."

"Catherine, go back home this instant. I'm ordering you to."

Catherine giggled.

"I refuse your order, Mrs. Palmer."

In front of them, the round gray dome of St. Paul's waited patiently under the clouds. She couldn't drag Catherine back by force but all her instincts were against taking her. If she had his daughter with her, Abse was certain to come after her. Anna would have to throw the girl off once they reached London. It was the only way. She would lose Catherine in the streets and let her find her own way home. She was old enough.

"Alright. If you absolutely must. Come on."

Anna had no idea where the road might be and judged it better to stick to the heath, where they would be harder to find. She picked up her skirts and hurried on, heading toward the distant outline of the cathedral. Catherine followed, keeping pace, and the two of them ran through frozen bogs, through reeds and grasses as high as their waists and up onto higher ground—dodging through stands of elms and oaks, the ground underneath sharp with acorns. They encountered a farmer on his horse and by unspoken agreement slowed their pace and began to talk loudly about the benefits to ladies of taking a walk. As soon as he was out of sight, they picked up their skirts and ran again, faster than before. The dome grew bigger and more distinct with every glimpse they caught of it as if it too was on the move, advancing to meet them.

They reached the top of a hill and Anna stopped, bent double, gulping in cold air that hurt her chest. Catherine had both hands clutched to her stomach and could barely speak.

"I've got a stitch," she gasped. "Let's rest. I can't go any farther."

The top of the hill was flat and dotted with smooth stones, carved with names and dates. They sat, recovering their breath, surrounded by sky on all sides, the great panorama of London spread out before them. Scores of steeples pointed up from between lines of slate roofs. To the east, plumes of black smoke rose in columns from factory chimneys. The river snaked its silver path through the middle of everything and the city sent up a distant blur of sound at odds with the sharp detail that met their eyes.

Catherine spread her arms wide and tilted her face to the sun.

"Isn't it wonderful, Mrs. Palmer? To be free."

"Let's carry on, Catherine. We're not safe yet."

Anna didn't feel free. She wanted to be far away from Lake House and unencumbered by Catherine. She jumped up from where she sat and hurried on down the hill, encountered a path and began to follow it. It grew wider and better trod as they went. Before long, the sound of a train whistle pierced the air. Anna saw the man-made glint of a railway line through the trees. The air took on a smell of smoke and baking bread.

At a ditch with a plank laid over it, Anna stopped. They were close enough to a marketplace to hear voices and the neighing of horses. She tucked her hair back into her combs and examined a tear in her skirt. The idea of being in a crowd frightened her. She felt as if she'd become different from other people while she was shut away, that they would know it just by looking at her. She forced herself to cross over the ditch, walk on to where the path ended by a ragged line of barrows and stalls and join the people, affecting a nonchalance she didn't feel.

Men and women were selling onions, pots and pans, old clothes from carts and ramshackle stalls. Anna and Catherine passed a man pattering about early birds and worms, his arm strung with watches on chains. Anna stopped and stared at a pyramid of oranges balanced on a sack on the ground, with a single cut half of the fruit glistening at the front. She felt as if she was seeing an orange for the first time. The color was full of life and heat, as if the sun had squeezed itself into it.

"Where shall we go?" Catherine said, raising her voice over the hubbub. "Now we're here?"

"I'm going to my sister's house in Wren Street."

"You never told me you had a sister."

"I've got four."

"No brothers?"

Anna shook her head.

"Are you hungry, Catherine?" Catherine nodded. "Then wait here a minute." Anna reached out and squeezed Catherine's hands. The flush on her cheeks had subsided; the girl was white again with shadows under her eyes. "Stay here and don't move."

Anna made her way on through the crowd, following a singsong voice until she caught up with the watch seller.

"Excuse me, sir."

He had ringlets in front of his ears and kind, brown eyes.

"Want to purchase a timepiece, missie? You won't regret it."

She pulled off her glove and held out her hand. The turquoise stones in her ring were bright in the sun, the gold coils of the snake shone.

"Will you buy this from me?"

"Take it off," he said. "Let's have a gander."

"I'm not taking it off until we agree on a price. It's gold and it cost ten pounds. I only want eight for it."

He took her hand in his, turned it this way and that, then brought her wrist to his mouth in a quick movement and bit the gold between his teeth.

"I'll give you five."

"Seven."

"You trying to put me out of business? Six pounds and ten bob on top for goodwill, miss."

"Done."

He let go of her hand and loosened the neck of a leather pouch around his waist, counting out the pound notes and four half crowns. She took off the ring and gave it to him.

"God bless," he said, his eyes curious, the ring already secreted somewhere out of sight.

Anna looked down at the bare fingers of her left hand. The ring had left no mark and she felt easier without it. She'd only expected to get four or five pounds for it—it had cost Vincent six. She pulled her glove back on, sliding the folded notes inside it, and felt a sharp pang of loss. She'd forgotten her knife, the little penknife from Egypt that Captain Newlove gave her when she was eight years old. Left it behind in its dark hiding place.

She stood for a minute among the shoppers and hawkers then walked a few steps farther away from where she had left Catherine—past a man selling brooms, another flicking at a pile of old books with a feather duster. She felt she ought to pinch herself to make sure she wasn't in a dream, a dream of escape from which she would shortly wake. They would be certain to have raised the alarm by now. She must hurry to her haven at Louisa's house. First, she had to rid herself of Catherine. Slip away out of this market and disappear into the streets of London.

Anna stopped and leaned on a plane tree. Its bark peeled up in strange shapes and shades that looked like maps of the moon. The air was filled with the twittering of caged birds. A line of a dozen or more thrushes were trapped in wicker baskets that swung from a wooden pole hung between two branches of the tree. Their song was piteous. She clasped her hands over her ears and began to retrace her steps, hurrying back by the stacks of books and piles of turnips, past heaps of kindling and slabs of churned butter. She must at least get some food inside the poor girl before she left her. Would find a way to give her a half crown as well.

Catherine was rooted to the spot where Anna had left her, her eyes darting in all directions, her body stiff. From a distance, she looked twelve years old again. She burst into tears when she saw Anna.

"Where have you been? I thought you'd abandoned me."

"Look!" Anna showed her the ends of the notes emerging from her cuff. "We have funds, Catherine. We can eat."

She bought an orange, asked the costermonger to cut it into quarters, and they ate in silence, sucking out the flesh, juice running down their chins. Anna ate the peel as well, chewing it up between her back teeth, the bitterness as satisfying as the sweetness. She felt as if she was eating life. At the edge of the market they stopped again, this time for two cups of green pea soup with chunks of hot bread. They sat on a stone bench by a water trough and ate—more slowly now. Anna finished first. She brushed the crumbs off her lap and tucked the remaining notes down inside her boot, tying the lace tight and straightening up again.

Catherine wiped the inside edges of the cup with her finger, licked the line of green sludge off it. She tossed her bread in the direction of a pair of wary strays crouched by an old crate.

"Come on, pusses," she whispered, holding out her hand to them. "Don't you love cats, Mrs. Palmer? I do."

Anna sighed.

"Are you ready, Catherine? We've got a long walk still."

"Of course I'm ready. I don't want to miss the Fasting Girl, Mrs. Palmer. I need to be at Vauxhall early. Will you come with me?"

"I suppose I'll have to. I can't let you go on your own. Come."

Beyond the market lay an area of terraced houses, the narrow, cobbled streets full of people. Women chatted over gates, boys rolled battered hoops or dragged puppies along on strings and men leaned on walls, smoking thin cigarettes. The women looked with quick interest at Anna's and Catherine's snagged skirts and ruined boots and the men turned their heads, their attention caught by some quality of excitement in them—by Anna's escaping hair and Catherine's pale, bluish complexion.

Anna walked fast and kept her eyes fixed on a spot a few yards ahead of her as she'd learned to do when she first came to London; you couldn't look at every person you passed or greet strangers, as you did around Dover. You had to see without seeing, otherwise you would drown in people.

Her pleasure at being on the streets, back in life, was spoiled by a constant terror—of hearing someone shout her name, feeling a hand on her shoulder. She tried to shake off the sense that anyone and everyone might apprehend her, drag the pair of them back to Lake House.

A little farther on, in a high street, Anna hurried Catherine by a man passed out drunk by the side of the road with his trousers open, pulled her past a woman clouting her child and a pickpocket stalking an old lady, walking close at her elbow. They carried on, over a canal with a boat gliding along it, past Moroni's ice warehouse—so wide it occupied three plots—past dank passageways and public houses squeezed between foundries and workshops, toward the new railway station.

"What should we say, if anyone asks?" Catherine said.

"Nothing. Just keep quiet and stay close to me."

"Shall I be your sister too?"

"If you like."

Catherine looked pleased.

"I always wanted a sister. You're so fortunate."

"You think so?"

"You've got four of them. And you're not imprisoned in your father's house."

"I don't have a father, Catherine. Or a house."

Catherine clapped her hands.

"You're like Aurora Leigh, Mrs. Palmer. She was an orphan too, 'in this unroofed and unfurnished world.'"

They turned into a wide thoroughfare of solid houses, their brass door plates and whitened steps gleaming. A constable walked along the other side of the street and Catherine waved at him. Anna grabbed her wrist and pulled down her arm.

"What did you do that for?" she whispered urgently. "Keep your eyes down and carry on walking."

It was too late. He'd crossed the road and was standing in front of them—so close that Anna could see the dried blood from a razor cut on his chin and the shine on the neck of his serge tunic.

"Excuse me, sir," Catherine said, smiling up at him. "My sister and I are lost. We are trying to reach Robin Street."

"Wren Street," Anna said.

The policeman set about explaining the way he would take himself. He took a long time over it, drew a map with his pencil and tore it carefully from his notebook. Anna pretended to study the map, her heart beating so hard she felt the policeman must be able to hear it.

She forced herself to turn and face him, smile her thanks. He winked at her, touched his helmet and stood aside to let them pass, looking after them for longer than seemed necessary.

She waited until they got around the corner then whirled toward Catherine, trembling with rage and fright, her hands on her hips.

"He might have arrested us. Taken me back! How dare you put us at risk?"

She could have slapped the girl. Catherine looked startled.

"Don't treat me like a child, Mrs. Palmer. If it wasn't for me, you wouldn't have been able to get away at all."

The little map bore no relation to the city they encountered. Roads led them in circles and each one looked the same as the last. Without the advantage of elevation, they couldn't see St. Paul's. Despite Catherine's pleas, Anna refused to ask further directions. She'd been to Wren Street many times and she had a sense of where it was, if not an exact one. Their steps slowed as they wandered past taverns and coffeehouses, putting off hawkers of buttons and beads, sidestepping beggars and drunks. Anna gave a penny to a woman sitting on the stone steps of a church with a baby at her breast, another one to a blind singer standing under a tree. She let Catherine put a threepenny bit in the hand of an old man in the tattered remnants of a naval uniform.

"God bless," he said, looking at them with rheumy eyes, raising his hand in a salute.

By the time they reached Wren Street, it was mid-afternoon. The sun had disappeared behind dense gray clouds and the temperature was dropping. The cold bit at their flesh; fragile sheets of ice were re-forming across the smashed puddles. Catherine was shivering so much she couldn't speak. They limped past a pair of housemaids huddled up to their suitors on the corner with their hands under the boys' coats. The street was narrower than Anna remembered. The houses stood nose-to-nose, the fanlights over the doors small and neat. Gas lamps illuminated cosy-looking drawing rooms where the curtains had not yet been drawn for evening, rooms that looked to Anna as if they sheltered harmonious, happy lives of a kind she had never really known.

"Come on, Catherine. Nearly there. I hope my sister is at home."

She reached number 6 and climbed down the area steps, clinging to the handrail, ignoring Catherine's protest that they were creeping in like Gypsies and ought to announce their arrival at the front door. Anna pushed her way through an unlocked door into the kitchen and breathed in its steamy fog.

"Clear off," said a woman standing at the range, replacing the lid on a pot. "I'm not buying. What have you got anyway?"

"Is Mrs. Heron in?"

The cook looked her up and down.

"Who wants her? The cat's mother?"

"Her sister. Tell her that her sister wants her."

They waited while she delivered the message then heard a shout and a pair of feet running down a wooden staircase. Louisa took one look at Anna and collapsed in the doorway, her crinoline tipped up like a shuttlecock.

On her knees in her bedroom, Emmeline made a vow. If God returned Catherine to her, she would believe in Him properly, as she had always known she should. She would fast every Friday, attend church twice on Sundays and embroider ecclesiastical vestments. Make a pilgrimage up a stony hillside on her knees, like the Catholics in Ireland. Become a missionary in Africa. She closed her eyes. "Dear God, if you have to take a life, please let it be mine. Take me, I beg you. Leave my little girl safe."

The commotion outside the door increased. Querios was shouting orders at Fludd. Martha Lovely's voice rose in protest, somewhere farther away. Fanny Makepeace's iron tread in the corridor made the boards shake. The house was in uproar. The sanctuary of her bedroom, the fringed mantel cover, the dusted rosewood expanse of the dressing table, the twin miniatures on the wall of her mother and father, was always under siege. Now it was breached entirely. There was nowhere she could get away from what had happened. She could go to Timbuktu and not escape it.

Emmeline buried her face in the baby dress, felt the soft linen against her skin, the raised pleats of smocking across the bodice, and inhaled the faint scent of cedarwood. It was her own fault. If she'd agreed to the outing, Catherine would still be here. Or they might be at the fair together, watching the dancing bear, the jugglers. She'd never enjoyed fairs herself and hadn't understood how much it meant to her daughter. Such a small thing to have granted, it seemed now. Emmeline made a solemn promise to whatever great power saw fit to witness it that if she was spared, she would grant Catherine anything. Always.

One of the patients, the Reverend's wife, had disappeared at the same time. Lovely had lost sight of the patient, she said, after slipping on the ice. Poor woman had searched everywhere before she returned distraught to report Mrs. Palmer missing. Catherine was out in the grounds at about the same time and there was no trace of either of them. The gatekeeper swore on his own daughter's life that the gate hadn't opened all morning, that he never took his eyes off it and that no one had passed on the road. No woman could climb the walls of Lake House. They looked low enough from the road but there was a ditch running round them on the inside that made them eight feet tall. The pair of them had vanished into thin air.

Querios was convinced that they were still somewhere in the house or the grounds. He'd had Fludd and the groundsman checking the bushes and glasshouses, the shrubbery. Indoors, the maids were searching the attic, the cellars. There were cupboard doors banging, the drag of bed legs on bare boards, drawers that hadn't opened in years squeaking in protest as they were hauled out on their runners and shoved back in again. No cries of delight, of discovery.

Emmeline knew Catherine wasn't hiding in a broom cupboard. She hadn't told Querios about Catherine's request to go to the fair. It wouldn't help anyway. Catherine hadn't said which fairground or even why she wanted to go. Emmeline hadn't thought to ask. Catherine wasn't a lover of spectacles. Tricks. She would have thought she'd hate to see monkeys smoking pipes, horses forced to rear up and walk on two legs.

She closed her eyes and asked God to forgive her wandering thoughts, to hear her prayers. She would accept anything in her life except that harm should come to her daughter. God had to agree that it was wrong for Catherine to suffer before she was an adult woman. Still a child, really. And it was so cold. Such a bitter, bitter day. The light already beginning to dim. She pressed the smock against her eyes, trying to ward off visions of Catherine lying in a ditch with her ankle broken or being kidnapped by the lion tamers at a traveling fair.

Sometimes she still missed her own mother. At this moment, she felt her absence as keenly as if she was a child lost in a strange place. And she was forty-two. Catherine wasn't yet sixteen. She was out in the world alone, unchaperoned except perhaps by a lunatic. Her father never noticed anything, had willfully refused to see what was happening with her. Emmeline threw the baby dress over her head and began to cry into the red satin bed cover.

The door opened. She heard Querios enter, felt him standing next to her, looking down at her.

"Emmeline, really. This is no time to indulge in the vapors." She remained on her knees, her arms spread across the soft warmth of the bed, her face buried in it. It seemed impossible that she would ever move again.

"I've got up a search party in the grounds. Benedict's gone to ask around in the village."

"It's too late."

"If all you can do is be hysterical, you'd better stay here."

"I'm not hysterical, Querios."

His voice softened.

"Don't worry, Em. She's probably set her heart on a bonnet or something."

"She's run away to London, Q. To a fair."

He tutted.

"Don't be ridiculous. What would a girl like Catherine be doing at a fair?" He shut the door sharply behind him.

"There are no girls like Catherine," Emmeline said to the empty air. "There is only Catherine." She started to howl.

TWENTY-TWO

Louisa was propped on a heap of cushions at the end of a couch, hold-ing a burnt rag to her nose. She was the beauty of the family with black hair that fell in good-tempered curls and creamy skin that she'd been at pains to protect from the sun. Her eyes were round and brown and her lashes curled upward, giving her an innocent look that verged on startled, as if everything caught her slightly by surprise.

"Catherine," Anna said. "Meet my sister, Mrs. Heron."

"Good afternoon, Mrs. Heron."

"This is Catherine," Anna said. "A friend of mine."

Louisa looked at Catherine without curiosity, nodded a greeting.

"I thought you were dead, Anastasia." With her small hands, the fingers sparkling with opals and marquises, the nails buffed to a shine, she folded the burnt rag into a flat, neat square. She leaned forward to where Anna sat at the other end of the couch and looked at her intently. "I've been through such torment, you can't imagine. I waited for you all that afternoon. I couldn't understand why you didn't come, thought you must be ill. Next day, I went to the Vicarage."

"You saw Vincent? What did he say?"

"He told me that you'd gone to stay with friends of his. That you needed rest. Peace and quiet. He was busy with a sermon so we didn't talk for long. The next time I went, no one answered the door." Louisa's eyes flickered toward her belly. "I thought perhaps . . . well, you can imagine what I thought. You're not, are you, darling?"

Anna shook her head.

"Lou, I . . ."

There was a tap at the door and the King Charles spaniel on the hearth squeaked in its sleep. A domed mirror over the fireplace reflected the parlor walls curved into a globe, a contained world like a stage set or a painting. A girl opened the door, admitting a waft of boiling fowl, and laid a baby between them on the couch. It was wrapped in a shawl with only its face showing. Louisa dabbed her eyes on the rag and looked at the infant.

"How could you?" she said to Anna. "Just disappear like that."

"I wrote to you so many times. I expected you every day. When you didn't come, I thought Vincent must have persuaded you . . . I was afraid he might have convinced you that there was something wrong with me."

"Vincent could never convince me of anything," Louisa said. "I begged you not . . . Well, it's too late now." She picked up the baby and adjusted the swaddling, pulling the shawl more tightly around its chest. The baby opened its eyes and began a protesting whimper. Its skin was irritated, flaky pink patches standing out on the cheeks, and a soft silken fringe of red hair escaped from the edge of a tight white cap. Louisa jiggled it impatiently.

"Shhhhh, Harriet," she said. "Meet your auntie Anna."

"Oh, it's a girl. Congratulations, Lou," Anna said. "You must be so happy."

"Yes."

Anna had the faint sense of oppression that she always felt with her sister, as if in her company she became a dilute version of herself. She'd rehearsed the escape again and again mentally but she hadn't thought much about what would come afterward. She'd trusted that things would take care of themselves if she could only get outside the walls of Lake House and reach her sister. Now she was here, she felt shabby and clumsy. Out of place.

Anna pulled her sleeves down over her wrists, trying to conceal their frayed edges, and clasped her hands together in case Louisa should notice that she wore no ring. Her boots had left clods of mud on the carpet. Anna felt mired in what had happened, as if she hadn't left it behind at all. She didn't know how to begin to explain it to her sister, how to ask for the assistance she needed.

She smiled at her. "Louisa, I . . ."

Louisa reached forward and plucked a twig from Anna's hair. Her nose twitched and a look of distaste flickered over her face. The folds of her shot silk dress shimmered from orange to gold and back again with every movement she made.

"If you have a bath, you'll look alright. I'll lend you something to wear. I was washing gloves when I heard your voice. It gave me such a turn. Did Vincent bring you here straight from his friends' house? You look so bedraggled. I thought at first"—Louisa put her hand in front of her mouth and laughed a light, incredulous laugh—"I thought you might have run away from something. You looked as if you'd been tramping across the countryside like a pair of navvies."

Catherine was sitting on a footstool fondling the dog's ears. She jumped to her feet, overturning the stool.

"That's exactly what we did do, Mrs. Heron. It was so romantic. We had to hide from everyone, even the milkmaids, until we got to London. Then we disappeared among the crowds. It's the best way to disappear, you know—in full view of everyone. I've read about it."

Louisa had stopped laughing.

"Anna, what is she talking about?"

Anna got up and went to the fire, leaned on the mantelpiece next to a photograph of a small, fair child, in a frame decorated with seashells. She looked into the steady, lively flames, the swept hearth contained behind a polished brass fender.

Louisa had always been unreliable. Reluctant to take responsibility. It was always Anna who'd insisted they walk all the way along to the lighthouse. Anna who'd had such a yearning for whelks that they had to stay out on the rocks past the time when they should have scrambled back to the beach. There was something else, tugging at the edge of memory. She couldn't remember what. Only that it was important.

She cleared her throat and turned to face her sister.

"I need your help. Vincent doesn't know I'm here, Louisa."

She related in brief the events since November, leaving out the vision of the boy. She wouldn't bring that up now. Louisa had always been frightened of what Anna saw.

"It's a madhouse. Can you believe that Vincent took me to a madhouse? The only person from outside I've seen since I got there is a photographer. His name—"

"It's not a madhouse," Catherine interrupted. "It's a country retreat. It promotes peace of mind."

Louisa rolled her eyes in Catherine's direction and lowered her voice.

"I suppose she's one of the inmates?"

"This is Catherine Abse. The daughter of the proprietor."

Louisa's eyes widened. "And you've run away with her? You want me to hide the two of you? Really, Anna . . . People see everything in this street." The sound of hooves colliding to a halt on the cobbles echoed up into the room and Louisa pressed the rag under her nose. "See who it is, Anna. I think I might faint again."

Anna went to the window. Her stomach churning with fear, expecting to hear the crash of the knocker on the front door at any second, she pulled aside a lace curtain patterned with bouquets of flowers and grapes. A cab had pulled up at the house opposite. A woman climbed out with a hatbox slung by its cord over her arm. A maid stood at the open door in readiness; the light from the sconces in the hallway spilled out into the dusk and made a halo through which the woman passed. The door closed, the carriage pulled away.

"It's nothing, Louisa," Anna said, sitting down, feeling weak.

"My nerves, Anna," Louisa said. "Please think of my nerves."

Louisa's priority was a quiet life, without interruptions from the past. Louisa had left Dover and their family behind when she married Blundell Heron, whom she'd met when he was on a holiday down there. She'd shed her past like a snake's skin—changed her way of speaking, her way of dressing. She announced after the wedding that she didn't want to come back to the harbortown except in her coffin and then changed her mind and said not even then—she'd be buried in London, thank you very much, with all the other people who'd come to make a decent future for themselves.

After Louisa left, things were different at home. The flint house grew dark with just Anna and her mother left in it. Amelia Newlove lit the lamps late, when it was already too dark to read or write. She said hot water was unnecessary and went to bed early, huddled under the eiderdown. She wore layers of flannel petticoats that smelled like the pawnbroker's shop and kept her good clothes, her good self, wrapped in linen tablecloths, sprinkled with peppercorns against the moth.

Decay triumphed anyway, creeping in from the outside. Tiles slipped from the roof and flints fell from the walls as the mortar between them crumbled. Wasps took over invisible spaces in the eaves for their nests, their industry mocking the human lives inside. The gate sagged on its hinges. Approached from the windblown garden, the house with its sacking over the windows looked mutilated, as if it had had its eyes put out.

Mrs. Newlove, when Anna tried to persuade her to get out, to cheer up, to take an interest again in life—said she could not, that Captain Newlove hadn't provided for her in life or death. Anna didn't respond. She hated criticism of her father when he was alive and she hated it more after he was dead.

Catherine had righted the stool and was still on her feet, clutching her elbows, her knuckles white.

"We're going to see the Fasting Girl this evening, Mrs. Heron. She has no appetites of any kind. She is one of my heroines. Can we go soon, Mrs. Palmer? It's after five."

The baby began to cry in earnest. Her face, the only part of her that was able to move, was scarlet, mouth stretched open, eyes squeezing out tears in rapid succession. Louisa rocked her impatiently, sighing in short, urgent breaths.

"What do you want from me, Anna?"

"I've agreed to take Catherine to see an amusement. Can we come back here afterward? I just need somewhere to stay for a few days."

"I don't dare think what Blundell will say. You know, he disapproves of . . ." Her face slackened then recomposed itself. "I'll do my best, Anna. For a night or two. I'll ask him."

TWENTY-THREE

The ground was littered with sweet wrappers and handbills, with flattened apple cores and pieces of potato skin. Catherine skipped as they made their way past jugglers and stilt-walkers and a man leading what he proclaimed to be a leopard, prowling at his heel on a silver chain.

"It looks like a dog, with paint on it. Did you know Mr. Darwin believes our dogs are related to the dogs in ancient Egypt? Can you imagine Mrs. Heron's spaniel trotting around the Pyramids?" Catherine laughed and put her arm through Anna's, squeezed it with sharp fingers. "I'm happy, Mrs. Palmer. Happier than I have ever been. I feel as if I could die now, because I am so happy. Do you ever have that feeling?"

Anna smiled back at Catherine. She felt the excitement too, couldn't help but share in some part of it despite a growing feeling inside that she must decide what to do. The firecrackers made her body start and her ears pop. The air was sharp with the smell of cordite, with burnt sugar and horse manure, overlaid with the sweet, musky odor of burning incense tablets. All around them, people strolled and laughed and jostled, bundled up in furs and mufflers, their faces lit by flares, grease lamps, braziers. It was good to be in a crowd. To be part of something.

They passed a costermonger shaking a perforated pan over the coals.

"Lovely chestnuts," he said, winking at her. "Nice an' 'ot."

Catherine stiffened and began to tug Anna along, pushing her way ahead through the throng.

"There she is," she said. "Oh, my Lord. Look!"

In front of them was a board propped on a tree, a painting of a dark-haired woman with sharp cheekbones. There was a queue of women and girls outside a marquee, a man announcing the One and Only, the Marvelous, the Miraculous, the Incredible, the Astounding American Fasting Girl, shouting through what looked like an ear trumpet. She had taken no sustenance this year, excepting the smell of flowers and exotic fruits. At eight o'clock this very night she would take a few drops of dew, brushed onto her lips with a feather. The Fasting Girl was indisposed after her journey, he added as they drew near. She would not speak to her admirers. They should not trouble her with questions.

"She'll speak to me," Catherine said. "I know she will."

"You go in. I'll wait for you outside. Go on—get in the queue. Here's the money."

"I'm frightened."

"Why?"

Catherine hesitated, her expression pained.

"All my heroines have come from books. I've never known one in real life."

"So?"

"I don't want to be disappointed, Mrs. Palmer. People in books are whatever you want them to be."

"She's a performer, Catherine. Like an actress."

"She isn't. She's just like you and me except that she lives off air and rain. She inhabits the spiritual realm."

"Roll up," said the man, bowing to Catherine. "Roll up, miss. Take the chance of a lifetime to see the Fasting Girl. Only sixpence."

Catherine paid the money and joined the line of women and girls. Anna waved at her and walked on. She'd never been to a London pleasure ground. Vincent disapproved of them. The traveling one that had come to Dover at Whitsun was a smaller, poorer affair with the same magician every year, pulling the same rabbit out of his baggy sleeve.

Anna paused by a low wooden stage lit with swinging lamps and found herself in a ring of people, their faces illuminated by the light reflected from the stage. In the middle of it was a girl with long, dark hair down her back, dressed for a hot climate in shimmering bloomers that were loose around her hips but tight over her calves and ankles and a flowing, soft shirt in the same pink-and-gold paisley print. She nodded at the audience for silence and began to bend her body over backward from the waist. She went farther and farther, curling her chest on and on in a snakelike movement until her head appeared between the silky ankles. Her face was looking at them once again, this time with her chin resting on the ground. The crowd roared their pleasure.

The showman brought a lamp closer and put it down by her feet. She had a needle between the toes of one foot, a length of thread held in the other. They fell silent as she lifted her head up farther between her knees, brought her feet together and threaded the needle. A scatter of applause went up as she righted herself, shook her hair into place again and faced them, expressionless. A man passed around a hat, the crown hanging off the rim. Anna dropped in a halfpenny and passed by, thinking about the girl, wondering where she had come from and why.

Louisa had hurried them out of the house the way they came in, through the kitchen. She'd talk to Blundell after he'd eaten his dinner, she said. She would get an answer from him by morning. She would leave the kitchen door unlocked and they must take off their boots by the range, creep up the stairs and sleep with the children in the nursery. Blundell never saw the children in the mornings so he wouldn't know anything about it.

Anna bought a slice of bread pudding from a boy with a tray on his head. He lifted it down and cut her a slice, sprinkled extra sugar on the top and passed it over on a square of paper. It was warm through her glove, fragrant with cinnamon and cloves. She ate it piece by small piece, exploring the raisins with her tongue, chewing the sweetness, feeling the warmth of it slide down her throat. There were peddlers everywhere—selling hoops, firecrackers, silk posies, things that might once have appealed to her but now seemed pointless. She finished the pudding and wiped her fingers on the paper, threw it down on the ground.

Wandering on, she found herself in a quiet part of the gardens where couples were consorting in dark corners, the women with painted eyes and lips, the men laughing loud and often. The moon was almost full, missing a sliver off the side as if someone had helped themselves to a slice. She ought to rejoin the crowd, return to the busy, lit area to wait for Catherine but the river drew her onward. The tide was high and the water gleamed with reflected lights from the boats anchored in the middle.

The smell of river water was rank and muddy, tinged with salt. The strains of the barrel organ had given way to the sound of waves from a tug's wake slapping on the embankment down below, the deep rumble of a ship's horn from farther upriver. Anna stood and stared at the shifting reflected light on the water. For the first time since she had jumped off the ice and onto the churned shore, she felt free. In the morning, she would be able to think and plan. In the morning, she would decide what she was going to do.

As she turned back to collect Catherine, her eye was caught by two people coming toward her from the other side of a flower bed. Anna stood, staring. The woman wore a short cape over broad, stiff skirts, a feathered bonnet, but it was the man who drew her attention. He was tall and dark, dressed in a long coat and smoothing his moustache with one finger. His head was bent toward his companion and as they walked the woman laughed and put her hand on his arm in a practiced gesture. Was this she? Was she looking at Maud Sulten?

Neither had seen her. Anna checked the urge to step out before them and drew back behind a tree, caught a drift of frankincense as they passed mixed with a sweet reek of violets. She stood motionless, gazing after them at the upright dignitary's hat, the plume of feathers that waved from a bonnet beside it, the head cocked at an angle.

She leaned on the old tree, feeling dizzy. Its rough, cracked bark pressed the flesh of her arm through her cloak. A pair of cold hands covered her eyes from behind and she screamed and threw them off.

"It's me," Catherine said. "Don't take on, Mrs. Palmer. You look as if you've seen a ghost."

At Lake House, lights burned in every room. The feverish search had given way to a vigilant waiting, a waiting focused on absence.

"It's like a wake," Emmeline said. "All we're missing is the body."

"For Heaven's sake, Em. There's no need to dramatize the situation." Querios and Emmeline were in the study, Querios pacing the floor and Emmeline hunched in a shawl by the grate, her laudanum bottle clutched in her hand.

"They're not here," she said. "We have to face it."

"She might have gone to Flo's," Querios said. "To her aunt's house."

Emmeline gave him one of her looks. "Unlikely. I can't persuade her there for a visit so I can't think why she would have run away to them."

"I'll call on them and find out," he said, his voice more optimistic than he felt. "Probably find her playing charades with her cousins, tucking into one of Flo's pies."

"You might," Emmeline said, bleakly.

Some hours later, in Chelsea, Querios Abse left the house of his sister-in-law, Florence Worth. He stood on the curb in the dark street, stamping his feet, trying to keep the murderous cold at bay. Catherine was not there and the mission had succeeded only in communicating alarm to the rest of the family. Catherine's cousin Henry had insisted on throwing on his greatcoat and setting off to walk the streets in search of her. Flo was hysterical and her husband had departed with a neighbor to report Catherine missing at the police station.

Querios felt defeated. He racked his brains, trying to think where his daughter could have gone. He was forced to admit that he really had no idea. A church bell tolled eleven and he remembered his other pressing difficulty. Mrs. Palmer was missing too. Was it possible that the two of them were together? He had thought he could feel no worse than he did but his heart sank a little further, at the prospect of informing Palmer his wife had absconded. He would put that off till tomorrow. Or longer, even. First thing in the morning, he would ask Makepeace whom the Palmer woman wrote to, who her friends were.

For now, he saw no option but to try to get home.

TWENTY-FOUR

The amber glass at the windows combined with the yellow mantles of the two lamps to create an otherworldly glow. Lucas St. Clair balanced on a wooden stool, his feet hooked on its rungs, a glass in his hands. He could relax in the darkroom. The dim, obfuscating light and the strong, sour smells released him from the obligation that he felt throughout his waking hours. The duty owed was not to his boss, Sir Harry Grieve. It wasn't even to the patients at St. Mark's. It was to some more demanding client—a broad notion of progress, betterment, a future that his hands must play a part in creating. Since Archie died, he'd known he must do something with his own existence. He could not waste it.

He'd returned late to Popham Street and eaten the sweating piece of Cheddar that Stickles had left out on a corner of the dining table. Decided against a baked apple studded with what looked like beetles and come upstairs to do some work. The first whisky hadn't enabled him to leave St. Mark's behind and he'd poured a second.

The pressure to discharge patients with a *cured* stamp in their file was increasing. Some were desperate to go, others wanted nothing more than to stay. That afternoon, a chap had banged his head on the wall, when Lucas told him he was discharged. The patient swore at him, shouted that he'd sleep on the bed of Father Thames before he went back to the workhouse. He was a young chap, about his own age—missing a hand, but he still managed to overturn Lucas's desk, trying to prove himself insane. Which he wasn't.

After that, he'd been to see Mrs. Ruth Mann in one of the women's wards. The beds were evenly spaced; the high, iron-framed windows cast a series of rectangles of light over the polished wooden floor. Mrs. Mann lay in her bed, her face looking more like raw meat than a female countenance. She was another of Grieve's candidates for immediate discharge back to her own family. The problem was, she did not have a family.

She peered at him through swollen eyes and reached for his hand.

"You've come to see me, Doctor."

"I have, Mrs. Mann. Are you any better today?"

"You're the doctor, aren't you? You tell me."

She began to laugh and stopped, lifted her hands to her face. "Ah, Doctor, it hurts. Everything hurts."

He'd prescribed antimony to calm her mind. It would stop her hurting herself further, for the time being, but it would not cure her. She had been brought from another hospital and there too she'd made determined efforts to do away with herself—forcing stockings down her throat, rushing headlong at walls and windows and swallowing glass. He wondered, sometimes, if self-killing ought automatically to be considered a crime or whether it ought to be respected as a choice some human beings made for themselves. All human life was precious beyond measure but for some of his patients life was a deeper torture than any hellfire the church could conjure. In the hospital, there was no way to depart life with dignity. No easeful lake or obliging steam train. And there was no guarantee of any amelioration either.

"Can you help me, Doctor?"

"I can certainly try, Mrs. Mann. I am trying to get you better."

She laughed again.

"I meant—can you help me end it. That's all I want."

His professional opinion was that time might cure her. Once she was past the change of life, her blood settled again, she might regain the desire to live. At the other hospital, she'd had her blood let—her neck bore the scars of repeated openings with the lancet—and been leeched, blistered. She was malnourished. She needed beef tea, port wine, egg custards. Perhaps an outing to a garden or a peaceful cathedral where her mind might expand under the soaring vaults. She was sick at heart, her husband dead and her children grown and scattered. Stickles might be able to comfort her, he had an instinct, with a cowslip brain tonic and—better—a listening ear, a few hours in a warm kitchen.

He was obliged to enter the diagnosis in the required section. He'd called it general melancholia but it was something deeper than that that ailed Ruth Mann. If Grieve had had an open mind, Lucas could have photographed her—studied her face properly and listened to its silent communication. As it was, he had to make a judgment based on hasty conversation and brief observation.

As he left her bedside and hurried on to the next, he felt frustrated by the limits to the help he could offer. Angry. He had more than a hundred patients under his care and was meant to see every one of them every day. Patients were discharged when still ill or confined beyond the time they should have been free. About half were not insane by any measure he would employ. They were debilitated by disease or hardship, driven to the edge of madness by life itself. He felt sometimes that he was not working as a doctor but as a custodian. A jailer for the people society had no use for—the old, the feeble and the brokenhearted.

Lucas stood and ran the tap at the sink, rinsing his arms up to the elbows. The talk to the Alienists' Association was a month away, he must begin on a rough draft of the presentation. But tonight, he would put St. Mark's out of his mind and prepare for his next visit to Lake House. He had been thinking about the girl from Regent Street, how she was in the picture and not in the picture. Shown and not shown. It was the complaint Mrs. Palmer had made—that she didn't recognize herself. He had pointed the camera at her competently enough but what did that mean, if she did not find herself in the image?

He picked the first image he'd made of her out of the wooden plate holder, intending to score his nail through it in a cross, peel up the collodion in four neat triangles. Holding the sheet of glass in both hands, looking at Mrs. Palmer's black face, her long, white hair falling over her shoulders down to her narrow waist, he experienced a curious sensation that he held a person between his fingertips. That it was important not to injure her. A longing came over him to see Mrs. Palmer again.

Lucas settled the plate back in the rack and set about mixing a solution of fresh collodion. Measuring out ammonium iodide, he mixed it with distilled water and watched it clump and cake in the bottom of the beaker. He liked the delicate tones of a solution higher in bromides. He added half the quantity of cadmium bromide, stirred it in with a glass rod, and held the container over a spirit lamp, keeping back from the rising fumes. Opening the collodion bottle, he trickled in the salts through a funnel. The mixture fizzed and subsided, turned cloudy inside the brown glass. He agitated the bottle and set it back on the shelf.

He had decided to alter his approach—to experiment with larger images, from close up. It would enable him to see patients more clearly and read more accurately what was exhibited on their faces. It might, he hoped, answer the question of how a person could be captured by a camera at the same time as they escaped it.

Lucas returned to his stool and drained his whisky. He sat nursing the empty glass until the church clock beyond his window chimed one. Timekeeping was the only use he had for the church; he did not resent its insistent message of the passing of the hours. He rose and left the room to prepare for bed. He would go to Lake House in the morning and request to photograph Mrs. Palmer again. He could see in every detail the picture he would make of her.

It took time to rope the carrying cases onto the seat of the cab, the stoppered bottles chinking against one another inside. The driver tried to insist that he strap the plate box on the luggage rack and looked disapproving when Lucas informed him that the box was of the greatest importance, that he would rather if necessary get rained on himself. The man thought he was a drunk, it occurred to him, as they lurched past the Angel and began the long ascent of the Hollow Way. He thought he carried his gin supply with him. He laughed and rested his head back on the worn leather. It was the first opportunity he'd had since Christmas to return to Lake House and he was impatient to arrive.

* * *

The maid's face fell as she pulled open the great front door. She looked past him as if she expected someone else then met his eyes with an agitated expression.

"It's not my place to ask I know, but is there any news, sir?"

"Nothing in particular. I've come for Mr. Abse."

Lucas smiled at her, passed through the dim hallway into the study to wait for Abse. He walked up and down the room, underneath the ledgers and leather-bound books on the shelves, threading a path between the curios that Abse seemed to be collecting, almost falling over a bowlegged ladder. A woman was wailing somewhere in the house.

When the door at the far end of the room opened it wasn't Abse but Makepeace who appeared. She had an air of triumph about her as she sailed toward him with one hand clutched over a ring of keys hanging from the device she always wore at her waist. It was a chatelaine. His grandmother used to have one and he'd always found it ominous. He disliked things being locked.

"Morning, Makepeace. Tell Mr. Abse I am here, would you?"

"Mr. Abse is engaged with a family matter, Dr. St. Clair."

He felt cheered by the prospect of avoiding an encounter with Abse. The fellow used up daylight with his ponderous conversation.

"No need to trouble him, in that case. I shall set up in the Fernery. I intend to photograph Mrs. Palmer first."

"You're too late."

He looked at his watch. It was ten o'clock in the morning.

"It is certainly not too late, Makepeace."

She smirked. "I think you will find that it is, sir. Mrs. Palmer has absconded."

Lucas felt as if he had walked into a lamppost.

"She can't have."

"I'd say the same myself but she has. She's gone, no one knows where, and she's taken the daughter of the house with her."

If she wasn't there, he couldn't photograph her. He could not absorb it. He had thought so much about the picture he was about to make, had imagined it in such detail, that in his mind it already existed.

"She was here last time I came."

Makepeace laughed and the buttons on her bodice rolled from side to side.

"See for yourself. I was on my way up to the guests' rooms. We're all at sixes and sevens. They haven't even had their breakfast yet."

He followed her up the elegant stairs from the ground floor, running his hand along the smooth, curved banister. Through the deserted dayroom and on across the dining room, where he consulted with patients over their photographs.

They continued—up a narrow staircase of thin and splintered treads along a low-ceilinged corridor of numbered doors, each with an observation slot at eye level. His head just cleared the bowing ceiling and the air was foul; used chamber pots stood outside some doors, discarded trays of food by others. Lucas felt a creeping sense of shame at the conditions, at the compromises involved in using a private house as an asylum. He'd never been to the patients' sleeping quarters before. It occurred to him that he really knew very little about Lake House.

Makepeace stopped at door number 9.

"See for yourself," she said, unlocking it and swinging it open. The door banged against the wall. She let the key fall back among its companions and jerked her head toward the interior. "Good riddance, if you ask me. But it is awful that Catherine's missing. Poor Mrs. Abse is beside herself."

Lucas took in a cold grate. A dormer window catching a reflected gleam of the morning's light and a pair of worn slippers placed neatly by the bed. Just looking into the room made him feel constricted. It was a case history, he told himself. Nothing more. He could have no personal interest in her. Mrs. Palmer was not only a patient but a married woman. He would use the time to make another image of Mrs. Button or Miss Batt. The disappointment wasn't lessened. He was flummoxed by his sense of loss. Spotting the photograph he'd made of her, on the mantelpiece, he ducked inside the room, picked it up, and took it to the window.

The black fronds of the fern she held were turning rusty brown. He hadn't washed the print for long enough. A fingerprint had bloomed in one corner. His own thumb made an illiterate signature on his work. The image intended to arrest time had changed even since he had presented it to her.

The picture looked different, in other ways. Her eyes, the direct appeal they made, announced her desperation to be free, he could see now. Her face was alive with unexpressed emotions that he hadn't been able to interpret but looked like a plea for help. He stopped, arrested by a thought that hadn't occurred to him before but suddenly seemed obvious. Perhaps it was not only the photograph that might alter. The viewer could change too.

As he went to replace the photograph on the mantelpiece, a scream came from outside the door followed by a heavy thump, a rattling of metal as if someone had hurled a handful of coins at the floor. He put back the photograph, took a last glance around the room, and stepped out into the corridor.

Makepeace lay in a heap by the door to the next room, keys scattered all around her on the boards. Her skirts had risen to show men's socks emerging from the tops of her Adelaide boots and a pair of thick white calves. She was moaning and his first thought was that her heart had failed. He kneeled beside her and felt for the pulse in her wrist. She opened her eyes and looked at him.

"Not me, you fool," she said, her voice choked and harsh. "It's Talitha. Help her, Doctor. Help her."

He got to his feet with a sense of dread and put his eye to the observation slot.

TWENTY-FIVE

Miniature smocks and pantaloons hung in neat lines on a clotheshorse by the side of the fire. Anna breathed in the pleasant, soapy smell of drying cotton and blinked at the light, strong against the nursery curtains. The sheet was fine and soft against her skin, the cotton pressed smooth. She reached for a flask of water on the bedside table and poured herself a glass. Catherine was still asleep, lying on her stomach in the other bed. The children and their nursemaid had gone.

She remembered the dream she'd had, drifting in and out of sleep as the nursery fire subsided. Lucas St. Clair had been making a picture of her. It was a wedding photograph; Anna had her hair piled high on her head, threaded with country flowers. As well as being the photographer, Lucas St. Clair was the bridegroom. He stood beside her, his own dark hair loose on his shoulders. The two of them were naked as Adam and Eve, without even the fig leaves, but in the dream she'd felt no shame—only a deep, insistent pleasure. She felt a stirring of it again.

The dream was so real, seemed more real than the morning she woke to. She wondered at the pictures her own mind could throw up as she got out of bed and walked in bare feet along a carpeted passageway to the bathroom. She filled the basin and washed herself all over with scented soap from a patterned dish. Letting the water run away through a brass grille at the bottom of the basin, she refilled it and splashed her face again and again with warm water. Then cleaned her teeth with clove-scented powder, combed her hair, and rubbed some of Louisa's cold cream onto her face. Reluctantly, she put on the dress Louisa had left out for her.

When she'd finished, she sat on the edge of the bath with the door still locked and put her head in her hands. She was ready, but she didn't know for what. She was not married to Lucas St. Clair—the thought prompted a sad, sweet pang—she was married to Vincent Palmer. Morning had come and she still lacked a clear idea of what she should do; what she *could* do. She might beg Louisa to conceal her here while she searched for some employment and a place to stay. Some women did live alone in rented rooms. But she would not be able to hide indefinitely from Vincent. They would still be married. She could confront him with the injustice of her incarceration, perhaps with her brother-in-law at her side to make sure she wasn't carted back to Lake House. She might even voice her suspicions that he had a mistress, if she dared. But then the best that could happen would be that she found herself back at the Vicarage.

Blundell called out a good-bye to Louisa, somewhere down below in the house. He sounded impatient. Anna didn't hear her sister's reply. She wondered what it was like to be Louisa. She didn't know, even wearing her clothes, using her toothbrush, her hairbrush, what Louisa's life was. What she felt when she opened her eyes, what she dreamed about. She never had done. Anna opened her sister's scent bottle, dabbed the glass rod on her wrists, and went down the stairs.

The dining room was empty. She took a poached egg from a covered dish and slid it onto a plate decorated with painted insects. They were the plates that they'd had in the flint house, brought from Germany by their father. Even when the days came when they were living on rice pudding and sago, Amelia Newlove refused to let her sell them.

Anna breathed in the smell of carnations on her wrist. It was the scent that their mother used to wear on what she called *occasions*—a powdery, musky smell. It reminded her of something that eluded her. Something that mattered. She had a sense that if she knew what it was, she would know what to do. She looked down at the bone handle of the knife resting on her palm and felt the familiar sensation of emptiness in her hands.

"You look miles away." Louisa was in the doorway.

"Good morning, Lou."

Louisa poured herself a cup of tea and pulled her chair close.

"Good morning, Anna. I only wish you were here in happier circumstances. Have you thought what you're going to do?"

"Not yet. Did you talk to Blundell?"

"Yes." Louisa averted her eyes. "You have to go to Vincent, Anna, and apologize. Plead with him to take you back. There's nothing else for it."

"I can't go back there."

"To bedlam?"

"To the Vicarage."

She hadn't told Louisa that she'd seen Vincent at the fair. Louisa wouldn't believe it. Anna could hardly believe it herself.

"You can't stay here," Louisa said, bluntly. "Blundell won't allow it."

Without her corsets, her hair loose on her shoulders, Louisa looked different. Her body had grown wide and round; damp patches seeped through from her breasts on each side of her wrap. There were lines at the sides of her eyes and shadows underneath them. The new baby was the fourth. Once, Louisa had been bony and brown as a Gypsy girl. It was the despair of their governesses, the way her skin absorbed the sun. Anna had an image of a pair of bare feet flashing up the path in front of her, the heels white with chalk, calves narrow as daisy stems.

"Can't you persuade him to take pity on me, Lou? I need a few days to work things out and I've got nowhere else to go."

Louisa put down her cup and stared into the tea leaves.

"I'm sorry, Anastasia. He said he'd be obliged to inform Vincent tonight in person if you're still here. Vincent has a case, he says. It was an eccentric thing to do—running off to a shipwreck."

Anna took a deep breath. She would have to explain more clearly to Louisa what had taken her on the mission. Get her to understand.

"I know it might appear odd," she said. "But I had to go, Lou. I saw something. I had a vision of a boy."

Louisa appeared not to have heard.

"This tea's cold," she said and jangled the bell in the air between them. "I'll get some more brought up. Where's Catherine?"

Anna paused.

"Still asleep."

Louisa had never wanted to hear about the visions. Once, Anna saw a tree full of angels. The tree was growing on the shore, out of the sand, and the angels were male, naked apart from feathery wings, their legs curved behind them like fishtails. It was the first time she understood that angels could swim, could breathe underwater. Anna ran all the way up the path to the house to tell Louisa and when she did Louisa slapped her in the face, even though Anna was past the age for slapping.

She'd stood in their bedroom doorway with one hand clutched stupidly to her cheek while Louisa went back to her book. She had the same sense now, that her sister could not or would not hear her. Anna shifted the plate in front of her, prodded at the egg. The yolk was congealed and her appetite gone. She put down her fork. She would tell Louisa about the other side of things. That at least she might be willing to understand.

"I believe that Vincent has betrayed me."

"Why do you say that?"

"I found a letter, from a woman. And last night . . ."

Louisa interrupted her.

"He has a mistress, you mean? Most men do."

Children's running feet thumped overhead and a wail went up.

"Louisa, listen. I can't trust him. When I spoke to him about the letter, he denied it. And taking me to Lake House, even if he meant it for the best—he tricked me. I have to stay away from the Vicarage at least until I can see some proper doctors and get the certificate to say that I'm well. Otherwise he could take me back there."

The maid came in and put a pot down on the table. Louisa got up and closed the door behind her, stood for a moment with her ear to the crack.

"Blundell isn't always understanding. He's even questioned my own state of mind. Mother's behavior at the end—it hasn't been forgotten, you know. He threatened last night that I'd be joining you at your asylum if I kept up the séances."

"You still go to Mr. Hamilton's?"

"Yes." Louisa poured the tea and they watched as steam rose from the wide, shallow cups. "I speak to Mother often, consult her. She's perfectly alright now. Pa came through once. Before Christmas, I heard another voice. Not that he could say anything, of course, but I heard his voice, just like it used to be."

"What do you mean? Whose voice?"

Louisa looked at her.

"You could come with me, Anna, when things are back to normal. It would help you."

"Help me what?"

Louisa ran both hands up over her face, into her hair. She tightened the wrap around her waist and stood up.

"For God's sake. Sometimes I think Blundell is right about our family." She sat down again and leaned in toward Anna with eyes full of trouble. "I can't go against his wishes, Anna. I don't dare."

Number 59 was the last in a new terrace, a small two-up, two-down that leaned against the public house on one side of it. The front door was narrow and sheltered by a porch. A laurel hedge sprouted behind the front wall, its broad leaves coated with soot that had been partly washed away by the morning's shower.

Anna stood in the road, looking at the house. She was alone; Catherine had woken with a fever, her eyes glazed, forehead burning. Anna had given her weak tea and left her in Louisa's care, promising to be back by lunchtime.

Anna made herself walk up the path. She was trembling, half expecting Vincent to lean his head out of the upper window. The knocker was in the shape of a woman's hand and had an iron bracelet on its iron wrist, the beads picked out in green paint. She lifted it, brought it down hard. And again. Once more. She stood and waited, her back straight, head up.

There was no sign of movement inside the hall, beyond the squares of violet-and-crimson colored glass in the door. Her fright began to lessen. Of course Vincent was not inside. No one was. She sat down on the low wall that separated the little front garden from the one next door. Men were rolling wooden barrels into the cellars of the public house and the boys she'd passed on her way had resumed their game; their shouts hung on the air. Her mouth was dry, her lips sore from the cold air.

Anna had thought about Maud Sulten's refusing to see her. She'd considered the possibility that they would quarrel or that Maud might deny all knowledge of Vincent. But she hadn't thought of this: that the woman might not be at home. Anna found herself staring at a wooden spinning top lying capsized under the hedge. It was faded, the sides dented from being bowled along by an insistent stick. A feeling grew in her that she had been here, outside the closed door, before. That she had always known this place, with its smell of smoke and yeast and impending rain, the damp chill from the brickwork coming through her petticoats and the air, that rang with cries and echoes.

She looked again at the spinning top and the feeling passed. The moment grew unfamiliar. She left, turning up a side road to the high street, to where a butcher called out his wares, standing under a row of hanging rabbits. Scraps of paper idled down gutters in the wind and a pair of soot-covered sweeps passed by on the back of a cart, their feet swinging.

Anna felt separated from other people. They hadn't met betrayal. If they had, they couldn't carry a cabbage under an arm in that casual way or laugh with that head-thrown-back freedom. She must face facts, she told herself. Louisa couldn't help. She had to think of something else. Anna wandered past an undertaker's and a grocer's shop and imagined herself going to Lucas St. Clair's hospital. She knew St. Mark's—it was not far from All Hallows and she'd often passed it, hurrying by to escape hearing the cries of the inmates from behind the high walls.

She put aside the thought. She felt certain, whatever Vincent said, that Maud Sulten did exist. That it was she whom Anna had seen with Vincent at the fair. Anna did not have a clear idea of what she'd say to Maud if she answered the door—just a feeling that they should know about each other. Even if Maud knew that Vincent had a wife, that was different from knowing that it was she. Anna. And if Anna met Maud and spoke with her, Vincent wouldn't be able to say she was imagining things. *Mad.*

She stopped outside a baker's, drawn by the smell of caraway, then stepped into the warmth, holding open the door for a harassed-looking woman pulling a boy by the hand. The woman thanked her, tilting her head to one side as she passed. She had a vivacious, pretty face with lips reddened by cosmetics. A silk posy was pinned on her cape.

Anna's eyes ranged over the sloping shelves at the back of the shop. Macaroons, slightly burned. Lumps of seed cake and square slabs of gingerbread—things she had taken for granted until a few weeks ago. On the other side of a curtain of beads, the baker lifted a tray of Bath buns out of the oven, all joined to each other.

"I'll have some of those, please. A dozen."

"Shan't be a minute, miss."

She'd give them to the children and have one herself. Catherine might like a couple, and Louisa. The bakery assistant pushed through the beads; they rattled back into place behind her. As Anna waited, she saw in her mind the short cape of the woman at the fair. The inquisitive angle of her head and the trays of silk posies the hawkers had tried so insistently to sell to her and Catherine. The assistant came back with a bag of buns and Anna handed over half a crown. She leaned on the counter while the woman counted out the change, slapping coins down on the scarred wood.

"You having a turn?" the assistant said. "You look queer."

"It's nothing. Thank you, ma'am."

Anna took the bag and groped her way through the door. She retraced her steps, hurrying down the side road, hugging the warmth of the buns against her chest. Turning the corner into Sebastopol Street, she was just in time to see the woman push open the gate of number 59 and walk up the path. Maud Sulten, if it was she, waved to a neighbor, unlocked the door, and let herself in, still holding the child's hand.

Anna leaned against the wall of the pub trying to absorb what she'd seen. She had two or three hours to get back to Louisa's house, collect Catherine and leave—with a plan. But she felt unable to think at all.

TWENTY-SIX

Anna and Catherine were in the nursery. Louisa had persuaded Blundell to grant them one more night, on the grounds of Catherine's not being fit to travel. Now they had to go. Catherine sat on the rug with her legs stretched out in front of her, stroking the dog's long ears. Anna perched on the side of a truckle bed, dangling a rag doll in her hands. The painted features had been almost rubbed away from the cotton face and the doll was floppy from use, the straight arms and legs limp inside a gingham dress. It had been Louisa's.

Anna's heart ached. The smocks airing on the fireguard, the smell of milk and soap and the soft hiss of a new log in the grate made the nursery seem a place of safety. But it wasn't.

Catherine had wept earlier when Anna insisted she must go back to Lake House. "You're the hysteric, don't forget, Mrs. Palmer. You're the escaped lunatic. Why should I be the one to go back?"

"You're fifteen. You're unwell. You have to go back to your family."

Catherine's face was febrile, her voice hoarse. She closed her eyes. "I won't go back without you. You'll have to drag me there yourself."

"I'm coming with you, Catherine. I can't stay with Louisa either."

Catherine began to cry again. "I don't want you to come back, Mrs. Palmer, really. Why doesn't she hide you here?"

"She can't," Anna said flatly. "Her husband won't let her."

"I hate him," Catherine said. "I hate all husbands."

Louisa was insistent that they must be gone from Wren Street before Blundell returned from the office that evening. She'd had a hectic, anxious look in her eyes since the morning and kept rushing down to the kitchen on trumped-up errands. She had promised to send doctors to see Anna at Lake House. "As soon as you get the certificate, Anna," she'd said, "everything will be alright. You can go back to Vincent and start again. Maybe a child will help. . . ." Her words had faded away.

Anna hadn't been able to speak, or even to look at her. Louisa was as powerless as she, and Anna felt sad for both of them.

The spaniel whined and thumped his tail on the carpet, looking from Catherine to Anna. His mouth hung open, displaying pink-and-black gums. Catherine kissed the top of his head.

"At least I'll see Ben again," she said. "I miss him. You'd like my brother, Mrs. Palmer."

Anna smiled. She must see the girl safely home, get her near the house. Once they got there, she would declare her own plans to her and hope that Catherine would understand.

The bus was full, the air soupy with breath and damp wool and the roof creaking from the weight of passengers on top. The team of eight horses tossed their heads and breathed vapor into the cold air, their eyes concealed behind leather blinkers. Anna found an empty seat and settled Catherine into it, wrapped in her cloak, her hands in her muff. She paid the conductor a shilling for the two of them and Catherine fell asleep almost immediately, her head bumping on Anna's shoulder.

Anna shivered. Louisa had insisted she keep on the cast-off dress. The skirt was too short and her ankles were in a draft. Lou had insisted on dressing her hair as well before they left, had arranged it in a fussy style like her own, with a parting running over the top of her head from one ear to the other, held in place with pins, talking all the while about how everything would turn out alright. Anna had her own dress in a paper parcel on her lap, tied with string. She would change, as soon as she got the opportunity. She couldn't do what she had to do in a dress that didn't feel right. That wasn't her own.

She gazed out of the window at a man in a barber's shop, his throat lathered. A board advertised Madame Lily, clairvoyant, *guaranteed to see your future*. Anna had disliked London when she first visited— thought it dry and overcrowded, with too much brick and blackened stone, too many hurrying people. The paved streets made her feet ache and the stench of the gutters was unrelieved by sea breezes. She hadn't understood how people could live with a smell like that hanging over them. But she'd grown used to the city quickly, grown to like the sea of people. Now she regretted the prospect of being far from London, buried in the countryside. But if Louisa couldn't help, she had no alternative. She couldn't trim hats, like Miss Batt, and she wouldn't go and stand under a gaslight, with all the other country girls who'd lost their way. She would never do that.

Anna had agreed with Louisa that she would go back to Lake House and wait for the doctors to come. But she had no intention of returning. She was going to deliver Catherine almost to the gates then hurry back to the village and pick up the stagecoach at the inn, traveling on along the great north road. Make her way to her eldest sister's house, in Northumberland. Lavinia would shelter her for a little while at least, once she heard what had happened. Her husband, Jim Lillywhite, was a mild man who fell in with Lavinia's wishes and had done ever since they married.

Far from London, Anna would be able to think clearly and decide what to do with her life. Currently, all she was certain of was that she would not return to the Vicarage. She was beginning to feel as if she had never known Vincent at all, as if she knew him better when he was a stranger, and once she married him, began to unknow him. One thing she was familiar with was his view on divorce. He told her the day before the wedding that he considered it a cardinal sin, that he would die before he would divorce.

Catherine's head slipped forward onto her chest. Her face looked younger than ever, her high white forehead blue-veined with the blood that pulsed inside. The wheel of the bus hit a rut and she opened her eyes and looked around, her expression startled.

"Where are we?" she asked, sitting up. "I was dreaming."

"What about?"

"The Fasting Girl." Catherine leaned her head back on Anna's shoulder, slipped an arm through hers. "I can't stop thinking about her. Do you think dreams can be more real than life, Mrs. Palmer?"

"Perhaps." Anna rested her head on the top of Catherine's. "What would be the nicest dream you could have for your life when you're a woman? Tell me about it."

Catherine began to talk about pomegranates and cypress trees, high-walled houses perched on top of mountains and terraces where fountains splashed in the night air. She smiled and her face looked restored.

"Next time I escape, Mrs. Palmer, it will be forever," she said.

They climbed down from the bus at Highgate and set off out of the village on the road that led to Lake House. The tall trees on either side of the way were black-limbed, glistening and still. The ice had thawed and the grasses and hedgerows looked subdued and ordinary, stripped of their glittering crystals, their coat of armor. They walked past the allotments, past a boy cutting the tops off Brussels sprouts, swiping at them with a sickle. Anna took Catherine's arm.

"Ben will be happy to see you home again," Anna said.

"I know."

"He must have missed you."

"Yes."

Catherine's voice was monotonous. Anna took hold of her hand and kissed it. They were within half a mile, she estimated, of Lake House. She would not go any nearer. She stopped in the road.

"Are you strong enough to walk alone from here?"

"What do you mean, Mrs. Palmer?"

"Catherine, I'm not coming any farther."

"I don't understand."

"I'm going to stay with my sister. Another one of them. I can't take you with me this time. And you know I can't come back to Lake House."

They heard the clip of metal striking on stones and both looked up. Makepeace was coming toward them along the lane, dressed in a black cape and felt bonnet and using a furled black umbrella as a walking stick. At the sight of her, Anna felt fear run through her like a tide.

She reached under her cloak for the St. Christopher and clenched her fingers around it, her hand pressed against her neck. St. Christopher was the patron saint of travelers. Silently, she asked him to help her. She would hand Catherine over to Makepeace and leave. She'd keep her distance, wouldn't get close enough for Makepeace to grab her.

Catherine's voice shook. "What's going to happen to me?"

"Nothing will happen, Catherine. Don't be afraid. You're going home."

Makepeace was approaching steadily—she had seen them now and her walk was more purposeful although still slow.

"Good-bye, Catherine," Anna said.

"I'm glad, Mrs. Palmer," Catherine whispered, "that you're not coming back."

Anna and Makepeace faced each other by the side of the road. Makepeace seemed shorter than she did in Lake House. Her eyes were swollen, their rims red, and something about her reminded Anna of another encounter, in another place.

"Good afternoon, Mrs. Makepeace."

"Miss Abse, Mrs. Palmer." She nodded at them in turn, drew a black-edged mourning handkerchief from her reticule and shook it out.

"What's happened?" said Catherine, in alarm. "Is it Mother?"

Makepeace shook her head.

"Mrs. Abse is prostrated. That will pass." She turned her head away and let out a sob. "But this . . . this will not pass."

The survivors from the wreck, Anna thought. Makepeace reminded her of the sailors. Their dazed faces and the sense that they inhabited a different reality. She had a growing sense of unreality herself. The white sky, the stillness and the shivering crows planted along the verges of the road, were dreamlike.

Makepeace stood as if rooted to the ground, the winter light reflecting off her stricken face. She had aged in only a couple of days and Anna felt a surprising stirring of pity for her. She wondered who had died. Hearing the rumble of cart wheels in the lane behind her, the soft clop of a single horse, she took a deep breath, still keeping her distance. She would make a dignified good-bye then run for it, all the way to the village, jump on the first coach that presented itself.

"I've brought Catherine back to her family, Mrs. Makepeace. I shall leave her with you."

"Very kind, Mrs. Palmer, I'm sure."

Makepeace's voice was iron hard. She put away her handkerchief and looked at Anna with something of her old mix of malice and resentment. Anna's legs were trembling. She was too close to Lake House, must leave while she still could. She kissed Catherine on both cheeks. The cart had pulled up behind them.

"I'm going now, Catherine. I'll write to you."

She hugged her a last time, turned, and ran headlong into the massive figure of Jethro Fludd.

"No," she shouted. "No."

The cart was filling the lane. She tried to dart around the other side of it but Fludd laughed, reached out one massive hand and caught hold of her arm. Leaving the cart standing, the reins of the horse hanging loose, he began to drag her along the road toward the gates as easily and carelessly as if she had been a puppy. Catherine ran along beside, weeping and kicking at his ankles, while Makepeace walked behind, looking on with an expression of dull satisfaction.

Fludd's grip was viselike, but Anna scarcely felt it. Her head was full of her sister. Makepeace and Fludd must have known that she and Catherine would be on the road, that they would be able to capture her. Only one person could have told them. Louisa.

TWENTY-SEVEN

Anna picked herself off the floor and shook out her cloak. Nothing in the room had changed. The slippers were side by side, the bed neatly made and the photograph still propped on the mantelpiece. She picked it up and scanned her white face, the fern, the weave of the canvas backdrop. She wasn't looking for herself. She was looking for Lucas St. Clair. A thumbprint had appeared in one corner, oblong and complicated, like a map of a maze. She fitted her own thumb over it.

Anna had been to his hospital, after she left Maud Sulten's house. She'd had an idea that she could appeal to Dr. St. Clair more freely outside Lake House, that he was the one person who might be able to help her. She wanted to see him. She got as far as the gates of St. Mark's, heard the cries floating over the walls, saw the high chimneys of the laundry, and turned around, feeling sick. She couldn't voluntarily step inside such a place. It might have been better for her if she had.

She replaced the photograph and hugged her arms around herself. The room was colder than ever; the chill seemed to issue from the walls. She sat down on the edge of the bed and pulled out the pins, undoing Louisa's work, returning her hair to its usual plain arrangement in a bun on the back of her head, held by her tortoiseshell combs. Collecting what remained of the money out of her boot, she lifted the leg of the bed, felt in the empty hollow with her fingers. She reached in farther with a hairpin and shook the frame. Only the handkerchief fell out. She wrapped the money in it and tucked it up as far as she could. She was distracted, wondering what could have happened to the knife and who could have found it.

Anna got into bed, fully dressed, lay still and looked at the watery light falling on the wooden panel on one side of the dormer, uncertain which seemed more unreal. The fact of having been outside Lake House. Or the horror of being back in it.

Lovely woke her, standing over her with a candle in one hand and a plate in the other.

"Bread and jam for dinner tonight, miss. Cripes. It's colder in 'ere than what it is outdoors." She put down the plate by the bed, brought in a scuttle from the passage and began laying the fire, crouched in front of the grate. "I didn't expect to see you back."

"I was bringing Catherine home and they caught me." Anna hesitated. "I have a feeling my sister may have been in on it."

Lovely's hands grew still as she turned her head to Anna.

"Don't tell me she let yer down?"

"She didn't let me down, exactly. It's just that she doesn't always see what is the right thing to do. Did you get into trouble, Lovely?"

Lovely shook her head as she resumed the construction of a small pyramid of twigs.

"I slipped over, on the ice. Took a moment to get my breath. I looks around and you've gone. Vanished into thin air. I never saw Miss Abse."

"Mrs. Makepeace believed you?"

"For now. They're short of hands, remember."

"I thought you'd help me if you could. But I didn't know if you could risk your job. Thank you."

The twigs caught, the kindling blazed. Lovely dropped single lumps of coal on the fragile heap of sticks and dusted her hands on her apron. She sat on the end of the bed and ran her feet in and out of her clogs.

"I'm about ready for a change, anyways."

"What's happened here?" Anna asked, seeing a black ribbon tied around the arm of Lovely's dress. "Has someone died?"

Lovely made an odd, inconclusive movement of her head.

"Is it—was it—old Mrs. Valentine?"

"No, miss. Not Violet."

Lovely led Anna into the corridor, opened the door of the adjacent room, and walked into it, holding the candle in the air. The curtains were closed and there was a cloth thrown over the mirror. As Anna's eyes adjusted to the gloom, she saw a pot of rouge on the washstand with a few spent matchsticks heaped next to it. She took the candle from Lovely and held it to a painting on the wall. It was a portrait of a man, dressed in a purple tunic patterned with gold. His eyes were piercing, his skin brown and he had a red dot between his eyes. He looked like a prince. Miss Batt's lover.

"Oh, no," she said. "No. Please. Say it isn't true."

Anna made herself look down at the iron bed pushed up against the wall. There was a form on it, covered in a sheet. The shape cast a shadow on the wall like a range of low hills, the outline trembling with the movement of the flame. The form itself did not move. Lovely stepped forward and lifted a corner of the sheet.

"She's at peace now, miss."

Anna brought the candle closer and saw a pair of dark eyebrows in a high white sky of forehead over Talitha Batt's curved, closed eyes. Lovely brought the sheet down farther. There was red pigment gathered in the cracks of Batt's purple lips. Anna pressed her hand against the cheek. It was waxy and unyielding, more solid than Batt had ever seemed in life. She touched her hair and took in the sight of the distinct, dignified profile, the pleated ruff high and tight under her chin. Anna felt empty. Too empty to scream or cry. Miss Batt was not there. Only a body remained.

"I done the best I could with her. Dr. St. Clair wanted to make a picture." Lovely twitched the cloth back over the face. "Now you've seen it, miss. Whatever they say downstairs."

Her voice was odd, almost angry. She pushed Anna back into her own room, dragged out the straw mattress and flung herself down on it, launched into the Lord's Prayer. Anna sat on the edge of the bed and waited for the Amen.

"How did she die?" she asked, after it came.

Lovely was under the blanket with her head hidden and only her feet in their woollen bed socks still showing.

"Like anyone else. Her heart stopped beating."

*   *   *

Anna couldn't sleep. She lay in the hollow in the mattress, listening to Lovely's breathing and to the silence beyond it. The wall between her room and Talitha's seemed to dissolve in the darkness; Anna pictured the three of them, three women lying side by side in their different states, all entombed in Lake House. Lovely, forced to work in it for her living. Herself, captured. She closed her eyes and prayed that Talitha was free. *Woken from the dream of life.*

Seeing her had made Anna think of her mother. Dying, Amelia Newlove became pretty again. Her face grew younger as her mind ranged over the years. She had an airiness about her, an absence. She mistook Anna for her own mother, asked her to sing to her, reached for her breast. Then she bit her, accused her of lying. Shouted at her that she had stolen away her child. She shouted all the time, while she still had the strength. Couldn't hear herself through the cork stoppers. Anna had stood at the door of her mother's dark room, holding on to the frame and feeling unsteady on her feet, in her self. The flint house was a ship, foundering.

"Shall we go for a picnic?" Amelia Newlove said, in her social voice. "Is the pony ready?"

After the shouting came the screaming.

"Where is my Antony? My baby boy? What have you done with him?" Incomprehensible reproaches and laments that disturbed and distressed Anna.

"It's the morphine," the doctor said. "Takes folk different ways. You mustn't blame yourself."

In death, her body was soft. Silent. Anna washed her hair and sponged her, sprinkled her with rosewater. She was tiny. Harmless. Anna could love her again as she once had. She took the St. Christopher from her neck and fastened it around her own throat. Arranged her mother lying on her side, one cheek resting on her clasped hands.

The funeral was as slight as the coffin. A handful of mourners, friends of Captain Newlove's, mainly. A spot in the overcrowded graveyard, the earth heaped high on each side of the path, the white void narrow, barely wide enough for the box. The wind colder than she ever felt it before. Afterward, without her mother in it, the flint house seemed becalmed—neither sinking nor floating. Anna didn't know what to do with possessions. With minutes. She didn't know how to live.

Hepzibah came, from Gloucester. Beatrice, from Portsmouth. Lavinia was confined and couldn't travel from Northumberland; she dispatched her eldest daughter, with her governess. Louisa came from London. Vincent sent condolences. He wasn't able to get away for the funeral.

Hunched around the drop-leaf table, quarreling, her sisters didn't seem like married women. Anna talked with her niece, took her down to the beach to collect shells. Her elder sisters had always seemed more like aunts.

No sooner was she buried than her mother arrived in Anna's dreams like an uninvited guest, refusing to leave. She was as big as the wind, filled every room she entered. She heaped her own coffin with soft black earth and planted it with bulbs; they grew tall and blue, turned into children. She came after Anna demanding to know what she had done with Antony.

That night, in her room at Lake House, Anna fell asleep and dreamed of her mother—alive again and asking her a question. In the morning, waking in the same position as she'd fallen asleep, she felt confused as she opened her eyes to the texture of the green wallpaper, the repeated pattern of thistles. Lovely had gone and she was alone.

"Who is Antony?" she said aloud.

Makepeace was at her table, twisting a length of black ribbon between her fingers.

"You wanted to see me, Mrs. Makepeace?"

"You owe us all an explanation. Mr. Abse is much disturbed. Mrs. Abse has come close to nervous collapse."

"I couldn't have brought Catherine back any quicker than I did."

"It seems you feel no gratitude toward your friends here. You've evidently made no progress in your state of mind."

As Makepeace's eyes bored into her, Anna pinched her own wrists on her lap. She thought of London, and imagined Madame Lily—gazing into a ball of cloudy crystal, perceiving the outline of things to come. The man getting up from the barber's chair, rubbing a hand over a newly shaven cheek and walking out into a shaft of winter sun. Of the woman in the baker's, helping herself to a bun and eating it absentmindedly as she stood behind a counter. Life had a place for her. She would return to it.

Anna lifted her own eyes and stared back at Makepeace.

"Being an escaped lunatic is hardly better than being a confined one. I intend to free myself properly."

"How'll you do that, Mrs. Palmer?"

"Not by writing letters. My sister did not receive a single one, of all those I entrusted to you."

Makepeace's lips twitched as her eyes shifted to the fireplace.

"Relatives are embarrassed when their lunatics write begging letters or arrive on their doorsteps. Most often, like your sister, they're able to persuade them to return. Mrs. Heron was anxious that you should believe that you came back of your own free will. That you shouldn't know that Mr. Fludd was waiting downstairs in the kitchen in case you changed your mind. He followed behind the bus all the way with the pony, Mrs. Palmer. Her husband insisted on it."

"You're lying, Mrs. Makepeace," Anna said, without conviction. She stood up and walked to the door. "I need to see Mr. Abse. I need to see him as soon as possible."

The cup and saucer sat unchanged on the mantelpiece; the arrangement of everlasting flowers was layered with cobwebs. Her eye fell on a piece of embroidery pinned to the wall behind Makepeace, unframed. It was a vibrant tableau of tropical flowers and insects. It glowed and shone as if it were the only living thing in the room. Miss Batt's work was complete—every last petal and stem finished.

Anna lingered on the threshold, overcome by weariness and rested her head on the doorframe.

"It is a tragic loss, the death of Miss Batt. We will all grieve her. But what about you, Mrs. Makepeace? You're not certified or imprisoned by your family. Will you remain now she is gone?"

Makepeace tightened the ribbon round her finger; the tip of it was purple, suffused with blood.

"This is my home. I shall never leave Lake House."

* * *

Alone in the room, Frances Makepeace sat motionless. The tears she had suppressed while Mrs. Palmer was there ran down her face. She wished she could feel something so simple as grief for her only friend. She felt more rage than sadness, rage at Talitha for leaving her without a good-bye. For taking her own life and abandoning her, Fanny, here in the barren world. Rage at Querios Abse, for being more concerned about what the newspapers would say if the story got out than he was about dear Talitha. And at Lucas St. Clair—for having made a photograph of the corpse. No living soul ought ever to see another person the way she had seen Talitha Batt, with her throat gaping open. To record it was nothing short of blasphemous.

Most of all—although she had an inkling that it was unjust—she felt enraged by Mrs. Palmer. All of this was her fault. Palmer had unsettled everything and everyone since she arrived and yet what was she? Nothing. Nothing but a naive young woman who'd never faced any trouble and who relied on a pair of striking eyes and a slender figure to get her through life. Frances hated her.

She opened the drawer under her table, extracted an envelope slit open along its top and pulled out a single sheet of paper. She read the letter again.

Dear Miss Sulten,

You do not know me. You may not even know my name. But I am writing to plead for your help.

I barely trust my own mind as I write this letter. I must know whether or not you are acquainted with Vincent Palmer, the man I married seven months ago. He swears on the Holy Bible there is no such person as Maud Sulten.

I don't inquire about the nature of the relationship but I need urgently to know—do you exist?

Yours truly,
Anna Palmer

Makepeace laid the letter on the table in front of her. She was back again where she could not tolerate to be, in the past. When Jack Makepeace first left her, she simply hadn't believed it. She stayed indoors, waiting for Jack to come home. Emptied a sherry bottle one morning, for the first time in her life, and another the following morning. She played the piano for hours on end. It would have been better for her if she had remained that way—sipping fortified wines and soothing herself with tunes. *Julia's a-weeping, On a summer's afternoon . . .*

How could Jack, a clerk, a man who gave his eyesight and his days to setting out the profits and losses of three spice traders, a man dedicated to the rendering of the world in precise quantities and values—behave as he did? He'd eaten the breakfast she'd risen to make him. Swallowed it down with the tea kept hot under the cosy she'd knitted. She saw him off, was still standing on the step when he reached the corner. He didn't look around. Frances went indoors again, feeling cheated. He'd owed her a wave, a backward look. That made her laugh, later. Laugh and cry.

It had been a year before she could step outside the house. As if it was not Jack who'd disappeared, but herself. She was ashamed to show her face in her own street, where she'd lived all her born days, even though it was his empty suitcase on the top of the wardrobe, his spare pair of trousers on the hanger. He who had sauntered off without so much as a good-bye.

After a year, she had a letter from the girl. Her name was Lillah and she hadn't known anything about Frances. "You don't know me," the letter began. "You may not even know my name." Lillah wrote to say she was sorry. Maybe it was a blessing, she said, that Fanny'd had no children. If she wanted to come and see Jack's child, she would welcome her. Perhaps, she said, they could be kin of sorts.

One July day, Frances opened her door and stepped out into the street as if nothing had happened, as if she'd never been married to Jack Makepeace but had remained Fanny Fitzgerald, as surely and blithely as when she was five years old. She made her way to the address on Lillah's letter, her reticule stuffed full, bobbing against her hip with each step. She walked up the tiled path and past a greengage tree laden with unripe fruit as if she was delivering a visiting card, which, in a way, she was. She pushed the rags soaked in oil through the letterbox. Struck a lucifer and made sure the last shred caught properly before she dropped it through the slot, the tips of her fingers stinging and blistering.

She crossed the road to watch. She'd meant to stay just long enough to be sure it had worked but she couldn't leave. An hour later, maybe more, she was still there, entranced by the leaping, scorching grandeur of the flames, their disregard for window frames, curtains, privet leaves. She couldn't contain the shouts that rose in her, the jubilation. The ringing bell of the fire cart finally made itself heard, in the distance. A crowd had gathered, staring sometimes at the house and sometimes at Frances.

It began to rain, a heavy summer rain; the first drops splattered like pancakes on the ground. The fire quietened and began to smolder and as the rain grew heavier a veil of steam went up over what remained of the little house. Some of the people raised umbrellas over their heads at the same time as the roof beam caved in. The window glass had melted and the greengages shriveled where they hung.

Fire setting, they called it in court. Arson. It didn't seem like that to her. It seemed to her she was returning to Jack the anger he'd ignited in her—that had scorched her from the inside, that was properly his. The sentence had been unjust. No one died. Only the dog. Jack hadn't even been there. Jack always got away, from everything. After prison came Lake House. It was worse than prison, being jailed by her own family.

It was time Maud Sulten knew the truth. Probably poor Maud had been the Reverend Palmer's common-law wife. Then Anna had come along and spirited him away, just as Lillah had stolen Jack away from her. Fanny had seen Lillah in the courtroom, two children clinging to her skirts. It hadn't seemed possible, that such a young girl could be the mother of Jack's children. A slender, pretty, foolish girl.

Frances Makepeace refolded the letter and copied the address onto a new envelope in her own backward-sloping copperplate that had never varied since she was a child. She folded Mrs. Palmer's letter into it and sealed it then crumpled up the original envelope and tossed it on the fire. The acrid smell of burning wax filled the air as the envelope caught and flared; a pink trickle dripped through the grate, slowing and hardening as it rolled out across the hearth tiles.

TWENTY-EIGHT

Emmeline reached for the salt cellar and shook it over her soup. Nothing came out but she felt a solid lump flying up and down inside. Hannah should have taken it back to the kitchen for drying out. She looked up to frown at her and caught her leaning on the sideboard with her eyes drooping as if she was half asleep. At a look from Emmeline, the girl straightened up and began to fill the water glasses.

Catherine had been home for three days. She seemed farther away than ever, sitting next to Emmeline with her elbows propped on the table, a book open on her side plate. Emmeline didn't have the heart to correct her. Querios was eating methodically, lifting regular quantities of soup to his lips. She wished he was nearer to her. She needed him beside her, not at the opposite end of the table. They needed to stand together.

"The days are getting longer, don't you think?" she called down the length of the table, over the cruet and the candelabra.

He looked up balefully, not at her but at Catherine. He'd begun to take notice of her since she came back although not in the way Emmeline had longed for. He was treating Catherine with a wary, wounded vigilance, as if their daughter was a dog that had bitten once and might bite again. And he spent longer hours than ever before shut up in the study with the paperwork, worrying himself about the magistrates.

"Did you hear me, Q?"

"Hmm? Fox has been at it again," he said.

"At what?"

"Bold as brass. The second female. There's only the cock left now."

Catherine kept quiet. Since she'd returned she'd said almost nothing about what she did or whom she saw while she was away from home. Emmeline found her silence more alarming than her rudeness had been. The fever had lifted but she was eating less than ever. Like a bird, as far as Emmeline could see.

"You've hardly touched your soup, Catty. I thought you liked soup."

"I don't, Mother. Not anymore."

"Well eat it anyway, darling. For my sake."

"What good will it do you?"

She'd come home changed. Not in the way Emmeline had feared— mangled, dead. Defiled. Not even wearing bloomers or smoking cigarettes or speaking in slang. It wasn't any of those things. She was filled with something private, as if she had a secret. Emmeline swallowed another mouthful of the soup. Without salt, it lacked flavor. The tepid temperature didn't help. She laid down her spoon. Catherine was back at home. Safe. That was all that mattered. Everything would be alright now.

God had fulfilled his side of the bargain, although He hadn't offered any indication of what He expected in return. Emmeline had started by attending Miss Batt's burial. She had an uneasy sense that her attitude toward the patients had been un-Christian and anyway she had always liked Miss Batt. The manner of her death was shocking, of course, but the way they rushed the poor woman into the earth had offended Emmeline. More as if they were disposing of the evidence than laying her to rest in eternal peace. It was a scrubby patch near the road encroached on by sycamore saplings—not anyone's idea of sacred ground. Fludd had dug the grave earlier in the day and had left the clods heaped messily on one side of the trench, a hefty spade stuck in the top.

The other woman had been buried there too. The bird woman, who fell to earth. And the one with the little twins. Emmeline had almost forgotten about her. That was a terrible, terrible tragedy, the way she leapt from the old bridge. Taking the babies with her. There ought to be something to mark the burial ground. A stone cross or a shaped yew—some somber, lovely thing. It was disrespectful, burying people like stillborn lambs.

Querios expected a scandal. There hadn't been one. The newspapers missed the story beforehand and the coroner returned a verdict of state of mind unknown. Miss Batt could have been buried in a churchyard, by daylight. But the brother insisted on committal in the grounds, after dark, just as if she'd been found guilty of suicide, as they'd feared she must be. The coroner had showed mercy. Emmeline saw Mr. Batt in the hallway afterward, swiping soil off his trouser cuffs, slapping at them with his gloves by the light of the sconces in the hall.

"As far as the family is concerned, my sister passed away a long time ago."

He boomed it out as if he was making an announcement to a great, invisible audience, even though it was only Querios standing there in front of him, in the shabby black jacket that he refused to replace. She'd been on the landing, on her way downstairs to bid the brother goodbye. She found she couldn't breathe easily all of a sudden. She'd turned around and gone back upstairs, slowly.

Emmeline reached for her glass and took a sip of water as Hannah reappeared, carrying the large willow-pattern dish; the room filled with the smell of mutton and sherry. Hannah served the meat from the sideboard and put down the first plate in front of Benedict, the chop plump and pale on a bed of creamed spinach.

"Thank you, Hannah," he said, smiling up at her, tucking his napkin in under his chin.

He took his philanthropy too far, thanking the servants, inquiring after their families, their health. Not that Hannah Smith had a family. Emmeline had taken her on from the workhouse, impressed by her serious, quiet demeanor. She'd wanted to give her a chance in life. Hannah was still standing next to Ben, ladling gravy. She had a flattened bulkiness about her at the front that was becoming impossible to mistake for weight gain or cumbersome clothing. Emmeline hadn't yet spoken to her about it. The right moment hadn't presented itself.

Catherine was holding her napkin over her nose. Querios glared at her. Emmeline had begged Querios not to punish her, persuaded him to overlook the incident and put it behind them. They had been in the study earlier in the day, the three of them, for his formal rebuke to their daughter. Emmeline had had the feeling Catherine was barely listening to Querios's admonishments and advice.

"D'you think it's right, Father?" she'd said, when he appeared to have finished. "Locking up women who are perfectly well? Depriving them of their liberty, for money?"

Emmeline had hurried Catherine out of the room, almost before the words were out of her mouth. She'd hoped that Querios hadn't been listening, but seeing his bloodshot eyes and air of scarcely suppressed rage this evening, she realized he probably had.

She caught movement out of the corner of her eye. Catherine had pushed aside her plate, was putting something to her mouth. Emmeline raised her water glass and stole a look at her. Catherine looked like an angel; so narrow and white. So self-contained. In her right hand, held lightly to her nose, was a rosebud. The silence in the room thickened to something ominous.

Querios banged his fist down on the table and the cutlery, the mustard pots and napkin rings and toothpick holders all jumped and rattled as if they were in a buffet car on a train.

"What do you think you're playing at, Catherine?"

Catherine opened her eyes.

"I'm not playing, Father. I am taking sustenance from a flower."

Her tone of voice was so sure, Emmeline felt a sudden ache in her heart. Catty was still a child. Still innocent.

"If you don't eat, Catherine, you'll d . . . become ill."

"I won't *die,* Father. Do we have any grapes?"

Querios was scarlet, his mouth open.

"Grapes! Why not pomegranates? Mangos? Why not . . ." He got out of his chair, grabbed the rose from Catherine's hand and flung it on the cloth. "I'll have you fed, if you don't stop this nonsense. In the treatment room. You'll soon get your appetite back then."

Benedict was on his feet at Querios's side, towering over him.

"You can't f-force her to eat, Father. It's wr-wr-wrong."

Catherine folded her arms over her chest and sat very straight, her face on fire. Before Querios could respond, there was a knock at the open door. Fludd stood there, dressed in a filthy old waistcoat made from moleskins, and grinning. Querios sat down. He lifted his tankard and took a long draft of beer before he spoke.

"Fludd. I wanted to see you."

"Yes, Mr. Abse? What were it concerning?"

Fludd had left Cornwall when he was a boy but his accent was so strong Emmeline could barely understand him, even though he must be forty now. He'd been taken on by old Mr. Abse and Querios refused to get rid of him even though just seeing him gave Emmeline the shudders. She took another sip of water, reached for Catherine's hand under the table and squeezed it.

"Fetch down the chair, Fludd. Put it back together, in the cellar. Just as it was."

Fludd nodded and left, his cap in his hands. Emmeline gripped the edge of the table, felt the immovability of the mahogany through the soft white linen. She waited until Fludd's heavy tread died away. She needed to compose herself, would ration her determination, not spend it all immediately. She spoke quietly.

"Querios, you cannot do that to our daughter. I am her mother and I will not allow it."

"What chair? What are you talking about?" Catherine said. She looked confused.

Querios ignored her.

"Not Catherine, Em. It's for the Palmer woman. She's a maniac."

"She's not!" Catherine shouted. "She's my friend."

Catherine leapt up and ran out of the room. Her feet pounded on the stairs and a door banged. Querios threw down his napkin and left without a word, heading for the study. Emmeline felt relieved that Querios was not intending to use the chair on Catherine. Nauseous, at the idea of its being brought back into service in the asylum.

Ben threw her a concerned glance, got up and patted Emmeline's shoulder. He didn't know what the chair was, she thought dully. Even he hadn't eaten his pudding. A dish of apple Charlotte lay untouched at his place.

"Catty'll be alright, Ma," he said on his way out of the room. "Why don't you take her away? It would do you both good."

Hannah cleared away the plates, the silver, the napkins, brushed off the bread crumbs; only the withered pink bud still lay on the white cloth.

The sound of hammering had been going on all morning, sending shudders through the floorboards, the walls, the soles of Anna's feet. It was unsettling. In the dayroom, Anna pulled her legs up under her on the window seat, feeling her toe through a hole in the end of her stocking. Talitha's green velvet chair remained empty, her embroidered shawl draped over its back. Featherstone was shouting that her husband was hiding outside in the shrubs, would shoot her if he caught a glimpse of her. She got down on her hands and knees, crawled from one end of the room to the other. Violet walked behind, clapping her hands and laughing.

"Cuckoo," she called. "Cuckoo."

Anna rested her forehead on her knees. She'd expected to be called in to see Abse before now, had wanted to ask Abse if she might attend Miss Batt's funeral, but they'd buried her already, Lovely said. At night. Anna had never heard of a burial taking place at night.

Catherine was on her mind. Anna wanted to know how the girl was. She held on to a slim hope that Abse would find it more difficult to call her a hysteric after she'd brought his daughter back to him. He might acknowledge her rationality, her moral sense. Might even want to repay his debt to her, for caring for Catherine. It was possible, she insisted to herself.

Anna felt underneath the cushion of the window seat for her work-bag. She had resisted picking it up, it would confirm that she was back, that time stretched ahead of her with nothing to fill it except stitches, but there was nothing else to do. The inactivity was torment and the routine—breakfast, prayers, turns around the airing grounds, luncheon—had collapsed with Talitha's death. Anna had barely seen Makepeace since the interview in her room.

She pulled apart the long looped handles and took out the fabric. The silks lay curled and helpless in leggy skeins in the bottom of the bag. Cerulean and navy, rust, silver, and sage. Rethreading the needle, she began to push it through the cloth. The stitching soothed her, numbed her mind. It was a consolation, however clumsy her fingers. An image began to form itself over the hours that followed. It was not a letter *V* that was taking shape beneath her fingers. It was an outline of rocks. With a stiff cross-stitch, she began work on the sea that surrounded them.

She hadn't known she'd made choices from the bag of colors Makepeace had thrust in front of her. She had reached in blindly, taken the first that came to hand. But she must have selected them more carefully than she knew. They were the right shades for the picture she found herself making.

The summons came late that afternoon. Makepeace appeared in front of her, heavy-eyed, and nodded toward the door that led down the stairs to the office.

"He wants you in the study."

Anna thrust the sewing back in the bag and left the room. On the landing, she paused and looked out the window at the old oak. Its steady, rooted presence reassured her. She took a deep breath and continued down the stairs.

She knocked confidently and opened the door. Abse was on his feet, looking out the window toward the lake.

"Mr. Abse?"

Certain that they met on new terms, as if for the first time, she held out her hand to shake his. He continued to gaze out over the lawn with his own hands clasped behind his back. She couldn't be sure if he had noticed her gesture.

"I wanted to see you, Mrs. Palmer," he said. "And for the purposes of this interview, I am speaking to you not as a guest but as a fellow human being."

She felt heady with relief.

"I'm so glad, Mr. Abse. I feel the same. Everything has changed."

"Indeed it has."

"How is Catherine? I'd hoped to see her before now. We spent so much time together."

At last he turned toward her. His face was gray, his chin above the line of whiskers sprinkled with white stubble. All the cheer and confidence, all the bombast, had departed.

"I suppose we must be grateful that you deigned to return her to us."

Anna felt herself falter inside at his sarcasm.

"I don't require gratitude."

"You don't? How very gracious." He paused, looked up at the ceiling. "Mrs. Palmer, you lured my daughter across the ice. Walked her for hours in the bitter cold—a tender, delicate girl, not an insensible lunatic who feels no pain. You imprisoned her in some unknown household before dragging her to an unsavory fairground."

Anna struggled to take in what she heard.

"Did she say that?"

"Catherine is young and impressionable. I was able to see beyond her account of events."

"I didn't drag her anywhere. She . . . I brought her back to you, Mr. Abse. That's what matters. She is safely back."

His face creased suddenly and he put his hands over his ears, began to rub them.

"When your husband first brought you here, Mrs. Palmer, I believed that you might have fared better in your own home." He laughed. "That you did not need a full retreat. How wrong I was. How utterly mistaken."

She opened her mouth to explain. Closed it again. She didn't want to make things worse for Catherine. But she must defend herself.

"Mr. Abse, that is not what happened."

"You believed that by abducting my daughter you could avenge yourself on me. It is as simple as that." He turned his back on her once more. "She has come home changed. Her head is full of ideas. Do you know, Mrs. Palmer, that she believes she can live on the scent of flowers?"

The lamps on the desk were still unlit. In the gloom, the towers of yellowing ledgers behind the desk resembled the chalk stacks out in the sea off the south coast.

"May I see her, Mr. Abse? Perhaps I can talk to her, persuade . . ."

"Enough," he bellowed, shouting right into her face, blasting her with sour breath and rage. "My own daughter thinks her father a common jailer. My most esteemed and reliable patient is dead. And you dare to tell me you don't want gratitude."

Anna took a step back. She felt more frightened than she had at any moment so far in Lake House.

Abse picked up a pen from the desk and smoothed the trimmed feather between his fingers. His voice when he spoke again was controlled and he did not look at her.

"I have written to your husband to request your transfer to another asylum. Until then, you will be treated for mania. We shall try every means at our disposal to help you. But moral insanity such as yours is most often beyond cure."

TWENTY-NINE

"Come along, Palmer."

Makepeace's voice was cheery despite the early hour, the bitter cold in the corridor. She walked in front of Anna, and Lovely came behind with the corner of her apron stuffed in her mouth. It was not yet light; the bell hadn't rung for breakfast. They walked past the treatment room, past the shower room and on, to a set of steep, curved stone steps. Anna followed Makepeace down, holding a rope slung from the wall like a banister, and arrived in a cellar, its floor scattered with straw, an old brick oven on one wall.

The room was filled with noise; a machine was running somewhere nearby. Fludd loomed out of the corner, dressed in a smith's leather apron. Anna gasped at the sight of him. He was adjusting a strange contraption, festooned with straps and attached to a long wooden arm. It was a chair. A high-backed chair, attached to the end of a wooden beam.

"What's happening, Lovely?" Anna's voice was a whisper.

Lovely shook her head.

"You'll be alright, miss," she whispered back. "It's the chair. It don't kill yer."

Makepeace cleared her throat. "This is the patient, Mr. Fludd. I think you recognize her."

Anna met his eyes, blue and intense, as he walked toward her. She shrank against Lovely, had time to feel the soft bulk of her, breathe in her smell of sweat and lye, before the man lifted her off the ground and with one movement thrust her into the chair. She kicked at him and tried to push him away with her fists. He laughed.

"No funny business," he said. "Not with Fludd."

He leaned his shoulder against her chest, pinning her in the chair while he tightened a belt around her waist, strapped her legs to the legs of the chair, her chest to its high back. His hair fell forward and Anna caught a glimpse of a scar on the back of his neck—a white circle that looked like teeth marks. Fludd stood up and the machine in the distance quieted. For a moment, everything was still.

"Have a care, Mr. Fludd," Lovely said.

Lovely, Makepeace and Fludd all stood back behind a wooden partition, and Fludd bent over a wheel. As he turned it, the chair started to move. Anna felt herself traveling around the brick walls of the cellar in a circle as if she was in an open carriage, the air cooling her face, her neck. For some slow-moving seconds, she felt nothing more than loneliness, a sense of herself in motion while the others remained stationary. The chair gathered speed, the room became round. The walls disappeared; corners, individual stones lost their solidity. She tried to grip the arms of the chair but her fingers refused.

Soon the chair was turning so fast she couldn't see anything, couldn't hold anything with her eyes. She tried to shout but nothing emerged; her mouth was open, she realized, her head thrown back against the chair. The air had become solid. It slammed into her, choked her, battered her body and then her mind. She was struggling to breathe. She felt nausea rising, turning her body liquid, her bones as formless as the spinning walls. She summoned the last scraps of will, tried again to scream and as she did so she felt the chair slowing. It came to a halt.

She heard Lovely crying, could feel something warm and wet on the seat. Anna was sitting in her own urine. She was sick, suddenly and violently. She half closed her eyes, waiting for the straps to be undone, the room to cease turning.

"All right, Fludd." It was Makepeace. "Get on with it."

The chair began to move again, in the other direction. She traveled backward. A panicked, choking wave rose in her chest but the chair turned so fast the sound was forced inward. It lodged in her head so she was the scream and the scream was she. Her head was thrown forward on her chest, the vomit gathered in her throat and choked her. She knew nothing but the impulse to fight, fight for air.

*   *   *

Anna was in bed. The walls were spinning around her, rotating in a way that made her sick. She reached out to still one as it passed by, saw a white hand appear in front of the blurred thistle heads of the wallpaper. The hand was moving too, it floated up to the ceiling; there was no still place. The thistles had turned to roses, green and thorny, each one different from the next.

She heard a door closing, saw a tray spinning on the chest of drawers that tumbled in space. A hot hand held her wrist. She understood; her skin no longer contained her—she had left her body and was rolling weightless around the room. Her self had been driven out of her. Anna felt a pure, detached sorrow that this was her life. Her path had been leading her here from the very beginning and she hadn't guessed. She had walked through the days in ignorance, without fear, and each one brought her closer to this one. Life had betrayed her.

On the second day, Makepeace instructed that she be kept longer in the chair.

"Five minutes each way, Mr. Fludd." Her voice was excited, as hard and jangling as her rings as she clapped her hands to indicate that he should commence. Anna heard herself whimpering as she was lifted into the seat. She didn't struggle, she tried to put her hands over her eyes, to block out the cellar walls, Makepeace's face, but Fludd grabbed her wrists, trapped them on the arms of the chair. She began to scream, but not for help. There was no help. The chair started to move.

When they lifted her out, she was lost in an impossibly large body. She couldn't find her lips or her tongue. Her feet and her head were on each side of her and her elbows were distant and out of reach. She was cold, colder than she'd ever been in her life.

After a week of the treatment, Anna stopped trying to remember where she was or why this was happening. She opened her eyes one dusky afternoon to a small bedroom and saw two candles lit on the mantelpiece. A photograph of a woman she didn't know. The loneliness was unbearable. She called for Louisa. For her mother. For any human soul. They were there, all of them, her mother and her sisters looking down at her from the top of the cliff and Anna was below, the tide turning and rising around her ankles. She grew silent, waded in the shallows, heard the sigh and suck of the water, knew the terrible emptiness of her open hands. Only her eye could hold the image of him as he sank. Her hands were useless.

She prayed for a sign. Anything at all. Nothing came. Nothing new. Only herself on the shore and then in the shallows. She saw the scene, the freezing water, the disappearing child, with a sense of detachment. She lived in the shallow waves, her hands trailing through the water, could experience it with her eyes closed or open, could hear the sighing waters over and under the echoes from along the corridor, feel the urgent emptiness of her hands around the cup Lovely pressed into them.

Dr. Higgins had instructed that she be purged, Makepeace announced. They were in the treatment room; Lovely had been sent out. Makepeace turned to Anna. She had rolled up her sleeves and taken off her rings. Anna closed her eyes as Makepeace took hold of her, pulling back her head and pinching her nose.

"Come on, Palmer," she said, as she poured chalky liquid through a spout down Anna's throat. "Open your eyes." She jabbed at one of them with her finger. "You're not a child, to be hiding away. Anyway . . ." Makepeace came closer, her face lowered over Anna's. "There is nowhere to hide. Not now."

Anna's bowels turned to water; she was left shut in the bedroom with the stench, the slops freezing in the chamber pot. Next day was another kind of emetic; she vomited until she thought her insides would spill into the tin bowl, stood up with black spots dancing in front of her eyes and at once collapsed on the floor.

Days later, Makepeace arrived in her room again, early. Anna walked behind her down the wormy boards, weeping silently and unstoppably, supported by Lovely's arm around her waist. The corridor grew narrower and darker every time she passed down it. It had once seemed long but now it was never long enough.

In the treatment room, Lovely brushed Anna's hair—slowly, with a patient gentleness in her big hands, smoothing the tresses with her palm between each brushstroke. Anna wished the moment could last forever.

"Enough of that," Makepeace said. "I'll ring if you're required."

Lovely left the room backward; the last thing Anna saw was her broad, concerned face. Anna closed her eyes, her ears jarred by each snip of the scissors. When she opened her eyes again, it was done. Her hair lay on the floor all around, in long, dark skeins, unaware of its severance and shining in the beams of sun that fell through the window. She felt the shock in her fingers as they ran over her head from her forehead to the nape of her neck. Makepeace doused Anna's head with water, came toward her with a bar of soap, an open razor.

"It's for your own good."

Her scalp, readied by shaving, was first blistered with hot irons. Later, it was frozen with crushed ice that had been packed in an India rubber cap. Anna saw herself as if from above, as if she floated over the woman she had been. She saw her own familiar body dressed in a calico nightdress, strapped to a chair in the treatment room. Saw Makepeace, pushing the ice down hard on her head, breathing heavily.

"What are you doing to me?" Anna heard herself say.

"Cooling the blood. Mr. Abse's orders."

The pain was sharp and jarring, as if something had come loose inside her skull.

Afterward, in the mirror at the washstand in her own room, her lips were as blue as cornflowers. Her scalp looked angry, the skin raised and red. The pain had changed. It was as solid as iron; it enveloped her from the inside of her head. She threw the towel over the mirror. The creature she saw in the glass was a stranger and the stranger frightened her.

Next, a week later, came the leeches, applied to her private places by Dr. Higgins. She was maniacal, he said, as he lifted her skirts, due to a disorder of the menses. He had renewed the certificate for her own safety. Anna didn't protest. She couldn't. It seemed to be someone else this was happening to while she watched from above, dispassionate and helpless. The bites oozed blood that would not cease.

* * *

After some days, she didn't know how long she had lain there, time couldn't be measured anymore in the old ways, they brought her out of the bedroom. Put her into the window seat in the dayroom, wrapped in a blanket. She still couldn't speak, she discovered. She couldn't respond to Lizzie Button's gentle inquiries. All she could do was look into Lizzie's brown eyes. She gazed at her for a long time until Makepeace stepped between them. Mrs. Featherstone laughed and sang to herself, tore the tassels off the edges of the curtains and scattered them on the floor like flowers. Talitha's chair was empty, waiting for her.

Anna no longer felt sorrow. She didn't feel anything. She was not there. She could smell sea air underneath the boiled cabbage and potatoes and feel the spray of surf sharp on her skin as she sat in the gloom of the dayroom. Eating a mouthful of herring at breakfast she tasted the whelks they boiled in seawater over driftwood fires. When the two friends quarreled, shrill and resentful, she heard the voices of children, playing.

She saw the sun on the chimney breast, over a far horizon, the water merged with the sky. The chalk shore turned pink and gold in its fiery light and she roamed it, up and down. The sky lay flattened and stilled on the sand, caught in the wet remaining lick of sea, the pink gleam of sunset brought to earth, the fire of it cooled. The sea could do that, could unify earth and sky. The sky over the earth was bereft, could not regard itself in the mirror of the sea, find itself rosily beautiful.

Not always beauty. The beach could be starkly ugly. The light muddy and neutral, overcast, the tide not in nor out and hard to know which way it traveled. The sea grumpy and recalcitrant. Sulking, midtide. It deceived, appeared to pause. Or ran away like a coward, a bully. Disappeared toward the far horizon and left everything scattered and stranded on the beach—translucent, twisted tails of weed or rope, expired jellyfish, flat with exhaustion—the sea departed as if it was a thief disturbed. Ebb tide spoke of death.

Sailors who died at sea had their tattoos cut off, the patches of skin brought back for their relatives. She heard these things as she heard the sea, without quite hearing them, as if they washed into her through her skin, soaked into her being. As if they had always been part of her and she could not rid herself of them.

Anna looked up to see if anyone else was aware of it. If anyone else knew that separate lives, separate worlds, could occur side by side, could mingle in every moment like night and day rolled into one. They were not. Miss Little and Miss Todd gazed not at each other but at her. Violet sat across the table and grinned at her with toothless gums. Lizzie Button pressed her to eat a slice of bread, to build up her strength. Put a morsel into her mouth with her own fingers. Anna pushed it out with her tongue when Lizzie turned away. Only Talitha Batt understood. And she was gone, stepped into her other life. Her real life.

In bed in the darkness, Anna prayed to Him to let her die properly. To allow her to depart her empty body. She was nothing more than a body. An irregular heartbeat. A series of painfully drawn breaths. She was a shell on the shore, the living creature inside gone. One night as she lay listening to her own breathing the hollow feeling gave way to a sense of enormity. Of a world inside herself that stretched backward and forward, that was impermeable, invulnerable. She was whole, peerless. They could do nothing at all to her, not now and not ever.

She lay holding the rough edge of the top sheet in both hands, pulled it up over her face in the darkness. Her self was contained within. The whole past was inside her, perfectly preserved, laid out in strange and awkward shapes like the world on the globe. She could turn it in her mind, fast or slow. Still it. It was always there. Even in her dreams, her world was inside her. When she was vomiting her innards into the tin bowl, it was not the least disturbed. Marriage had not enabled her to leave it behind or to forget. Nothing ever had or ever would. She could not mislay anything in her mind. She kept everything, inside, recorded for all time on a globe that spun faster and faster, whole continents of time whipping past, oceans of love, forests of regret and rocky hopes, all blurred and run together.

It was the next morning that he came. Restored to life, his flesh white against the pale sand, his eyes round and brown. He sat with his legs stretched out in front of him, festooning a sand castle with flags of weed, armoring its entrance with mussel shells. Anna could hear him breathing as he concentrated on sorting the shells, black and pink, large and small, whole and broken. The boy stood up, wandered into the shallows. His feet disappeared into the running waves. His hair blew in the wind and he laughed as the spray flew in the air, falling on him like rain. She watched as the water soaked his smock and the lace-edged waves rolled back, beckoning, sucking the ground from under him. That was her own voice, speaking to him. Calling his name. Anna heard herself laughing with delight and disbelief, and looked around.

The beach shifted, turned into a breakfast table. The rocks were loaves, the fish sprats, stranded on a platter. Button was watching her with eyes full of care. Anna looked around for the boy but he was gone. She heard herself calling his name. She was surprised.

"How do I know his name?" she asked.

Button shook her head. Her face dissolved, her teeth were made of chalk.

He came more and more. At the bottom of the cliff or the top, surrounded by flowers; sea lavender and tamarisk, samphire and saxifrage. The wind blew in his curling, fiery hair and carried away his voice. She strained to hear whether he laughed or screamed, whether it was he who cried out or the gulls gliding on the currents above. His voice and theirs mingled in the firmament. It was only above that anything was firm. That the stars were fixed in their proper places, ready to reappear each night.

There he was again, staring at the horizon. His chin pink with dribble. His legs planted in the sand. That lilt again. Running into the waves, not understanding what she understood, had always understood. His feet always wet. A governess voice. "Look at you, soaked through." The voice was pleased, liked the daring, the darling, the not-listening wildness of the boy. His boots with their own tide running over the toes in white wavy lines. His pantaloons sodden, chafing on white thighs.

He was in the bath in front of the fire, splashing with his fists, his little penis floating upward. In the morning before it grew light she heard him singing to himself. Long stretches of song like a skein of silk unraveling from his mouth. She listened from her dark bed, puzzling over the mystery of the roses, while he talked to companions unseen, in a language unknown.

Was it him she heard or was it the sea? Its persistent silent call, its hypnotic slush and splash, its irregular rhythm. Deceptive. Sly. She eavesdropped as it talked to itself, as it murmured and cursed and lamented. Its monologue echoed the one in her head, the wish sounds, the whispers, the sighings and drawings away, rushings toward and retreats. Sometimes, occasionally, the sea rejoiced.

Anna didn't know anymore if she remembered or imagined him. She didn't know where he came from or where he had gone. He was there. They lit fires between the rocks, threw pods of seaweed on the flames to hear them explode, shouted with fear and laughter. The next day, he was gone. Their fires, the charred sticks, the ash, the branched, burned strands of weed, washed away. The sea was its own night. It covered things over, forced forgetting. Erasure.

And now he came in ways not as shapely as memory. He came as a feeling, a feeling she would have missed if she hadn't been expecting him. Waiting for him. He was present in the smell of boiled milk. The sight of a round-tipped spoon or a pair of canvas shoes on the cloak-room floor. He appeared in her dreams. She was in the flint house at a round table with him on the other side in a high chair. His ears were too big for his head and his limbs pliable and pale. Clumsy.

He came as absence. Silence, where his voice had been. A morning blankness. Her bed was a ship adrift on the oak floorboards, the sea creaking and shifting all around, the wind rattling the windows, howling in the chimney. The roses obscured. Their mother, weeping in the dark. Antony.

Anna rose from the bed and felt with her toes for the slippers. The insides were cold, the leather damp. The room, the house, was silent. As she had so many times before, she pulled the blanket around her and dragged the chair to the window, looking out at the gleam of mauve on the horizon, the opalescent skies. The oak tree emerged from the dawn and waved to her, arms swaying above its fractured, anchored trunk. The bridge was there, still and waiting. Faithful.

She pressed her forehead against the glass as the birds began to sing. The loudness of their calls, the way they resounded in the air, made her think of spring.

THIRTY

The morning sun poured through the long, dusty windows, its abundance a reminder of grander, more expansive times. Vincent Palmer felt in his pocket and gripped the sovereigns between his fingers. He found the feel of money in his hands uniquely reassuring, despite the imperative not to *lay up treasures on earth*. He supposed money was the reason behind Abse's letter.

The maid nodded at the only empty chair and left without a word, as uninviting from the back as from the front. Vincent dusted his handkerchief over the seat and arranged himself in an attitude of relaxed alertness, his silver-topped cane standing between his knees, moustache newly blackened with a comb-in Colombian preparation. It was the day after Ash Wednesday and in the interests of humility he hadn't entirely erased the ashy cross from his forehead.

He wondered again why the fellow had written. If Abse intended to pronounce Anna cured, Vincent wouldn't stand for it. Even if Anna was restored to rationality, which he doubted, he couldn't risk returning her to the Vicarage before he had dealt with Maud, dispatched her and the boy back to Ireland. He would have to be firmer with Maud this time and make clear that it was to be a permanent move. There would be a better climate for the lad away from the noisome streets and morals of London. Unadulterated milk, bread, et cetera. He'd write, visit once a year if he could.

"'A virtuous woman is a crown to her husband,'" he said aloud, as the door opened. "'But she that maketh ashamed is as rottenness in his bones.' Good morning."

The entire household appeared to have lost the power of speech. Abse glanced at him as if his presence was no more than he expected and headed straight for his desk. Vincent didn't rise from the chair. He had to maintain God's dignity in his dealings with the world. He projected his voice across the acreage of frayed Persian rug.

"Bless you, Dr. Abse, for caring for the vulnerable on this earth. 'The righteous shall flourish as a branch.' How is my poor, dear wife?"

"It's Mister. Not Doctor. I expected you before now, Reverend. Didn't you get my message?"

"I received your note. I have been too occupied with the parish to travel out of London. I hope Mrs. Palmer is improving?"

Abse left his desk to stand in front of Vincent. His fists were clenching and reclenching and his hair, which he always wore coaxed up the sides of his head, was brushed downward. He looked older, Vincent noted with satisfaction.

"We run a quiet house, Reverend, for quiet patients. As I said in my letter, your wife will be better suited elsewhere."

"What are you trying to say, sir?"

Abse began to mither on about mania and a regrettable chain of events. Something about his own daughter, a foolhardy escape. The instrument, what was more, of a fatal incident. A clock in a far corner suggested that it was four-twenty. It wasn't later than ten. Vincent had departed early, intending to travel from Lake House straight to Sebastopol Street and discuss travel arrangements with Maud. She had written again to the Vicarage, the envelope reeking of violets. *As a jewel of gold in a swine's snout, so is a fair woman which is without discretion.*

Vincent used his pulpit voice to halt Abse midflow.

"I can hardly be blamed, sir, if an errant daughter takes it into her head to elope. I don't want the inconvenience of finding another establishment. My wife needs correction for her disturbed ideas but she is not a drooling idiot like some of the ones I saw here on my first visit. She is, after all, Mrs. Vincent Palmer. It takes a great deal to anger me but you, sir, risk doing just that."

"And I, Reverend, would be grateful if you'd settle your account with us," Abse said. "And take your wife away with you today."

Before the words were out of his mouth, the door burst open and a pitiful creature entered the room. The face was battered, the skin scabbed. At the sight of the head, Vincent flinched. He had the impression of a convict, bound for Australia.

"Vincent. You have come at last."

She came toward him and fell on her knees on the rug at his feet. He restrained himself with the greatest difficulty from using his cane to keep her at bay and looked around for Abse, who had left the room.

"I don't ask to come back to the Vicarage, Vincent," she said. "All I ask is that you get me out of this place. You can turn me onto the streets—I'll go to one of my other sisters, I'll find some employment somewhere. But don't leave me here."

Anna was rocking back and forth, begging him to have pity, making a display of herself. She prostrated herself in front of him.

"Vincent, please. I implore you."

Vincent leapt off the chair, almost tripped on a curling rug, and retreated to the far end of the room, pressing his back against a row of soft, disintegrating spines. He seized the bell on the desk and began shouting for assistance. He'd made a mistake about Anna. He had thought her overwrought, nervy—but it was now apparent that she was disturbed to the point of mania. The mother could have let him know as much before she passed away, if she had chosen. The sisters must have been in on it too. Deceivers all. The muttered objections to her removal from certain of his parishioners, his household, were offensive.

Abse returned, licked one finger and began riffling through papers at his desk.

"There's three months owing. Further amounts for the extra treatments. We are not a charity, Reverend."

Vincent felt in his pocket. He gripped the coins between his fingers to prevent any telltale chinking.

"In my hurry to see my unfortunate wife, Dr. Abse, I find I have left the house without funds. I regret to say that I cannot remove Mrs. Palmer at present since I am unable to settle the bill."

Anna wailed again and as she left the room, escorted by an attendant, looked at him for the first time. Amid the ruined flesh of her face, her eyes were clear, their curious blue-green shade more vivid than he'd noticed since the first time he met her. An uncomfortable twinge of remorse, like heartburn, rippled through Vincent's chest. He looked toward the heavens as he raised his hand in a gesture of farewell to her. He could not be expected to find words of comfort when she had distressed him so.

Alone with Abse again, Vincent felt his composure returning. He ran a finger along the stiff, smooth curves of his moustache and assured the chap that if further treatments were needed, he had no objection. It was more than he could stand, he said, to think of dear Anna lost to him in this way. Crueler than if she had died.

Abse appeared unconvinced by his display of solicitude.

"I won't keep you, Reverend. Your wife will remain here until you pay up. Not a day longer. Good day to you."

Vincent helped himself to his feet with his cane and settled his hat on his head as he settled the matter in his mind. Anna's eyes had been cool. Almost contemptuous. She hadn't lost her mind entirely and there was no knowing what she might do or say if released. He couldn't allow the Bishop to see her, despite His Lordship's pressing request.

"It may be some time before I am at liberty to return, Dr. Abse," he said. "It is Lent and I am much occupied with spiritual matters."

He departed down the hall, controlling a powerful urge to break into a run.

Querios Abse, back at his desk in the study, reclined in his chair and sighed. He wished he had never admitted Mrs. Palmer. The credentials of the doctors who'd signed the papers had struck him as bogus. And he hadn't liked the cut of Palmer's jib from the start. Pompous ass.

The thing with patients and their relatives, his father had drilled into him from as young as he could remember, was that it was business. It wasn't personal. Just business. It had become personal, with Mrs. Palmer. She had enraged him, stealing away from Lake House under his very nose and taking Catherine with her. Bringing the child back with a headful of foolish ideas. Dangerous ones.

Since her return, Querios hadn't wanted to treat Mrs. Palmer, he admitted to himself. He'd wanted to punish her. Frighten her. That was the only purpose the chair had ever served. Terror. He'd had recurrent nightmares about it as a boy, hearing the cries of the patients rising from the cellar. As a man he'd sworn to himself it would never be employed in any establishment he controlled. Mrs. Palmer had turned him into a monster. And if the magistrates saw the chair, he'd have no chance.

Querios pictured Reverend Palmer's smug face, heard again the way he addressed him as "Doctor," and a sharp ringing started up in his left ear. He was damned if he would discharge the Reverend's wife without getting the money he was owed.

He opened the study door and shouted for Fludd.

"Dismantle the chair," Querios said, when he arrived. "Put it back in the attic. On second thought, Fludd, burn the confounded thing."

The light was ideal, white and abundant and diffuse. Holy, Lucas St. Clair might have thought, if God hadn't shown himself at Balaclava not to exist. He put down his pipe on the bench and stepped into the dark cupboard. The silver bath was ready, the larger glass plates polished, free of dust or fingerprints. The new bottle of collodion had lost its milkiness and turned thin and translucent as whisky. It would pour clean and even over the glass. He pushed the cork back into the neck of the flask as the door to the fernery opened.

A woman in a bonnet stepped over the threshold, looked around her and appeared to sniff the air. She didn't see him behind the amber window of the cupboard. Walking to the far wall, she raised a hand and rubbed away a patch of condensation on the glass, peering out through a curtain of papery hydrangea heads on the other side. She straightened up and crossed the brick floor to the stove, hugging her arms around herself.

Lucas knew he ought to announce his presence to Mrs. Palmer but he felt reluctant to move. He had a sensation of his eyes as a lens, of the dark cupboard as a camera, and his whole self the sensitized plate receiving an impression.

He stepped out of the cupboard and her hands flew to her face.

"I'm sorry," he said. "I didn't mean to alarm you. . . ."

The woman lowered her hands. It wasn't she. It was another person, disfigured by livid green and purple bruises and with numerous dark scabs at her temples. Her skin was gray, her lips cracked. They'd sent someone else. He felt again the flooding sense of disappointment at the absence of Mrs. Palmer.

"I'm sorry. I was expecting another patient."

"Were you?"

He looked again. Her eyes were the color of the sea, vivid and startling in the light that bathed them both. He cleared his throat.

"I'm sorry. It's a pleasure to see you again, Mrs. Palmer. How are you?"

"My appearance shocks you, Dr. St. Clair."

"Yes. It does."

Abse had informed him that Mrs. Palmer had developed full-blown mania. Lucas hadn't believed his account of violent attacks inflicted on her own flesh, resistance to treatment. Mrs. Palmer showed no indications of mania in the previous portrait, only of a mild hysteria, and in talking to her, he'd found her perfectly rational.

It seemed that Abse might be right, for once. The injuries were dreadful. Could they really be the result of her own hand? He had a moment's sickening suspicion that they might not be and put the thought out of his mind. He wanted to make images of the patient as she truly was, he reminded himself. If that was the challenge, how she appeared was immaterial.

Mrs. Palmer was wandering around the walls of the old glasshouse, touching the tips of the new ferns that were beginning to curl their way out of the mortar.

"Sailors," she said, walking back toward him. "Sailors crave the sight of green things. The things of the earth. The world becomes more precious to those who are removed from it."

"Sailors may return," he said. "Find land again."

"Yes."

She was standing in front of him, close enough for him to see the expression in her eyes. He could see it but couldn't read it. A twig scratched at the glass roof and they both looked up.

"If you don't wish to be photographed now, Mrs. Palmer, I understand."

"Dr. St. Clair, I am more sane than I have ever been in my life. And yet—I look like a madwoman."

"No," he protested. "I don't think you do."

"It's alright. You needn't try to spare my feelings. I have a mirror. I know that I look like someone from a battlefield. And I know that my mind is in full health."

She sat down in the posing chair looking at him straight and steady. He'd grown used to the bruises and scabs. All he saw were her eyes. The shape of her mouth. He had another jolt of feeling that this time was desire for her. She was still beautiful.

"Make the picture. I have nothing to lose."

The light had shifted even since she arrived—become cooler and more blue.

"Last time we met, Mrs. Palmer, you said that you couldn't find yourself in the photograph I'd made of you."

"It wasn't me."

"I wanted to make another attempt."

"Please do."

"In that case, with your agreement, I would like to make a more detailed study of your face. Closer in and using a larger plate."

"My face?"

"Yes."

She untied the ribbon of her bonnet. Her head was covered with a plain white scarf; short locks of hair emerged at the sides and on her neck. The bruises and burns were more stark without the shade of the bonnet; his stomach lurched at the sight of them. Some looked indeed as if they might be the marks of his own profession. He resisted the urge to go to her, touch her. He was not a man in the company of a woman. He was a doctor testing a theory with a patient.

"Are you sure, Mrs. Palmer? Shall we proceed?"

She nodded, reached into her bodice and pulled a silver necklace over the high collar. It was a St. Christopher, small but solid-looking, the figure of the saint standing out in relief.

"I am ready, Dr. St. Clair."

The air was warmer under the camera's cloth. A paleness swam on the ground glass, soft-edged and luminous. Lucas tracked the lens, felt its reliable, familiar mechanism, pulled it steadily toward him until the outlines of eyes and cheeks and chin took shape. She did not fill the frame. He shifted the tripod forward and forward again until he was closer than he had ever been to anybody before, behind a camera, until her face filled the glass.

The crown of her head was resting on the bottom of it, the upward, even curve of her chin was at the top, with the silver medallion poised above like a full moon. He took his magnifying eyepiece to the ground glass. In her eyes, sections of the iris radiated from the pupils like the petals of a flower. Upside-down, he recognized in them the renewed appeal she was making to him. He wanted to respond to it. He wanted to help her. Tightening the focus knob, he emerged from the velvet tent and went into the dark cupboard to prepare the plate.

His hand shook as he poured the collodion, nursing one sharp corner between thumb and forefinger. He drained the excess back into the neck of the flask, clumsily, slid the plate into the silver bath and watched impatiently as it turned opaque and was ready for use. The picture he was about to make was going to tell the truth about Mrs. Palmer.

What it would be, he did not know.

The light dazzled Anna's eyes and the sound of the gravel underfoot hurt her ears. The sky was bigger than she'd ever realized and the airing grounds, that had once seemed constricted, now appeared vast. One wall was covered with a tangle of stems festooned with silvery seed heads. In front of it, plump scarlet hips and haws stood on the naked, thorny stalks of a rosebush. Underneath, a clump of snowdrops had pushed their way through the black earth, shown their modest white heads. Anna stared at them, wondering why she had never before seen the beauty of the plants with such clarity.

"It seems a little warmer," Mrs. Button said. She was waiting on the path in front of Anna.

"Yes." Anna's voice sounded rusty in her ear.

She caught up with Lizzie Button and walked behind her. The paths between the beds of shrubs weren't wide enough for two to walk comfortably together. Button's hair was growing. A dark line of it emerged below her bonnet and brushed the collar of her cape.

"I'm glad to see you regaining your strength, Mrs. Palmer," she said, over her shoulder.

"Thank you, Mrs. Button."

A robin was following them, bobbing from twig to twig. Button stopped and dug in her pocket, scattered crumbs on the ground. The bird landed on the gravel, claws splayed, and began to retrieve the scraps of bread with darting, nervous movements of its head.

"I envy him," said Button. "He can fly away."

"We will be free one day," Anna said, with a sudden, strong sense that it was true. "You will and I will."

Button sighed.

"You have your life ahead of you. Every day is a torment to me. Every minute of every day."

She resumed walking and Anna followed.

"Mrs. Button, I've wanted for a long time to express my condolences."

Button's back stiffened. "For what?"

"The infant you lost."

Button groaned. "What do you mean, Mrs. Palmer? My son's one year old, strong and well."

"I'm so sorry. You used to grieve so . . . I thought he must be lost."

Button turned to face Anna, looking unlike any Lizzie Button she had ever seen before. Her cheeks were flushed, her eyes shining.

"Of course I grieve. I was dragged from him when he was just two weeks old. They brought me here. I've got three other children. Girls. My oldest's nearly seven. I miss her even more than the baby."

"I didn't know," Anna said. "Forgive me."

Button lifted her shoulders in the navy cape, lowered them, and shook her head.

"I don't like to speak of them. Not in here. They are the dearest and best girls you could imagine, Mrs. Palmer. My angels."

They carried on walking. Four children. The same as Louisa. She couldn't have imagined Button had a family, people relying on her. She hadn't seen her as a woman with a life before Lake House. A life after it. How could she have been so blind?

"What is your son's name, Mrs. Button?"

"Albert."

They paused by a bush covered with pale starlike flowers while Mrs. Button bent to her bootlace. On the far side of the beds, Miss Todd stood like a statue, holding her palms toward the sky. Miss Little had gone, exiled by an uncle to Colney Hatch. A crow shrieked out of sight and Lizzie Button straightened up, snapped off a sprig from the bush, and tucked it into Anna's buttonhole.

"I always wondered about you, Mrs. Palmer. About why you were here."

Anna breathed in the intense sweetness of the buds. Sighed.

"For a long time, all last year, I had a vision of a boy, drowning. After the great storm, I heard of a boy brought from the water still breathing. I went to the site of the wrecked ship, trying to find him. Offer assistance. My husband thought—he believed I must be in a disturbed state of mind." The words sounded alien to Anna, as if someone else spoke them. Why was she here? She had never truly understood.

"And did you? Find him?"

"He wasn't there. I still see him, Mrs. Button, but he's alive now. Playing. Singing."

Anna smiled at her and Button nodded, her bonnet slipping back and forth on her head.

"You appeared so disturbed when you arrived. You shunned company. Didn't put two words together at table. We all thought you'd committed a crime."

"What kind of crime?"

Button hesitated.

"Murder, some of them said. Don't take it too hard, Mrs. Palmer. I didn't believe it, nor did the late Talitha."

Anna began to frame her objections, ask how they could possibly have imagined such things, and stopped. She must have appeared strange, with her refusal to talk to anyone, her conviction that she was utterly unlike any other woman there. Her belief that her husband would see sense and come for her, or that her sister would rescue her, had been deluded. Anna felt a fleeting pity for the self that had first come to Lake House.

It began to rain, a drizzly dampness settling on their bonnets and shoulders, and the gate on the other side of the airing grounds opened. Lovely waved, her shawl drawn up over her head. It was strange that Anna had thought Lovely plain when they first met. She wasn't plain. She was vivid and strong and alive, standing in the rain, frowning and gesticulating.

"Come along, my beauties. Yer'll catch yer death."

Miss Todd and Mrs. Button went ahead and Lovely and Anna walked behind them. Heavy splashes began to fall as they hurried along the side of the house, soaking through Anna's cotton scarf, wetting her cheeks, mixing with the tears that were falling again, onto the soaked gravel. Lovely took her arm. Everyone seemed to believe she needed an arm to lean on.

"Alright, miss?"

"When I get out of here, Lovely, will you come with me?"

"To the Vicarage?"

"No. I'm never going back there."

"Where, then?"

"I don't know, yet. I'll know soon." She would know soon, Anna felt sure. Things were changing in her as surely as they were changing in the winter garden. "Will you, Lovely?"

"I might do. You've got visitors inside, miss. Gentlemen."

Lovely helped her out of her cloak and up the stairs, then showed her into the dining room.

The table looked naked without the oilcloth and two men were sitting at it with their backs to the sideboard. Both got to their feet as she closed the door behind her and reached out their hands to shake hers.

"Mrs. Palmer?" said the older one.

"Yes. I'm Anna Palmer."

"Dr. Frank Fairclough. This is my colleague Dr. Brewer. Mrs. Palmer, please accept our apologies. Your sister asked us some time ago to call on you but we understand from Mr. Abse that you have not been well enough to see visitors."

Dr. Fairclough was ruddy-cheeked, one eye drooping below the other. He had a rumpled, human look about him, as if he had known trouble himself and might be able to sympathize with other people's. His good eye regarded her with intensity as Anna pulled out a chair and sat down opposite the two men. Dr. Brewer, young enough to be Dr. Fairclough's son, looked at Anna with undisguised pity.

She addressed herself to the older man, propping her elbows on the scarred mahogany and clasping her fingers together.

"Is that what Mr. Abse told you? At any rate, I am quite well now."

"Do you feel strong enough to answer questions?" said Dr. Brewer, his voice gentle. "Mrs. Heron hoped that we could ascertain your state of mind. She has asked us to help you."

"We are indeed here to help you, Mrs. Palmer," said Dr. Fairclough. "At the same time, you will appreciate that we are doctors. That if we find you to be unwell, we will be under a professional duty to report that fact."

Anna looked at the black-and-white photographs on the wall next to the fireplace. Her eye came to rest on the portrait of Violet Valentine, her bird cupped in her hands. These men could help her, of that she felt sure. Could help any one of them. She pictured Talitha Batt as she had been at the sideboard, on the very first morning after Anna had arrived. Heard again the pain in Lizzie's voice not half an hour earlier, when she spoke of her children.

"There is something you can do to help me."

"If we can, we will," said the younger one.

"There is nothing wrong with my mind." She looked across the table at them, steadily, meeting Dr. Fairclough's good eye. "Nothing at all. But there is someone else in this place who urgently requires your aid. Will you interview her as well as me?"

Dr. Fairclough laughed.

"Mrs. Palmer, we are not here to consult with every inmate. Only to assess your own state of mind."

"The fees cover only one consultation," Dr. Brewer said. "And this is the third time we have made the journey. Does the lady have means?"

"No, I don't believe she does."

Anna made a decision. She rose, clenched her nails into the palms of her hands, and before she could change her mind walked toward the door of the dayroom. She put her head around the door. Makepeace wasn't there nor Mr. Abse. She went to Lizzie, took her hand and led her into the room.

"They're doctors, Lizzie. Proper doctors. They can pronounce you well." Anna turned to the men. "Her need is more urgent than mine. Please tell my sister that I shall free myself in my own way. She needn't worry."

Closing the dining room door behind her, she went to the window seat of the dayroom. She sat down and stared at the pictures on the wall opposite, at LM in her convalescence, feeling as bleak as at any time since she had first arrived.

THIRTY-ONE

Lucas St. Clair had brought the plate back to Popham Street in one piece. He'd fixed it that same night and applied a coat of varnish in the calm and order of his own darkroom, inhaling the scent of lavender oil and sandarac as the flame of the spirit lamp flickered over her mouth, her eyes. It was important not to let the glass get too hot when drying the varnish. It could crack or the edges could burn your fingers, impelling you to drop it. He did not want to drop her. He had the sense that the plate, in some primitive way that contradicted the scientific nature of the medium, that the plate *was* her.

Sitting on the stool, holding it carefully by the edges, he marveled at the way her face filled the large sheet of glass. Wondered if it had been proper to approach as close as he had. He felt as if through the medium of the camera he had touched Mrs. Palmer, held her face in his hands.

When the weekend arrived, he made a dozen sheets of albumen paper, coating them with egg white and salt that had been strained and strained again then left for a week to cure. Stickles made egg nog from the yolks, had the hiccups all Sunday. The papers dried smooth and glossy. Lucas brushed on the silvers, freshly mixed, one midweek night after work. He saw the pearly patina in the amber light of the dark chamber, sniffed its blank promise, and marked the backs in pencil with a cross. Having flattened each piece in the press, he stored the sheets in a light tight box interleaved with blotting paper.

And then he had hesitated. Opportunities came and went; fine days passed unexploited. The picture mattered too much to him, he dimly perceived. When he had made the print, he would have to look at it and analyze it, not as a photograph but as a means of diagnosis. And that was the difficulty. Everything about the way Mrs. Palmer looked on the plate suggested mania. But in his heart, he did not believe she was suffering from mania.

The talk to the Alienists' Association was only weeks away. Mrs. Palmer awaited his findings. He could not delay any longer. On a sun-warmed Saturday morning a full fortnight after his visit to Lake House, he pulled on a pair of cotton gloves and brought down the printing frame. The box of sensitized paper. The plate itself. In the yard at the back of the house, he secured the plate on top of the paper in the frame and offered the whole contraption up to the light, balanced on an old trestle left by a previous tenant. The sun fell on his own face as he waited in the shelter of the south-facing wall. He closed his eyes and offered his winter-white flesh to its rays. It was March; the days were getting longer. A leggy shrub blossomed on the far wall; a crop of gold flowers, sodden by the previous night's rain, lay on the stones underneath.

He watched through the glass as the paper began to respond to the light, darkening under the clear parts of the plate. He felt the habitual anxiety about making a successful print; the trick was to leave it long enough for the blacks to become richly black but not so long that the whites became fogged. After half an hour, he pulled out the paper and slid it into a tray of hyposulfate to halt its development. With a pair of tongs, he began to agitate the paper, rocking the edge of the dish, sending liquid in waves over Mrs. Palmer's face. The photograph looked almost larger than life, as clear as a pre-Raphaelite painting by one of the disciples of realism. Her eyes stared at him from underwater, then they darkened and were lost. Overexposed. He went back upstairs to wash his hands then came down and tried again.

The second print was still too dark and the following attempt too light—revealing just a pair of eyes on the paper and the medallion at her neck. The St. Christopher medallion, the old man bent over a staff, a child on his shoulders. Lucas stopped, arrested by the odd nature of the image. He would keep it. The accidental could be interesting. His next attempt was scuppered by a blemish in the weave of the paper. He carried on. The problems that arose in printing were ones that could be solved—technical issues that demanded nothing more from him than steady effort and patience. The larger challenge, proving the truth of the theory, lay ahead.

He plunged the fourth print into the fix and rocked the dish, willing the image to respond to the cyanide, to cease responding to light, to remain as it was. It did. He carried it upstairs and set it to wash. Mrs. Palmer floated under the surface, bobbing up with the flow of the water, rising as if for air. Her irises were a rich brown black, the whites of her eyes clean and bright, the lashes separate and stark as pen lines. The grain of her skin was a fine, silvery sand. Her parted lips, their outline slightly darker, looked as if they might speak. The light on her face was stronger from one side, illuminating the curve of her cheek, the highlights on it, and casting the other into a graded shadow.

The bruises and scabs defaced her. Abse had said they were self-inflicted but seeing them on the print, looking at them under the magnifying glass, Lucas doubted it. The scabs were blister marks, clumsily inflicted and kept open too long. Higgins was a disgrace to the profession. The old charlatan ought to have retired years ago. The bruises ranged in a row on her cheeks looked like fingerprints from a hand a great deal larger than her own.

The fumes in the darkroom were making him nauseous. He pegged the print on the line strung across the bench, made his way downstairs and threw himself in the wing chair. He lit a match with wrinkled, waterlogged fingertips and held the flame to the tobacco in the bowl of the pipe as Stickles entered the room.

"Didn't you hear me knock, sir?"

"Hello, Stickles. Didn't hear a thing."

She handed him a plateful of anchovy toast. He took a bite and grimaced as he felt the sticky paste on the roof of his mouth.

Lucas tapped ash out on the side of the plate and got up to pour himself a whisky, appreciating its clean, deep sting on his tongue and in his throat. He'd made the image he dreamed of making. Now, all he had to do was interpret it by comparing the signs on Mrs. Palmer's face with those in the textbooks. He fetched his dog-eared copy of Morison from the shelf and sat with it on his knees. He expected to open

The Physiognomy of Mental Diseases, study the illustrations within its pages and compare them to the face of Mrs. Palmer, looking for the signs of mania, the peculiar expression of the countenance and the eyes that the physician described. But he found that he could not.

Anna stood at the sideboard, rubbing the back of a spoon with a rag loaded with a paste of salt, vinegar and flour. She'd taken on some of the small jobs that Talitha used to do—cleaning silver, stacking plates, sweeping the hearth. She found relief in it, the same relief that she now understood Miss Batt must have obtained. It enabled her for minutes at a time to forget where she was.

She heard the dining room door open and looked up to see Catherine's mother, Mrs. Abse, coming from the dayroom. She looked as if she limped but watching her Anna realized that she did not. It was more that her entire locomotion seemed impeded and difficult. She reached Anna, her face creased in a frown, and stood next to her. Mrs. Abse looked down at the cleaned spoons lying in a nest and picked up one.

"Good afternoon, Mrs. Palmer," she said. "I hoped to find you alone." She put down the spoon and looked at Anna.

"It's my daughter, Catherine. Would you talk to her? Try to bring her to her senses? I am so terribly worried about her."

Anna licked her dry lips. She'd been afraid that Mrs. Abse bore some sinister message from Querios Abse. Anna's fear of the chair was ever present, even though the treatments had ceased as suddenly as they began.

"Catherine?" she said. "I'd like nothing more than to see her. What ails her, Mrs. Abse?"

"I wish I knew. Would you mind coming now? I see you are occupied but it's just that my husband is . . ."

A harsh noise sawed into the air from the other end of the room as Makepeace cleared her throat.

"Do you think that's advisable?"

They both turned to face Makepeace as she crossed the floor, from the other door.

231

Emmeline Abse's voice was suddenly surprisingly commanding.

"If I didn't think it advisable, Fanny, I wouldn't be suggesting it. Please attend to your duties. If you can." She looked back at Anna, her tone softened, almost pleading. "If you wouldn't mind coming with me, Mrs. Palmer?"

The Abse parlor was shabbier than Anna might have imagined. The piano lid was open to reveal yellowed ivories, thinned at their tips. A cracked glass case held a half-melted posy of wax flowers, and the mantles of the lamps were obscured by soot. Catherine lay back on a chaise longue. She wore a wintry green dress that hung off her thin frame and had a large shawl pinned around her shoulders despite the warmth of the room. Beside her on a low table was a plate of black grapes. Anna tightened the cotton scarf over her head as she walked toward her.

"Hello, Catherine."

Catherine clapped her hands, half rose from where she lay, and sank down again.

"Where have you been, Mrs. Palmer? And what on earth has happened to your hair?"

She looked too fragile to hug; Anna bent and brushed her cheek with her lips, took her cold hands in hers. Catherine's pearl ring was slipping off her finger and her nails were tinged with blue.

"I wanted to come and see you before but I wasn't permitted."

Mrs. Abse retreated toward the door.

"I'll leave you girls to talk."

Catherine and Anna looked at each other, Catherine's eyes glistening with unshed tears.

"What has my father done to you, Mrs. Palmer?"

"I'm alright, Catherine. The treatments are over now, you needn't worry about me. But what's happened to you? Have you been ill?"

Catherine averted her eyes. Her ears poked through her hair; her white skin was dry.

"Nothing's *happened* to me. I'm conquering my appetites, Mrs. Palmer."

She held out the plate of grapes. "Have some. I had to promise to finish these."

Anna took one and felt its cool, moist plumpness between her fingers.

"You look ill."

"I am so tired of being talked to about myself. Where's your hair? You were so pretty before."

Anna put her hands to her head again and felt the bristles through the cotton scarf.

"My hair will grow back. It's already starting to."

She ate the grape and handed a stem of them to Catherine. Catherine picked one off, began to peel it in irregular strips, licking her fingers as she went.

"Have you finished 'Aurora Leigh'?" Anna said. "Would you like me to read aloud to you?"

"Not really. I don't want to finish it." Catherine put the peeled grape down on the plate and they sat in silence. Catherine's face was wistful, lit on one side by the light from the parlor windows. Anna felt a twinge of guilt. She hadn't thought much about Catherine since they returned and the girl was so altered it was as if months, not weeks, had passed.

"Catherine, please. Tell me what's the matter."

"You might as well go now if you only want to bully me."

"I don't. I want to help you if I possibly can. We're friends, aren't we?"

Catherine giggled and for a moment she looked girlish, like herself again.

"We were sisters for three days. I wish it had been longer. You're the only sister I ever had."

Anna lifted her hand and kissed it. Catherine sighed.

"Talk to me, Mrs. Palmer. I have never known the truth about another human being."

"I haven't either."

"You must have done. Having all those sisters. A husband."

"No. I don't think I ever have. I never really had a husband. And my sisters were much older than me. I've always felt alone, especially when I was a child."

"You could take up reading. The people in books never desert you."

"Catherine?"

"Yes?"

"Was it the Fasting Girl? What happened, when you saw her? Did she speak to you?"

Catherine nodded, twisting her ring, pushing the pearl to the back of her finger and around to the front again. "There was a man there most of the time but I was alone with her for a minute at the end. She spoke to me then."

"What did she say?"

Catherine stared down at her hands, her face a deepening pink.

"She asked if I had any food. She said she was starving. I went out and bought a baked potato for her. When I came back, the man wouldn't let me in. I tried to get past him, I told him she only wanted to warm her hands on it, but he chased me away. He threatened to call the police."

"The poor woman. She looked half dead, in that picture we saw."

"She is dead. I read about her in my father's newspaper. She died on the boat on the way back to America."

A clock somewhere out of sight chimed gently as Catherine sat back in the chair and looked at Anna defiantly. Anna felt a surge of frustration with her and checked it. She made her voice neutral.

"Why are you trying to be like her?"

"I don't know."

"Fasting isn't living, Catherine. It's more like dying. What happened to all the adventures you planned?"

Emmeline, passing the time in the sewing room while Mrs. Palmer was with Catherine, couldn't settle. She went to the window, sat down, rose again. She couldn't take up her mending or close her eyes for a doze. A door banged farther down the passage and she jumped up and put her head round the door to make sure Querios hadn't returned early. The corridor was empty—she saw only Hannah's skirts sailing around the landing and down the stairs.

She returned to the sewing room window. She half expected the gray sky outside to come collapsing down on all their heads. The old oak tree, the line of waving willows by the lake, seemed unaware of her transgression, unaware that on this ordinary day the world had turned upside-down. She reached into her sewing bag and took a drop of laudanum, squeezing the pipette over her open mouth. Querios would not be back until suppertime. There was nothing to fear.

Catty had left her book balanced on top of the chest. Emmeline picked it up and felt the weight of the thick pages in her hands, the soft binding. The pages were falling away from the spine. It was Catherine's favorite, "Aurora Leigh."

She opened it at random and began to read.

> *For he, a boy still, had been told the tale*
> *Of how a fairy bride from Italy*
> *With smells of oleanders in her hair*
> *Was coming through the vines to touch his hand.*

She put down the book. Ben was right. Catherine needed to travel. She would take her, herself. They would go to Italy. The thought made Emmeline feel tall and straight. Just to think it changed something inside as if already she had traveled to a strange land and become a more intrepid version of herself.

They would go on a tour. If she had to defy Querios's wishes, so be it. She was past the age where it befitted a woman to obey her husband's every wish. She had that advantage at least.

THIRTY-TWO

From the dark garden, Emmeline saw a light burning in the study. Querios was still in there.

He was demoralized by the death of the bird. He had come back late from his appointment with the accountant and found the silver peacock lying on the ground in the run. He came indoors with it, holding it in his hands, brought it right into the bedroom as Emmeline was getting dressed for dinner, gazing at it, shaking his head and repeating that it was still warm, that he didn't understand. There were no marks on it—nothing at all appeared to be wrong with it.

He'd cursed the fox all through dinner, reached again and again to have his tankard refilled by Hannah Smith, despite the looks Emmeline shot him from the other end of the table. She'd wanted to raise the trip with him before the meal, must inform him of her plan before speaking of it to Catherine—but she couldn't.

Catty looked fragile at the supper table, like a creature newly born that had not yet grown its skin or fur, the layer it needed to be able to live in the world. She'd rallied after the visit from Mrs. Palmer but eating her own supper Emmeline had been certain she saw Catherine's hand move to her sleeve. She suspected it concealed slices of ham.

Now, at close to midnight, Emmeline pulled her cloak tighter around herself and crept around the wall of the house, walking on the compromised ground where the grass met the gravel in a messy scatter, feeling the stones through the soles of her satin slippers. She'd hardly known what she pulled onto her feet but she recognized them by the narrow fit, could see their gleam in the starlight.

Until five minutes ago, she'd been in bed—listening for the creak of the floorboard, the squeak of the sash window, the muffled thump as it slid back down the runners. She was praying that she would not hear them, tonight. When they came, she got out of bed in the dark almost as if she sleepwalked and made her way down to the side door, turned the key.

Catherine's window was on the south side of the house. Emmeline crouched down and began to feel around on the ground, moving her fingers underneath fallen leaves, tracing the sinewy roots of the magnolia. She felt something clammy and jumped with fright as it leapt out from under her hand. A frog. She wiped her fingers on her cloak, trying to rid her skin of the memory of the cold, moist contact. She resumed the search and found nothing. No ham. No biscuits or bones. Only stones.

Her knees hurt. She stood up and stooped down to rub them, glanced up at the window. She felt as if someone was watching her. It was impossible. Catty would have had to be leaning right out of the upper window in order to see her underneath. Turning to go back indoors, she heard a rustling in the shrubbery. Had Catherine thrown something over there? Emmeline stepped over the grass and parted the stiff architecture of the rhododendrons with her hands, feeling a branch catch at her hair.

She got down on all fours again and crawled underneath the canopy, reading the damp, soft earth with her fingertips. She inched onward, absorbing the chill into her hands and breathing in the smell of decay and life mixed. The shoes, her best ones, were pinching her toes. She kicked them off and sat back on her heels with a perverse satisfaction at the idea of the oyster satin smeared with leaf mold, the rosettes from the Paris atelier unraveled.

The explosion startled her—the noise so close by it seemed almost upon her. She couldn't immediately think what it was. In the silence that followed, it came to her. Querios was out with his gun. He was drunk. Could hurt himself. She grabbed hold of a branch over her head and began to pull herself to her feet but the branch bowed under her weight, shook and bent to the ground. The gunshot came again like a series of sharp, coordinated fireworks and she lurched over on her side, sprawling on the ground. She heard her own scream, harsh as the cry of the fox. Reaching into the darkness, she put her hand to her leg and found it sticky and hot. The pain was so extraordinary, so unbounded, it brought the same awe as she'd felt in childbirth, that a human body could contain such agony.

The explosions had ceased and been replaced by the sound of feet running on gravel. Someone shouted her name and she became aware of a disturbance, close by, of the branches. A swinging lamp. Querios's face loomed over hers, close enough to kiss. She reached up and touched him. Her fingers left a bloody mark on his cheek.

"Q," she said as she passed out. "It's you."

Anna sat at the breakfast table, daydreaming about the clifftop at Dover, in spring. Covered in wildflowers, a tangle of scarlet poppies, of bee orchids, daisies, celandines, mallow. She felt the upward spring of the ground underfoot and sniffed in the strong, earthy fragrance. Heard the sea far down below, hushed and tamed by distance, mixed with the human-sounding agitation of the curlews. Saw herself, walking toward the lighthouse. With Lucas St. Clair.

She looked up. Makepeace was watching her from the far door, which led along the treatment corridor. It was late. The sounds from downstairs—china being stacked in a stone sink, brooms banging on the skirting boards, the clink of cinders in dustpans—had ceased. The voices had fallen quiet too; the others were gone, departed for the airing grounds. The two of them were alone, surrounded by silence and sunlight.

Querios Abse hadn't been seen for three days. There had been comings and goings downstairs, raised voices and hushed ones. Anna had been worried about Catherine but Lovely shook her head when she asked. It was Mrs. Abse, she said. She'd had an accident. She was confined to the Abse quarters, being waited on by her daughter. Mr. Abse had ordered fresh beef tea made every morning. He was hanging around in the parlor, the dining room. Calling Dr. Higgins out to her every day. He hadn't set foot in his office. None of them had been paid, come Friday. Mrs. Makepeace was in charge, as far as they knew.

Lovely had brought Anna a different dress that morning. It had a heavy black skirt and bodice that looked as if it might once have belonged to Makepeace herself. She could put it on or stay in her room, was the message that came with it. Anna was wearing it now. She shuddered again at the feeling of it, the fabric coarse and greasy against her skin.

Makepeace approached her.

"What are you doing, still here? You ought to have gone out with the others."

Makepeace was standing so close behind her that Anna could feel the woman's breath on the back of her neck. Her spine prickled.

"I'm just sitting here. Thinking."

Makepeace laughed a scornful laugh.

"Well, Mrs. Palmer, I'm sure you've got plenty to think about."

Anna turned around to face her.

"Why do you hate me?"

"I don't hate you. I don't feel anything at all about you. Guests come and go. We remain. The staff and the family."

Anna pushed her plate away. The kidney had grown cold; it sat there, rubbery and dead-looking, on the crazed china.

"Mrs. Makepeace, I'd like to have my own dress to wear. The old velvet one that I had when I first came here. Could you send it up for me? I can launder it myself if necessary."

"Mr. Abse doesn't buy good food just to have it fed to the pigs, Mrs. Palmer. Eat your breakfast and forget about your pretty dresses."

"It's not a question of it being a pretty dress. Don't you understand? It's just that it's mine, Makepeace, and I feel better when I wear my own clothes. I want it back."

"I want it back." Makepeace imitated her accent, exaggerating the Kentish lilt. "We all want things back, Palmer," she said. "But we don't always get them."

Anna lifted her tin mug and took a mouthful of water. She felt strong again. Stronger than she ever had, she understood with a faint sense of surprise. She would not allow Makepeace to bully her.

"If you have no sympathy with the patients, you have no business working in a place like this, Makepeace. I am going to do something about it when I get out of here."

Makepeace came toward her again.

"You're not going to get out. You've let down your husband. Your family don't want you."

Under the coffee, the other smell leaked from the pores of her skin, strong and sweet. Anna sniffed it and glanced up at the set face, the folded arms. She understood something about Makepeace and felt an unexpected pity for her. Her voice, when she spoke, was soft.

"My family do want me, in their own way. It's yours, isn't it, Mrs. Makepeace? It's your family that don't want you. I'm sorry."

As their eyes met, Makepeace raised one hand and slapped her face. Tears of shock sprang to Anna's eyes. She stared straight ahead of her, willing them not to fall.

"You can't hurt me, Makepeace. Nothing you can do can hurt me."

Makepeace lunged forward again and swung her arm at Anna's head—so hard and fast that Anna fell off the chair. She sprawled on the floor among the crumbs and the dust, her head spinning with the impact. Getting to her feet, she rubbed the arm that she'd fallen on, felt her face with her fingers.

"Give me my dress back."

Makepeace had stationed herself at the sideboard and was slinging spoons one by one into the wooden cutlery box.

"Make yourself scarce," she hissed. "Get out."

Alone in the dayroom, her head still reeling, Anna picked up a magazine and sat down with her hand pressed over her aching jaw. She tried to re-enter her daydream of Dover in spring but the mood had gone. She sat, staring into space. She'd allowed herself to believe that Dr. St. Clair would come back, that he would pronounce her well and her mind as whole as she knew it to be. That he would call Abse into his own study and tell him there had been a mistake and that if he wanted a certificate of her sanity Dr. St. Clair would sign it himself, photograph or no photograph. Lucas St. Clair hadn't come. Nothing she hoped for, longed for, occurred. She closed her eyes and begged for a sign of what she should do.

The others trickled back into the room, talking loudly, their voices and faces enlivened by the air. Mrs. Featherstone was joking with Violet. From across the room, Lizzie smiled at her. Anna roused herself. The sign had not come. She'd prayed in vain.

The magazine was still on her lap. It was a new one, only a month old. She found herself reading about a ship moored in a northern port called Liverpool. The ship remained at anchor at all times, a mission for sailors. There was a chapel in what had been the captain's quarters, bunks where they could sleep. They could get food or a new pair of boots, collect their letters or find someone to write one for them. She read the article from the first word to the last and when she'd finished she sat and stared at the engraving of the chapel. "Unto Us a Child Is Born" it said, carved into the rafter over the heads of the sailors.

There would be a purpose for her in a place like that. Even if she did what Lovely did—washed floors, served meals, fetched and carried. Talked to people and treated them like human beings. *I have work for you.* The idea was a lodestar, a point by which to orient herself. She tore out the pages and, as she folded them into the ugly bodice, breathed in the sharp, hopeful tang of newsprint mixed with the stale pall of the fabric.

Makepeace would not triumph over her. Nor Vincent. Nor Abse. Anna got out her embroidery and began to stitch, her mind racing. By the time the bell rang for luncheon, the cambric was worked all over with a small, auburn-haired child in flight, jumping from the rocks onto floating chunks of chain stitch in white silk. She'd done the work without knowing she did it, without a picture in her mind and what had presented itself was her vision. The boy. It was almost finished. She tied a knot, bit off the thread and followed the others back into the dining room. The air was warm, sweet with the smell of baking buns rising from the kitchen.

THIRTY-THREE

Lucas St. Clair cleared a bowl of walnut shells plus several piles of *Medical Times and Gazette* and the *Photographic News* off the table and dumped them on the floor. Dusting the table with a napkin, he looked at the window and contemplated cleaning the glass. It would take too long. He'd come to his dining room for the light, wanted to see what he was doing by the clear, white light of day. Filtered amber—the forgiving yellow tinge of the dark chamber—was unscientific. He set down a stack of photographs and began arranging them in lines.

When he had finished, he turned his back on them and stood at the window looking out into the small garden without seeing it. The smell of boiling citrus was coming up from the kitchen, making his eyes water. Life went on. Marmalade would appear and Stickles would hold the jar upside-down, remark on the superior setting qualities of Seville oranges. Maddox would marry. Produce small, broken-toothed versions of himself. Birthdays would roll around. The next was his thirtieth and he wanted it behind him.

Life would go on for him—would continue to race, amble and lope along. *Screw your courage to the sticking point! Summon the blood!* His father's voice would continue to echo in his ears, urging his sons to feats of bravery in sailing boats, among birds' nests, on horses. Bellowing at them as they lined up their tin soldiers to advance. Advance.

Lucas had taken the month off from St. Mark's. He'd informed Harry Grieve that he had to have time to build up the evidence for his ideas. They'd been in a corridor at the time and there had been an incident on one of the noisy wards; shouts and screams of patients and keepers

242

echoed off the tiled walls, bounced in the air. He'd run into Grieve by chance and known as he saw him coming toward him that he must act. He stood in front of him, blocking his progression.

"I have to take a sabbatical, Sir Harry. I need time to work on my theory. If the ideas hold good, I intend to change my practice and use photography in diagnosis with every patient." He'd had to raise his voice to be heard but as he was halfway through, the commotion on the ward died down. His own voice was the only one ringing out along the corridor. "I'm not willing to continue working like this. I believe we are selling patients short."

"You may be better fitted to a different kind of establishment, St. Clair," Grieve said, frostily. He sighed and clapped him on the back. "Although I grant that you've done good work here, young man. Excellent work, in its way. I'll get another chap in for a month and after that we'll talk again. I wish you all the best with your experiments, misguided though they are. Enjoy your holiday."

Since that morning, he had worked harder than at any time since his university finals. Every shirt he owned was stained with silvers and his fingers looked as if he wore black gloves. He had barely slept but he didn't feel tired. He was on a campaign.

He had made photographs of his sister, Beth. Of Stickles. Of his cousins, the twins Melody and Melissa. His godmother sat for him and his next-door-but-one neighbor in Popham Street, a lawyer's wife keen on watercolors who always expressed interest in the sun paintings, as she termed them. He didn't quarrel with her, hadn't time to explain that they were not paintings, that that was the whole point of photography. He'd made images of the woman's eighty-year-old mother and the mother's French companion. At Lake House, he photographed the most recent patient, Mrs. Jane Featherstone, followed by Mrs. Button, again, Mrs. Valentine and—at the specific request of Mrs. Abse—her daughter, Catherine. The girl couldn't have been less like her father.

He'd made visits to the two other private asylums in which he had permission to make images and photographed women with hysteria, epilepsy, puerperal fever. Mania and habits of intemperance.

In all, there were thirty portraits. The beauty of them, their scientific significance, was that he'd made every image using the large-format plates measuring eight by ten inches and had photographed every sitter in the same way as Mrs. Palmer. Persuaded each to wear a white scarf over their hair and a plain, dark gown. Free of props, against a blank background, only their faces spoke from inside the oval frames. No recent coiffure or flash of diamonds or intrusion of potted palms contributed to the statement of the mind of each individual.

Once he'd made all the images, he'd set about printing them. He'd had to buy the albumen paper ready-made. It was expensive and not as good as the paper he prepared himself but it was adequate. The cost of materials had cleared him out. He'd told Stickles there was no money for meat this month or coffee. Only whisky, bread and cheese and whatever she needed for herself downstairs.

He was allowing himself an early drink. He took a mouthful and picked up the first picture. It was his sister, Beth. Her pointed, doubtful face, as large as life, gave him a sense of looking more closely at her than she had intended or allowed. He could see in her downcast eyes the signs of incipient melancholy. He replaced the picture and picked up the next one.

Violet Valentine. He brought her closer to the window. Her skin blurred at its edges as if the wrinkles reached into the atmosphere around her, as if her face was not flesh but time. Her bird had died at New Year and despite the acquisition of a replacement, Violet had not been the same since. Next on the pile was one of the patients from The Laurels, the asylum south of the river. Her name was Sunday. There was a rueful, resigned understanding in her eyes that Lucas might have construed as wisdom. Yet this was a woman who'd taken the life of her own child.

The restrictions he'd imposed—the close perspective, the white scarf over the hair and dark gown below—had the opposite effect from what he'd expected. Instead of making the women look more similar, the restricted palette accentuated the differences between them. His neighbor, the artist Mrs. Mallinson, had presented herself as a beatific, eyes raised to a far horizon—looking at God himself, if the fervor of the expression was to be believed. Stickles looked out with dancing eyes; her expression, vivid and mischievous, mimicked mania. Stickles had started to cook. She'd taken to bringing up soups on trays, dishes of roast potatoes, bread and butter pudding, homely fare that she said cost next to nothing and claimed would do him good.

He'd brought the picture of Talitha Batt downstairs although he was undecided over whether it belonged in the set or not. Looking at it took him back to that day at Lake House. He'd wanted to leave the whole sorry business behind but had made himself stay. Waited while Lovely cleaned her, scrubbed the walls and the floor. She didn't wail or weep, just got on with the job. He had the feeling she was more sorry than any of them. Lovely had wanted to dress Talitha Batt in her usual high pleated collar but he insisted on a chemise for the picture. Photography was the art of truth, not of advertisement.

The camera had looked unsentimentally at the injuries. The coating of white powder on her face ended just below the chin. Below it, framed by the lace trim of the chemise, the throat was open from one side to the other in a violent smile, the severed windpipe like an end of macaroni. The knife was still clutched in her fingers when they found her, its pearl handle flooded with blood. He put the picture on one side. Lucas had a feeling that Miss Batt would urge him to include it but he was not certain that he had her courage.

He had placed the picture of Anna Palmer in the top row. The bruises and scabs gave her the air of a textbook madwoman from the old days, a caricature. They were absences on the plate, clear spaces on the glass where there ought to have been flesh. After some consideration, he'd filled them with ochre and graphite. He'd restored her skin to what time would restore it to anyway and made another print. Lucas still did not believe Abse's claim that the wounds were self-inflicted.

He'd had a further idea after he'd believed the whole process was finished. He had reinstated the print he made of Mrs. Palmer before correcting the plate. The same photograph, unretouched, was on the table now in the third row. It looked like a different woman.

The pictures covered the table, the faces looking up in three long rows. Grave eyes, light ones, troubled ones and intent ones, gathered together in one indiscriminate family. Lucas took a last, long look at them and went into the parlor. He threw himself into the chair, relit his pipe and clamped the slender stem between his teeth. He had one leg over the arm of the chair; the foot wagged urgently and silently in the air where it hung.

THIRTY-FOUR

Emmeline was convalescing in Catherine's bedroom. Querios Abse thought he heard the sound of laughter coming through the floor-boards from the bedroom above. He sat up in bed, adjusted the bolster behind him and lit the candle. A board creaked overhead. Women's voices. Then another sound that might have been weeping leaking through the blank ceiling, seeping through the cracks in the plaster. Then laughter again.

It was unsettling. Querios stretched his hand over the cold expanse of cotton on Em's side of the bed, felt the uninterrupted contact between the top sheet and the bottom one. He brought his hand back and laid it over the solid warmth of his own chest. He missed her. Sometimes, between sleep and waking, he reached out for her and then remembered, readjusted himself to what was. Emmeline alive but injured and at his hands—all because of the blasted bird.

Everything was different. He and Benedict ate alone at one end of the dining table. Catherine spent all her time with her mother. Catty wore eccentric costumes—bloomers one day, a red velvet scarf wrapped around her head another, Em's old opera slippers on bare feet. She appeared at odd hours of the day and night, made brief responses to inquiries, and disappeared again, bearing plates of short-bread or almond pudding, trays of soups and jellies up to the sick-room, all fancifully decorated with leaves or berries for which she had rooted around in the garden. She treated him coolly.

The fact of the matter was, she spoke as if he was the child and she the head of the household.

"Mother's tired," she would say, putting her head around the door of the sickroom when he tapped for admittance. Or, "Not now, Father. We're talking." It irritated him, but since, as she seemed silently to remind him, he had been the one to cause the injury, Querios felt at a loss to protest. Everything would return to normal once Emmy was better.

Benedict had been a comfort. He was easier to get on with when it was just the two of them. The work the young man was doing at the ragged school was admirable, if you stopped to think about it. Some of the lads arrived starved and half-naked. They only came for the food, the warmth of the fire, Ben said. Spent their time playing, throwing chalk around the room, and generally being children when, in the world, they had to act like men. A proportion settled to their studies.

Boys graduating from the school were employed by makers of guns, canes, cabinets, matches, blacking, shoes, cards, locks, ink, watches, emery cloth, gold lace, violin strings. They'd found work with paper stainers, bookbinders, type founders, ivory turners, engravers, jewelers, smiths, printers, bricklayers, horsehair pickers.

They had a new benefactor, a man who'd never been to school himself yet made a fortune in patent remedies—a liver powder that Querios in actual fact had used on occasion. The philanthropist wanted to give a chance to young boys. They were looking for premises in order to start a boarding school.

"What about Lake House, Father?" Ben had joked. "It would fit the b-bill perfectly."

Benedict's stammer seemed mainly to have cleared itself up. Querios had told Emmeline it would. Children did get better so long as you didn't interfere too much.

There was one consolation for him in the accident. It had driven the magistrates out of his mind. He could barely remember to anticipate their next visit unless he spotted the note he'd written himself on the desk, listing the preparations still to be made. The list was too long to tackle now and somehow he didn't have the heart for it. When he tried to work on the figures he could not remember what the information related to, had no more idea what they meant than if they had been hieroglyphs or Hebrew.

Lately, Querios Abse felt like that about all of his life. That he could not recognize it, that it did not belong to him except by accident, by some mistake at the lost and found, and that his allegiance to it was ended.

The whistle blasts, three long, distant shrills, startled everyone. Violet threw her shawl over her head and whimpered that her time had come. Lizzie Button dropped to her knees. Mrs. Featherstone grabbed a curtain and began to wrap herself in it, turning in circles until she disappeared in a shroud of frayed brocade. More blasts pierced the air, louder this time and from nearer by. The air seemed to tremble with them.

Anna ran to the window, kneeled on the seat, and tried to pull it open. The frame refused to budge; it was nailed shut, she saw, like the bedroom window. She pressed her nose against the glass. The sky outside was thick and low, the sheep gathered in one corner of the field with their heads up. Men's voices hung on the air, along with the sound of wheels turning on gravel.

The door opened and Lovely came toward her at a noisy run, tying her apron strings over her stomach. She stopped in front of Anna with her face alight with excitement and laid her hands on Anna's shoulders.

"It's them, miss."

"Who?"

"The magistrates. It's yer chance to speak out."

"I can't."

"Why not? You've got to."

Anna's heart began to pound.

"I can't. I'm too frightened. Of the chair."

Lovely's face was urgent. She glanced over her shoulder and shook Anna lightly.

"You oughter be more frightened of staying here the rest of yer days. It's yer chance, miss."

She ran out of the room in her small, quick steps, her clogs bouncing on the boards, back toward the patients' rooms. As the door closed, Mrs. Featherstone stumbled; the curtain hooks tore away from the rail and she toppled to the floor, still wrapped like a mummy. A cloud of dust rose, filling the air. Anna helped her out of the tangled cloth and sat her in Batt's chair. Mrs. Featherstone's eyes were terrified.

"Don't worry, Mrs. Featherstone," Anna said, her own heart thumping with terror, her voice high and unfamiliar. "No one is after you. The magistrates have come to help you. To help all of us. Sit down and be patient."

A smell began to seep into the room, like a bonfire. Anna made herself return to the window seat. It was true that she was frightened of the chair. She was terrified of being strapped into it again, kept there for as long as Makepeace's whim demanded. But Lovely was right. It was her chance. The only one remaining to her. She had to take it.

She would speak calmly. She must make an impression without appearing to be a hysteric. She must speak slowly and make sure they understood. Not so slowly as to try their patience. If only she had her own clothes. Her hair. She ran her hands over the bristles on her head and groaned. Hearing a tinkling sound, she looked up. Makepeace was in front of her, her keys swinging on their holder.

"Mr. Abse says you're to see the gentlemen. I don't know why, I'm sure. There's others here more deserving to give an account of themselves."

Anna jumped to her feet, goose pimples rising on her flesh under the scratchy dress. She swallowed and tried to keep her voice level.

"Where are they, Makepeace? I will speak with them."

Whistles shrilled again and Makepeace's mouth twitched.

"I told him we should introduce Miss Todd. Or even Button. But he doesn't listen to me. He never did."

"Take me to them."

Makepeace turned on her heel and walked toward the door without a backward glance. Anna followed, her heart pounding faster than ever. As she passed Lizzie Button, Button reached up from where she sat and caught at Anna's skirt.

"Don't go, Anna. It's a—"

"I must, Lizzie."

She hurried past her—through the dining room, where a maid was engaged in a violent sweeping of corners and on past the linen store, the wardrobe. As she walked, she rehearsed her appeal. She would speak on behalf of the women of England, any of whom could suffer this same injustice. No. She would convey only her own case—her personal experience. She took a breath and changed her mind again. She would speak unemotionally, as a man might, as if she explained the case of a friend and was barely concerned about it herself at all. No . . .

They were outside Makepeace's room. The door stood ajar. Makepeace pushed it open with an expression of disgust.

"The patient's here," she said loudly, gesturing for her to enter. "As per instructions."

Anna stepped into the room and looked around. It was empty. A cup of coffee sat untouched on Makepeace's table and some other odor hung in the air, sweet and thin. As she opened her mouth to protest, a man stepped forward from behind the door and clamped his arm around her waist, his hand over her lips. It was Fludd. He forced her down onto the chair. Makepeace smiled as she stooped in front of Anna and pressed a cloth over her nose and mouth.

The cloying smell filled Anna's head. She saw Fludd's blue eyes, intent on some purpose and felt her limbs trapped in the vise of his hands. Makepeace's voice was distant, too far away to make out what she said or for it to matter. Anna's eyes slid past her to a host of spotted butterflies dancing over gold and purple and scarlet petals.

The magistrates were used to being delayed in reception rooms. It was generally acknowledged that a quarter of an hour was fair play and all three men, as the twentieth minute approached, had begun to fidget with their cuff links and drain the dregs of their sherry glasses.

Sir John Earle was once again leading the party; he had Mountford-Smith with him and a new chap, Hogben, on his first inspection. Querios Abse stood between them and the door. The signal from Makepeace, two rapid shrills, long pause, two more quick blasts, had not come. Querios rocked on his heels.

"Won't you take another glass?"

Thumps came through the molded plaster ceiling. As one, the magistrates glanced upward. Sir John Earle straightened his wig and got to his feet.

"Thank you for the refreshment, Abse. Now, if we could proceed."

He pushed straight past Abse and set off from the study, Abse hurrying to get in front of him on the stairs. Sir John had been to Lake House before on several occasions. It was he who had described the airing grounds as "dismal" and suggested carriage rides for the guests, bemoaning the lack of recreation.

"How many d'you have at present, Abse?" Sir John said, on the landing. "Numbers up at all? Any improvement on cures?"

He had a way of curving his mouth as he spoke, as if the curt smile could take the sting out of the words. Querios assumed his most dignified voice.

"The figures are in the ledgers, Sir John, all in the proper order. Ready for your perusal. I believe our cure rate is as good as anybody's, although there is, as you would expect, wide variation within the different classes of disorder."

"We don't need chapter and verse, old chap. Just a fair sample. I've got an early dinner date in town."

They were at the top of the stairs. Makepeace had had more than enough time to straighten things out and to take the agreed steps. He must have failed to hear her signal, Querios told himself. He grasped the handle, flung open the door to the dayroom and flattened himself against the wall of the landing.

"After you, gentlemen."

He followed the magistrates into the room. The sight met his eyes like a physical blow. One of the curtains lay in a heap on the floor. Button was on her knees, praying. Violet Valentine called for her mother. Featherstone cowered on what used to be Talitha Batt's chair, her face covered in smuts. There was no sign of Makepeace.

"Looks like a battleground in here, Abse," Sir John remarked pleasantly.

"Is there a piano?" came an eager voice from behind. "Any caged birds? The room doesn't appear to offer sufficient diversion."

Button jumped up off her knees. She got in front of Sir John before Querios had a chance to prevent it and stood twisting her hands together, the charred piece of wood clasped under one arm.

"Sir. It's not right. There's a patient who wished to speak with you. She's been taken from us this very minute."

From the dining room beyond, Querios at last heard the signal. Two short blasts. Long pause. Two more. The magistrates glanced at each other as Makepeace hurried across the floor toward them. Her eyes were dull and her cap askew.

"This lady fancies injustices at every turn, Sir John," she said, getting hold of Button's arm, thrusting her to one side. "She's not herself."

She made a gesture as if she brought a bottle to her lips, winked at the men. Querios could smell the gin from where he stood. The magistrates had remarked in the last report on her "unwearied kindness." All a charade. He turned his head away and made a sudden, overdue, decision. He would dismiss Fanny Makepeace as soon as he found a replacement. Might even do it before he found someone else.

Button had bobbed around Makepeace and stood in front of Sir John again, flushed to the roots of her hair.

"I have never taken alcohol in my life, sir. You must find Mrs. Palmer. Speak with her."

"I commend you for it," Sir John said, drily.

Hogben was watching, holding his new notebook open with one large thumb, a look of foolish sincerity on his face. The grandfather clock in the corner struck the quarter hour and the party moved on and followed Makepeace through the dining room. Querios brought up the rear. The magistrates showed no interest in the linen stores, the wardrobe. They passed the treatment room and although Hogben seemed inclined to linger and ask questions, Sir John did not. He sneezed more than once, brought out a fine white linen handkerchief from his pocket and passed it under his nose.

"Herbs, Sir John," Querios said. "To freshen the atmosphere."

Sir John's aristocratic nose twitched. "Smells like rot to me," he said. "Have you made the investigations that we talked about?"

Outside the seclusion room, Sir John stopped.

"What's going on here?"

Querios spoke confidently. Almost dismissively. "Nothing, sir. We rarely have recourse to any form of restraint. We prefer to employ more up-to-date methods with our guests."

"Really?" said Sir John. "In that case, what's that noise?"

In the silence that followed, Abse heard moaning coming from inside. He looked at Fanny Makepeace for an explanation.

"A melancholic turned maniac, sir," she said to Sir John. "She was determined that you'd done her wrong. Got it into her head to wreak some kind of vengeance. She's been sedated for her safety and for yours."

Querios couldn't immediately think who she was talking about. He could only stand and watch as Sir John stooped to the observation window and pulled back the wooden shutter. He remained in that awkward-looking stance for some time before standing up with a sigh. As Sir John straightened his long, lean body, Hogben bent his short, stocky one to the observation window, then stood up looking flustered.

"I say, Sir John. This can't be right."

"Can't it?" Sir John said. "Pray do explain, why not?"

After Mountford-Smith had also satisfied his curiosity, Querios stooped and looked into the room. It was smaller than he remembered, lit only by the light that filtered around the edges of a barred and shuttered window. Something lay on the floor—a large bundle of cloth, or an old sack. As his eyes adjusted themselves to the half light, the bundle first twitched, then raised itself to a sitting position. He saw a white hand, a flash of bright eyes before it collapsed down again onto the padded canvas. It was Mrs. Palmer. She was in a restraint waistcoat, a gag at her mouth. He stepped back, feeling off-balance. Fanny continued to avoid his eye.

Sir John sneezed again; his wig tipped back on his head, showing a second fringe of silver hair underneath it, sparser and straighter than the one on top. It wasn't too late to retrieve the situation, Querios told himself. There was no law to say noisy patients should not be secluded for their own good, restrained in a humane manner if necessary.

"Best place for her," he said.

Sir John made no response. He looked at his watch, turned on his heel and set off back down the corridor as if he owned the place. Abse had no option but to hurry behind him.

*   *   *

The sand was rough against Anna's skin, the waves shushed and murmured in her ears. She must have fallen asleep on the beach. She couldn't hear him, chattering to himself. Where was he? She should have been watching him.

Anna tried to sit up but her own arms refused to help her. She raised her head and saw a flash of a silver wig, heard men's voices. The sound of the waves died away. She must tell the men something, she knew, if she could only remember what it was. Trying to right herself, get her bearings, she collapsed again. Her head was heavy, her eyelids weighted with shells.

Someone was touching her. She opened her eyes and saw Lovely's face.

"Let me sleep." The words dissolved in her mouth, ran down her chin. Lovely pulled her into a sitting position and propped her against the wall. Lovely slapped her face, then loosened the band around her mouth. The corners of her mouth were stinging. Lovely untied the bonds at her back and her arms returned to life.

"Swaller it, miss."

Anna could smell something familiar and bitter. Lovely pressed the rim of a china cup against her lips and tipped liquid into her mouth. It was cold on her tongue. Coffee. She opened her eyes again and looked around. She was in a narrow room, one she'd never seen before. Curious that such a large house should contain so many small rooms. Like the chambers of the nautilus. The floor under her feet and the wall behind her back were soft, as if she was in a dream still. She had been dreaming about something. Something that left her heavy, waterlogged with some imagined or remembered grief.

Lovely shook her again and pinched her cheeks.

"You're going to speak to them."

"Speak to whom?"

She sounded drunk. She laughed. Lovely slapped her again, harder.

"It ain't a joke, miss. Get up."

Lovely pulled Anna to her feet, held her up with one strong arm and walked her, half stumbling, back along the treatment corridor, through the dayroom and down the stairs.

* * *

From outside the office door, Anna could hear Querios Abse and other, unfamiliar voices. Lovely lifted her apron, wiped Anna's chin with it.

"Now, miss. This is it. Here's yer chance."

Lovely opened the door, pushed Anna through it in front of her and closed it behind the two of them. The study expanded in front of Anna; the floor rocked and tilted under her feet. She reached for something to steady herself and found nothing.

The room looked as if it had been ransacked. Scores of ledgers had been taken down from the shelves, set out across every available surface, some laid open, some stacked in piles. Abse was there, standing behind his desk, in the company of three other men.

One, leaning back in his chair with his long legs stretched out in front of him, wore a silver wig. He had curved brows that precisely mirrored the curve of his eyelids, steady, doubtful eyes and a spotless white stock tied at his neck. A younger man, bursting his buttons, stared at her with his mouth hanging open. A third sat with his fingers linked under his chin.

The youngest man broke the stillness; he got out of his chair and carried it forward to where she stood.

"Do sit down," he said. "You appear a little unsteady. On your feet, I mean."

"Thank you."

She took hold of the back of the chair.

"You're wandering, Mrs. Palmer. You know you shouldn't be down here." Abse's voice was jovial, tense. "Lovely, take her back upstairs."

Anna glanced at the window and saw a flurry of snowflakes outside, colorless against the thick sky.

"I want to speak to the magistrates, Mr. Abse."

Her heart had slowed now that she was here in front of them. She could feel it beating strongly in her chest. Abse approached the man in the silver wig, who sat leafing through a ledger.

"I apologize, Sir John, for the interruption." He thumped down another armful of files. "Patients' particulars. Daily observations. It's all here. The weather seems to be worsening but I hope you may at least cast an eye over the paperwork without jeopardizing your dinner date." He raised his head. "Off you go, Mrs. Palmer. You're disturbing the gentlemen."

"I have a right to speak with them."

"I say, Sir John," said the young one. "Oughtn't one to hear . . . ?"

The snow was falling in earnest, thickening, the flakes huge and clumsy in their descent. The door opened behind Anna. She heard Makepeace enter and clear her throat in a parody of indignation. Anna tightened her grip on the chair. The man in the silver wig, Sir John, sat up straighter, adjusted his stock. He was so engrossed in the file, so intent on his reading matter, he had not noticed that she was there. Abse called across the room.

"Remove her, Mrs. Makepeace."

Sir John crossed one long leg over the other as he turned another page.

"Do sit down, Mrs. Palmer," he said. "Take your time. When you are ready to speak, I am ready to listen."

"My name is Anna Palmer."

"A little louder, if you can," Sir John said.

"They say the best place to start is at the beginning, Sir John. My problems began before I arrived at Lake House, when I married a dishonest man." As she heard the words, she felt a lightening of her whole self. It was true. She had barely known it herself until she said it aloud. She had married a dishonest man. She breathed and resumed. "I married a dishonest man. Mr. Abse had no hand in that. But when that man brought me here, on false charges of hysteria, Mr. Abse was only too happy to oblige and serve as a jailer.

"I was brought here without my consent or knowledge and kept here against my will. Mr. Abse claimed it was a place where a woman might find solace. I did need solace, Sir John. I needed it more than I understood at the time. But there has been no solace here. And if I was not ill when I arrived, I was likely to have become so afterward."

She swallowed. The young man leapt forward again and handed her a glass of water. She smiled at him.

"Thank you."

"Go on," said Sir John.

"When I tried to protest against my detention, they called me hysterical. I had either to go along with my imprisonment and surrender my life, or to speak against it and be told I was a lunatic. I have been made sick with powders. Frozen half to death in a cold shower. Tortured in a whirling chair. My hair, which had never been cut, has been taken from me.

"The person given the title of matron offers petty cruelties in place of the kindnesses that might make life tolerable. She turns to a treatment of her own. Mr. Abse knows what happens."

Abse banged his fist on the desk. "She's a maniac, unsuitable for Lake House. I requested her removal some time ago. Husband doesn't want to know."

"Be quiet, Abse," said Sir John.

"Some of us here are not ill at all. And those who are don't get any better. Miss Talitha Batt, whom I was proud to call my friend, met her death in this shabby prison. Mrs. Lizzie Button is a mother, parted from children whom no one could love as well as she does. Mrs. Valentine, whom you saw upstairs, deserves better than this at the end of her long life.

"All I want is to be allowed to leave. I have nothing that can be taken from me, apart from life itself. I have lost my reputation. My health. I have come close to losing my mind. As close as I will ever come."

She turned her gaze to Abse.

"For that, I am grateful to you. You have shown me that except by the will of God, I will not be destroyed. Not by powders or potions, not by spinning chairs or cold showers or locked doors or petty cruelties. Not by razor blades or confinement or blows. Not by boredom or hopelessness. Nothing short of murder can kill me."

She stopped. She had finished.

"Thank you, Mrs. Palmer," Sir John said.

He rose to open the door for her; his eyes met hers and he nodded his head up and down, slowly, for a long time.

THIRTY-FIVE

Anna walked alone back up the stairs, through the empty dayroom, the dining room. Beyond the dining room, by the stairs to the patients' rooms, she paused. She heard no footsteps. No sounds of crying or laughter. No rain falling indoors. Only a deep, muffled silence. She walked down the corridor, past the linen room and tried the door to the clothes store. It was unlocked. Pushing her way in, she rummaged in the pile of garments until she caught a glimpse of sea green. She pulled out her own dress and held it up, creased but intact. Hugging it against her, she slipped up the stairs.

Her door was open and the fire in the room lit. The air held a faint, aromatic smell and dried lavender flowers were scattered over the hearth. She gathered up a few and crushed them, bringing her fingers to her nose, breathing in the pungent scent. Through the window, snow was thickening the branches of the trees, piling on top of the railing to the field and the backs of the huddled sheep. "A dishonest man," she said aloud. "A trickster."

She undid the skirt and bodice, then stepped out of Makepeace's black dress, kicked it away from her into a corner and put on her own. The familiar, worn velvet grew quickly warm against her skin. Filling the mug, she took a long drink of water then sat down in front of the washstand. She pulled the towel away from the mirror and looked at herself. Her hair was soft and spiky like the fur of a cat. Smoothing it down on her head with one palm, she examined her face. The bruises had faded and the scabs were gone from her forehead. She rested her fingertips in the round pale scars they had left behind, felt the bone strong and hard under the warmth of her skin.

It occurred to her that she wished that Lucas St. Clair had been among the people in the room. She wanted him to know what had happened to her, that she was of sound mind and hadn't been broken. Anna still had the feeling that she knew him, more deeply than through the exchanges that had passed between them. That in other circumstances they could have been not Dr. St. Clair and Mrs. Palmer but man and woman, with nothing and everything between them.

He'd been nervous when he made the close-up picture of her. She wanted to see what he saw, pushing the camera so near she could smell the chemicals from inside the wooden box, had almost believed that the lens would make contact with her skin. Pulling the St. Christopher out from under her bodice as she had for the portraits, she let it hang over the neck of her dress, round and solid as a moon.

Anna leaned in to the glass. Her breath softened the reflection, misted the mirror as if she looked at an old photograph of herself, from another time. Her eyebrows were dark, her eyes clear and direct. Something had changed in them since she arrived. Something had been settled, some question answered, and it showed. Her mouth was soft. She didn't look either like a lunatic or exactly as she had when she came to Lake House. She looked like her own older sister. Not Louisa or any of the others. Her own, wiser self.

Her eyes traveled to the silver circle that gleamed under her chin. It was luminous, the figure standing out in relief. She lifted it closer to the glass and stared at the old man walking out of the waves, bowed under the weight of the child on his shoulder. She'd worn it since the day her mother died and she had never properly seen it. It was growing, filling her field of vision, obliterating the room, the green thistles on the walls, the lingering smell of lavender. Anna felt weary. So weary she could not remain where she was. She crossed the floor and lay down on the bed.

She was in Dover. In the flint house. It was bitterly cold, the milk frozen in the jug on the breakfast table. She tested it with a spoon; the crystals were sharp and thick on her tongue, the liquid underneath watery. Their mother was in bed with a migraine and a hot brick wrapped in flannel. Amelia Newlove shouted down the stairs that the children should go out, get some fresh air. Give her some peace and quiet.

Anna thought about peace and quiet, struggling with her blue coat. About what it meant. The buttons were too big for the buttonholes and her fingers stiff. The back door was open: Louisa had gone on without her. She got one button done up and ran through the glasshouse, sniffing the dry, fragrant smell. Through the garden, holding her hands tight over her ears to keep the cold from getting inside her head. There was no wind and the air was frozen like the milk. It felt solid with cold.

She came fast down the path, slipping and sliding, the chalk layered with ice, the bushes tearing at the skin of her hands. Reached the bottom, her head rushing with the downward plunge, feeling dizzy. Inspecting the beads of blood that stood up on her palm, she put her hand to her mouth and tasted her own blood, then felt with her teeth for the tip of the thorn and pulled it out. All the time, Anna was aware of a silence. A silence that should not have been. When at last she looked up, she cried out.

The sea was solid in front of her. It was pale and stilled, shut under a lid of ice with its top turned white. It was angry underneath. Raging at the imposed stillness. She knew that. Anna was frightened. She called for Louisa and heard nothing back but her own voice dying on the air. She walked toward the sea, tested the uncertain edge through the toe of her boot, keeping just a small part of it in her sight. She dared not look to the horizon, wished she had stayed in the flint house and never seen it. It was an evil omen, like in the Bible—a sea of glass. *And before the Throne there was a sea of glass like unto crystal.*

She hadn't been thinking about him. She never did. He was just there. Always there. Trailing them, crying if they left him behind. Falling asleep on the sand, in a corner of the garden, anywhere. She wasn't thinking about him.

And then she saw him. Standing on top of the chalk stack, the low one, closest to the cliff at the edge of the bay. He was there, with his spinning top in his hand. He threw the top out over the ice as if he tossed a ball. It sailed a short distance through the air, then fell and bounced and skidded on the surface. He watched it fall, observed its sliding path. Then he jumped, his face creased with smiling. He flew through the air, landed, paused for a moment as he imagined he would, as if he arrived on solid ground. He stumbled, slid half from view, slowly. Anna saw his face change, the expression turning from joy into puzzlement. He slid farther and disappeared. His hair was there for one last arrested moment, bright against the colorless matter of the sea ice. Then gone.

Anna ran along the hard strip of exposed sand, scrambled and crawled along the rocks to where he had been, farther out around the edge of the bay. The ice wasn't solid there. It was in jagged pieces with cracks between them. She climbed down onto the largest of them, under the rock, pushed her hands down though the crack, felt the bite of the water closing on her hands. Felt their emptiness as they sought and did not find. She was shouting at the top of her voice. No sound came. After a while, the cold drove the breath from her chest; she couldn't shout, couldn't breathe, could only whisper. She stayed there, plunging her arms down into the water, dragging her hands through it, her fingers spread. There was nothing. Her hands were empty. Only her eyes still held him. She turned back, crawled on her hands and knees, along the beach, up the path, through the garden.

She was in bed; the roses turned gray. Her hands were raw and grazed. She couldn't feel anything. She should have been watching. It was her fault. Every night in her dreams the sea entered the house, it filled the rooms, to the ceiling. She lived underwater, hearing nothing from the land but fragments, exploding.

In the days that followed, as the ice melted, she waited at the top of the cliff, lying on her stomach, hanging over the edge and watching. Looking for something, she didn't know what, searching with her eyes, willing something to appear from the opaque waves, to emerge, float up, become whole again.

One morning, the old man was down on the shore, bent over and digging for worms, in his wading boots that came up to the tops of his legs, his stooped shoulders in his usual navy jersey, his long, white hair blowing out in the wind. He pushed his toe into the sand, explored with it. He kneeled down as if he was praying and stayed there as the tide turned and began to run in around him. After a long time he rose, with something in his hands.

He laid the bundle, it could have been cloth, an old coat lost in the sea, waterlogged, heavy and limp at the same time, or a dead bird, a bird that fell from the sky, he laid it over his shoulder and he walked out of the sea, past the path that adults never took and up through the cut passageway.

By the time he reached the top, Anna was waiting for him at the gate, hiding. She followed him into the house; he kicked open the front door, walked straight in, water leaking from his boots with every step. There was something on his shoulder. An arm, hanging down against his back. The top of a head. Curled hair the color of sand.

The old man reached the kitchen, took off his cap and dropped it on the table. He leaned forward and as he did so the bundle on his shoulder contorted, the head rose. Antony lifted his head and looked at her, his blind eyes open, his face blue, the features thickened.

After that, there were only noises. The ship's bell, ringing and ringing. Louisa, crying. The sound of hammering, of nails being driven into wood, slow and somber. Adult voices. Her mother's screams, that drowned out the sea. Antony was gone. His bowl and spoon were gone, his smocks and shoes. His singing in the morning. His name was gone. They were not allowed to speak it. Erased from the air, from their mouths. From everywhere.

Anna lay on the narrow bed for a long time, listening to the thickening silence. As the light disappeared, she stood up and went to the window, resting her elbows on the sill. On the other side of the glass, huge broken flakes still drifted downward, obscuring the boundary between the lake and the shore, blanketing the shallow mound under the sycamores. In the whiteness, the bridge had disappeared. Nothing moved but the snow.

THIRTY-SIX

At the Pall Mall Club, Lucas St. Clair stood at a podium in front of the members of the Alienists' Association. More had turned up than had been expected. The organizers had brought in extra chairs and still a line of men were standing at the back leaning on the wall. Lucas rested his hands on either side of the lecture stand and breathed in the club-room smell of leather and beeswax, a smoldering ash log.

"Good evening, gentlemen. Some time ago, a distinguished doctor proposed that the new art and science of photography had application in the diagnosis of madness. I became interested in this idea. We all agree that we stand in grave need of tools to improve our capacity to diagnose mental distress.

"I have devoted myself to researching the theory for the last year. And I would like to propose that you join me now for the final stage of my inquiries. I have drawn my own conclusions but I do not expect that you take my word for it. I invite you to make your own experiment this evening, in this room.

"What you see on the walls here are photographic portraits of women. As you can see, all are devoid of the badges of wealth and beauty, even of industry. Any one of them might appear to be a patient. But not all of the sitters are patients. Some are inmates at private asylums. Others are healthy women of sound mind—members of my own family and household and of friends' families and households.

"I am asking you, as experienced doctors of the mind, to assess which is which. But before you start, I want to raise a further question. Is it possible that some of the women pictured here fall into both categories? I mean to say, is it possible that any are both inmates of asylums and in sound mind? Or vice versa?

"I have numbered each one but left them otherwise unmarked. Please note which individuals you believe to be the lunatics. And which are as sane as you and I."

The photographs were ranged in two long lines along one wall of the stately drawing room. Anna Palmer was there, twice. Violet Valentine. Lizzie Button. Talitha Batt, in life and in death. In between were photographs of the artist, Mrs. Mallinson. Stickles. Of his mother, her face shadowed with the grief that had afflicted her since Archie was cut down. Of Beth. Sunday. Catherine Abse. The identical twins, Melissa and Melody.

Every man in the audience took up his invitation to study the portraits more closely. They got to their feet with a prolonged shifting of chair legs, some protesting that they'd come for answers not more questions, others eager to prove their faith in the technique. The atmosphere changed as they began to look at the images. A hushed tone entered the discussions as the alienists found themselves looking at people, at individuals, and as the burden they carried—the responsibility and difficulty of making judgments about a fellow human—descended on them.

Several clustered around the second, retouched picture of Anna Palmer from which she gazed out clear-skinned and clear-eyed. Others crowded around them, believing that they must be missing the image that was the key to the whole experiment. Few lingered in front of the first, unretouched image of Mrs. Palmer in which the dark scabs and bruises dominated her face.

It was an hour before they were back in their seats, comparing notes, holding sheets of paper annotated with numbers and potential conditions. After an initial quarrelsome discussion, it became clear that there was no agreement among the doctors about who was suffering from mental disease and who was not. Only on two pictures had the gentlemen been unanimous. Mrs. Anna Palmer, in the unretouched image, was a lunatic. Mrs. Anna Palmer, free of scabs and bruises, was not. They disagreed only over whether she was one woman, photographed at intervals, or two different women. They similarly disagreed on the question of the twins.

By the time Lucas took the podium again, the mood was unsettled.

"Gentlemen. I began my inquiries with a firm belief in the potential of photography to take us farther down our path of helping the sufferers of mental distress. As some of you know, I've staked my professional reputation on this point—no one wished for its truth more than I. But the evidence does not bear out the theory. My research shows that although the photographic portrait can bring amusement, diversion and solace to those suffering from mental disquiet—as it can to any other member of the public—the hope that it can be used as a diagnostic tool is unproven."

A belligerent roar broke out among the bearded and black-jacketed audience; sounds of disapproval, mingled with disappointment, rose to the tobacco-colored ceiling. St. Clair waited until the hubbub died away. He felt anger too. No one could have tried harder than he to make the idea work. But it did not. The theory he had cherished for so long, had tried to uphold and enlarge, had perished. Perished on his own dining room table as surely as if it had never lived.

"Our aim tonight is not to prove one man or another right or wrong, but simply to shoulder our burden of pushing on with research, with widening our small circle of understanding of the human mind—in health and in sickness. Our quest is worthwhile and wrong turnings must lead us in the end to right ones.

"Gentlemen, I have one further point to make. I firmly believe that photography might yet prove its worth—in treatment. The discussions prompted by the images, the opportunity for patients to define themselves by them, or to contradict them, the potential for these ideas will inform my further investigations."

Maddox was sitting in the front row. He stood up and began to applaud; one or two others followed. The noise sounded like hammering from far away. Like demolition. Lucas gathered his notes and stepped down from the podium, began to take down the photographs from the walls, starting with Mrs. Palmer. The alienists were shrugging on their coats with the help of the cloakroom attendants, their voices lively with the fact of the evening being over, with waiting carriages. Harry Grieve was there, Lucas saw with some surprise. Two of the younger alienists argued still about whether or not Lucas's mother was deranged, standing between the fire bowls that lit the entrance to the club. It was snowing heavily outside.

Before leaving, Lucas stopped by the book of questions in the entrance hall. On the page where a year earlier he had posed a question—*Can photographs be effective in diagnosing disorders of the mind?*—he wrote his own answer, in a neat italic hand.

Fallaces sunt rerum species. The appearances of things are deceptive.

Lucas walked back to Popham Street, carrying the photographs in a portfolio under his coat. He put them down on the table in the dining room. Stickles had left out a tray of ham sandwiches, some pickled cucumbers. He climbed the stairs to the dark chamber. He'd left the collodion unstoppered, he saw. The air was full of the smell of ether. The solution was exhausted, thin and dark red. He emptied the bottle down the drain. On an impulse, he lifted the yellow shade off the lamp and turned up the wick. The dark chamber, by ordinary light, was dusty and the walls marked with black fingerprints. Rectangles of zinc—where he had patched the boards to prevent light leaking in from below—shone under his feet.

He set about rinsing and drying the measuring cylinders, empty bottles, and developing dishes. He put away the thermometer, the scales and the printing frame, swept the floor and hung on the line the last couple of prints from the wash. He spent a long time emptying and discarding and rinsing and when he'd finished, he dried his hands, sat on the stool, hooked his feet up under him and did nothing at all.

The theory had failed. It had failed utterly. The proposition to which he had devoted a year of his life was null and void. He felt flat. Relieved, as well. He could let go of it, and have time to consider other things. He would leave St. Mark's anyway. He could not stay. He'd find a new job—perhaps out of London. The lamp flared and died, the reservoir of oil empty.

The moon cast a shadow of the plane tree onto the wall. For an instant, Lucas desired to set up the tripod and make a photograph of the stark, reaching limbs, the complication of embracing arms reaching into the room. He didn't move. He watched as the moon was enveloped in cloud and the shadows softened and disappeared. Sitting in the darkness, he saw something else. It wasn't Maddox who wanted to get married. It was he.

Lighting a candle, he took the photograph of Mrs. Palmer, the second one, into his bedroom. He set it on the table by his bed, where he would see it for as long as his eyes remained open, would see it again when he woke. In the morning, he would go to Lake House. He would go and visit her. He owed her an apology. He might yet be able to help her.

THIRTY-SEVEN

Water dripped from the gutters and the branches. The line of snow on the ledge outside Anna's window looked brittle, the surface lacy with holes. The fire was not quite out; a few embers glowed from under a soft blanket of ash. Lovely arrived later than usual with a jug of cold water, her face worried.

"What's the matter?"

"It's Makepeace, miss. No one can rouse 'er. She's not dead—Cook held a mirror to her mouth."

She stepped outside the door and came back in with Anna's boots, put them down in the front of the hearth.

"Thought you might like to have these. Make your own way downstairs, miss. Mr. Abse says we've got to manage the best we can. The magistrates are still 'ere, they couldn't get away last night. He's having breakfast with 'em, in the study."

Anna washed from head to toe after Lovely clumped her way off down the corridor, humming. She put on her own dress again. Laced up her boots. Someone had cleaned them—the salt stains were gone. On impulse, she unlaced them again, took the money from the bed leg and hid it inside her boot. Afterward, she sat down on the bed, looking at the open door. She felt afraid to walk through it. She pinched her hands, reminded herself that she was a Newlove girl. Could endure more than any boy and was tough, resourceful.

She went down the stairs to the dining room and paused outside the door. Someone was singing inside. A lullaby. She pushed open the door. The breakfast table was laid as usual with tin mugs, the few

269

spoons. Lizzie Button sat in her place at the far end of the table, in the seat where Anna had first seen her. She had a child on her lap. A long, pale infant, with thin, fair hair parted over a fragile skull. She held him stiffly as if afraid he would break.

"Lizzie!"

Anna sat down next to her. The piece of wood was on the table, still wrapped in its shawl.

"I'm going home, Anna. Those doctors spoke with my husband. They told him his mother was wrong about me. That I wasn't any danger to anyone, let alone my own children."

"Is this your Albert?"

"Yes. He doesn't know me." Lizzie hugged him closer. She kissed the top of his head and began to cry.

"What if my girls don't know me either, Mrs. Palmer?"

A fair-haired man with prominent eyes, his hair cut like a monk's across his forehead, arrived in the doorway. He had a small girl on each side of him—both dressed in identical coats, their wrists protruding from the sleeves—and another in his arms, asleep. The smaller girl ran to Lizzie and grabbed her skirts, buried her face in them, and began to wail. The other stayed where she was, not moving, as if she was made of stone.

The man nodded at Anna.

"Come on, Elizabeth," he said. "Let's go home."

Anna remained at the table. It was quiet without Makepeace's ringing footsteps, her sawing cough. The only sound was of dripping from outside and occasionally a muffled sliding of something dislodged, slipping; melting snow fell past the window in great lumps. A little woman, dark and quick and neat, came in bearing a platter. Anna stared at her as she put it down on the sideboard and she looked back pleasantly.

"Good morning, miss. I'm the Cook. Care for a piece of bacon?" She lifted the lid. "It's nice and warm still."

The others began to arrive and Cook nodded at her and departed. The rashers were crisp and strong and salty. Anna ate slowly, helped herself to tea, poured a cup for Mrs. Featherstone and rose from the table still feeling as if she was in a dream. The dayroom was dim and disorderly, the chairs out of their usual positions and the bags of handwork scattered. The curtain lay on the floor. The residents sat singly and in pairs and the atmosphere was subdued.

Anna pulled Talitha's chair back to its usual spot, plumped up the green velvet seat and folded the fringed, embroidered Indian shawl over the back of it, then changed her mind and threw it over her own shoulders, breathed in the faint scent of naphthalene. "This is no place for a young woman, Mrs. Palmer. For any woman." She heard Miss Batt as clearly as she had heard her the first time. Anna sat down on the window seat, feeling the silken tassels of the shawl, rolling them between her fingers. She didn't read. She didn't sew. She didn't talk to Violet or Mrs. Featherstone or Miss Todd. She was waiting.

She didn't wait long. An hour later, the door was kicked open and Makepeace struggled through it. She had on two capes, one on top of the other, and dragged a carpet bag behind her. She looked disheveled, as if she had dressed in a hurry. Under her arm was a piece of tapestry in a black lacquer frame. Makepeace stopped in front of Anna and rummaged in her reticule with a ringed hand. Her hair was freshly dyed, the top of her forehead stained brown, and in her eyes was a look of triumph.

"Letter for you," she said, thrusting something in her lap. "You have my most sincere commiserations, Palmer."

She hurried on toward the other door, passed through it and Anna heard the bag thump down the stairs, step by step. Anna looked down into her lap. The scent of violets rose from the letter and the handwriting, round and loopy, was familiar. She pulled out a single sheet of paper and held it for a moment still folded in her hand. Opened it.

"Miss, I thought I knew the gentleman you mention but I was wrong. I never did understand why everything had to be secrit. Please come to me as soon as you are able. Maud."

She turned it over. The envelope had been steamed open; the flap lay limply against the pink body of it. The sender had written her name across the back. *Mrs. Maud Palmer.* She felt dizzy at the sight of those three words but with what she didn't know. Was it dismay? Or was it hope?

*   *   *

Violet's new bird had gotten loose. The others were chasing it, a note of fear in their laughter. It was ten-thirty, by the grandfather clock. Anna slipped out the door of the dayroom and down the stairs, lifted her cloak from the pegs in the cloakroom. She had to breathe unbreathed air. Take in the letter alone and think her own thoughts. Even the confines of the airing ground would be preferable to the dayroom.

The side door was unlocked. She let herself out and walked along the back of the house in slanting sunlight. The snow was melting on the path, sliding down between the gravel; it dripped from the branches of the trees, lay in shallow-edged drifts on the turf. At the window of the study, she came up close to the glass and peered through. Behind the stacks of books and papers, Abse sat at his fortress desk with his hands cupped over his ears as if he was trying to hear some faint and distant music. He looked up as she hurried away but made no sign of having seen her.

The gate to the airing ground stood open. She paused and looked in, at the walled enclosure, the grid of narrow paths and the wall of bricked-up windows along the far side. A robin hopped toward her, expectant, its head cocked. Glancing around her, Anna walked past the gate, quickening her step, her soaked feet carrying her on—under the trees and down across the grass. She reached the field, unchallenged, her heart beating painfully in her chest. The ewes were ships, their pregnant bellies swaying over dainty feet as they regarded her. She kept on—walking swiftly until she reached the edge of the lake. The level was high and the water fresh-smelling, moving all over. The trees were broken into hundreds of pieces across the surface, an undone jigsaw puzzle.

As she looked, a bellow thundered through the air, from behind her. It sounded like a wounded sheep. Anna turned and looked up the long snow-covered slope toward the house. In the distance, at the top, stood Fludd, legs akimbo, staring straight at her. He set off toward her, walking, not running, his stride purposeful. Anna's mind felt hard and sharp and clear. The sheep were still gathered around a trough of hay, eating peacefully; there was no one else anywhere in sight. She ran to the bottom of the field, turned, and still running made her way along the bank until she reached the coppice of trees.

The holly berries were gone; the red-stemmed bushes in tender, new leaf. There was no path through the thicket, no obvious entry point. She pulled her cloak up over her head, tightened it around her and launched herself into the sharp, snagging holly branches, the stems of dogwood. Snow showered down on her from the leaves, wet and heavy. Her gloves were soaked and her fingers cold. She fought her way on through the tangle of growth, panting, struggling to breathe. She dared not look behind her but kept going, forcing her way through beeches that were still brittle with brown leaves, though silky sheathed buds emerged underneath.

Anna reached the other side with her wrists and fingers bleeding and stood for a moment, gasping for breath, pulling thorns and brambles out of her cloak and hair. She raised her head and looked at the white bridge, shimmering, its reflection trembling on the water below.

There was something odd about the bridge, close up. It looked not as if it was made of white stone, as it appeared from the house, but more like wood. Painted wood. And she couldn't see the way onto it, only the front of it. She ran toward it, still panting, reached the bridge and stopped. She looked behind it, dreading what she would see. Catherine was right. It was not a bridge. It was nothing more than a piece of scenery. A two-dimensional, painted façade, its wooden back green with mildew.

A noise came from the undergrowth, of branches cracking and tearing, followed by a bellow of pain and a curse. Anna heard herself whimpering with fright. She stared at the bridge for a second then kicked the post at the end. It didn't move. She took hold of the post with both hands and tried with all her strength to shake it. It didn't shift even a fraction. It was solidly lodged in the ground. The balustrade over the top of the arches led in a smooth, undulating white line to the far bank. It was wider than it looked from the house. As wide as her own foot. It would have to serve.

Anna hoisted her skirts above her knees, got hold of the post with both hands and pulled herself up onto the support propping the back of the bridge. She scrambled along it, got both feet onto the top of the balustrade. For an instant, she paused, crouched down, looking at the dark, opaque water. She was a strong swimmer but not in skirts and a cloak. Not in icy water.

"You! Stop there!" Fludd's voice was right behind her.

She undid her cloak and threw it down in the water. She could hear him panting, hear him coming nearer.

"Stop right there, missy. No funny business." He laughed.

Anna raised herself so she stood upright and inched her front foot around, turning her body to follow. She began to walk, like a trapeze artist, one foot in front of the other, touching her toe to her heel, both arms stretched out to her sides.

A hoarse shout came from behind her. Another profanity. As she neared the center of the lake, she felt the bridge shake. She stopped, trembling so violently that she almost lost her footing. Don't look back, she whispered to herself. She straightened again and resumed her passage over the water, her eyes fixed on the far side of the lake. As she stared in the direction of the gleaming silver birches, a figure appeared on the sandy bank in front of her. It was a man, dressed in sailor's trousers, ragged and navy blue, and wearing a patched jacket. His beard and hair were long enough to catch the breeze and his feet naked on the melting snow. He stretched out his hand toward her.

"Come to me."

His voice was a deep bell note on the air. Anna could feel the breeze in her ears and on her skin, smell the clean, absolving odor of the water. The air around her supported her as if she floated in its light. She walked surefootedly, felt her way along to the very end of the white ledge until she was close enough to leap to the shore.

She landed more heavily than she expected. The snow had almost gone and the earth was covered with primroses. Anna brushed off her hands and got up to look on His face. There was no one there. Jesus had disappeared. She lifted her skirts and ran—up the sloping ground under the sheltering canopy of the trees and on toward the city on the horizon, the dome of St. Paul's, the roar and tides of the streets.

* * *

In Sebastopol Street, Anna turned in through the gate of number 59, lifted the metal hand knocker, let it fall. She didn't have the sense that she'd had last time, of having been there before. She was chilled to the bone, felt she could go no farther, that if the door didn't open she would simply slump to the step.

The door opened immediately, as if someone had been waiting for her just the other side of it. Maud Sulten was shorter than Anna— dark-haired and dressed in a red wrap, belted at her waist, her feet in embroidered green slippers emerging from the bottom of the robe. For a minute, neither of them spoke. They looked at each other, eyes locked. She had never known a stranger so perfectly, Anna had time to think, before the woman smiled.

"You must be Anna," she said, taking her frozen hand and clasping it between her own, drawing her over the threshold. "Come in and warm yourself. I was expecting you. I've got the kettle on."

Anna followed the woman down the passageway and into a sitting room where all the seasons bloomed at once—snowdrops, roses, lilies, poppies, chrysanthemums, poinsettias, in pots of artificial flowers. There was a crash and she looked down. A small boy grinned up at her from the rug in front of the fire, colored bricks flying and skidding and bouncing into the corners of the room from the castle he had just demolished.

His eyes were dark, his skin waxy and his little face serious for its years. Something about him was familiar. Anna sat and watched as he played. The room was cozy and enveloping; she felt strangely at home, listening to Maud clattering gently in her kitchen. She eased off her boots, her soaked stockings, wriggled her toes in front of the flames.

"Here we are."

Maud stood in the doorway with a teapot and a pair of flowery cups on a lace cloth on a tray. She put the tray down on the table, took the lid off the pot and stirred the tea, around and around.

"The thing is, Anna," she said. "I love him."

"Your boy? Of course you do."

"Not just our boy. I love Vincent. Foolish old goat that he is. I wouldn't have married him otherwise."

THIRTY-EIGHT

Emmeline curled the toes of her right foot inside one of Querios's slippers. She rotated her ankle in a small circle clockwise and then anticlockwise. The movement was coming back to her leg, despite the swelling that lingered. There was a tap on the door and her face creased into a frown. She found herself strangely reluctant, even now, to sack the girl. Hannah Smith had trained up nicely and had made herself so useful in the sickroom after the accident. Present when she was needed and absent when she wasn't.

Emmeline gave herself a mental shake. She had to do something. Hannah's bulk had become impossible to ignore and her time must be near. Catherine didn't seem to see it, which was fortunate.

"Come in," she called.

Hannah Smith stood in front of her, puffing lightly.

"You wanted me, ma'am?"

Hannah was wearing a pink dress, the bodice flattening her breasts into a broad band of flesh across her chest, her belly standing out before her in a proud mound. Emmeline thought she saw movement in it, a rippling interruption underneath the fall of sprigged cotton. She jerked her eyes away, remembering the feeling of kicks and stirrings, of independent life inside oneself, safe from harm. For a moment, she wanted to invite Hannah to sit down and take the weight off her feet, rest a little.

Such foolishness. Emmeline composed her face, tried to convey in her voice both severity and kindness.

"Yes, Hannah, dear. I've been meaning for some time to speak with you."

The door opened again and Benedict came in, looking warily at Emmeline, dumping a pile of books on the table.

"Hello, Mother," he said. "How are you today?"

"Ben, darling. I have to talk to Hannah and then . . ."

Ben and Hannah Smith were in front of her, standing shoulder to shoulder, almost touching. Both of them with that look of youth visible only to those who have lost it. Why was she thinking of "them"? Both? Emmeline felt suddenly, horribly exposed. The expression on Hannah's face wasn't apprehension. It was pity. Benedict looked at her with the same sorry, proud air. Her mind swam with the effort of understanding.

Emmeline cast her eyes around for her workbag, her laudanum, assistance in any form.

"Not now, Ben. I'm speaking with Hannah."

"Mother. We've got something to tell you."

Ben knelt down by the side of the chair and took hold of her hand, looked up into her eyes. Preoccupied with Catherine, how long had it been since she had noticed her son? The whiskers on his cheeks followed the same line as Querios's and there was silver in his hair at the temple. Even children aged, if they lived. It was obvious of course and yet so difficult to believe. She struggled to hear the words swimming around her ears.

"I'm sorry, darling. What did you say?"

"I said that Hannah and I are going to be married."

Emmeline struggled to get to her feet and, feeling a sharp pain in her bandaged leg, collapsed back into the chair.

"Utterly impossible," she said, summoning every last scrap of authority over her child, her servant. "You wouldn't understand, Benedict. The girl is *enceinte* quite apart from anything else." She turned her eyes to Smith. "I am so very sorry, Hannah. You will have to leave today. I will provide references, a character for you. I always liked you, you know."

Hannah swayed and groaned. She cupped her hands under her belly and a flood of liquid coursed out from under the hem of her dress, trickling off the edge of the rug and onto the floorboards. Her waters had broken. Emmeline looked down at her treasured silk rug, that

Smith had so often cleaned. Hannah sat down heavily on the chaise longue and gripped her knees, her face contorted and her knuckles white.

"Oh, ma'am, I'm so awfully sorry. We wanted to tell you but there was Catherine missing and then you had the accident and couldn't be troubled."

Catherine had entered the room and was standing looking at all of them. She wore one of the dresses they'd chosen for the trip to Italy and was losing the haunted look she'd had all winter. She'd become bossy and practical in the sickroom; she was going to be a poet, not marry one. They planned to travel through France first and arrive in Italy by train. Emmeline had sold her mother's diamond brooch to finance it. She must prevent Catherine's knowing anything about this business with Smith.

"Catty. I am having a private talk with your brother."

Catherine had the same look on her face as Ben. It was a careful, kind expression.

"Yes, Mother. I'm just going to sit with Hannah for a minute. I think she may need some help."

Emmeline felt another lurching shift in what she thought she knew. Hannah gave a long groan that rose at the end then subsided. Emmeline moaned too. Ben had hold of her arm, had somehow lifted her to her feet.

"Go and rest, Mother."

He propelled her toward the door and finally, Emmeline understood. She was dreaming. It was the only answer.

Emmeline limped out of the room. She had forgotten her stick and her leg had begun to throb painfully. Grasping the newel post, she pulled herself up onto the first stair and then the second. On the landing, she stopped to rest, sat on the stool placed there for the purpose since her accident. Emmeline sat for some time, thinking about babies. She had loved hers more than anything in this strange world, she concluded, and did so still, despite anything that might happen. Anything at all.

Through the window, in the distance, she could see a figure appearing to walk across the top of the sham bridge. It was a woman, wearing only a blue dress, no bonnet or shawl, her arms held out on either side. She hesitated in the middle, swayed, and for a minute Emmeline held her breath, thinking she was going to fall. The woman regained her balance and continued, jumping off the end with a bold, airy leap.

The door flew open, below. Catherine ran into the passage with the bell in her hand, ringing it hard and fast. Catherine looked up and caught sight of Emmeline on the stairs.

"Oh, Mother," she said, "isn't it the most wonderful thing ever? I've been longing for this day to come."

Catherine's face was radiant, as beautiful as she'd ever seen it. She looked like a woman. As Emmeline watched, she disappeared down the stairs toward the kitchen, shouting for Cook. A minute later, Dr. St. Clair pounded up the stairs and rushed into the parlor, rolling up his sleeves. Cook followed on his heels with a kettle in her hand and there was Catty again, with her arms full of sheets.

It was the longest and the strangest dream Emmeline had ever had. She must tell Querios about it. She got to her feet, ascended the last stairs, and, leaning on the wall, made her way along to her own bedroom. The old man, Septimus Abse, was standing by the door with a letter in his hand. She looked again. It wasn't Septimus. It was Querios. She limped up to him and put her arms round him, rested her face on his chest, and felt the beat of his heart. She was not dreaming. She was as far from dreaming as she had ever been. She must give him the news, before he heard the animal cries coming from the parlor.

"Come and sit with me, Q. I have something I must tell you," she said, opening the bedroom door.

"No, Emmeline," he said, looking down at the letter. "There is something that I must tell you."

THIRTY-NINE

Vincent Palmer held the notes for his sermon in front of him on his lap, rolled like a scroll, which he considered the most dignified way of carrying paper. He delivered his sermons as if they were spontaneous but he prepared them minutely beforehand, knew the rhythms he would strike, the metaphors he would employ. It enabled him to deliver them to maximum effect, and with maximum sincerity, as if they were part of himself, as if he spilled his own blood for the congregation.

It was a particular honor that the Bishop had chosen to be present on the fifth Sunday in Lent and one that could only be explained by His Lordship's appreciation of blood ties, however tenuous. In his note, His Lordship had again made reference to Mrs. Palmer, indicated that he hoped to meet her. He wanted to look her over, evidently. It was the Bishop's candid opinion, Vincent suspected, that if Anna was not fit to be a clergy wife he should pack her off to the country for good. Disencumber himself.

The sermon, the last in the Lent series, was on the sin and punishment of Gehazi. Its theme was mortification and Vincent believed it the best he had ever penned. Not so much a sermon as a statement, a distillation of everything he believed, everything he was as a man as well as a priest. He felt a shiver of excitement at the prospect of being able at last to display his true worth to the Bishop.

From the robing room, he could hear the congregation pouring in through the large doors at the back of All Hallows. He could hear the whispered admonishments of mothers to their children, the odd cry from a baby too young to know where it was. He felt ready. He'd had a light breakfast of poached eggs and a pot of tea and blackened his moustache with the Colombian powder. He was as prepared as he would ever be.

Clearing his throat, scroll in hand, Vincent strode to his place at the side of the altar. The Bishop was installed in the front pew, he saw, with room to stretch his legs if he cared and away from the hoi polloi, who could smell unpleasant, even and in fact especially on days of notable religious significance. A deep organ note wheezed into the church and the first hymn commenced.

The singing fell away, and the curate read the first and second lessons. There was some form of disturbance at the back as Vincent climbed the steps to the pulpit to deliver the sermon. At least a handful of worshippers generally had to be rebuked for arriving under the influence. He would discover afterward who the miscreants were, couldn't see them clearly enough to deal immediately with them. Arriving in the pulpit, he spread his hands in a gesture of humility and of welcome, nodded to the congregation, and bowed deeply to the Bishop. Then he began.

"Dearly beloved. All around us, in our streets and places of work, even in our own homes, we see examples of sinners. Brothers and sisters in Christ who have strayed from the path of righteousness. Consider Gehazi, who although he walked this earth almost two thousand years ago, was prey to the same temptations. . . ."

The protesting creak of the church door cut in on his words, heralding, no doubt, a further disturbance at the back. He stopped and let the silence that grew in the church speak for him, composing his face into a gargoyle frown, to make clear his displeasure. When the silence was once again complete, he continued.

"And the question that Gehazi raises for us today, the question that echoes down the generations, is thus . . ."

The latecomers had failed to understand his unspoken instruction. The rumpus at the back was growing and as he raised his eyes from his notes, two figures began to walk down the nave toward him. It was a pair of females. One all in red, the shape of an hourglass. The other tall and slender in a sea-green dress. They approached him like a couple coming to make their vows—slowly, their backs straight, heads up, and their gait measured. Between them a small figure took light, skipping steps. It was his shrill voice that pierced the hush pervading All Hallows.

"Father!"

Vincent leaned on the pulpit, groped in his head for the right lines. Silence. Nothing. "Oh Lord," he said to himself. "Why hast thou forsaken me?"

The pair had halted. Anna was standing by the Bishop, so close she risked stepping on the hem of his robes. What on earth was she doing here? Vincent frowned down at her and in the silence another voice came. It echoed off the stone walls, the cerulean glass in the high windows, the closed eyes of the saints. It was Maud's stage voice, sweet and ringing, and it had in it a breaking sorrow that pierced him as surely as if a nail had been driven through his flesh.

"Vincent. Which one of us is your lawful wedded wife?"

He could not stop now. He would not stop. Not while the Bishop was in the congregation. The congregation, for the first time ever, were riveted, every last one of them alert and listening with not a whisper arising from the furthest corner of the church. Even the babies were quiet.

Vincent caught the Bishop's eye and saw that his face was frighteningly, unnaturally composed, displayed no emotion whatsoever. The goodwill was entirely gone from it, Vincent noted.

How dare women try to create confusion in God's house? Bringing sordid carnal matters under this sacred roof? Vincent lifted up his eyes to the Lord and, as a greater disturbance erupted, with cries of protest and calls of "shame," the help he sought came to him. He felt his fists unclench and heard authority return to his voice, that authority that came from a greater power. With it came the words. Everything was there, in the Bible. All of human experience and all of human trouble. Old man Job had known it well.

"The days of affliction have taken hold upon me. My bones are pierced in me in the night season: and my sinews take no rest."

Some of the parishioners were laughing, some jeering. One woman wept. Vincent looked down and saw the Bishop departing with Maud and Anna, all three of their hems trailing on the stone floor and the boy skipping beside them.

Vincent raised his voice higher, lifted it to the rafters in joyful worship; God would hear him if man could not.

"I stood up and I cried in the congregation. I am a brother to dragons, and a companion to owls."

FORTY

The waves lapped delicately, coaxingly, beyond their toes. They soaked into the sand, made and remade their lacy trim. Louisa stooped, picked up a shell. It was pink and brown, shaped like a baby's cradle with the cover drawn up. She added it to the collection in her palm, all of the same type, the same shade.

"Does it have to be so far away, Anna? I don't know anyone who's ever been to Liverpool."

"I'll come back and visit, Lou. Or you can come and see me at the sailors' mission, when I get settled."

"Why don't you stay in London? Help me with the children? Blundell said he wouldn't mind—now there's no cause for embarrassment. He always knew there was something odd about Vincent."

Anna sighed and drew the toe of her boot along the sand, picked up a chalk pebble.

"I'm not cut out for domestic life, Lou. I never was."

"It's not right that you should go alone."

"I'm not going alone. A friend is coming with me."

"You mean the housemaid?"

"She's not a housemaid," Anna said, raising her voice over the clamor of gulls nesting on the cliff behind them. "She was an attendant."

Anna had on a new dress. It was made of velvet, thick and soft, sea green, with mother-of-pearl buttons up the bodice. It was the same as her old ones except that the lace collar was round instead of pointed. Louisa had insisted on having it made for her by her own dressmaker. The woman was working on another, in turquoise, for Anna to take

284

with her. Anna's hair had grown long enough to frame her face, would soon be long enough to put up in her combs. People had started to look at her again, the way they always had, as if they'd had some slight shock.

The sound of the waves washed into her ears, washed through her. She turned over the pebble of chalk in her hand, felt its cool, damp certainty against her skin, its softness and its history. They'd come to lay Antony to rest. To say good-bye to him and speak his name to the sea breezes, let them carry him all over the world like the sailor he would surely have been.

Anna and Louisa had traveled to their childhood home by train from London, just the two of them, barely speaking as they steamed through the lines of little houses, through the fields of Kent, past hop fields and windmills and over the muddy expanse of the Medway, the carriage crowded out with families, luggage, boxes, dolls. It was May and England was in bloom, the apple trees decked with pink-and-white blossom, the hedgerows waving with foxgloves and honeysuckle. Anna and Louisa took a cab along the coast road from Dover, then asked the driver to wait in the lane.

The flint house was empty and further decayed even in the year since Anna had left. The roof beam was bowing, the glasshouse by the back door collapsed into the long grass. The lawn was covered in daisies and shreds of sacking still flapped in the breeze from the upper windows. They sat on the grass and shared a bottle of lemonade that Louisa produced from her bag.

"Shall we?" she said, getting to her feet.

"Yes," Anna said. "Let's go down to the water."

They walked down the path to the beach, arm in arm. Neither of them had said his name. On the beach, they stood in silence, looking out at the chalk stack, the sea lapping gently around it. The tide was going out, the sand soaked and clean like a sheet of blank paper.

"It wasn't my fault, Lou. That Antony drowned."

"No one ever said it was your fault." Louisa's voice was subdued. "It was an accident."

"Yes. It was an accident."

Louisa took Anna's arm as they walked along the shore, looking down at the shells and smooth, rounded pieces of green and brown glass that the tide had deposited on the sand.

"I wasn't allowed to talk to you about it, Anastasia. No one was. Mother thought you were too young to remember. But you remembered better than anyone."

Even over the tang of salt and grass, Anna could smell her sister's carnation scent. It was strange that Louisa wore their mother's scent. Louisa hadn't altogether succeeded in leaving behind the past. Hadn't altogether wanted to, perhaps.

They turned and walked back to the path cut through the chalk cliff, shook the sand from their skirts and walked back up to the top, to where the view was startling and endless, the horizons of Europe visible in the distance. With the breeze loud in their ears, they embraced, drawing the sea air deep into their selves, their skirts blowing in the wind.

"I'm sorry, Anna," Louisa said, in the cab on the way back to the railway station. She gripped Anna's hand with her small white one and wiped a tear from her eye. "I've never been much of a sister to you. Too busy with my own troubles, I suppose."

"It's not too late, Lou. We've got our lives ahead of us."

"You're going so far away."

"We can write."

"Yes," Louisa said. "I'd like to get letters from you. To know about your life."

"And I'd like to know about yours."

Louisa reached into her pocket and drew out a small pearl-handled penknife.

"I want to give you this. Remember? Father gave us each one when you were quite small. Mother didn't think we ought to have them." Louisa laughed. "You can use it to open my letters to you. In Liverpool."

The high wrought iron gates were propped open, the gatekeeper's hut empty. Anna walked down the steep, banked drive under the tall trees, their branches edged with tender green buds. Lake House looked as if it had been notified of the change of season. Doors and windows were flung open; sounds of sawing and hammering came from inside. A black cat sat on the porch, licking a paw.

Anna stopped at the studded front door and peered into the dim hall. The smoke-darkened oil paintings that once hung there were gone and she could hear the shrill, insistent cry of a newborn from somewhere inside. She wouldn't knock on the door. She would make her own way down to the kitchen, find Lovely inside wherever she was. Lovely had wanted to meet her in London but Anna had been determined to come back to Lake House just once, as a free woman. To arrive when she chose and leave as she pleased. It was necessary.

She walked around the side of the house to the back, her feet crunching on the gravel in the still air. There was nobody to be seen inside Abse's study. The high shelves were empty but the fox looked out unperturbed from inside his glass case, tail lifted.

Anna leaned against the warm brickwork of the house, felt the sun on her face and her blood running fast and free in her veins. Life was returning. Returning to the world and to her. The banks of the lake shimmered with cow parsley and bluebells. She walked down over the grass under the trees and on through the field. The lambs were large, butting at newly shorn ewes and gamboling with each other. She carried on down to the lake and breathed the muddy freshness of the water, trailed her fingers between the round pads of the waterlilies, then sat down on a log.

Farther along the shore, beyond the coppice, the white bridge looked as delicate and exquisite as ever, casting its daylight moons on the surface of the water. It seemed to offer two ways across—one over the water, through the air, and the other under the surface of the water, in its still reflection. Anna got to her feet and looked at the far bank, at the point where she had jumped off the bridge and landed among the primroses. She searched it with her eyes, saw nothing but the slope, the trees, the dance of new leaves under the sun.

It was time to get Martha and go. She held her skirts with one hand and climbed back up toward the house. Reaching the path, she turned to head for the front door then changed her mind and walked the other way. The gate wasn't padlocked. She opened it and stepped into the walled garden, broke off a branch of white lilac, pressed her face into its cool, damp fragrance. Among the blossom, on the air, she caught a drift of pipe tobacco.

Her feet were soundless as she walked along the narrow brick path edged with box. Lucas St. Clair was in the fernery, sweeping the floor. He threw down the broom and went into the dark cupboard. She watched as he wrapped bottles in cloths, stowed them in a case, bending and rising, his pipe between his teeth, his face appearing and disappearing through the amber glass.

As he emerged from the dark cupboard, Anna tapped on the fernery window. Lucas looked up, emerged from the cupboard and came to where she stood. He brought his face close to the glass and she could see his long whiskers and the startled expression on his face, see his lips shaping her name. Lucas hurried to open the door.

"It's you," he said. "I can hardly believe it."

"Hello, Dr. St. Clair."

She brought up her hand to shade her eyes.

"They told me you'd gone," he said.

"I have gone. I've come back for Martha Lovely."

They stared at each other. The silence was sweet and empty. He looked down at the tripod he held in his hands, folded it and laid it on top of a wooden case standing by the door.

"I owe you an apology, Mrs. Palmer."

"What for?"

"Something I thought was true, that I no longer believe."

"I never saw the picture. The close-up one. I probably looked like a maniac."

He frowned.

"No, you didn't. You didn't at all."

Anna looked past him, into the fernery. The canvas background lay rolled up on a trestle; the stove was unlit. The carved chair had gone and the walls were dotted with the bright, unfolding skeletons of ferns.

"What are you doing here?"

"Packing up, Mrs. Palmer. Lake House is closing down. Abse lost his license and sold it to be turned into a school."

"I know. Catherine visited me before she went abroad with her mother. I've been staying with my sister until I go north."

"North?" A shadow passed over his face that was not to do with the moving clouds, that came from the inside. "You are going away?"

"Yes. I am traveling to Liverpool. I'll be working at a sailors' mission."

Their eyes met.

"Your husband will accompany you, I suppose."

"No. Martha Lovely's coming with me. We're going together. I am not married, Dr. St. Clair. I didn't know it but—well, I've found out that I never was legally married at all."

His face changed again. It took on a hopeful look.

"The photograph is beautiful. I'd like you to have a copy. Do you have an address, where you're going?"

Anna smiled. She breathed the scent of lilac and lifted the spray of blooms in the air between them.

"Why don't you make another?"

The sun was warm on his back. Lucas felt its heat through the cloth and thought that it reflected something that had already warmed inside him. Mrs. Palmer—Anna—was in front of him. Her head floated in the sky below. Her feet, in an old pair of boots, emerged from the hem of her long skirt and the world, the green curve of it, balanced itself on them. Her eyes looked intently at something. Someone. She looked at him. She saw him through the cloth.

Lucas adjusted the dial one last time until his focus on her face was as sharp as the lens could make it. Then he rose and emerged. The light was so brilliant outside the cloth that for a moment he couldn't see anything. He blinked and recovered himself, replaced the lens cap, and inserted the dark slide.

"Are you ready?"

"Yes. I'm ready."

Lucas pulled the cap off the lens and stepped into the picture, by her side. He could feel her living self next to his, the warmth of her arm where it made contact with his, and his own joy at facing outward from the picture, with her.

He would not smile. If a photograph could indicate anything at all of the movement of a mind, he wanted this one to announce that this was the moment in which they lived and had their being. And that he understood that by the time he moved back to the camera, replaced the lens cap so that only his human eye still beheld Anna Palmer, it would be gone.

ACKNOWLEDGMENTS

With thanks to my wonderful agent, Ivan Mulcahy, without whom this book would not have been written. To Laetitia Rutherford, also of Mulcahy Conway literary agency, for all her help. To my much-valued acquiring editors, Samantha Martin and Francesca Main, and to their passionate successors, Alexis Gargagliano and Jessica Leeke. To Maxine Hitchcock for her steady support and to all at Scribner and at Simon & Schuster UK. To my friends and fellow writers Andie Lewenstein and Linda Leatherbarrow and to generous readers Lynne Wallis, Birgit Kleeberg and Cate McRae.

Above all, thanks to my husband, Mike Goldwater.

ABOUT THE AUTHOR

Wendy Wallace is an award-winning journalist and writer.

Her journalism has appeared in magazines and newspapers, including *The Times*, *The TES*, *The Guardian* and *The Telegraph*. In 2001, she was Education Journalist of the Year.

Her book on life in an inner-city school, *Oranges and Lemons*, was published by Routledge in 2005. *Daughter of Dust: Growing Up an Outcast in the Desert of Sudan* was published by Simon and Schuster in 2009.

Her short stories have appeared in anthologies published by Methuen and Iron Press.

She lives in London with her husband and has two sons.

Visit her website at www.wendywallace.co.uk and follow her on Twitter @slangular.